short SUNZEN!™

VOLUME 2
BY SUSUGI SAKURAI

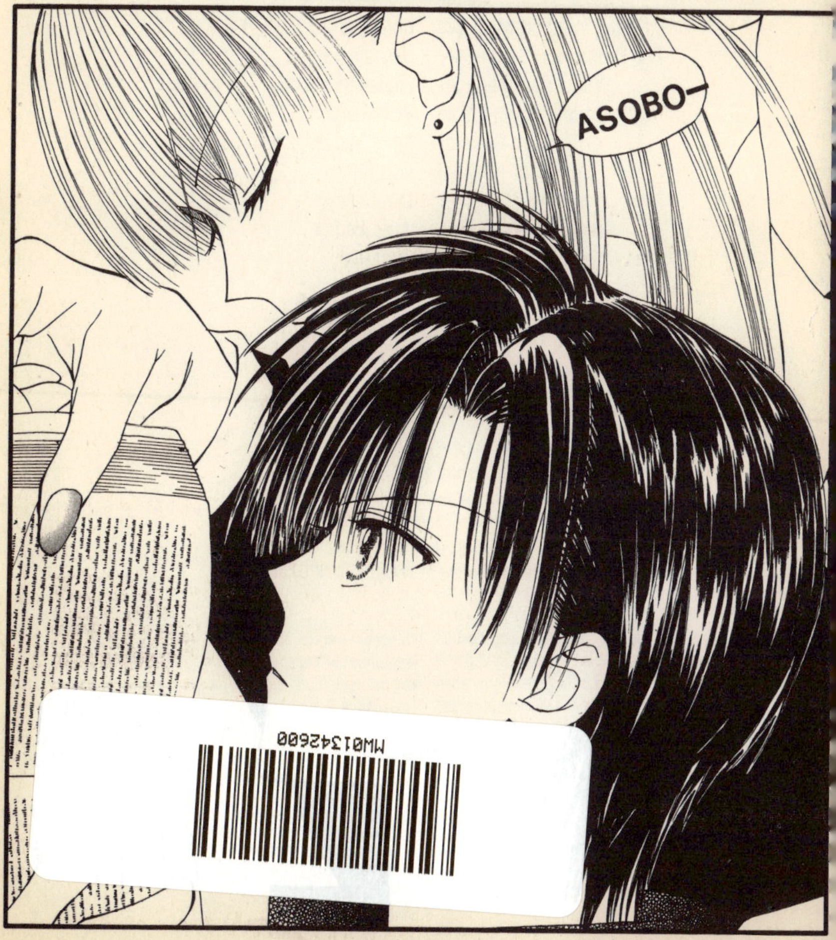
ASOBO—

Short Sunzen! Volume 2
Created By Susugi Sakurai

Translation - Kristy Harmon
English Adaptation - Zachary Rau
Retouch and Lettering - Star Print Brokers
Production Artist - Vicente Rivera, Jr.
Graphic Designer - Jose Macasocol, Jr.

Editor - Stephanie Duchin
Digital Imaging Manager - Chris Buford
Pre-Production Supervisor - Lucas Rivera
Production Manager - Elisabeth Brizzi
Managing Editor - Vy Nguyen
Creative Director - Anne Marie Horne
Editor-in-Chief - Rob Tokar
Publisher - Mike Kiley
President and C.O.O. - John Parker
C.E.O. and Chief Creative Officer - Stu Levy

A  Manga

TOKYOPOP and are trademarks or registered trademarks of TOKYOPOP Inc.

TOKYOPOP Inc.
5900 Wilshire Blvd. Suite 2000
Los Angeles, CA 90036

E-mail: info@TOKYOPOP.com
Come visit us online at www.TOKYOPOP.com

SHORT SUNZEN ! by Susugi Sakurai © 1998 Susugi Sakurai All rights reserved. First published in Japan in 2001 by HAKUSENSHA, INC., Tokyo English language translation rights in the United States of America and Canada arranged with HAKUSENSHA, INC., Tokyo through Tuttle-Mori Agency Inc., Tokyo
English text copyright © 2007 TOKYOPOP Inc.

All rights reserved. No portion of this book may be reproduced or transmitted in any form or by any means without written permission from the copyright holders. This manga is a work of fiction. Any resemblance to actual events or locales or persons, living or dead, is entirely coincidental.

ISBN: 978-1-59816-938-6

First TOKYOPOP printing: May 2008
10 9 8 7 6 5 4 3 2 1
Printed in the USA

VOLUME 2
BY SUSUGI SAKURAI

HAMBURG // LONDON // LOS ANGELES // TOKYO

short INTRO!

Satsuki Kurokawa is a rather rough and tumble high school senior who acts more like a gang member than a young lady. Along with her best friend, Aya Sendo, she attends Tama High, a school feared more for its ability to produce top fighters and delinquents than its ability to churn out graduates. Though they're often misunderstood as never-do-well's by the outside world, the biggest misunderstanding is between the two of them. You see, Aya is totally head over heels in love with Satsuki, and she has no clue! Will Aya ever be able to confess his love? Round Two begins...

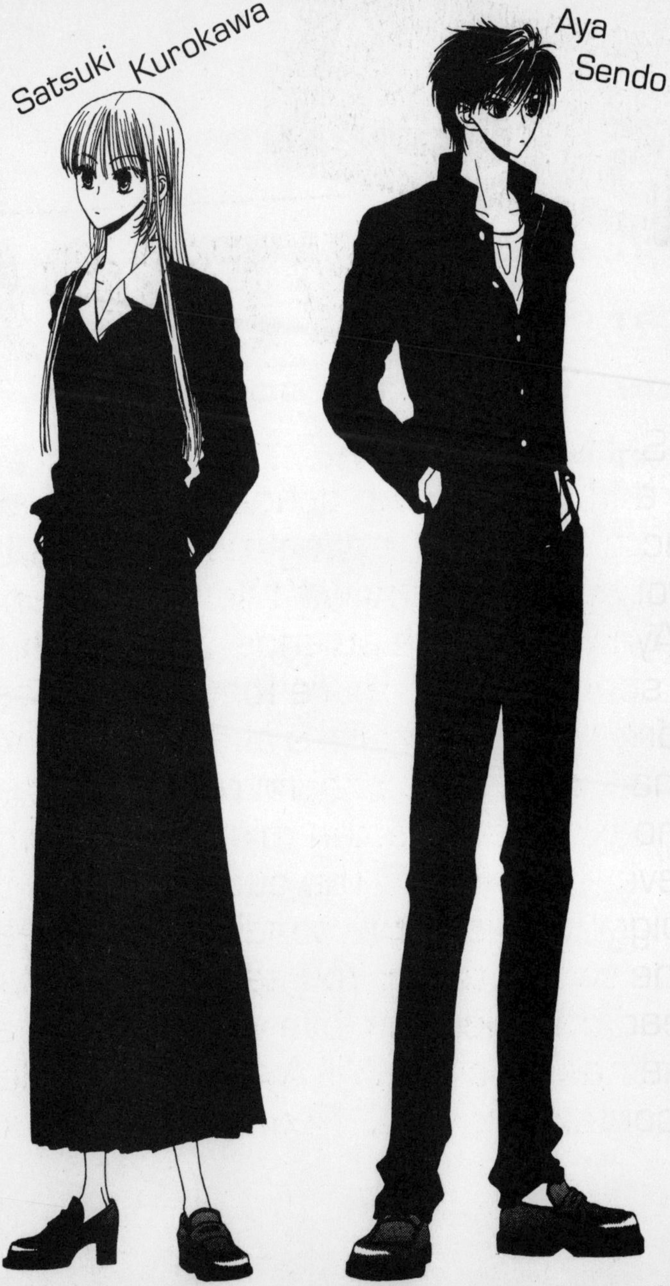
Satsuki Kurokawa
Aya Sendo

CONTENTS

SHORT SUNZEN! 7

SHORT PREFACE! 8

A CON ARTIST IN THE BOILER ROOM .. 159

SHORT POSTSCRIPT! 203

GLOSSARY 204

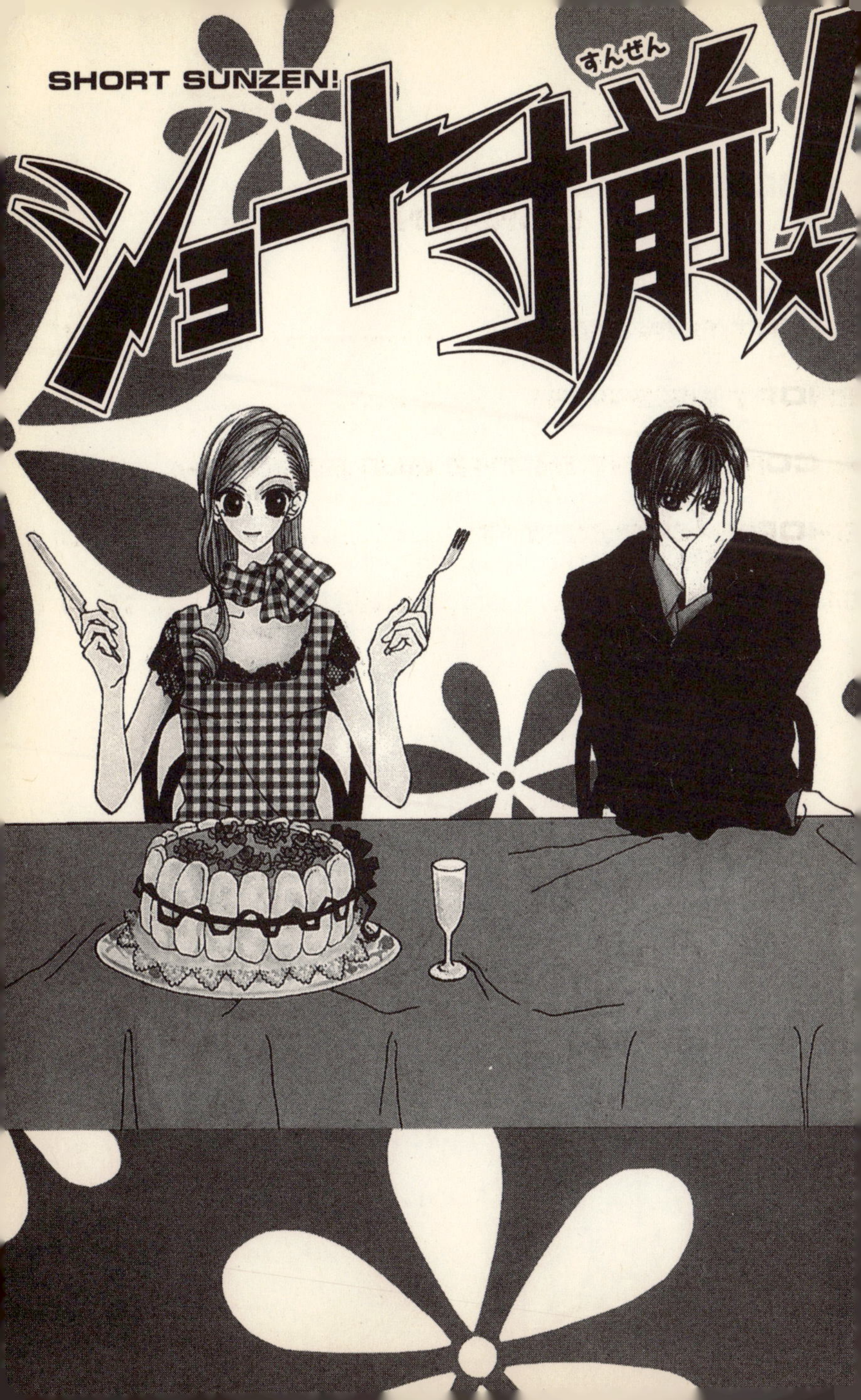
SHORT SUNZEN!
ショート寸前(すんぜん)!

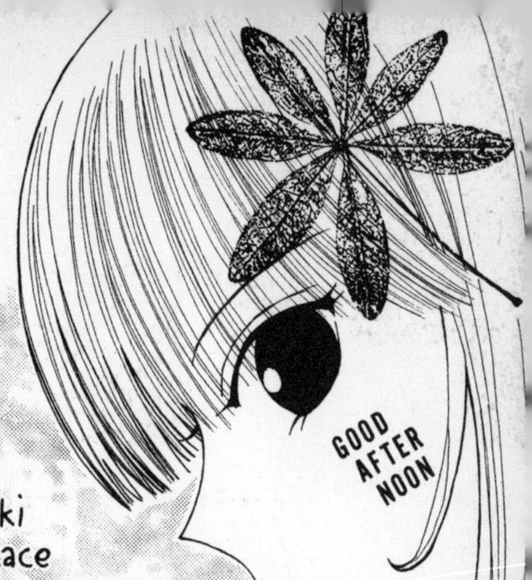
GOOD AFTER NOON

SHORT PREFACE!

Hello! It's been a while. Thank you for buying and reading this book. Volume 2! I'm happy we made it to volume 2! The story of Satsuki and Sendo this time takes place from summer to winter. It seems so exciting and fun! I'm envious! I am still fumbling towards the deadline with a carrot dangling in front of me (Ha ha)! And in the end, I probably won't even get to eat the carrot! Oh, I wish I could go to a concert. As I write this (March '01), the Spring Live concert series (Bump of Chicken, Kururi, Weezer, Seagull Screaming Kiss Her Kiss Her, Yurayura Teikoku) and summer festivals (Fuji Rock Festival, Rising Sun Rock Festival, Summer Sonic) hang in front of me as bait to keep me working. No, no! I mean, the only reason I can keep working is because of the people around me. If everyone enjoys the book, then all the work will have been worth it. (Ha ha ha!)

And that is just the preface.

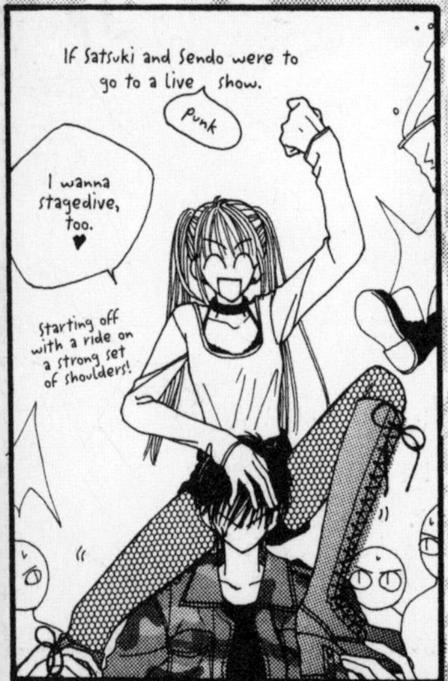
If Satsuki and Sendo were to go to a live show.
Punk
I wanna stagedive, too. ♥
Starting off with a ride on a strong set of shoulders!

I wish someone would give me a ride their shoulders!

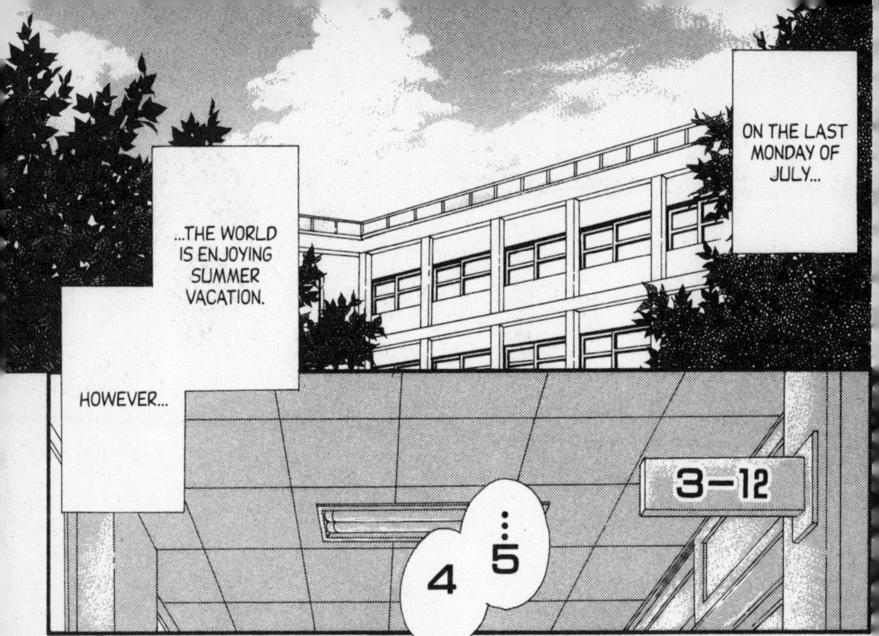
ON THE LAST MONDAY OF JULY...
...THE WORLD IS ENJOYING SUMMER VACATION.
HOWEVER...
3-12
...5
4

Note: see translators notes, page 204

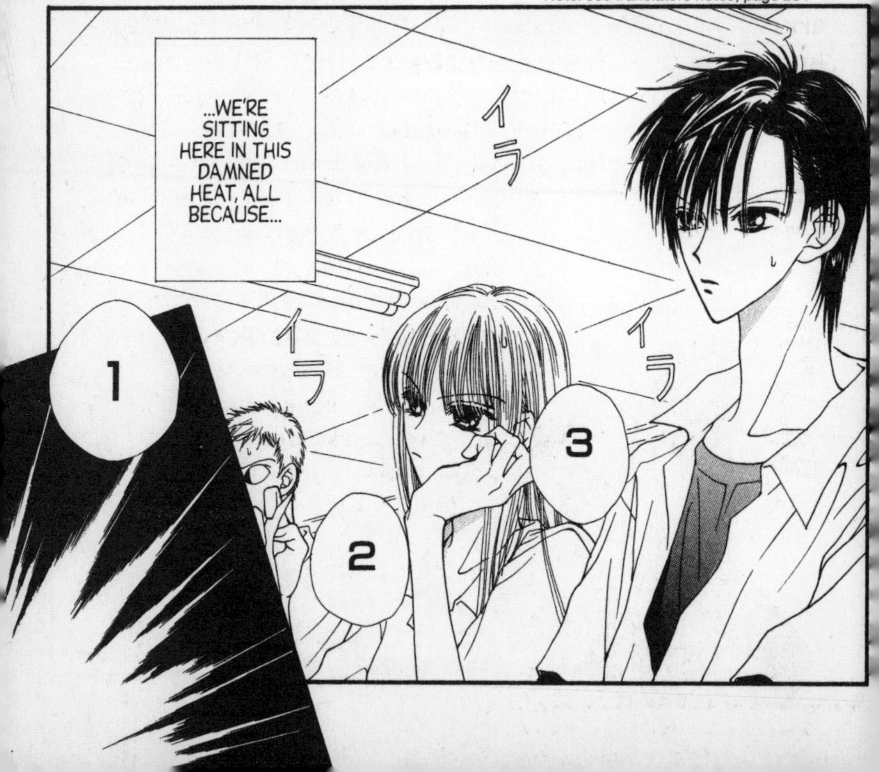
イラ
...WE'RE SITTING HERE IN THIS DAMNED HEAT, ALL BECAUSE...
イラ
3
イラ
2
1

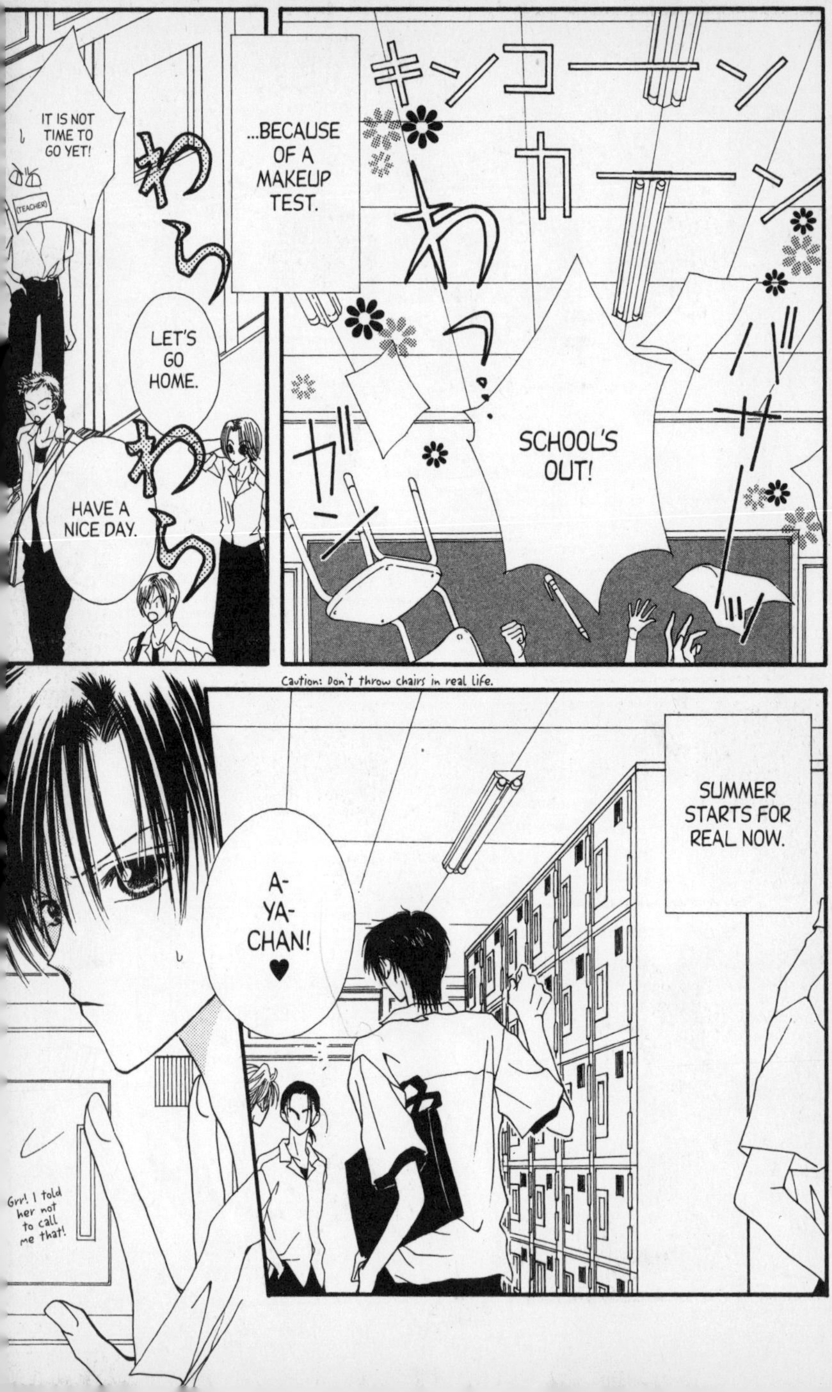
キーンコーンカーン
わぁっ!!
SCHOOL'S OUT!
ガッ
バサー
...BECAUSE OF A MAKEUP TEST.
Caution: Don't throw chairs in real life.
IT IS NOT TIME TO GO YET!
(TEACHER)
わらわら
LET'S GO HOME.
HAVE A NICE DAY.
SUMMER STARTS FOR REAL NOW.
A-YA-CHAN! ♥
Grr! I told her not to call me that!

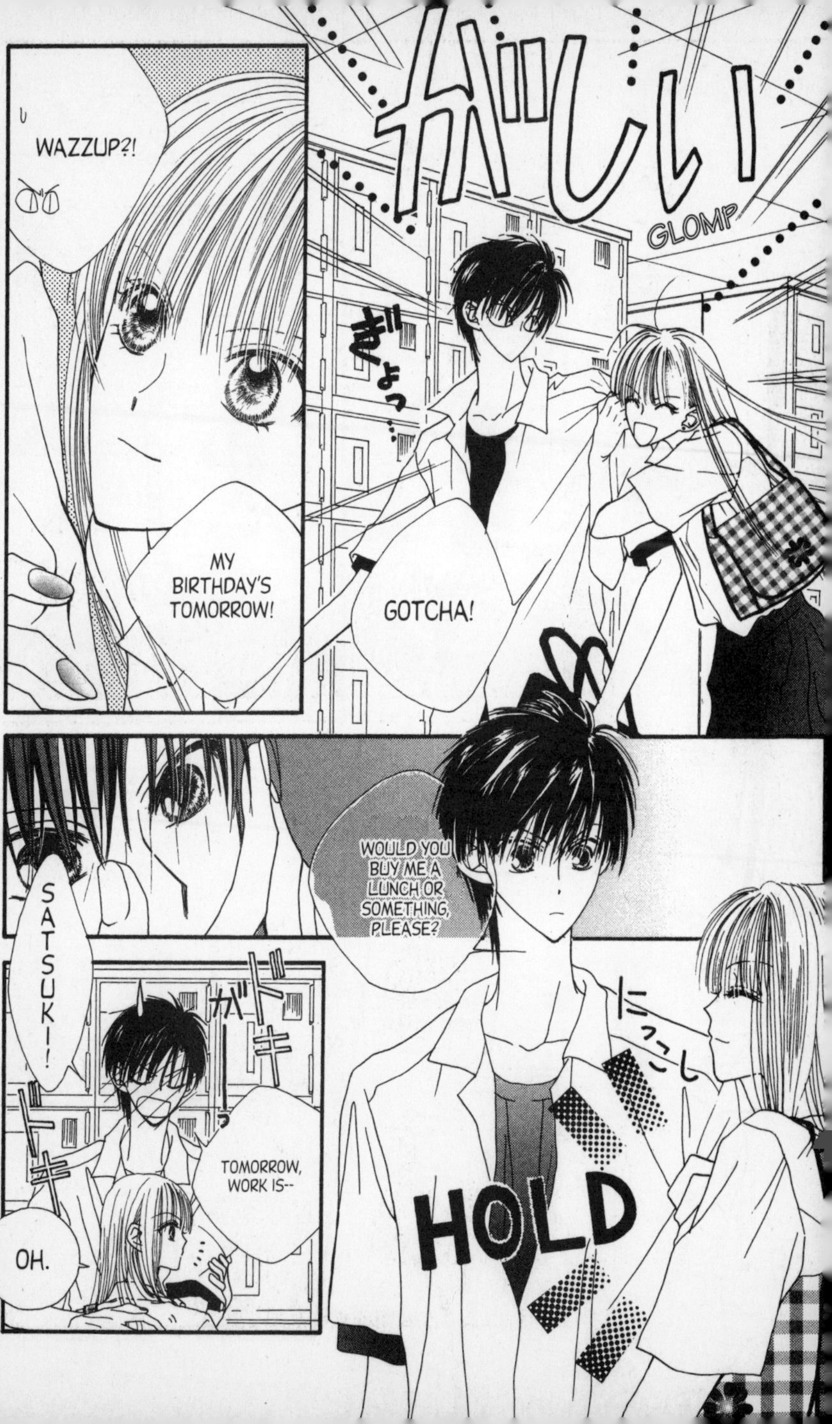
がしぃ
GLOMP
ぎょっ…
GOTCHA!
WAZZUP?!
MY BIRTHDAY'S TOMORROW!
WOULD YOU BUY ME A LUNCH OR SOMETHING, PLEASE?
にっこし
HOLD
SATSUKI!
ドキ
ガ
ドキ
TOMORROW, WORK IS--
OH.

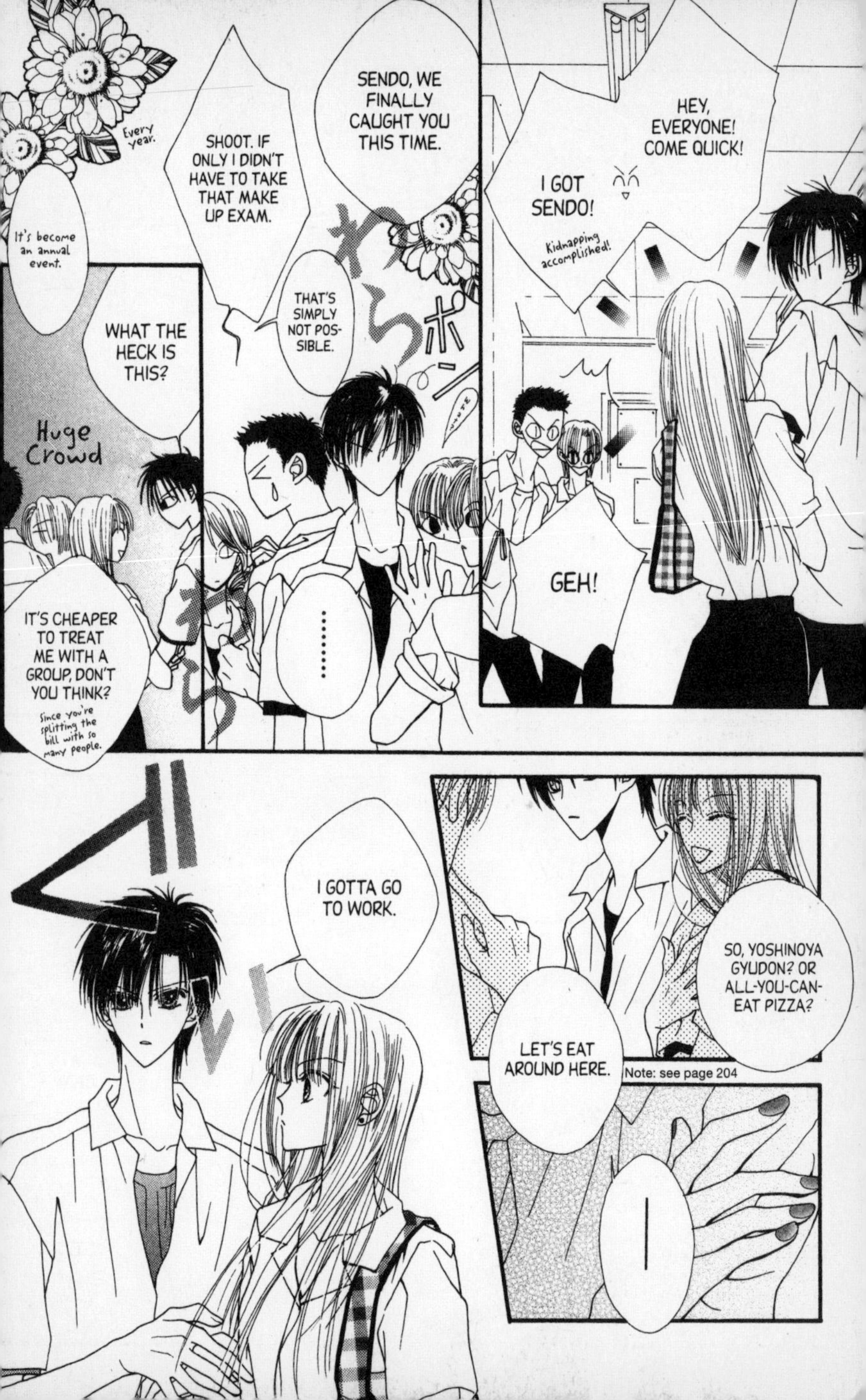
HEY, EVERYONE! COME QUICK!
I GOT SENDO!
Kidnapping accomplished!
GEH!
SENDO, WE FINALLY CAUGHT YOU THIS TIME.
SHOOT. IF ONLY I DIDN'T HAVE TO TAKE THAT MAKE UP EXAM.
THAT'S SIMPLY NOT POSSIBLE.
......
Every year.
It's become an annual event.
WHAT THE HECK IS THIS?
Huge Crowd
IT'S CHEAPER TO TREAT ME WITH A GROUP, DON'T YOU THINK?
Since you're splitting the bill with so many people.
SO, YOSHINOYA GYUDON? OR ALL-YOU-CAN-EAT PIZZA?
LET'S EAT AROUND HERE.
Note: see page 204
—
I GOTTA GO TO WORK.

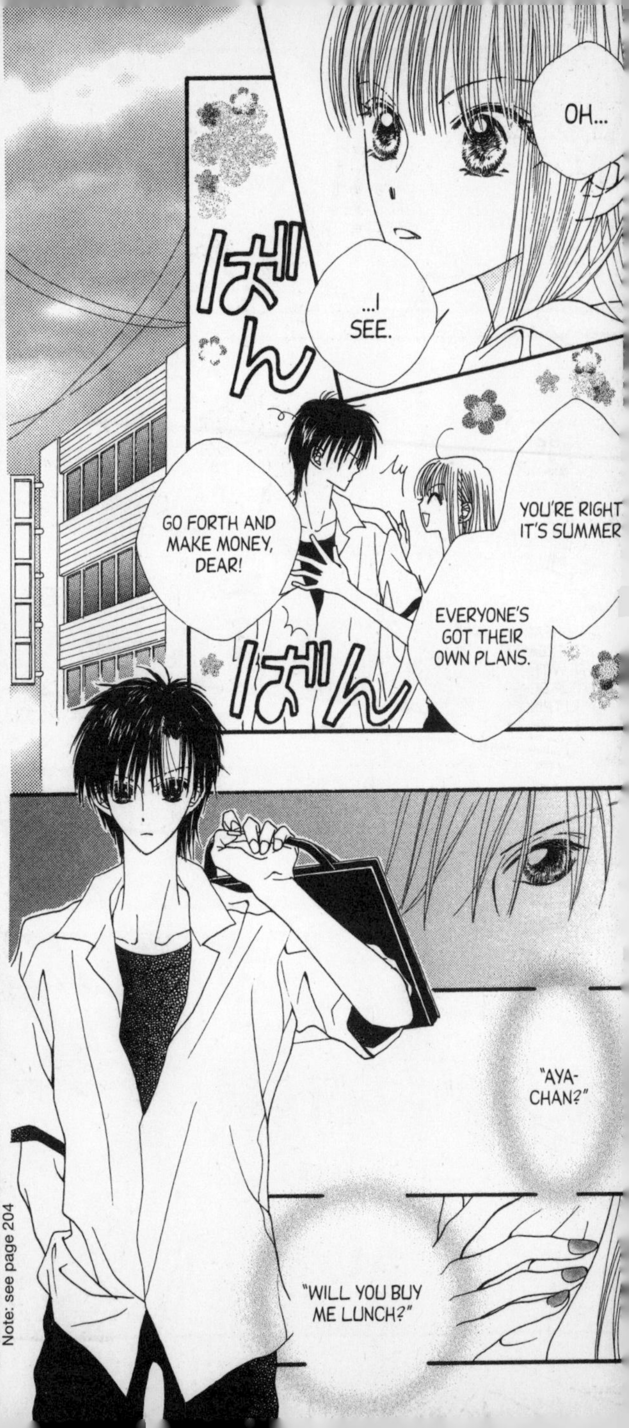
OH...
...I SEE.
ばん
YOU'RE RIGHT IT'S SUMMER
EVERYONE'S GOT THEIR OWN PLANS.
GO FORTH AND MAKE MONEY, DEAR!
ばん
"AYA-CHAN?"
"WILL YOU BUY ME LUNCH?"

Note: see page 204

WARDROBE

So, will you let me play with this space again? Play dress up.

Whether you feel nostalgic or embarrassed, you can read it or leave it. It's up to you.

OMAKE.

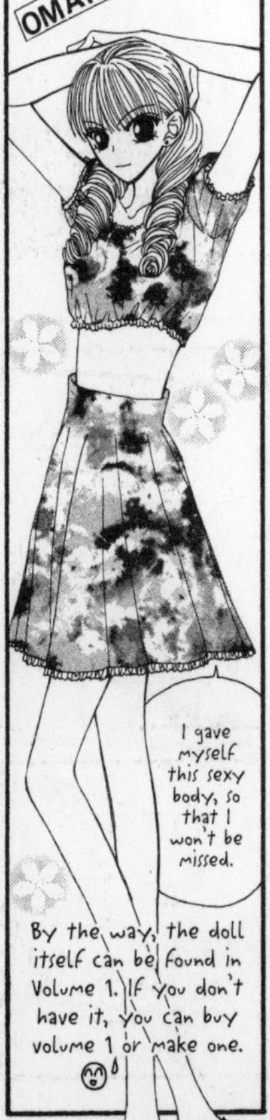
I gave myself this sexy body, so that I won't be missed.

By the way, the doll itself can be found in Volume 1. If you don't have it, you can buy volume 1 or make one.

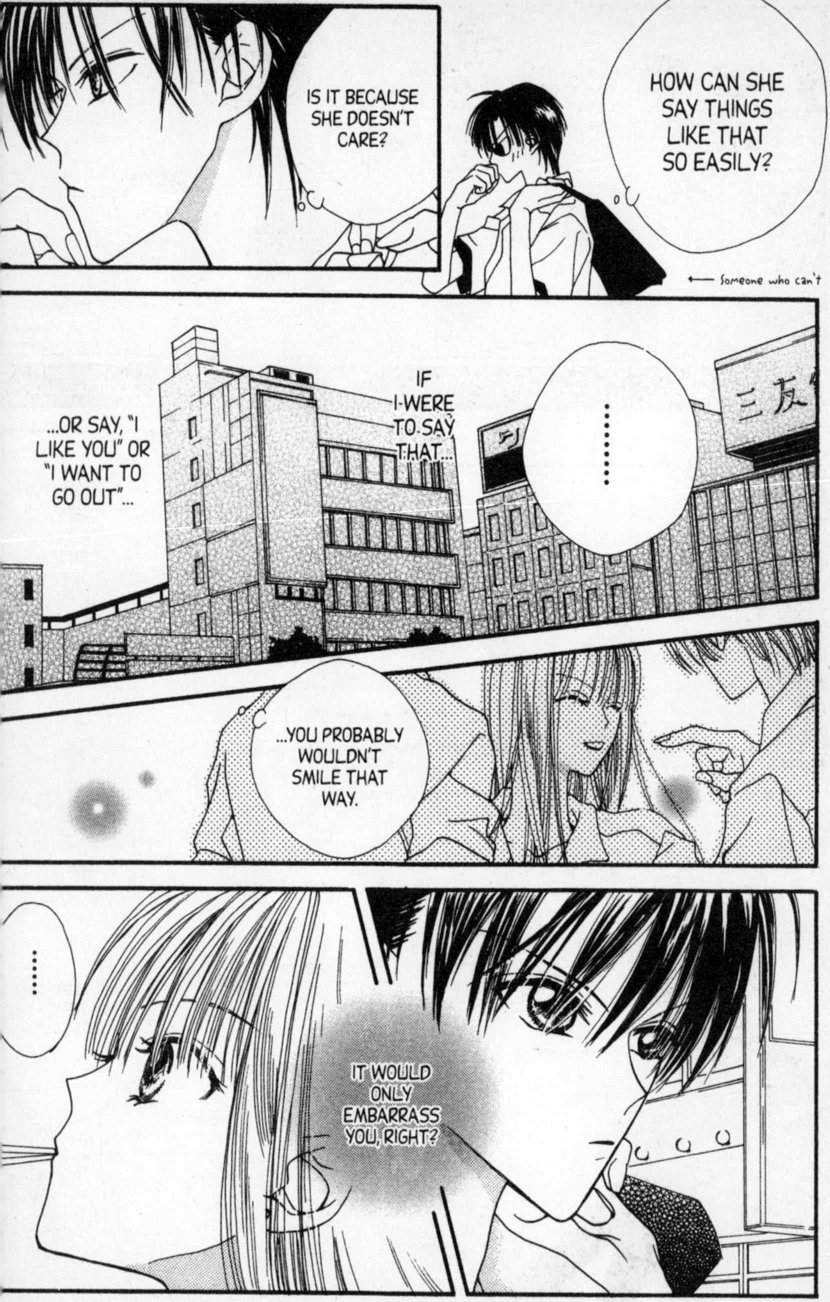
HOW CAN SHE SAY THINGS LIKE THAT SO EASILY?
← Someone who can't
IS IT BECAUSE SHE DOESN'T CARE?
三友
......
IF I WERE TO SAY THAT...
...OR SAY, "I LIKE YOU" OR "I WANT TO GO OUT"...
...YOU PROBABLY WOULDN'T SMILE THAT WAY.
IT WOULD ONLY EMBARRASS YOU, RIGHT?
......

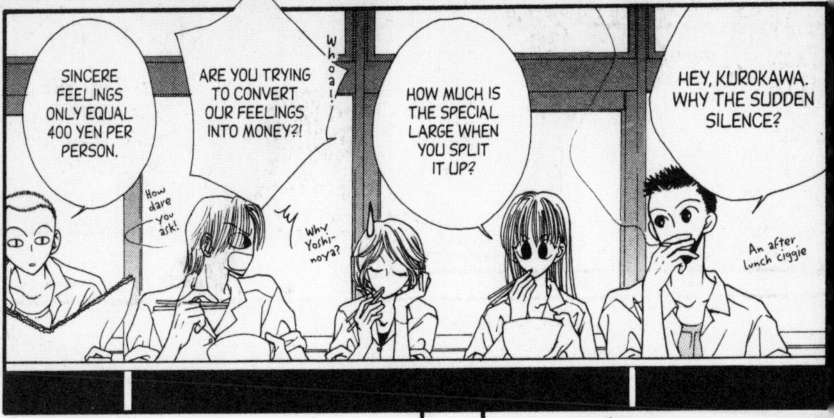
HEY, KUROKAWA. WHY THE SUDDEN SILENCE?
An after lunch ciggie
HOW MUCH IS THE SPECIAL LARGE WHEN YOU SPLIT IT UP?
Why Yoshi-noya?
Whoa!
ARE YOU TRYING TO CONVERT OUR FEELINGS INTO MONEY?!
How dare you ask!
SINCERE FEELINGS ONLY EQUAL 400 YEN PER PERSON.

Note: see page 204

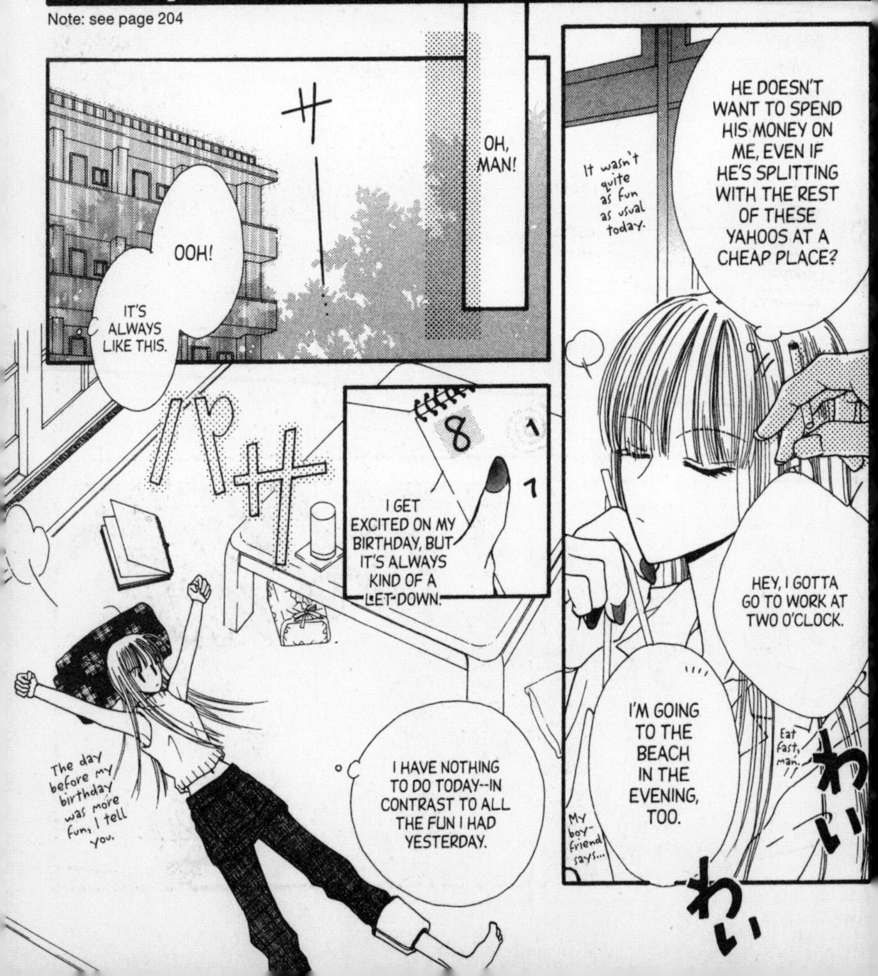
HE DOESN'T WANT TO SPEND HIS MONEY ON ME, EVEN IF HE'S SPLITTING WITH THE REST OF THESE YAHOOS AT A CHEAP PLACE?
It wasn't quite as fun as usual today.
HEY, I GOTTA GO TO WORK AT TWO O'CLOCK.
Eat fast, man.
I'M GOING TO THE BEACH IN THE EVENING, TOO.
My boy-friend says...
わい
わい
OH, MAN!
OOH!
IT'S ALWAYS LIKE THIS.
8
1
7
I GET EXCITED ON MY BIRTHDAY, BUT IT'S ALWAYS KIND OF A LET-DOWN.
I HAVE NOTHING TO DO TODAY--IN CONTRAST TO ALL THE FUN I HAD YESTERDAY.
The day before my birthday was more fun, I tell you.

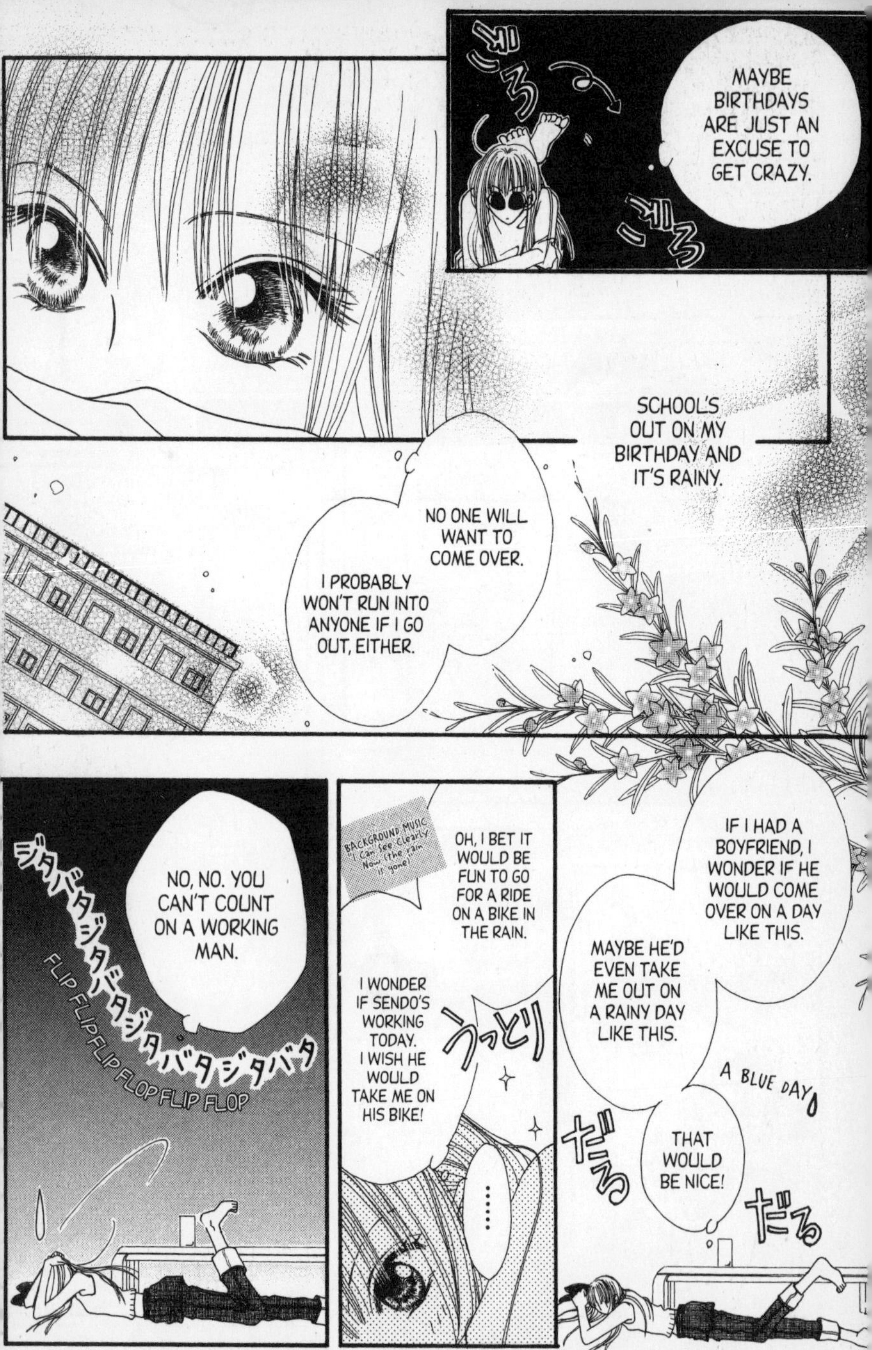
ごろ
MAYBE BIRTHDAYS ARE JUST AN EXCUSE TO GET CRAZY.
ごろ
SCHOOL'S OUT ON MY BIRTHDAY AND IT'S RAINY.
NO ONE WILL WANT TO COME OVER.
I PROBABLY WON'T RUN INTO ANYONE IF I GO OUT, EITHER.
IF I HAD A BOYFRIEND, I WONDER IF HE WOULD COME OVER ON A DAY LIKE THIS.
MAYBE HE'D EVEN TAKE ME OUT ON A RAINY DAY LIKE THIS.
A BLUE DAY
THAT WOULD BE NICE!
だる
だる
BACKGROUND MUSIC "I Can See Clearly Now (the rain is gone)"
OH, I BET IT WOULD BE FUN TO GO FOR A RIDE ON A BIKE IN THE RAIN.
I WONDER IF SENDO'S WORKING TODAY. I WISH HE WOULD TAKE ME ON HIS BIKE!
うっとり
......
NO, NO. YOU CAN'T COUNT ON A WORKING MAN.
ジタバタジタバタジタバタジタバタ
FLIP FLIP FLIP FLOP FLIP FLOP

No worrying!

Note: see page 204

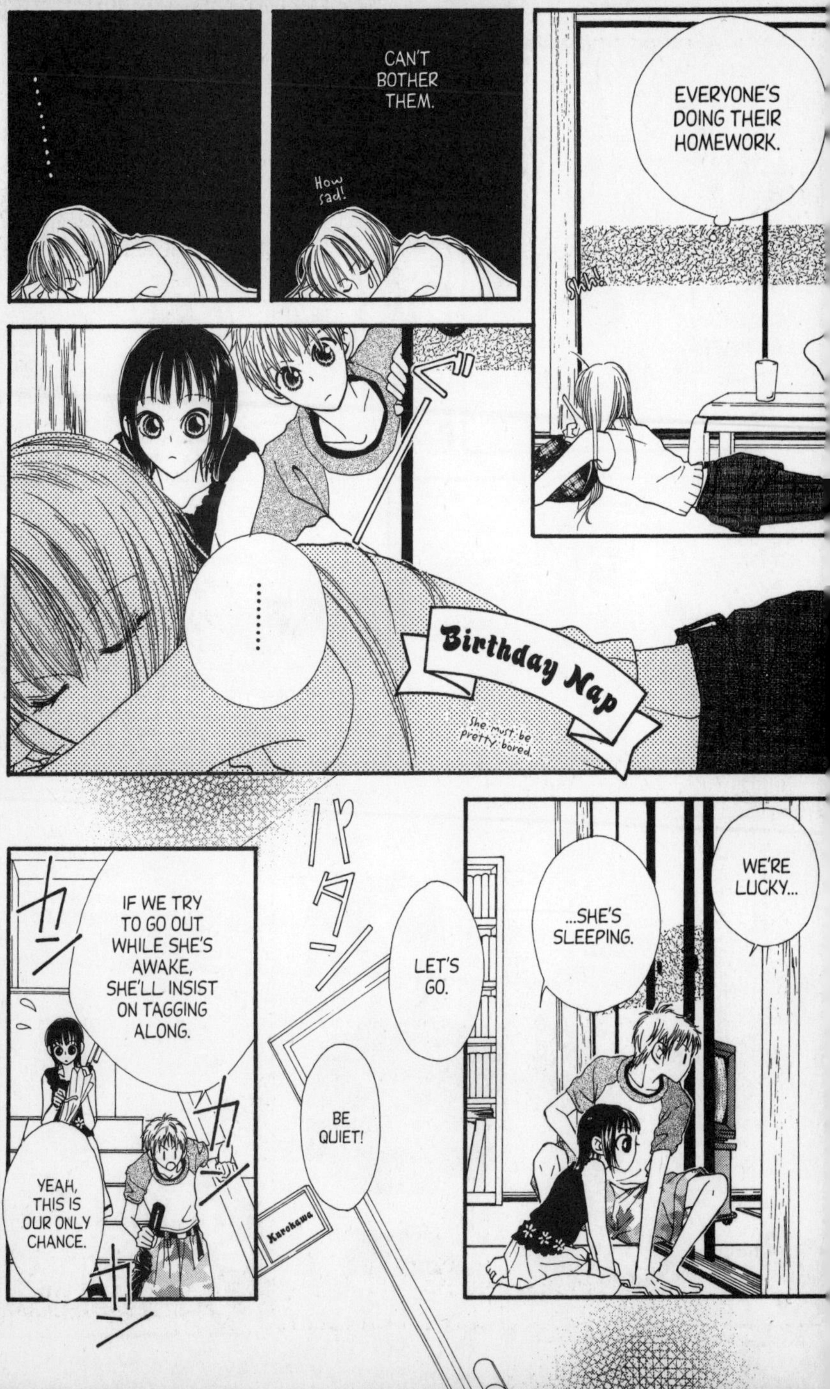
EVERYONE'S DOING THEIR HOMEWORK.
CAN'T BOTHER THEM.
How sad!
......
Birthday Nap
......
She must be pretty bored.
WE'RE LUCKY...
...SHE'S SLEEPING.
LET'S GO.
BE QUIET!
IF WE TRY TO GO OUT WHILE SHE'S AWAKE, SHE'LL INSIST ON TAGGING ALONG.
YEAH, THIS IS OUR ONLY CHANCE.
Kurokawa

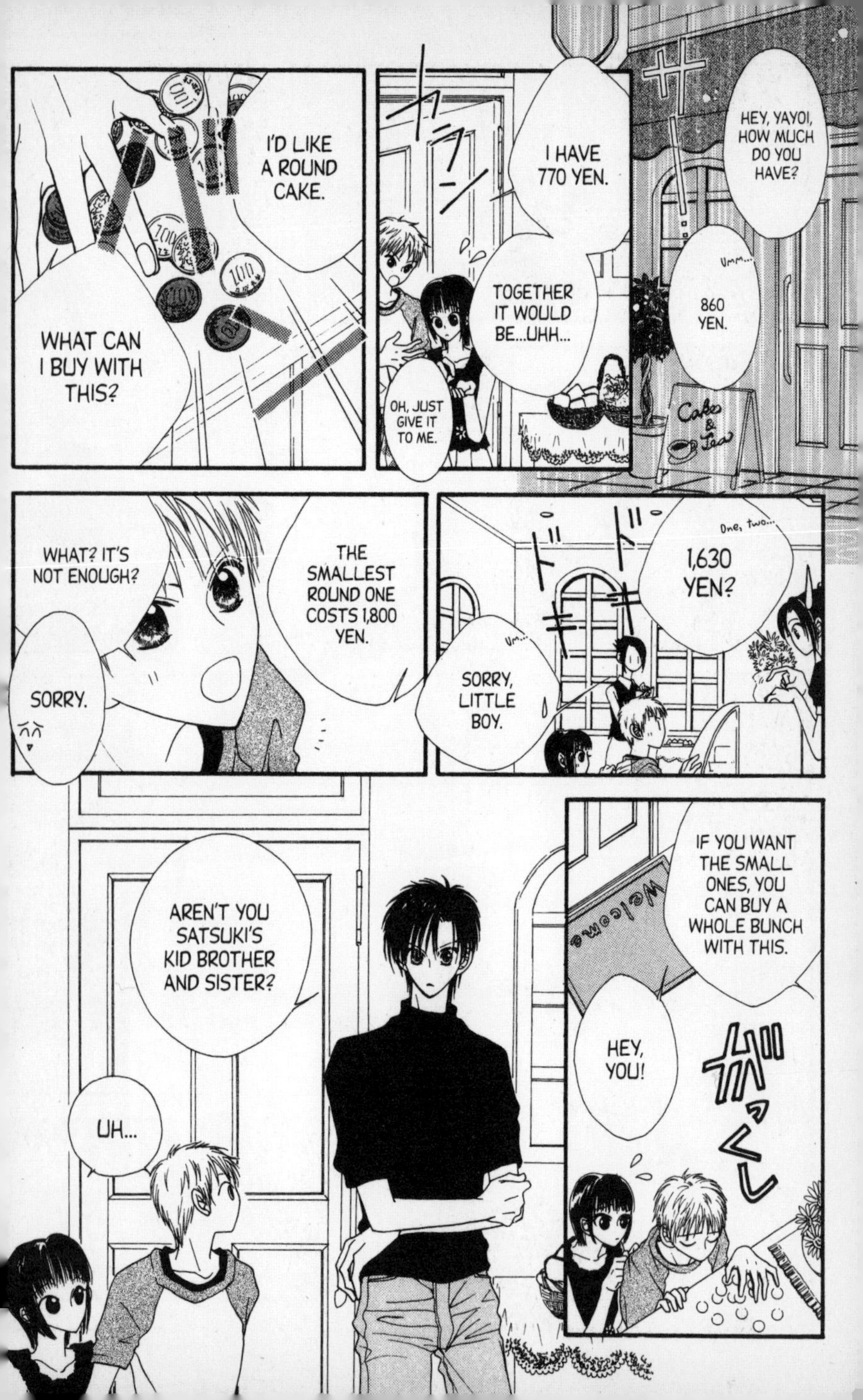
HEY, YAYOI, HOW MUCH DO YOU HAVE?
UMM...
860 YEN.
Cakes & Tea
I HAVE 770 YEN.
TOGETHER IT WOULD BE...UHH...
OH, JUST GIVE IT TO ME.
I'D LIKE A ROUND CAKE.
WHAT CAN I BUY WITH THIS?
One, two...
1,630 YEN?
Um...
SORRY, LITTLE BOY.
THE SMALLEST ROUND ONE COSTS 1,800 YEN.
WHAT? IT'S NOT ENOUGH?
SORRY.
IF YOU WANT THE SMALL ONES, YOU CAN BUY A WHOLE BUNCH WITH THIS.
HEY, YOU!
AREN'T YOU SATSUKI'S KID BROTHER AND SISTER?
UH...

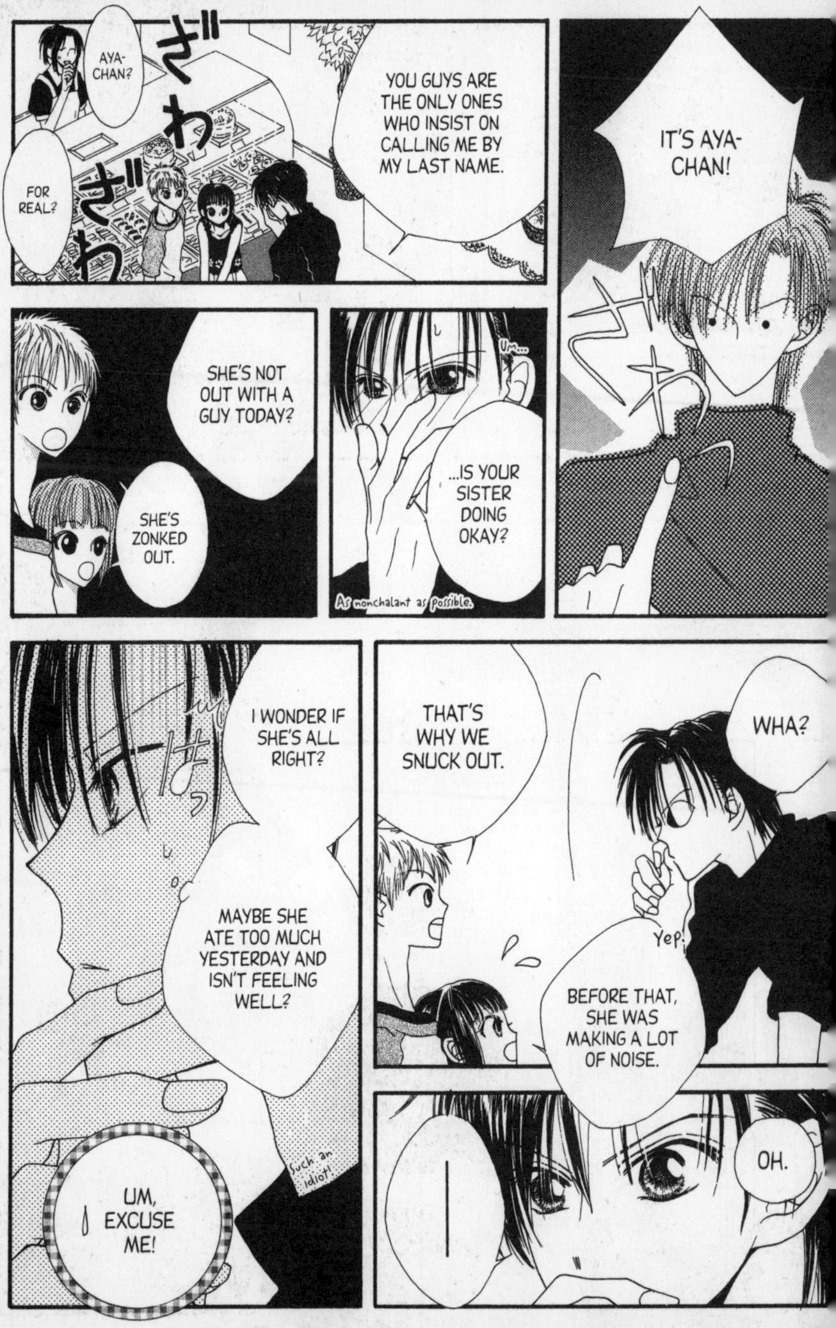
IT'S AYA-CHAN!
ざわ
YOU GUYS ARE THE ONLY ONES WHO INSIST ON CALLING ME BY MY LAST NAME.
ざわざわ
AYA-CHAN?
FOR REAL?
Um...
...IS YOUR SISTER DOING OKAY?
As nonchalant as possible.
SHE'S NOT OUT WITH A GUY TODAY?
SHE'S ZONKED OUT.
WHA?
THAT'S WHY WE SNUCK OUT.
Yep.
BEFORE THAT, SHE WAS MAKING A LOT OF NOISE.
OH.
I WONDER IF SHE'S ALL RIGHT?
はっ
MAYBE SHE ATE TOO MUCH YESTERDAY AND ISN'T FEELING WELL?
Such an idiot!
UM, EXCUSE ME!

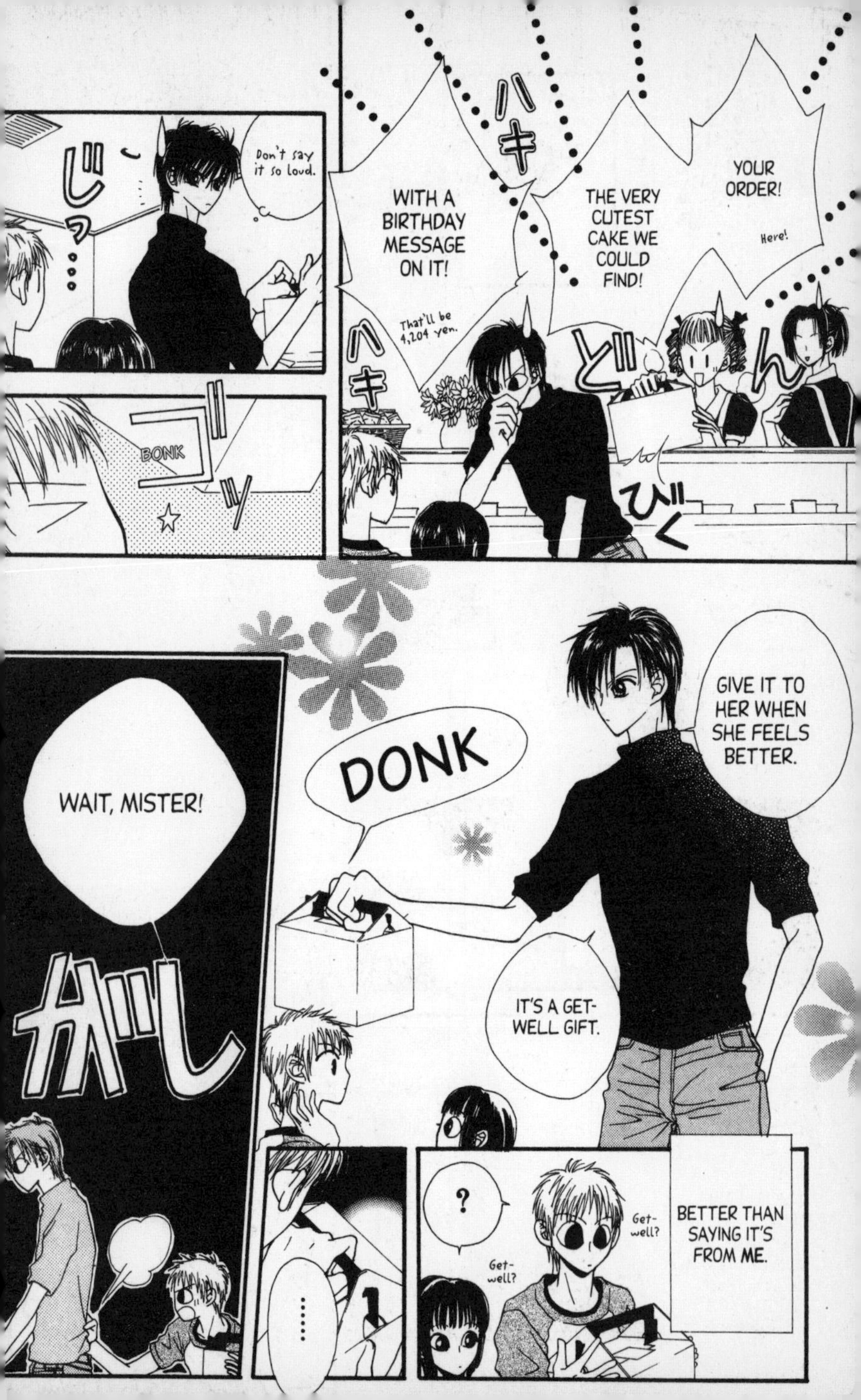
YOUR ORDER!
Here!
THE VERY CUTEST CAKE WE COULD FIND!
WITH A BIRTHDAY MESSAGE ON IT!
That'll be 4,204 yen.
ハキ
ハキ
どん
びく
じっ…
Don't say it so loud.
ゴッ
BONK
GIVE IT TO HER WHEN SHE FEELS BETTER.
DONK
IT'S A GET-WELL GIFT.
BETTER THAN SAYING IT'S FROM ME.
Get-well?
Get-well?
?
……
WAIT, MISTER!
がし

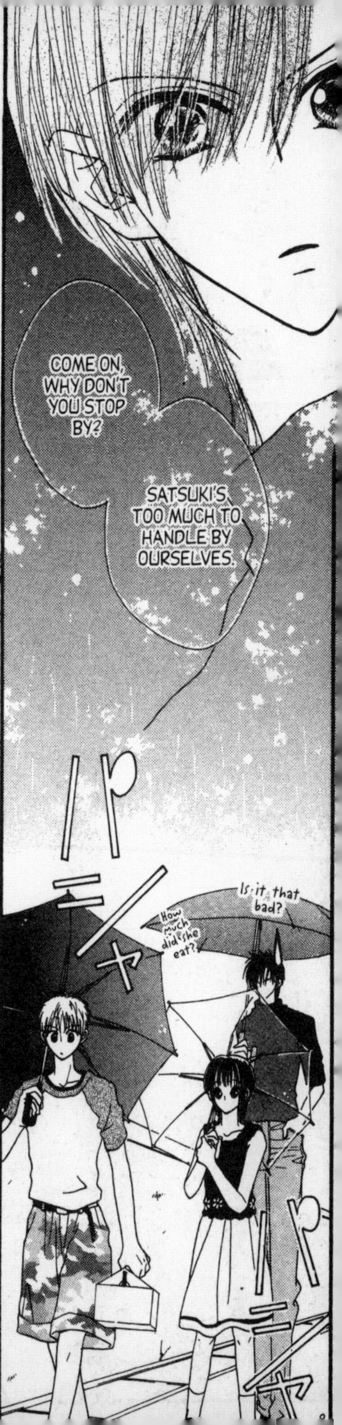
COME ON, WHY DON'T YOU STOP BY?
SATSUKI'S TOO MUCH TO HANDLE BY OURSELVES.
Is it that bad?
How much did she eat?

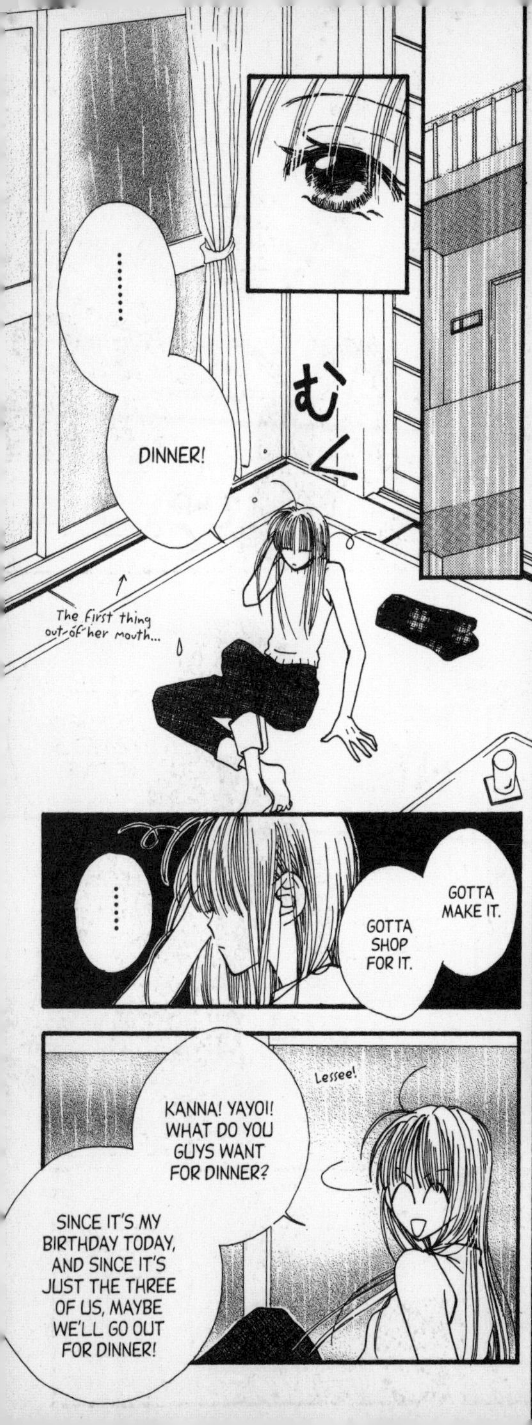
むく
......
DINNER!
The first thing out of her mouth...
GOTTA MAKE IT.
GOTTA SHOP FOR IT.
......
Lessee!
KANNA! YAYOI! WHAT DO YOU GUYS WANT FOR DINNER?
SINCE IT'S MY BIRTHDAY TODAY, AND SINCE IT'S JUST THE THREE OF US, MAYBE WE'LL GO OUT FOR DINNER!

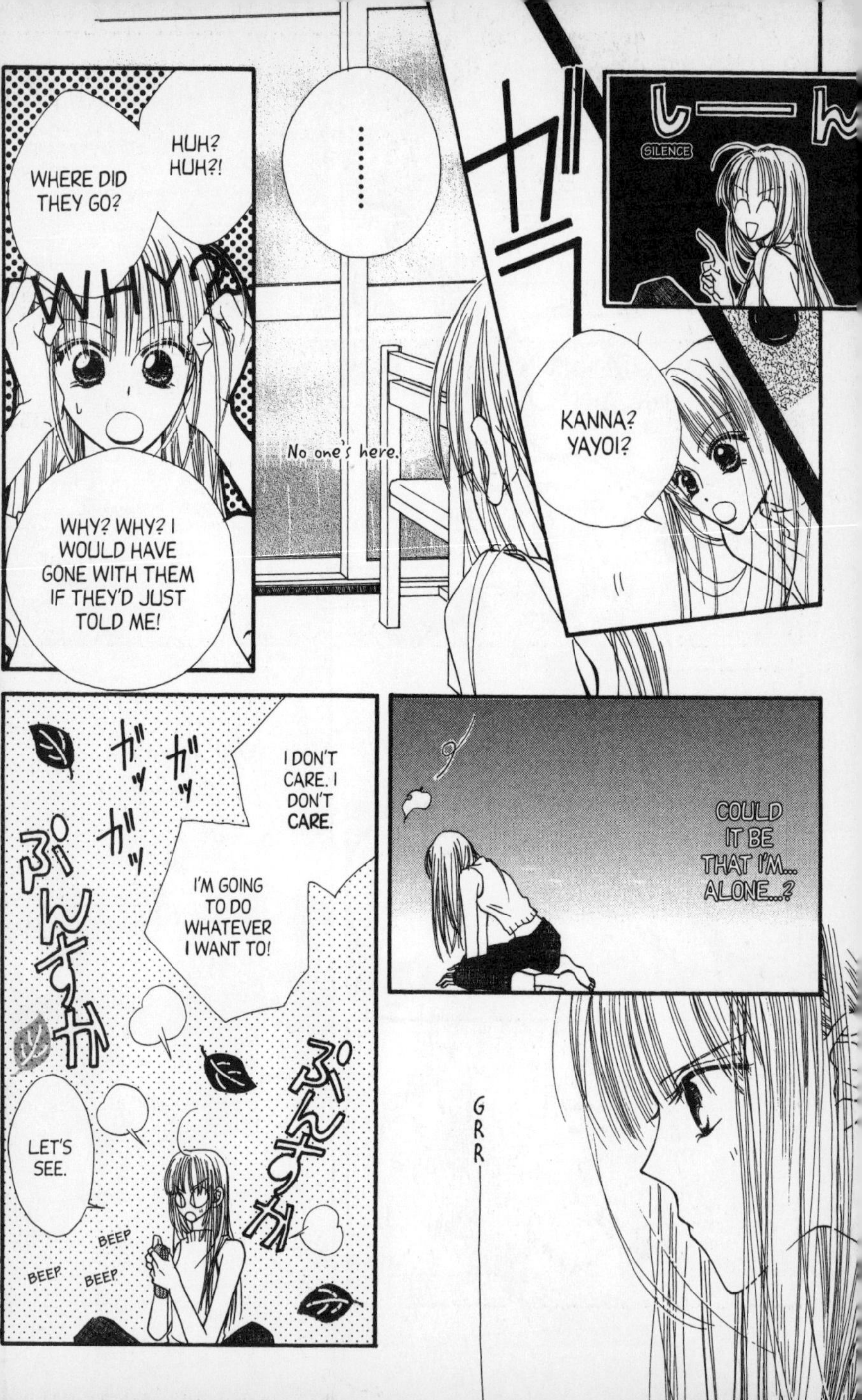
SILENCE
KANNA? YAYOI?
......
No one's here.
HUH? HUH?!
WHERE DID THEY GO?
WHY?
WHY? WHY? I WOULD HAVE GONE WITH THEM IF THEY'D JUST TOLD ME!
COULD IT BE THAT I'M... ALONE...?
GRR
I DON'T CARE. I DON'T CARE.
I'M GOING TO DO WHATEVER I WANT TO!
LET'S SEE.
BEEP
BEEP
BEEP

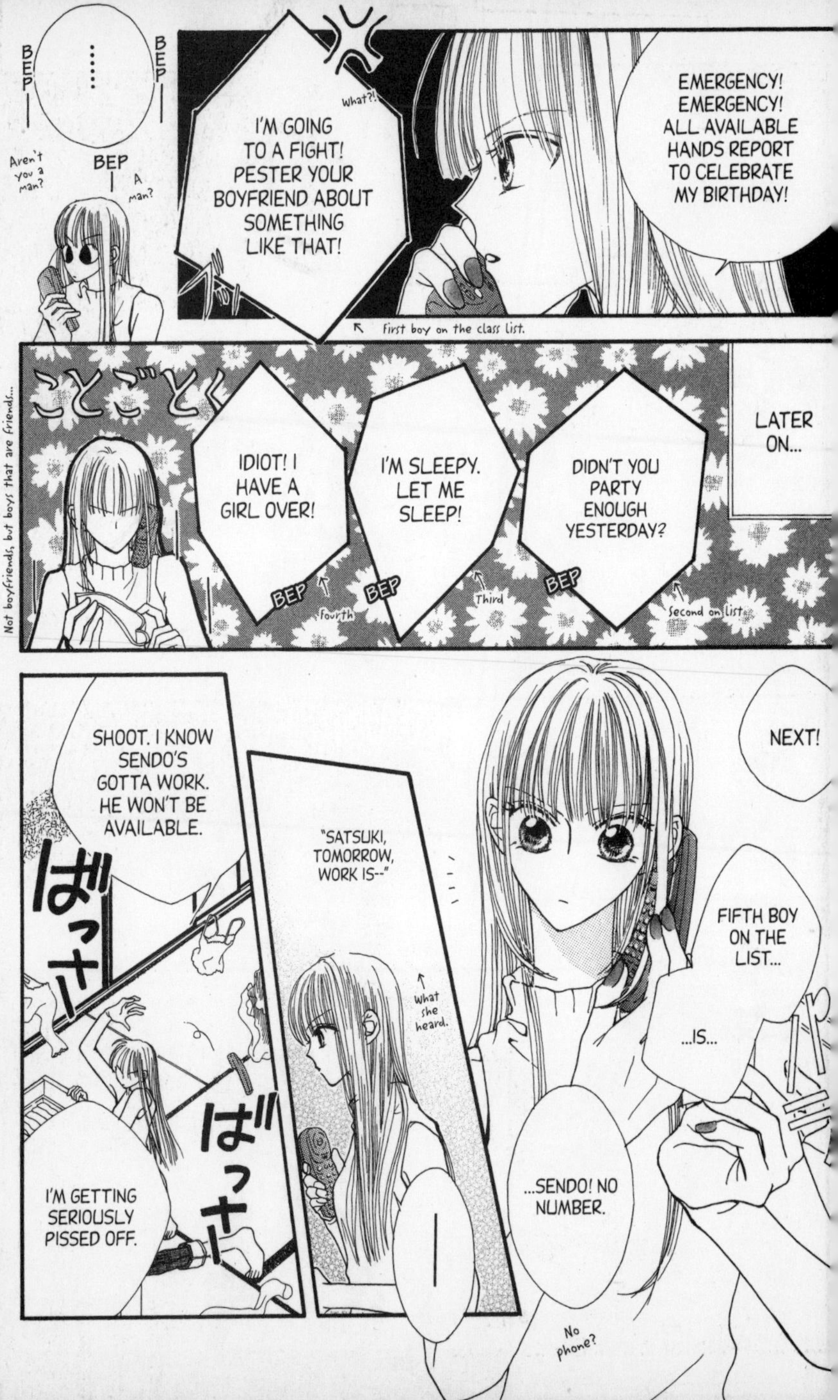
EMERGENCY! EMERGENCY! ALL AVAILABLE HANDS REPORT TO CELEBRATE MY BIRTHDAY!
What?!
I'M GOING TO A FIGHT! PESTER YOUR BOYFRIEND ABOUT SOMETHING LIKE THAT!
First boy on the class list.
BEP
BEP
......
Aren't you a man?
BEP
A man?
LATER ON...
DIDN'T YOU PARTY ENOUGH YESTERDAY?
BEP
Second on list
I'M SLEEPY. LET ME SLEEP!
BEP
Third
IDIOT! I HAVE A GIRL OVER!
BEP
fourth
ことごとく
Not boyfriends, but boys that are friends...
NEXT!
FIFTH BOY ON THE LIST...
...IS...
...SENDO! NO NUMBER.
No phone?
"SATSUKI, TOMORROW, WORK IS--"
What she heard.
SHOOT. I KNOW SENDO'S GOTTA WORK. HE WON'T BE AVAILABLE.
ばっさー
ばっさー
I'M GETTING SERIOUSLY PISSED OFF.

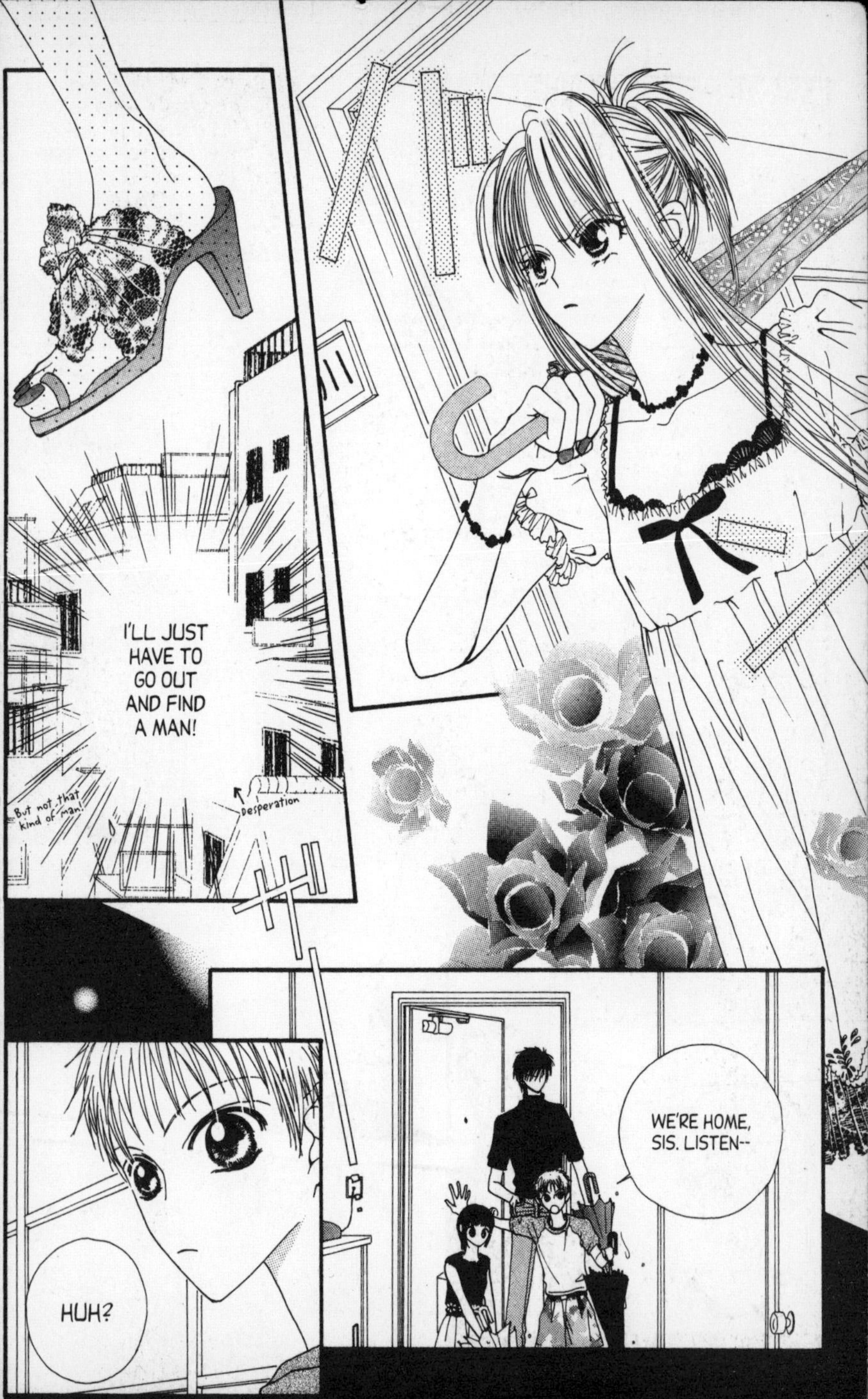
I'LL JUST HAVE TO GO OUT AND FIND A MAN!
Desperation
But not that kind of man!
WE'RE HOME, SIS. LISTEN--
HUH?

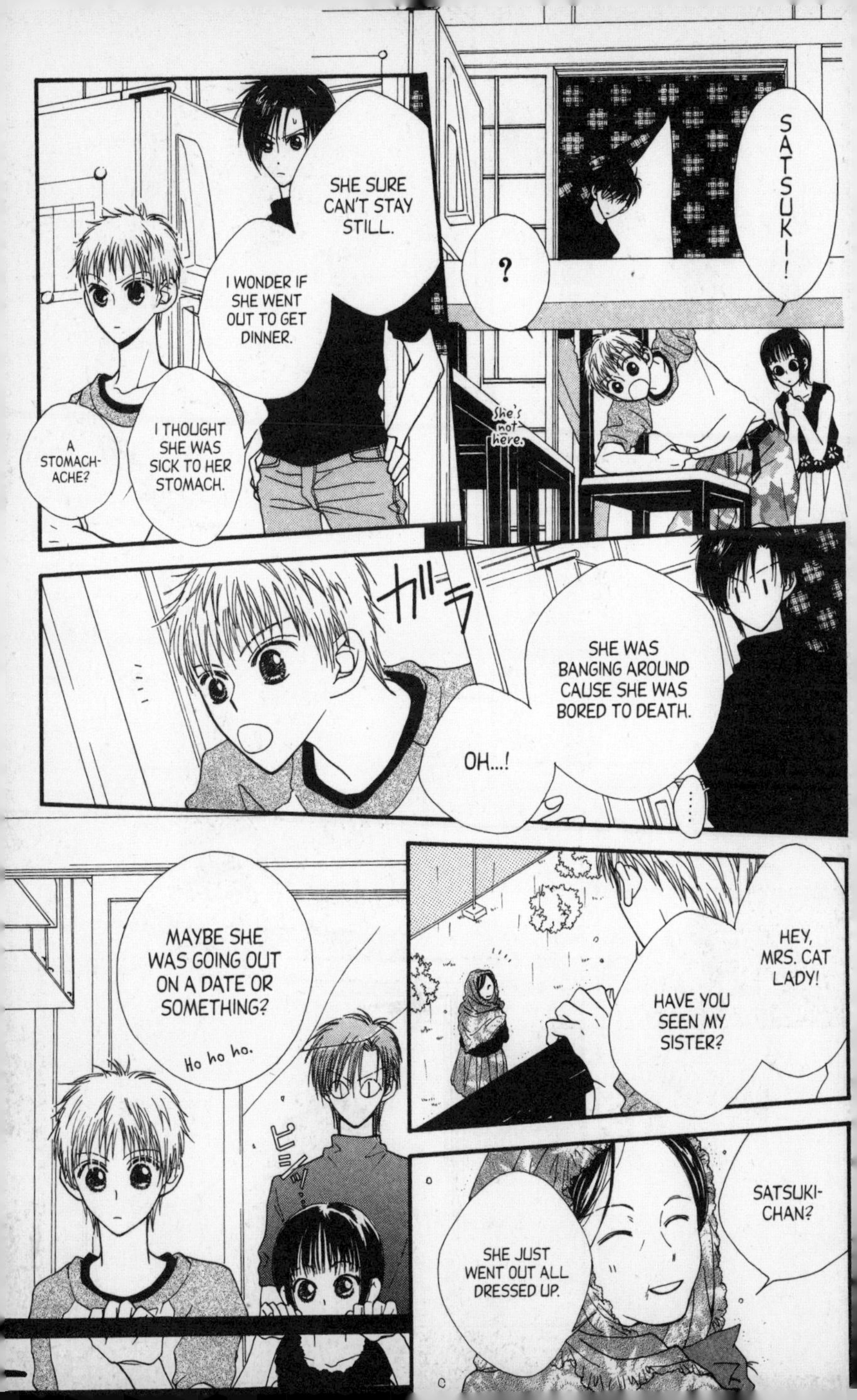
SATSUKI!
?
She's not here.
SHE SURE CAN'T STAY STILL.
I WONDER IF SHE WENT OUT TO GET DINNER.
I THOUGHT SHE WAS SICK TO HER STOMACH.
A STOMACH-ACHE?
ガラ
SHE WAS BANGING AROUND CAUSE SHE WAS BORED TO DEATH.
OH...!
.....
HEY, MRS. CAT LADY!
HAVE YOU SEEN MY SISTER?
SATSUKI-CHAN?
SHE JUST WENT OUT ALL DRESSED UP.
MAYBE SHE WAS GOING OUT ON A DATE OR SOMETHING?
Ho ho ho.
ピシッ

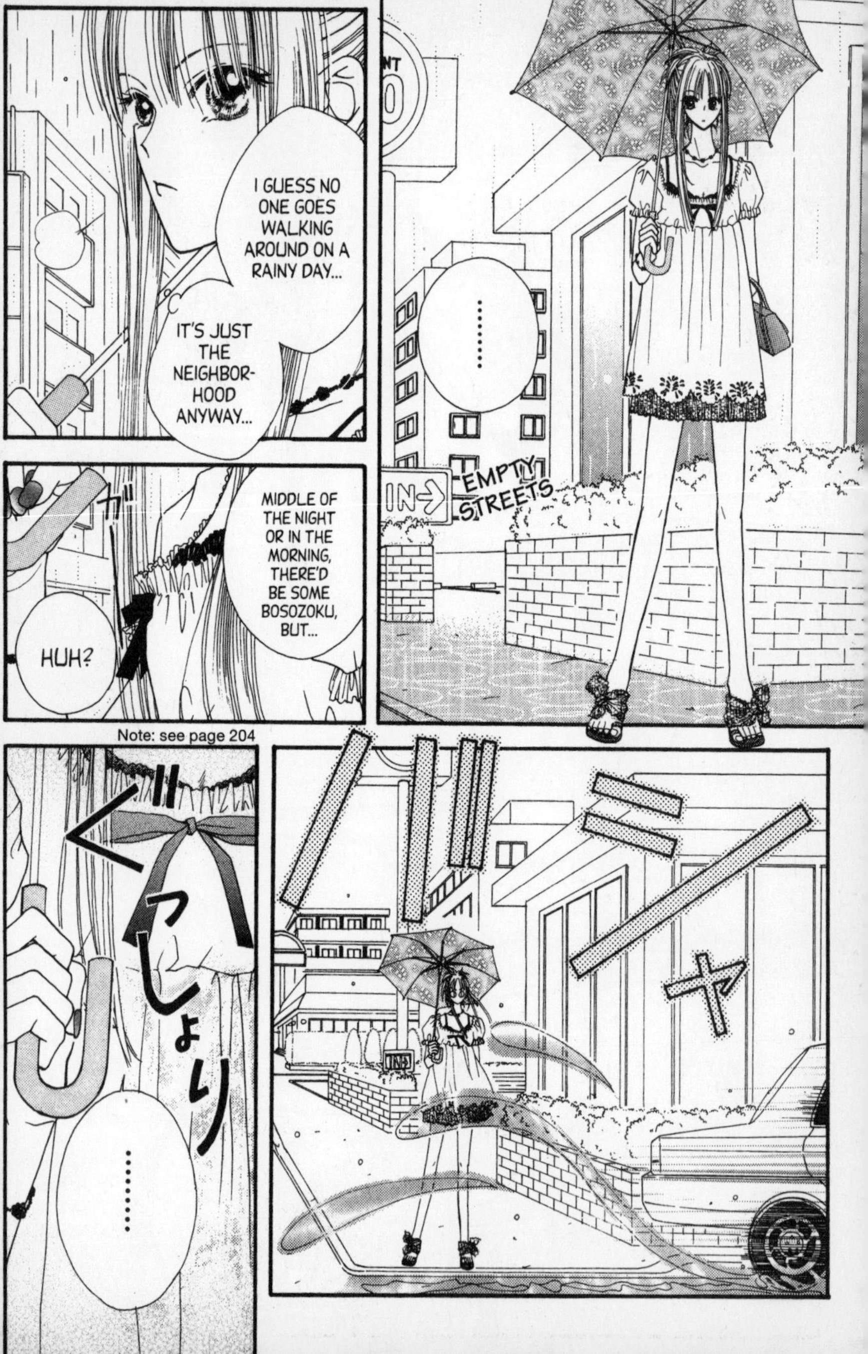
......
IN
EMPTY STREETS
I GUESS NO ONE GOES WALKING AROUND ON A RAINY DAY...
IT'S JUST THE NEIGHBORHOOD ANYWAY...
ガ
MIDDLE OF THE NIGHT OR IN THE MORNING, THERE'D BE SOME BOSOZOKU, BUT...
HUH?
ぐっしょり
......
Note: see page 204

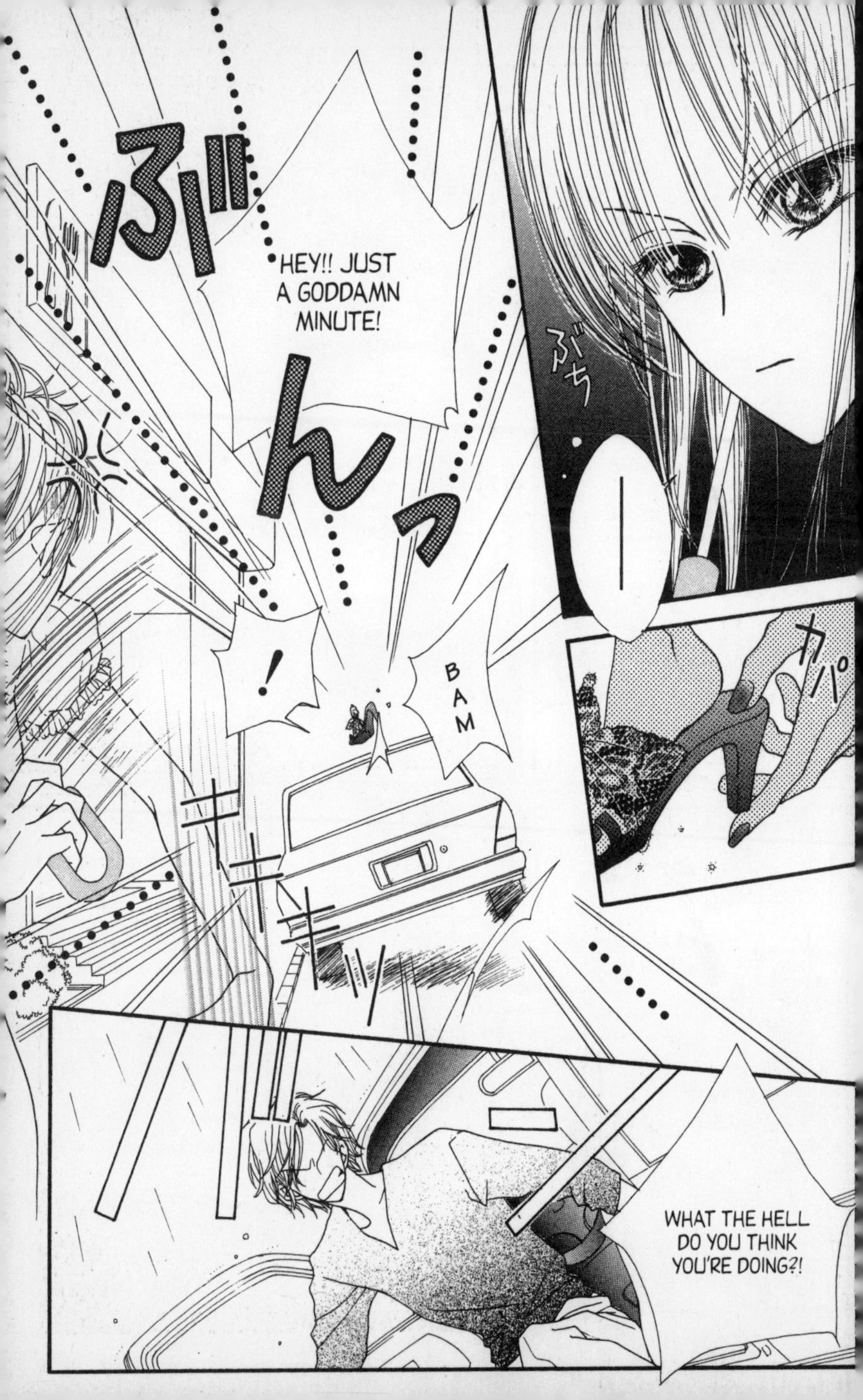
ぶち
カパ
ぶんっ
HEY!! JUST A GODDAMN MINUTE!
!
BAM
WHAT THE HELL DO YOU THINK YOU'RE DOING?!

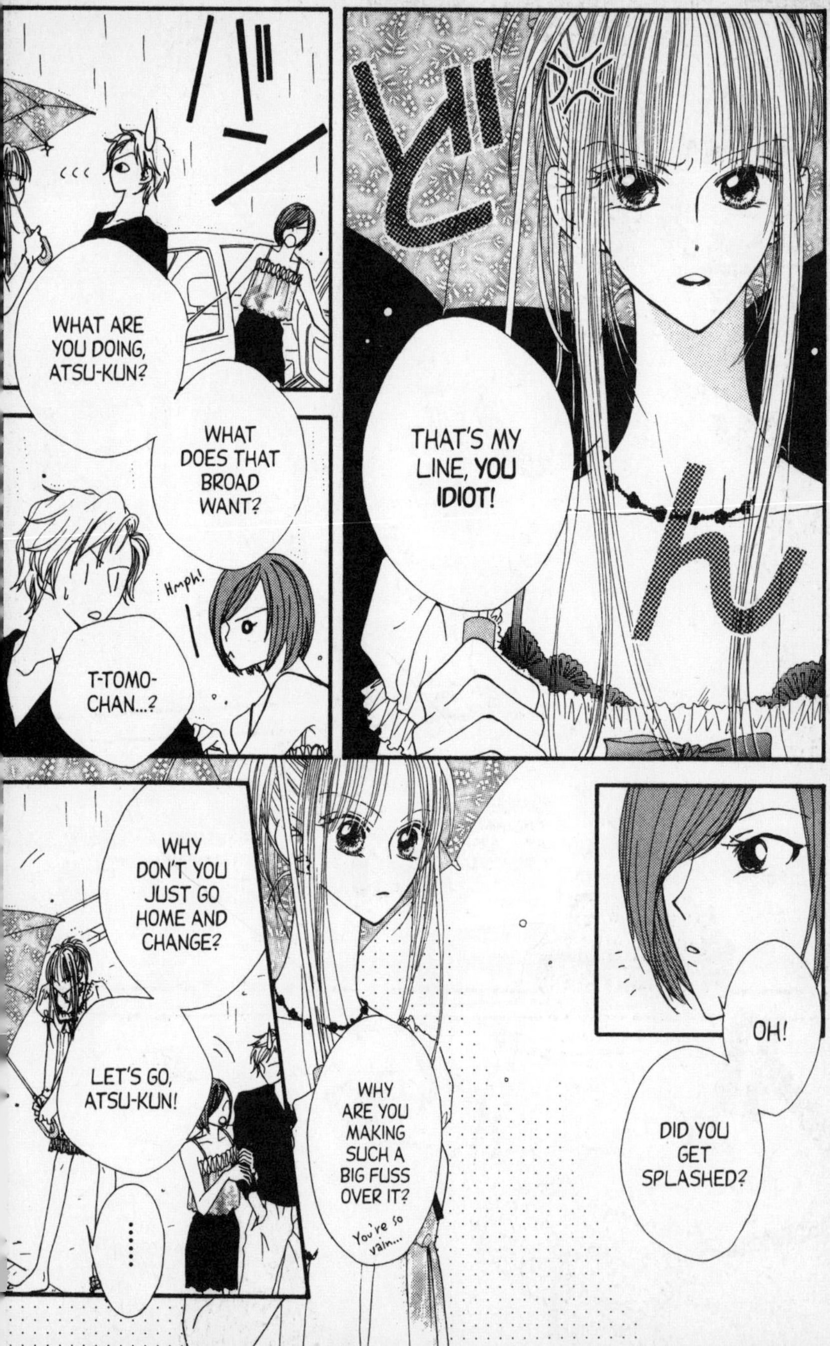
THAT'S MY LINE, YOU IDIOT!
WHAT ARE YOU DOING, ATSU-KUN?
WHAT DOES THAT BROAD WANT?
Hmph!
T-TOMO-CHAN...?
OH!
DID YOU GET SPLASHED?
WHY ARE YOU MAKING SUCH A BIG FUSS OVER IT?
You're so vain...
WHY DON'T YOU JUST GO HOME AND CHANGE?
LET'S GO, ATSU-KUN!
......

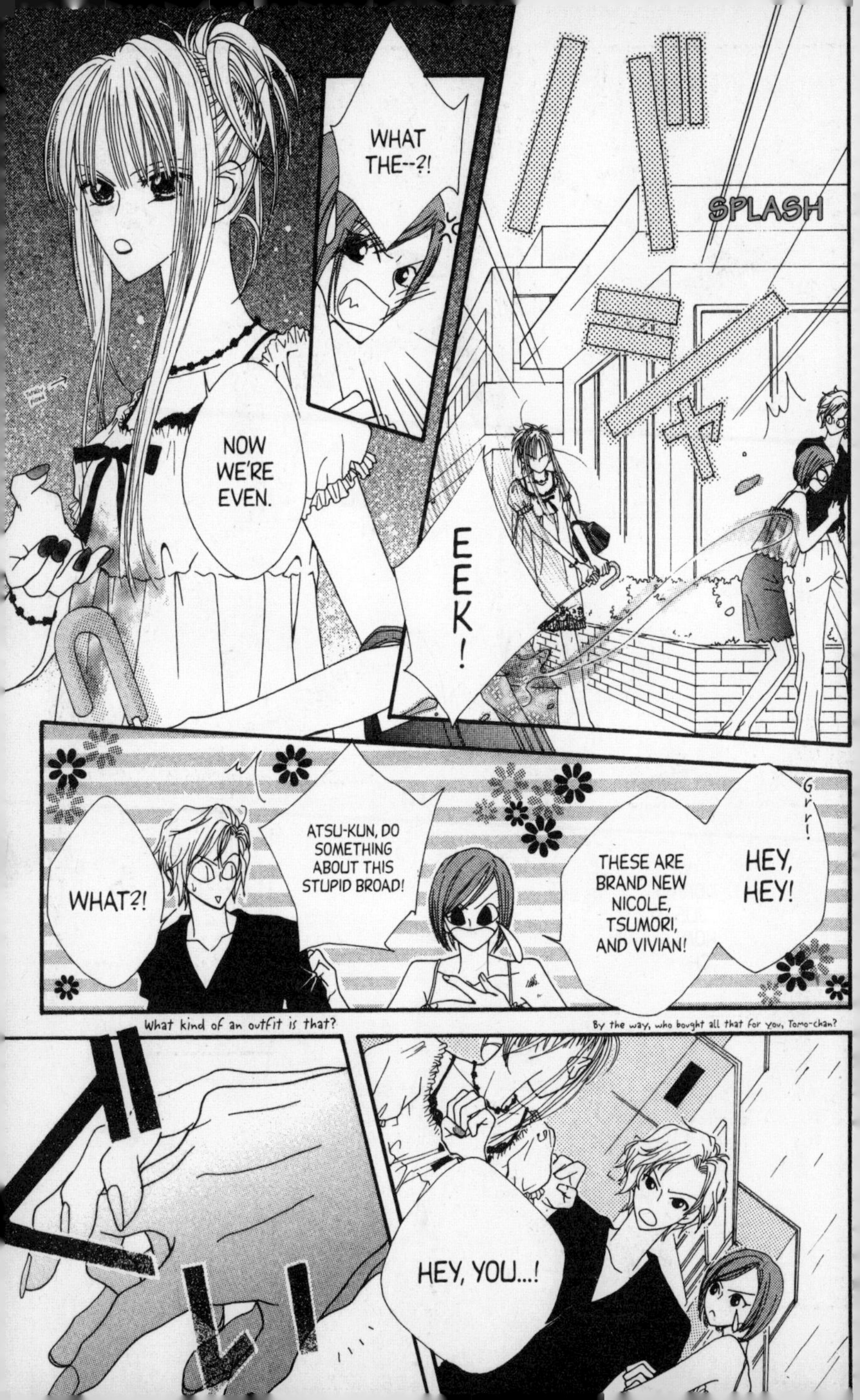
SPLASH
EEK!
WHAT THE--?!
NOW WE'RE EVEN.
Grrr!
HEY, HEY!
THESE ARE BRAND NEW NICOLE, TSUMORI, AND VIVIAN!
ATSU-KUN, DO SOMETHING ABOUT THIS STUPID BROAD!
WHAT?!
By the way, who bought all that for you, Tomo-chan?
What kind of an outfit is that?
HEY, YOU...!

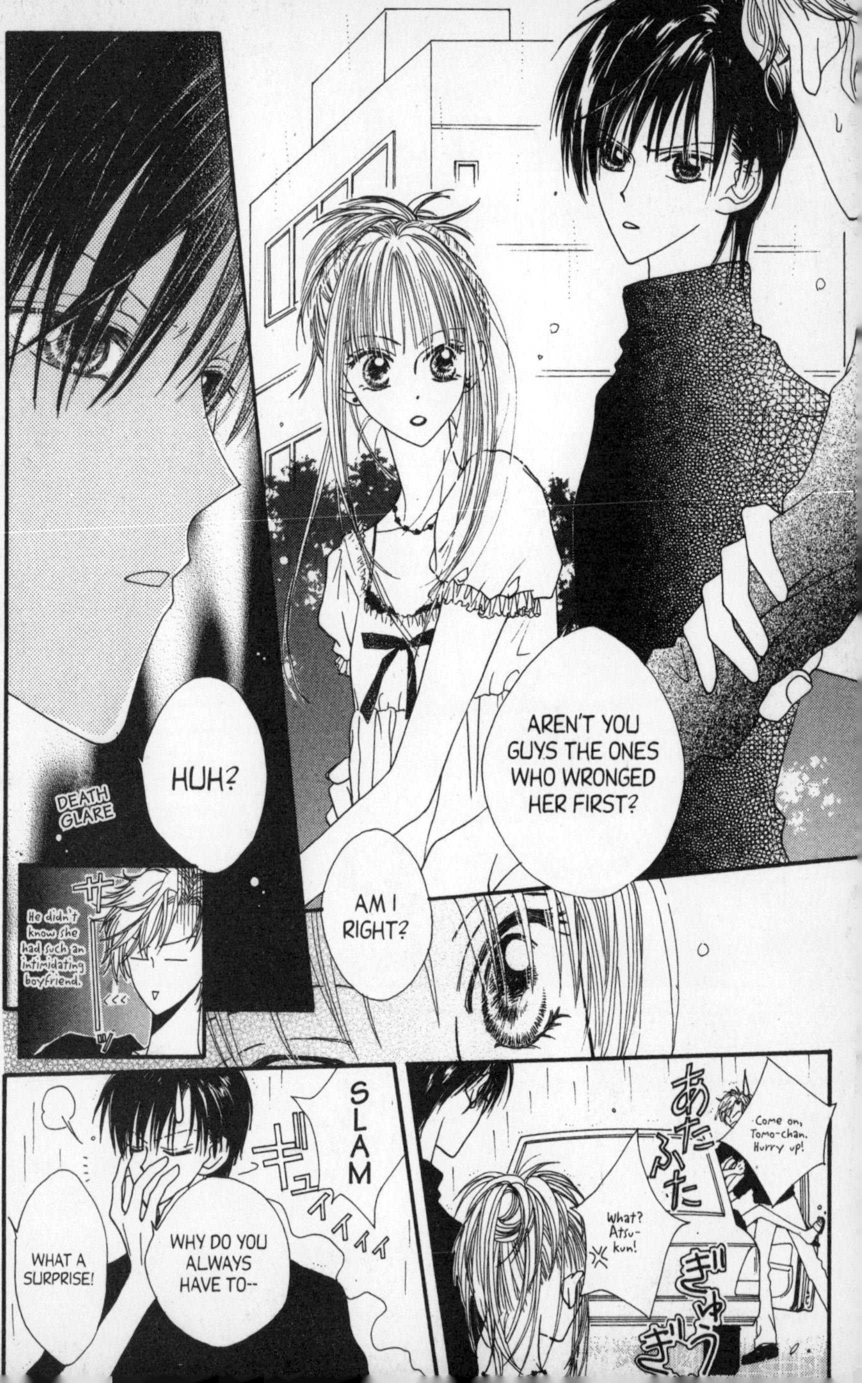
AREN'T YOU GUYS THE ONES WHO WRONGED HER FIRST?
AM I RIGHT?
HUH?
DEATH GLARE
He didn't know she had such an intimidating boyfriend.
サーッ
Come on, Tomo-chan. Hurry up!
あたふた
What? Atsu-kun!
ぎゅう
SLAM
ギュイイイイ
WHY DO YOU ALWAYS HAVE TO--
WHAT A SURPRISE!

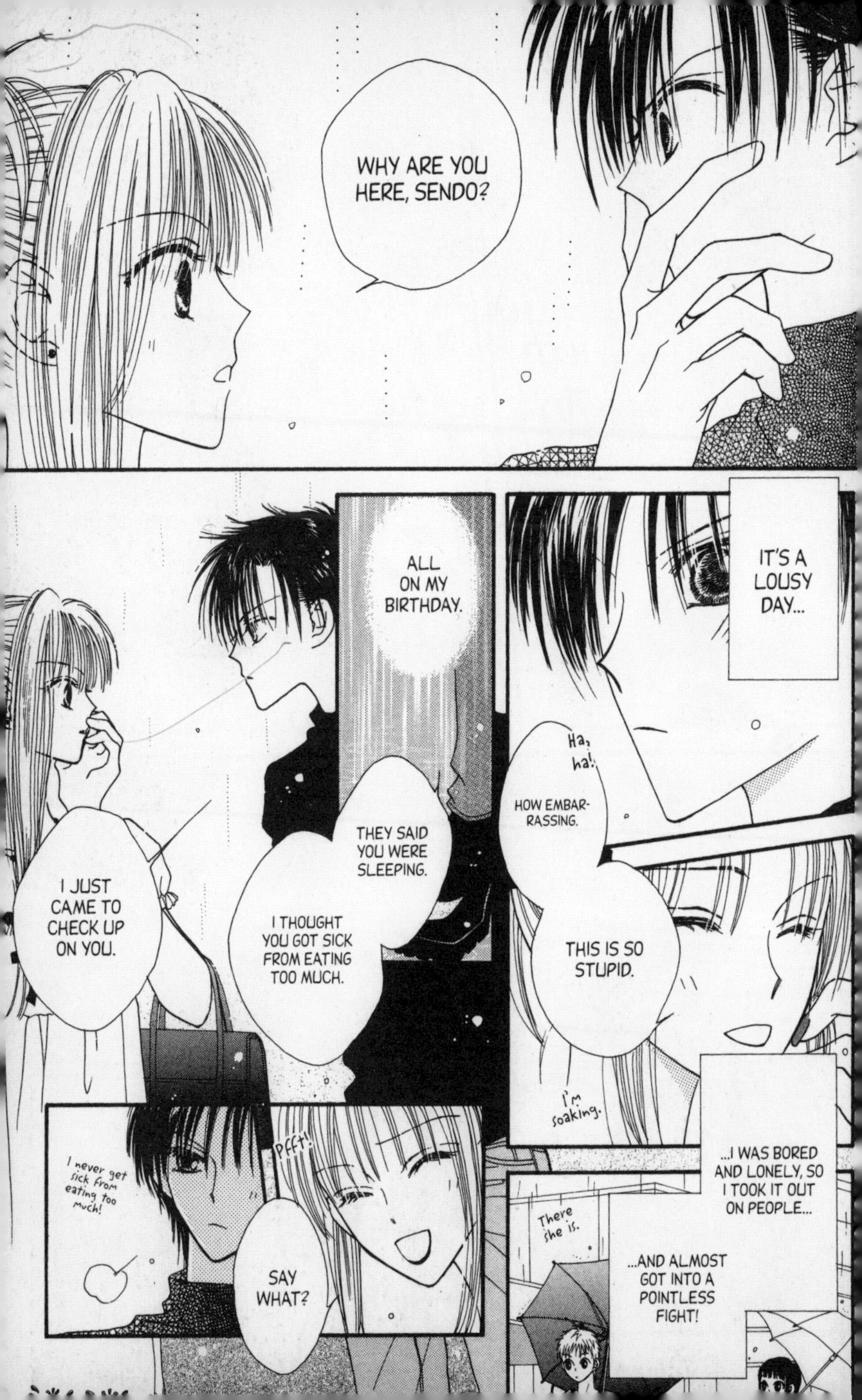
WHY ARE YOU HERE, SENDO?
IT'S A LOUSY DAY...
ALL ON MY BIRTHDAY.
THEY SAID YOU WERE SLEEPING.
I THOUGHT YOU GOT SICK FROM EATING TOO MUCH.
I JUST CAME TO CHECK UP ON YOU.
Pfft!
SAY WHAT?
I never get sick from eating too much!
Ha, ha!
HOW EMBARRASSING.
THIS IS SO STUPID.
I'm soaking.
...I WAS BORED AND LONELY, SO I TOOK IT OUT ON PEOPLE...
...AND ALMOST GOT INTO A POINTLESS FIGHT!
There she is.

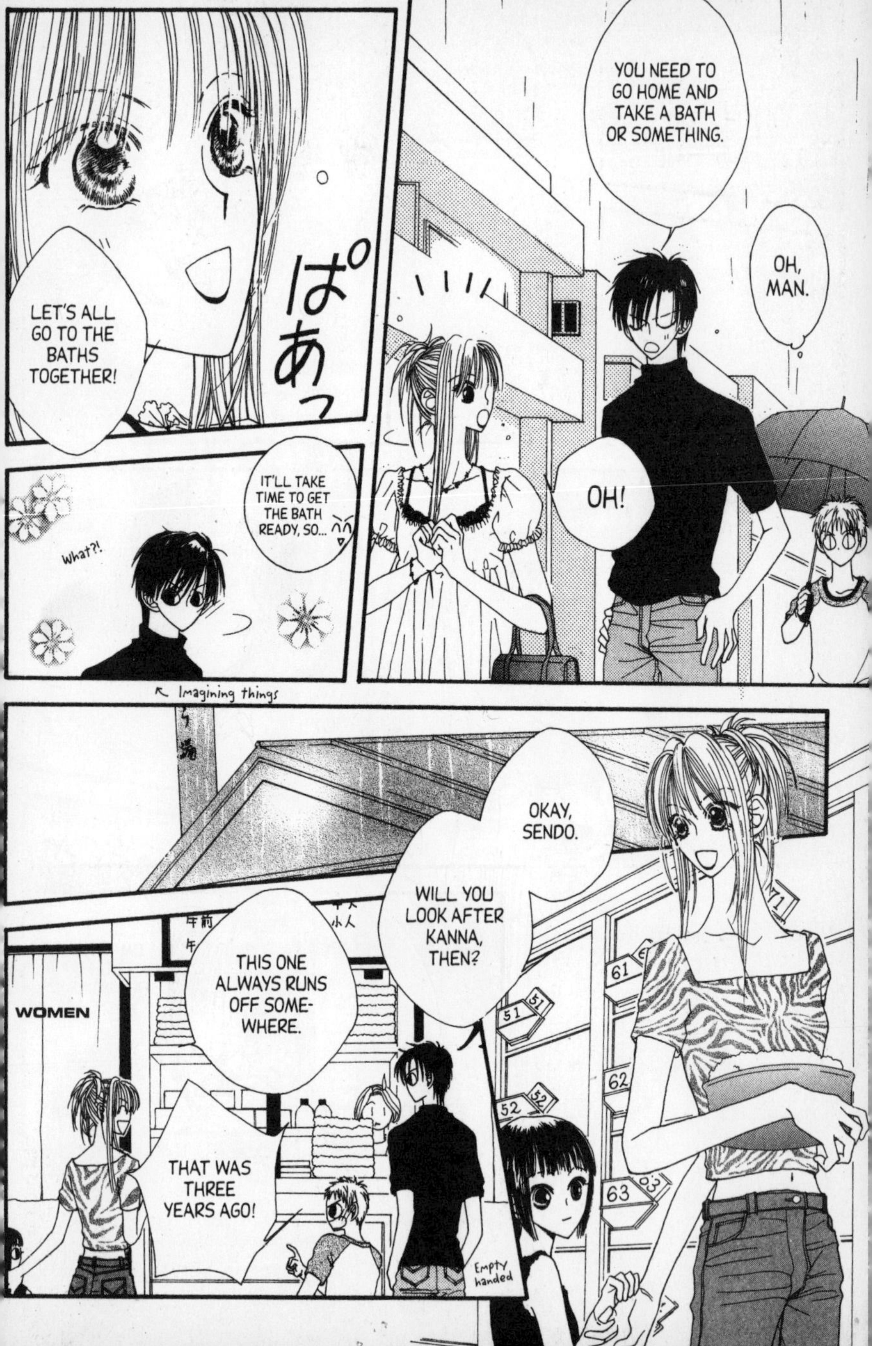
YOU NEED TO GO HOME AND TAKE A BATH OR SOMETHING.
OH, MAN.
OH!
ぱあっ
LET'S ALL GO TO THE BATHS TOGETHER!
IT'LL TAKE TIME TO GET THE BATH READY, SO...
What?!
↖ Imagining things
OKAY, SENDO.
WILL YOU LOOK AFTER KANNA, THEN?
THIS ONE ALWAYS RUNS OFF SOME-WHERE.
WOMEN
THAT WAS THREE YEARS AGO!
Empty handed

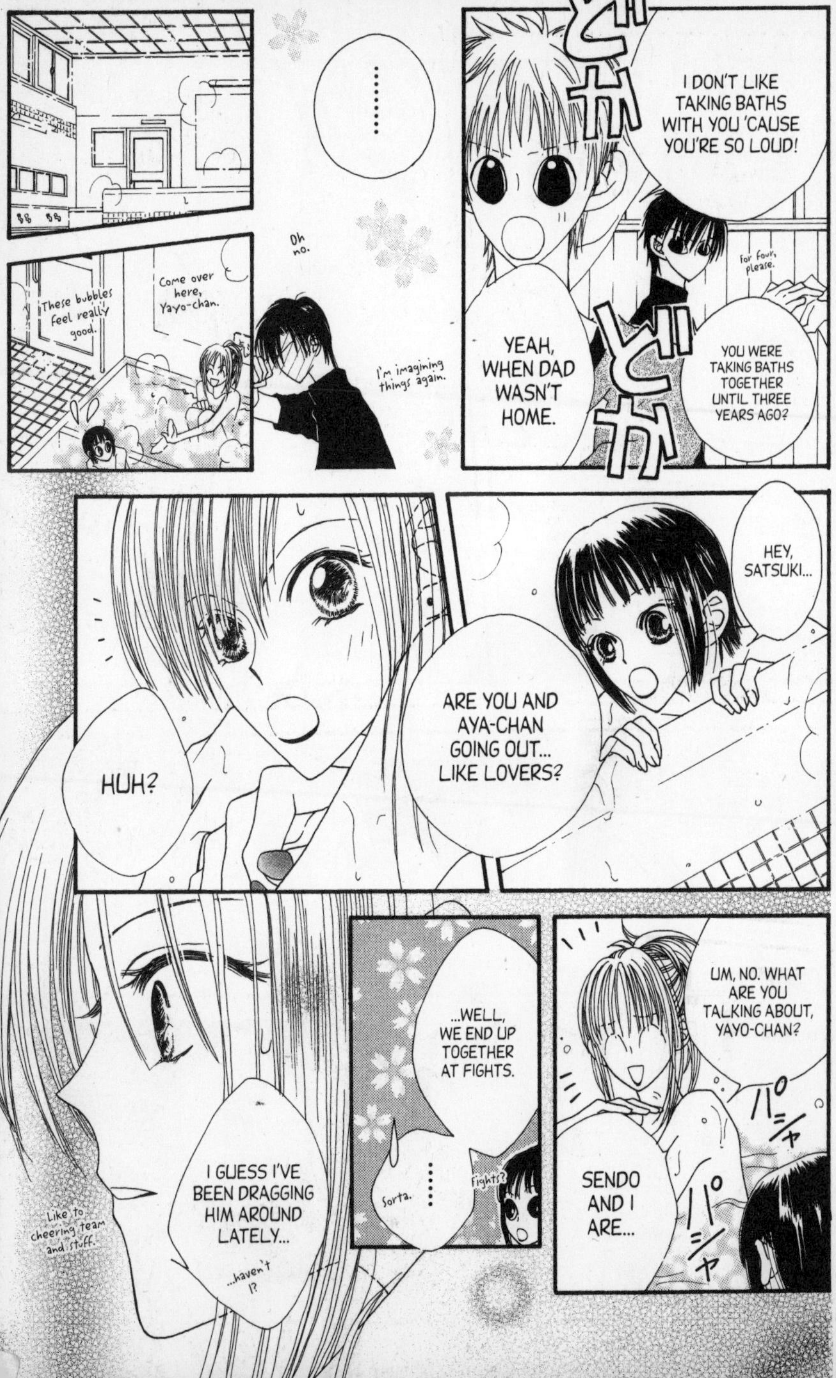
どか
I DON'T LIKE TAKING BATHS WITH YOU 'CAUSE YOU'RE SO LOUD!
For four, please.
YOU WERE TAKING BATHS TOGETHER UNTIL THREE YEARS AGO?
どか
YEAH, WHEN DAD WASN'T HOME.
......
Oh no.
Come over here, Yayo-chan.
These bubbles feel really good.
I'm imagining things again.
HEY, SATSUKI...
ARE YOU AND AYA-CHAN GOING OUT... LIKE LOVERS?
HUH?
UM, NO. WHAT ARE YOU TALKING ABOUT, YAYO-CHAN?
パシャ
パシャ
SENDO AND I ARE...
...WELL, WE END UP TOGETHER AT FIGHTS.
Fights?
......
Sorta.
I GUESS I'VE BEEN DRAGGING HIM AROUND LATELY...
...haven't I?
Like to cheering team and stuff.

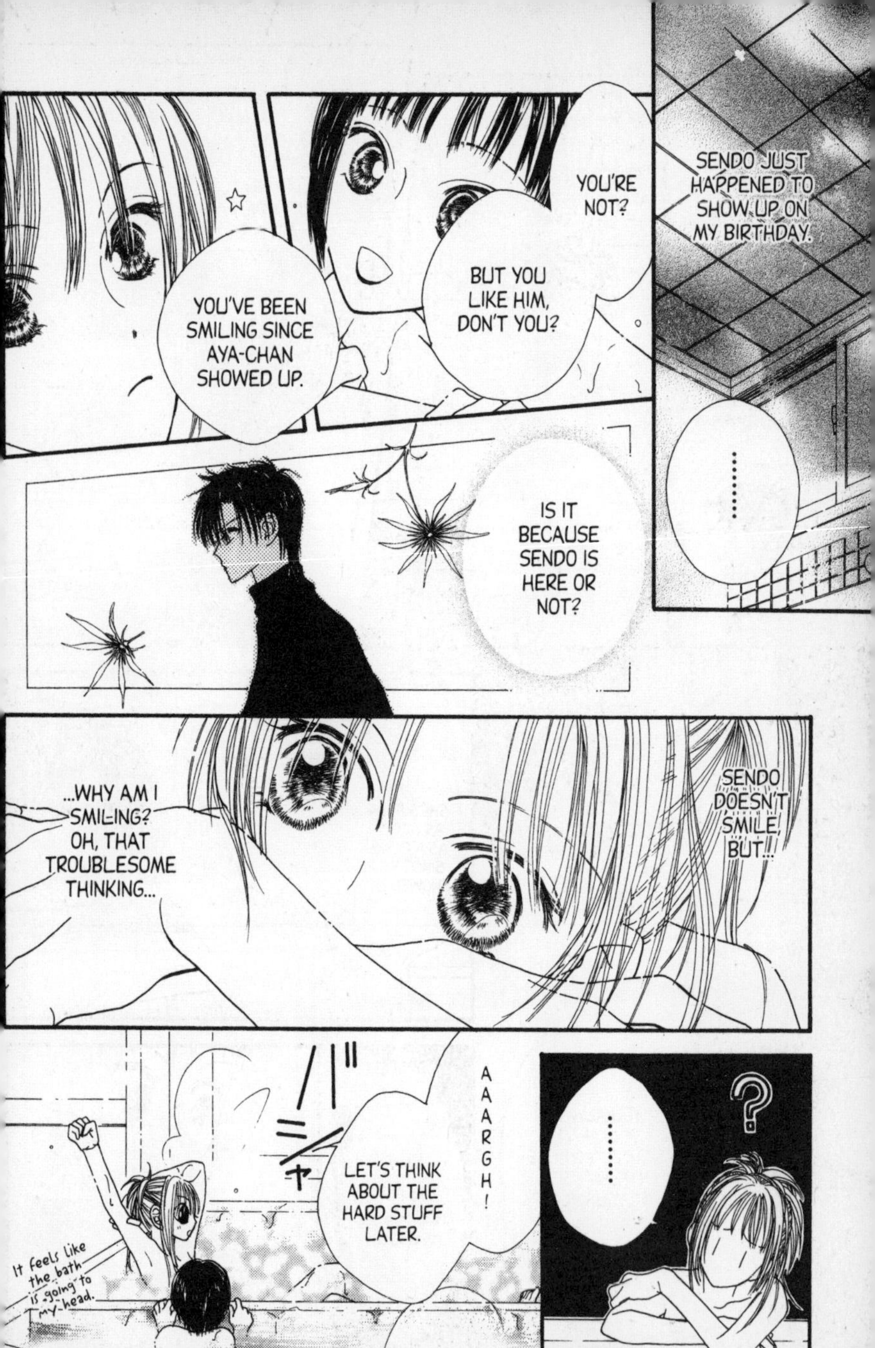
SENDO JUST HAPPENED TO SHOW UP ON MY BIRTHDAY.
......
YOU'RE NOT?
BUT YOU LIKE HIM, DON'T YOU?
YOU'VE BEEN SMILING SINCE AYA-CHAN SHOWED UP.
IS IT BECAUSE SENDO IS HERE OR NOT?
SENDO DOESN'T SMILE, BUT...
...WHY AM I SMILING? OH, THAT TROUBLESOME THINKING...
?
......
Thinking isn't her strong suit.
AAAARGH!
LET'S THINK ABOUT THE HARD STUFF LATER.
It feels like the bath is going to my head.

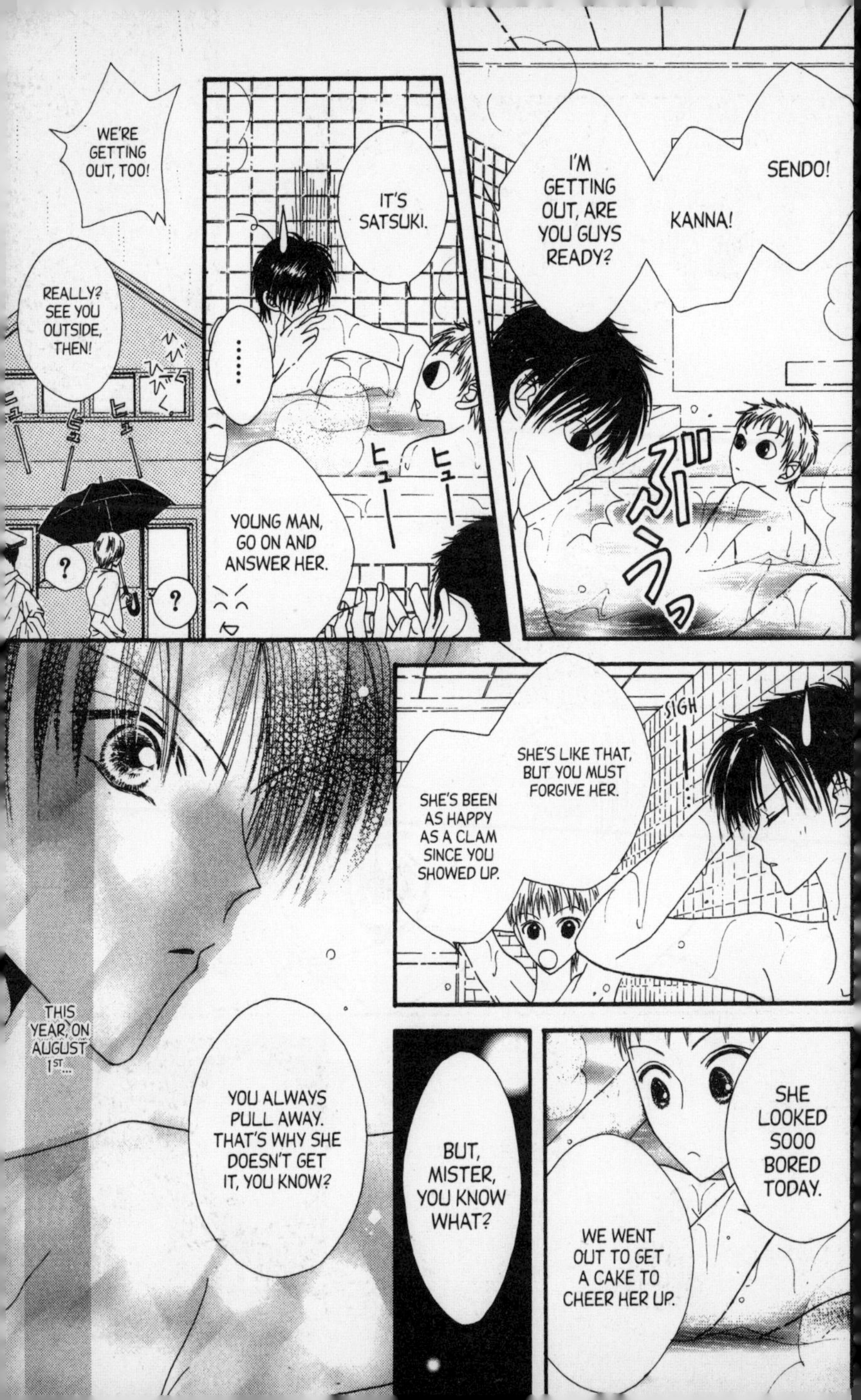
SENDO!
KANNA!
I'M GETTING OUT, ARE YOU GUYS READY?
ぶんっ
IT'S SATSUKI.
......
YOUNG MAN, GO ON AND ANSWER HER.
ヒュー
ヒュー
WE'RE GETTING OUT, TOO!
REALLY? SEE YOU OUTSIDE, THEN!
?
?
SIGH
SHE'S LIKE THAT, BUT YOU MUST FORGIVE HER.
SHE'S BEEN AS HAPPY AS A CLAM SINCE YOU SHOWED UP.
SHE LOOKED SOOO BORED TODAY.
WE WENT OUT TO GET A CAKE TO CHEER HER UP.
BUT, MISTER, YOU KNOW WHAT?
YOU ALWAYS PULL AWAY. THAT'S WHY SHE DOESN'T GET IT, YOU KNOW?
THIS YEAR, ON AUGUST 1ST...

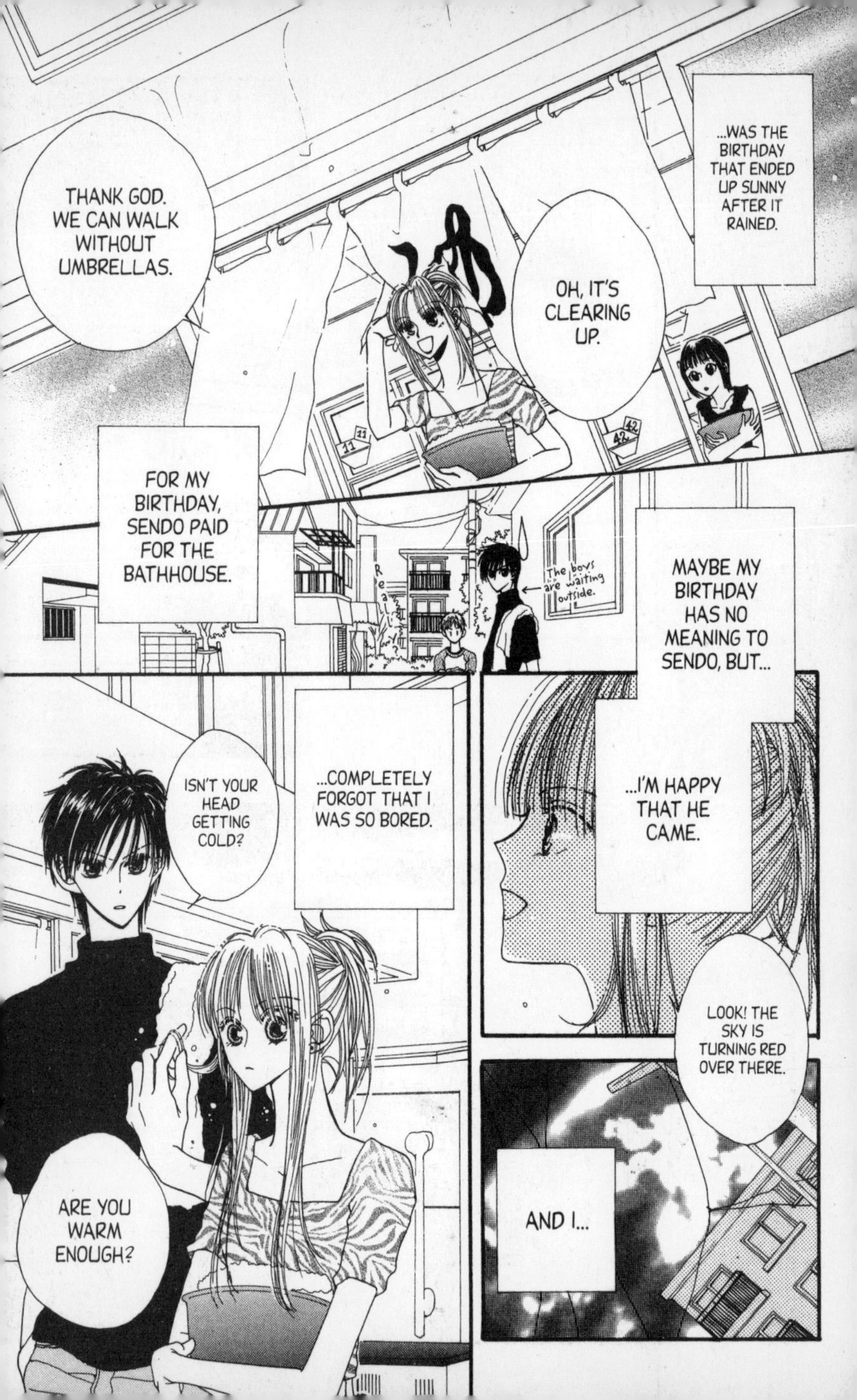
...WAS THE BIRTHDAY THAT ENDED UP SUNNY AFTER IT RAINED.
OH, IT'S CLEARING UP.
THANK GOD. WE CAN WALK WITHOUT UMBRELLAS.
FOR MY BIRTHDAY, SENDO PAID FOR THE BATHHOUSE.
MAYBE MY BIRTHDAY HAS NO MEANING TO SENDO, BUT...
The boys are waiting outside.
Really?
...I'M HAPPY THAT HE CAME.
LOOK! THE SKY IS TURNING RED OVER THERE.
AND I...
...COMPLETELY FORGOT THAT I WAS SO BORED.
ISN'T YOUR HEAD GETTING COLD?
ARE YOU WARM ENOUGH?

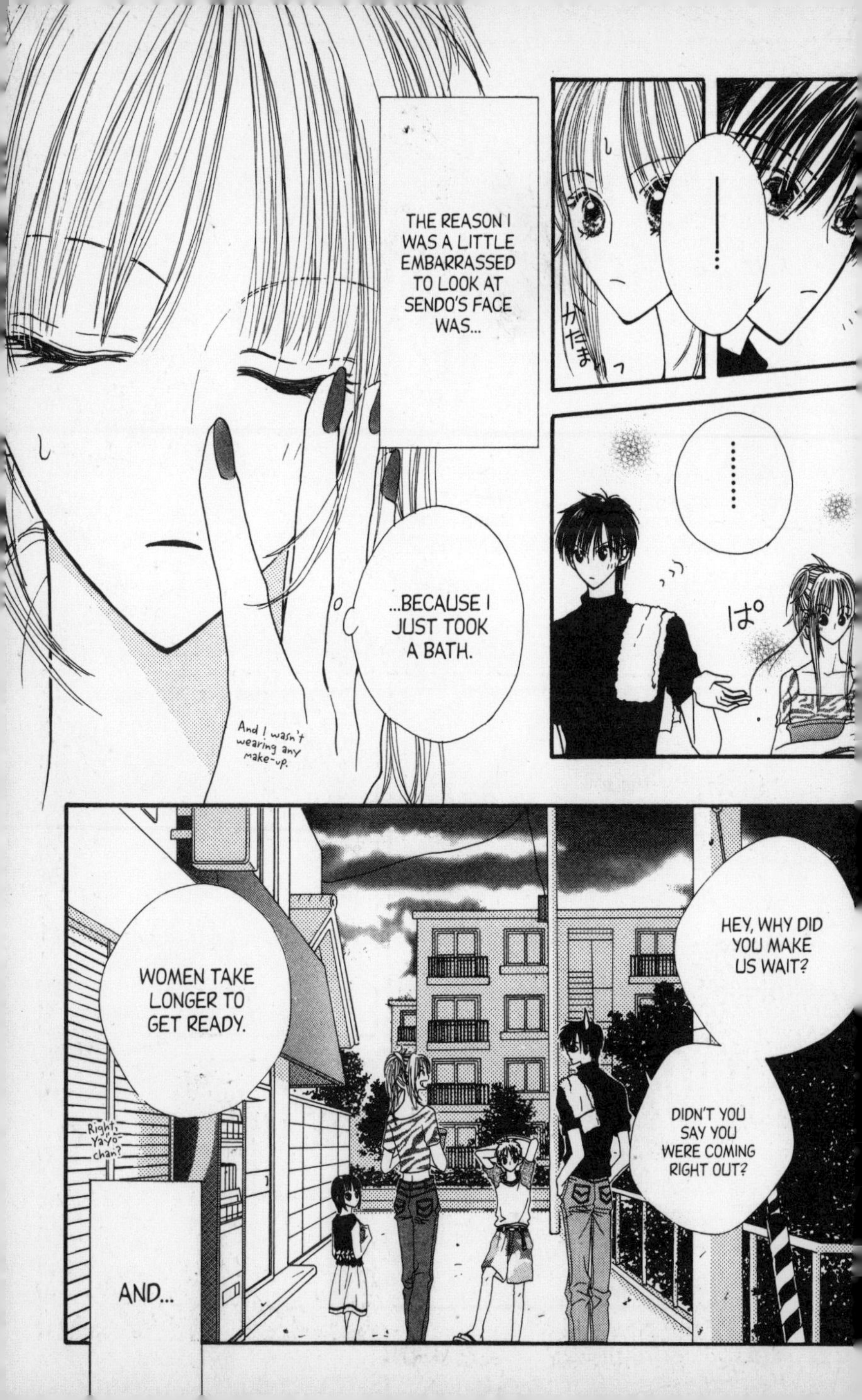
!...
かたまっ
......
ぱっ
THE REASON I WAS A LITTLE EMBARRASSED TO LOOK AT SENDO'S FACE WAS...
...BECAUSE I JUST TOOK A BATH.
And I wasn't wearing any make-up.
HEY, WHY DID YOU MAKE US WAIT?
DIDN'T YOU SAY YOU WERE COMING RIGHT OUT?
WOMEN TAKE LONGER TO GET READY.
Right, Yayo-chan?
AND...

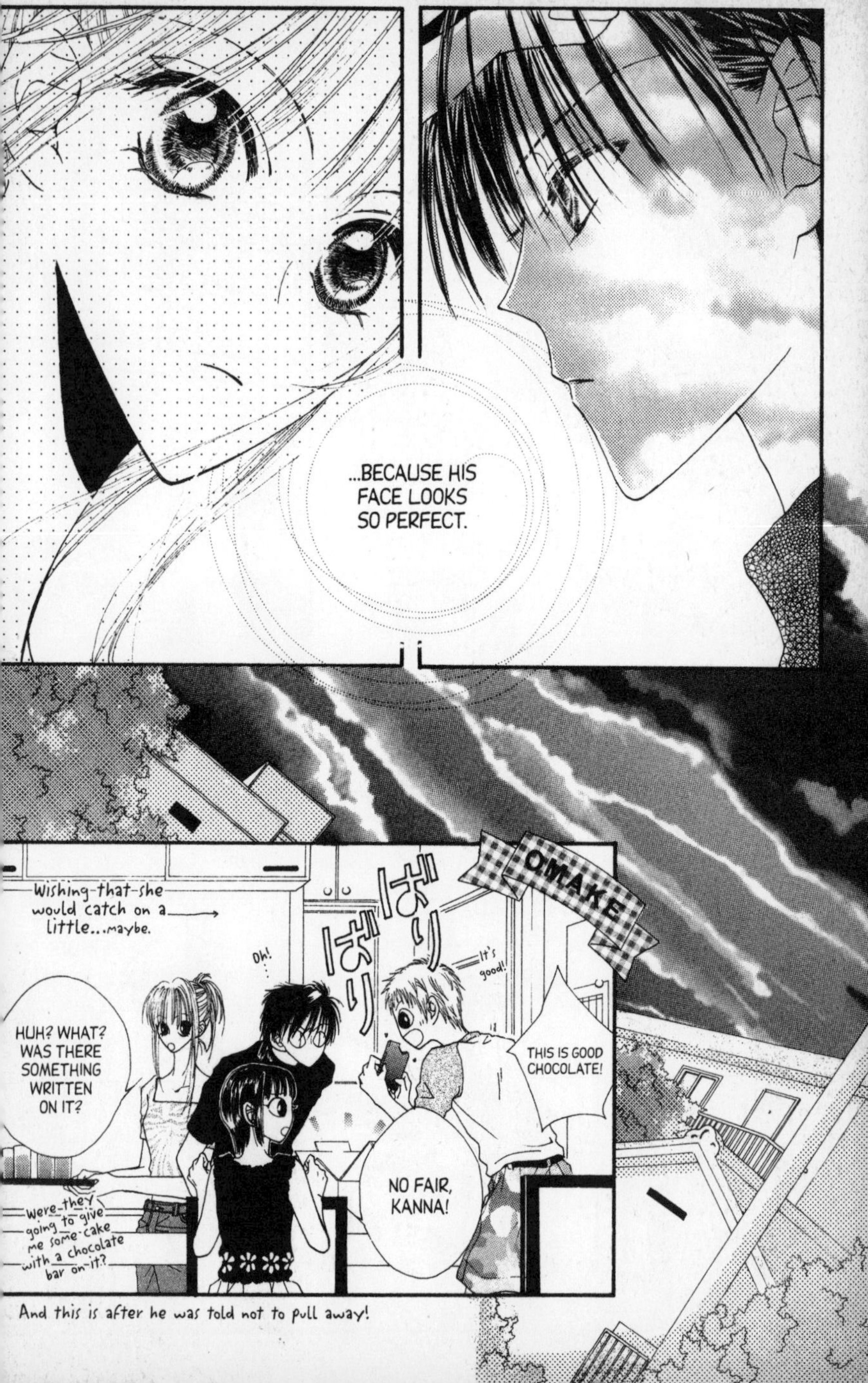
...BECAUSE HIS FACE LOOKS SO PERFECT.
OMAKE
ぱり
ぱり
It's good!
THIS IS GOOD CHOCOLATE!
NO FAIR, KANNA!
Oh!
HUH? WHAT? WAS THERE SOMETHING WRITTEN ON IT?
Wishing that she would catch on a little...maybe.
Were they going to give me some cake with a chocolate bar on it?
And this is after he was told not to pull away!

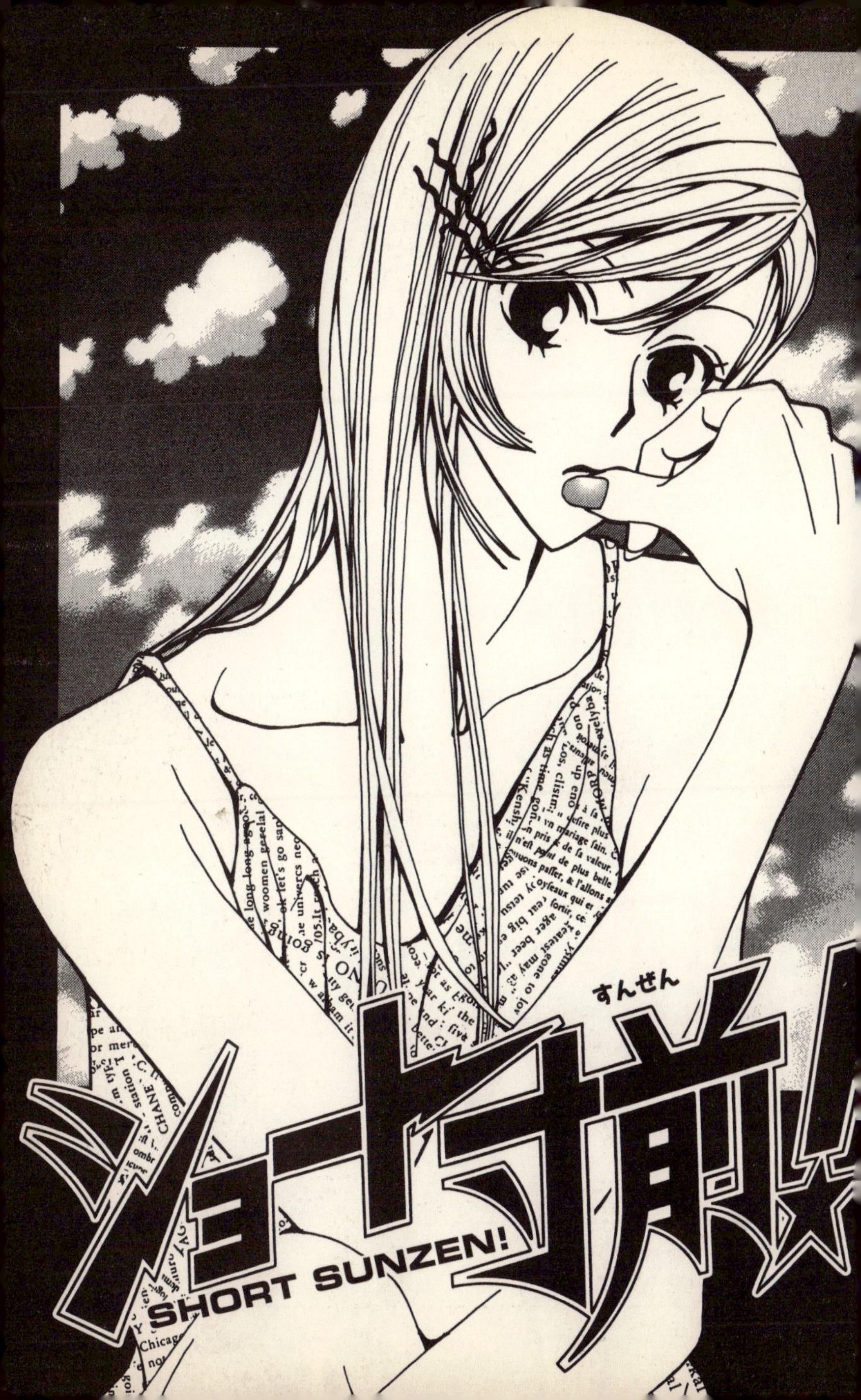
すんぜん
ショート寸前
SHORT SUNZEN!

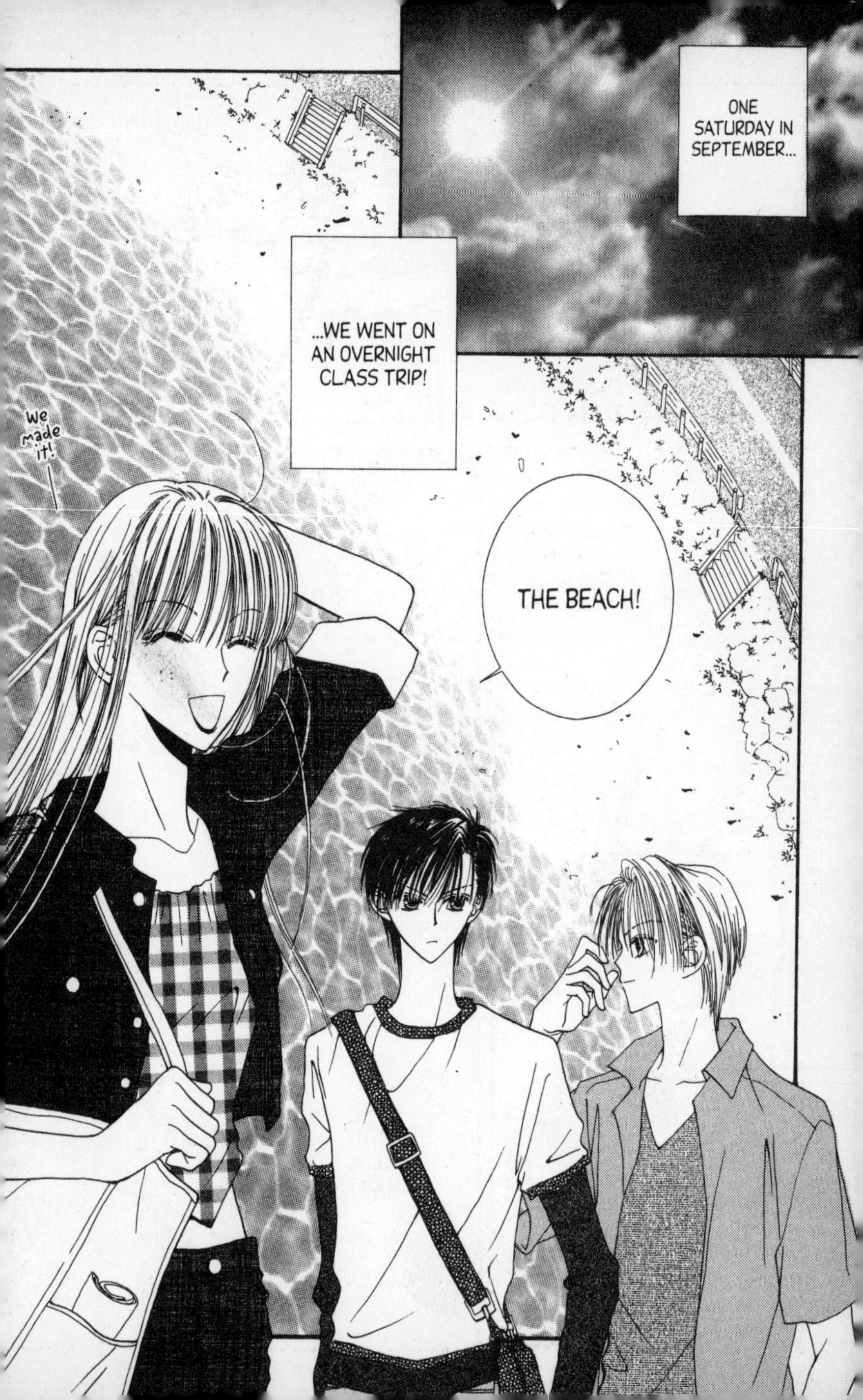
ONE SATURDAY IN SEPTEMBER...
...WE WENT ON AN OVERNIGHT CLASS TRIP!
THE BEACH!
We made it!

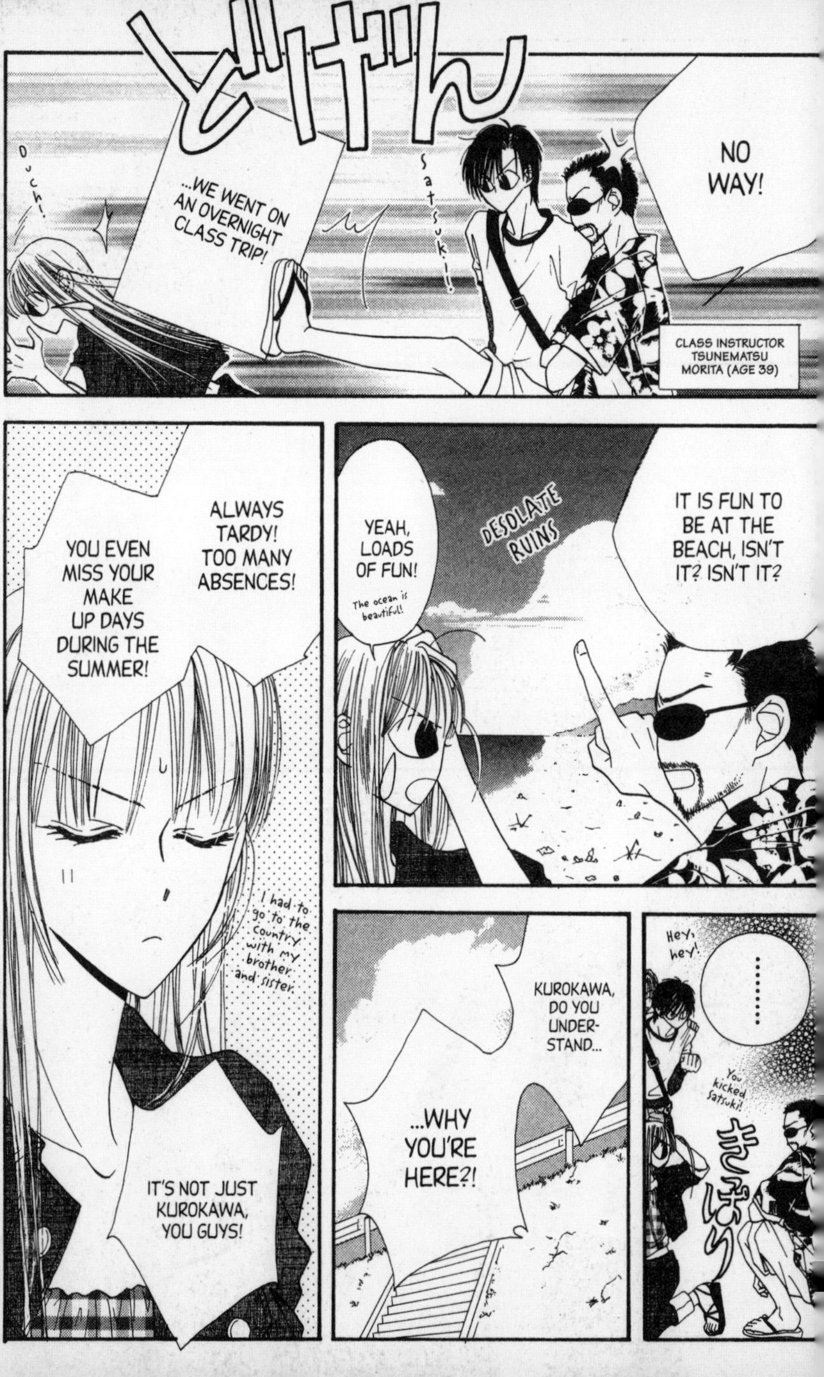
NO WAY!
CLASS INSTRUCTOR TSUNEMATSU MORITA (AGE 39)
Satsuki!
どげん
...WE WENT ON AN OVERNIGHT CLASS TRIP!
Ouch!
IT IS FUN TO BE AT THE BEACH, ISN'T IT? ISN'T IT?
DESOLATE RUINS
YEAH, LOADS OF FUN!
The ocean is beautiful!
Hey, hey!
......
You kicked Satsuki!
きっぱり
KUROKAWA, DO YOU UNDERSTAND...
...WHY YOU'RE HERE?!
ALWAYS TARDY! TOO MANY ABSENCES!
YOU EVEN MISS YOUR MAKE UP DAYS DURING THE SUMMER!
I had to go to the country with my brother and sister.
IT'S NOT JUST KUROKAWA, YOU GUYS!

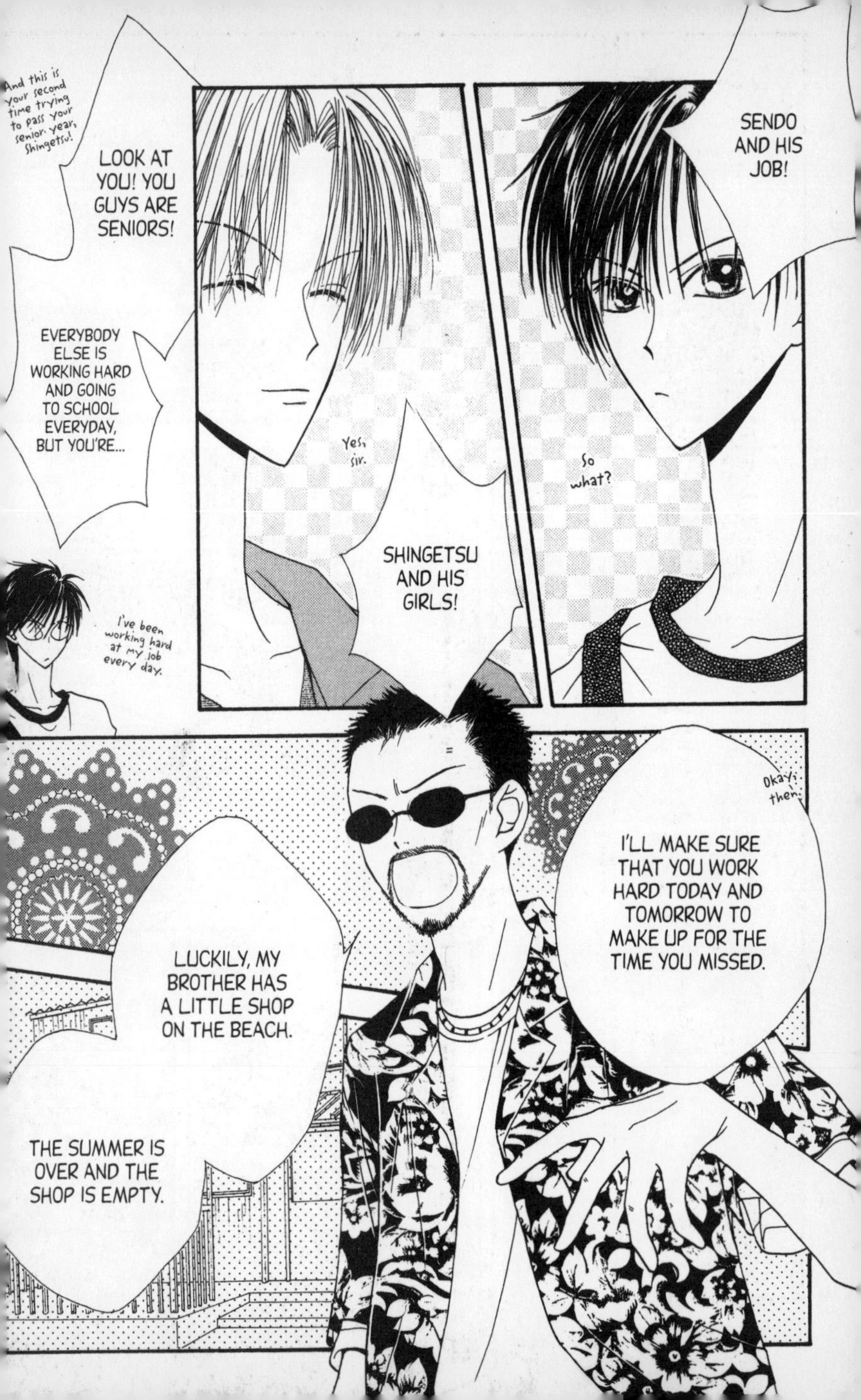
LOOK AT YOU! YOU GUYS ARE SENIORS!
And this is your second time trying to pass your senior year, Shingetsu!
EVERYBODY ELSE IS WORKING HARD AND GOING TO SCHOOL EVERYDAY, BUT YOU'RE...
SHINGETSU AND HIS GIRLS!
Yes, sir.
SENDO AND HIS JOB!
So what?
I've been working hard at my job every day.
LUCKILY, MY BROTHER HAS A LITTLE SHOP ON THE BEACH.
THE SUMMER IS OVER AND THE SHOP IS EMPTY.
Okay, then.
I'LL MAKE SURE THAT YOU WORK HARD TODAY AND TOMORROW TO MAKE UP FOR THE TIME YOU MISSED.

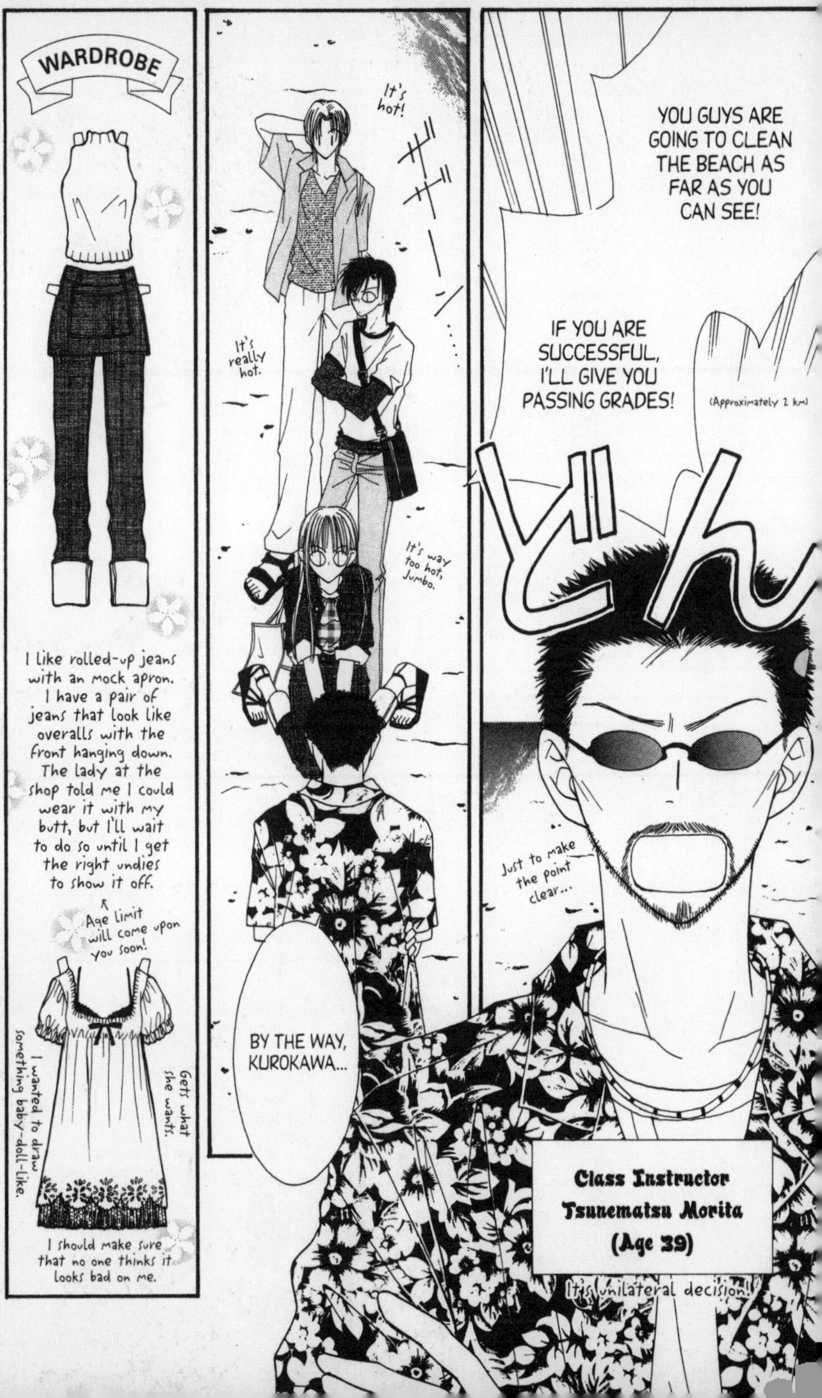

YOU GUYS ARE GOING TO CLEAN THE BEACH AS FAR AS YOU CAN SEE!
IF YOU ARE SUCCESSFUL, I'LL GIVE YOU PASSING GRADES!
(Approximately 2 km)
Just to make the point clear...
Class Instructor Tsunematsu Morita (Age 39)
It's unilateral decision!
It's hot!
It's really hot.
It's way too hot, Jumbo.
BY THE WAY, KUROKAWA...
WARDROBE
I like rolled-up jeans with an mock apron. I have a pair of jeans that look like overalls with the front hanging down. The lady at the shop told me I could wear it with my butt, but I'll wait to do so until I get the right undies to show it off.
Age limit will come upon you soon!
Gets what she wants.
I wanted to draw something baby-doll-like.
I should make sure that no one thinks it looks bad on me.

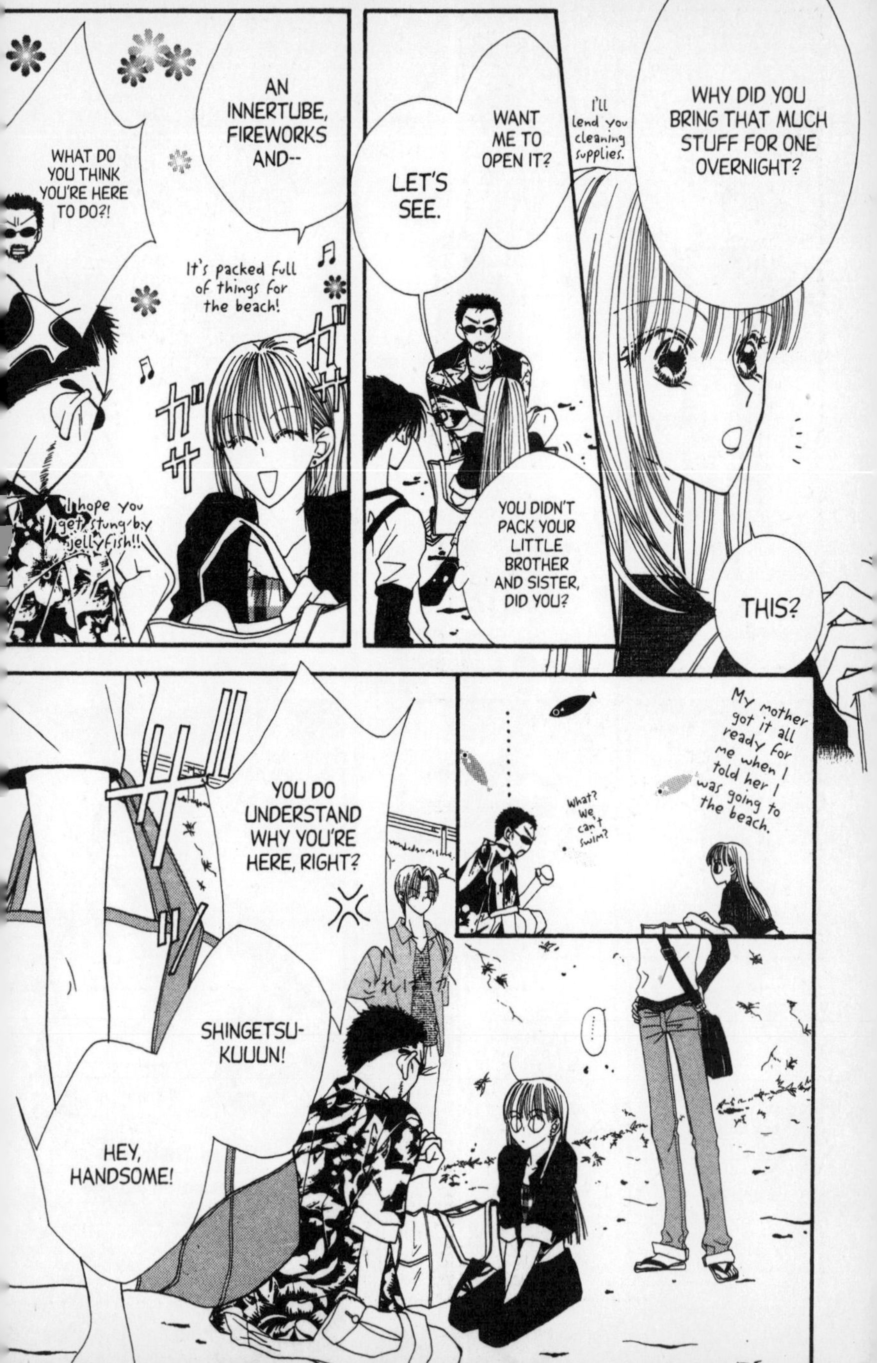
WHY DID YOU BRING THAT MUCH STUFF FOR ONE OVERNIGHT?
THIS?
I'll lend you cleaning supplies.
WANT ME TO OPEN IT?
LET'S SEE.
YOU DIDN'T PACK YOUR LITTLE BROTHER AND SISTER, DID YOU?
AN INNERTUBE, FIREWORKS AND--
It's packed full of things for the beach!
ガサ ガサ
WHAT DO YOU THINK YOU'RE HERE TO DO?!
I hope you get stung by jellyfish!!
My mother got it all ready for me when I told her I was going to the beach.
What? We can't swim?
YOU DO UNDERSTAND WHY YOU'RE HERE, RIGHT?
...
SHINGETSU-KUUUN!
HEY, HANDSOME!

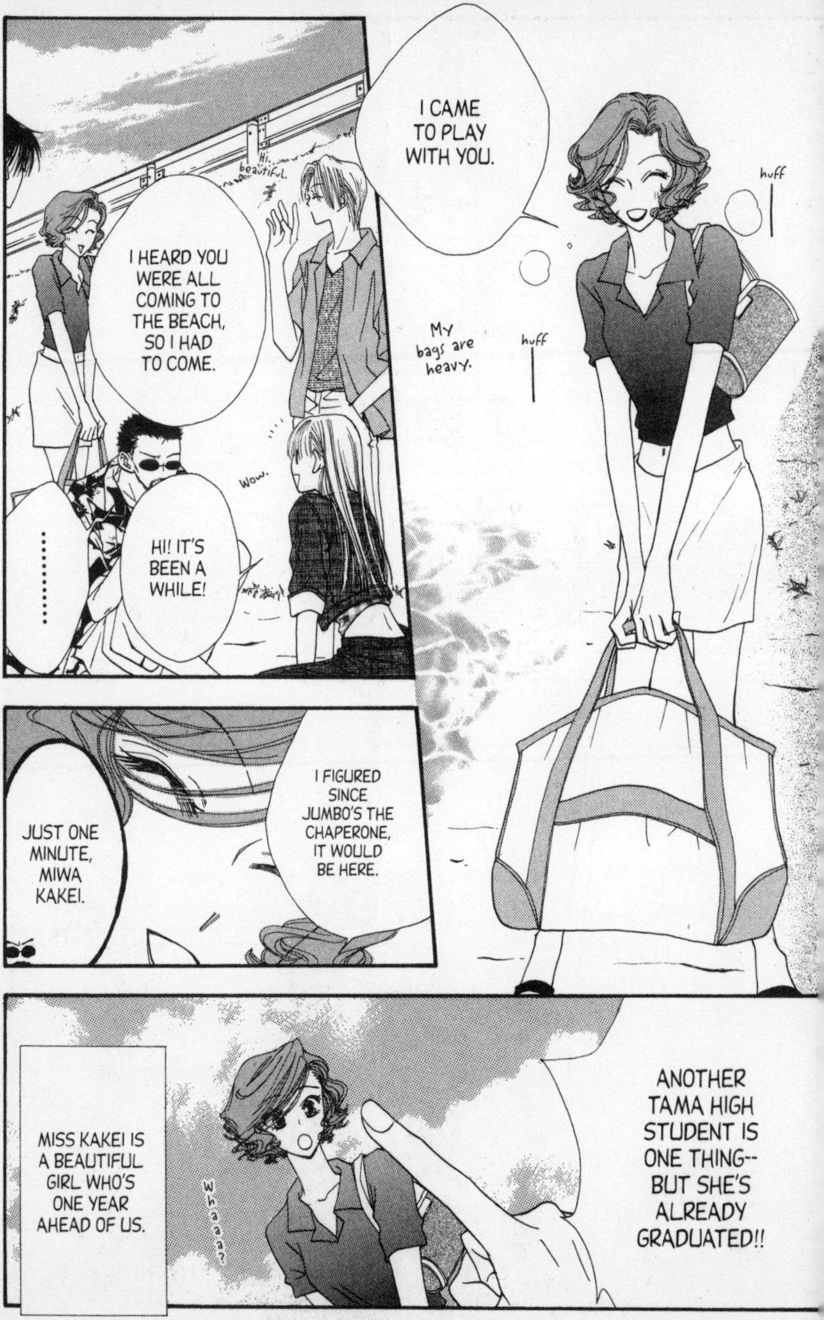
I CAME TO PLAY WITH YOU.
huff
My bags are heavy.
huff
Hi, beautiful.
I HEARD YOU WERE ALL COMING TO THE BEACH, SO I HAD TO COME.
Wow.
HI! IT'S BEEN A WHILE!
I FIGURED SINCE JUMBO'S THE CHAPERONE, IT WOULD BE HERE.
JUST ONE MINUTE, MIWA KAKEI.
ANOTHER TAMA HIGH STUDENT IS ONE THING-- BUT SHE'S ALREADY GRADUATED!!
Whaaa?
MISS KAKEI IS A BEAUTIFUL GIRL WHO'S ONE YEAR AHEAD OF US.

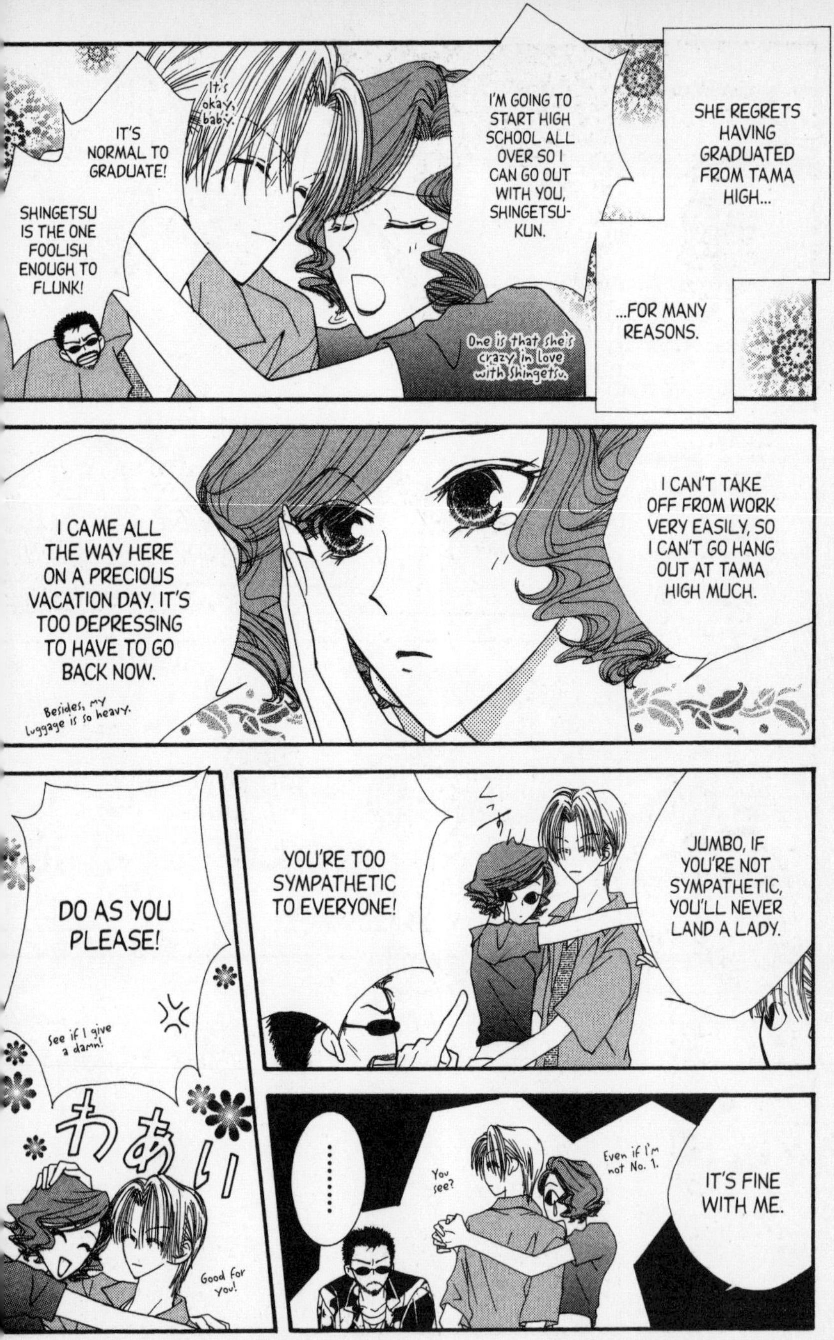
SHE REGRETS HAVING GRADUATED FROM TAMA HIGH...
...FOR MANY REASONS.
I'M GOING TO START HIGH SCHOOL ALL OVER SO I CAN GO OUT WITH YOU, SHINGETSU-KUN.
One is that she's crazy in love with Shingetsu.
It's okay, baby.
IT'S NORMAL TO GRADUATE!
SHINGETSU IS THE ONE FOOLISH ENOUGH TO FLUNK!
I CAN'T TAKE OFF FROM WORK VERY EASILY, SO I CAN'T GO HANG OUT AT TAMA HIGH MUCH.
I CAME ALL THE WAY HERE ON A PRECIOUS VACATION DAY. IT'S TOO DEPRESSING TO HAVE TO GO BACK NOW.
Besides, my luggage is so heavy.
JUMBO, IF YOU'RE NOT SYMPATHETIC, YOU'LL NEVER LAND A LADY.
YOU'RE TOO SYMPATHETIC TO EVERYONE!
IT'S FINE WITH ME.
Even if I'm not No. 1.
You see?
......
DO AS YOU PLEASE!
See if I give a damn!
わあい
Good for you!

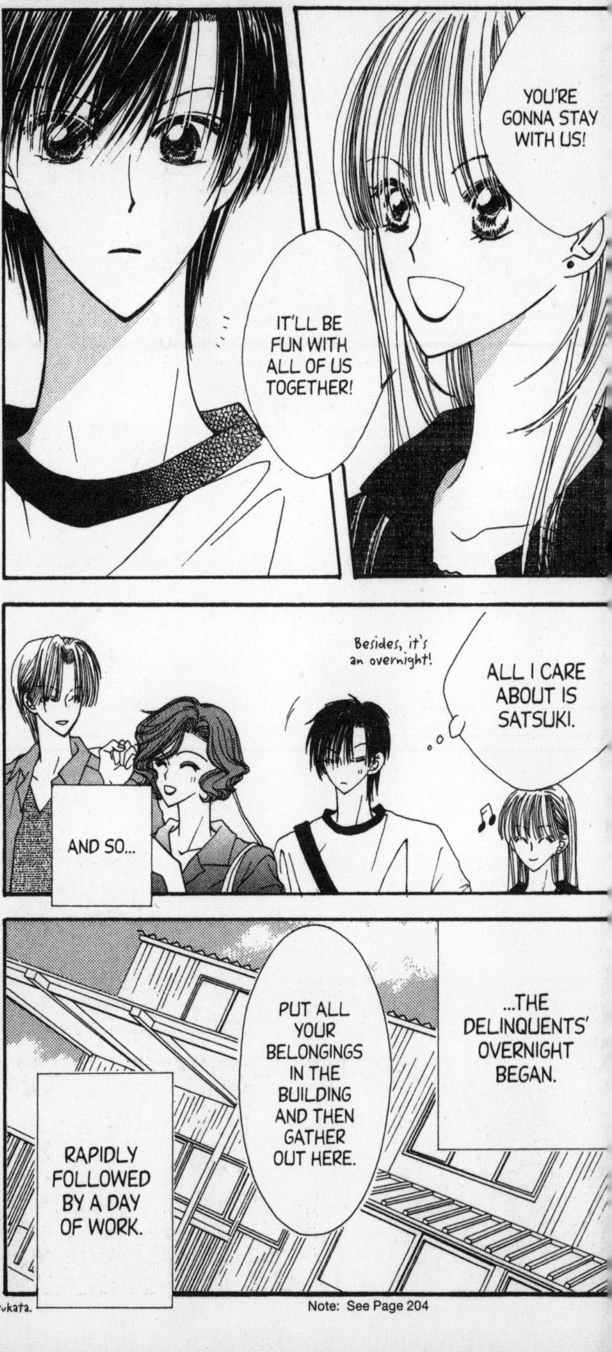
YOU'RE GONNA STAY WITH US!
IT'LL BE FUN WITH ALL OF US TOGETHER!
ALL I CARE ABOUT IS SATSUKI.
Besides, it's an overnight!
AND SO...
...THE DELINQUENTS' OVERNIGHT BEGAN.
PUT ALL YOUR BELONGINGS IN THE BUILDING AND THEN GATHER OUT HERE.
RAPIDLY FOLLOWED BY A DAY OF WORK.

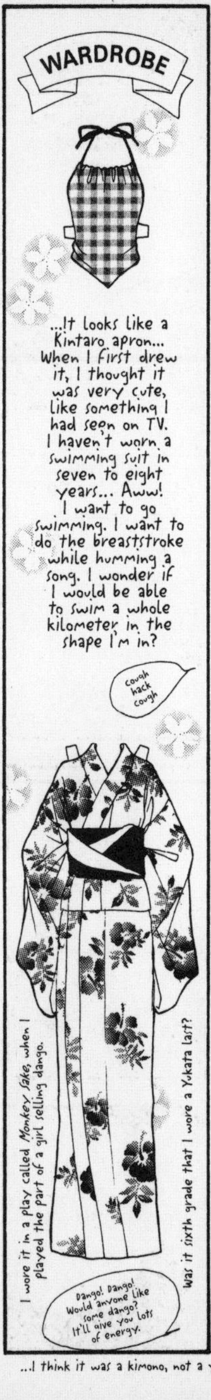
WARDROBE
...It looks like a Kintaro apron... When I first drew it, I thought it was very cute, like something I had seen on TV. I haven't worn a swimming suit in seven to eight years... Aww! I want to go swimming. I want to do the breaststroke while humming a song. I wonder if I would be able to swim a whole kilometer in the shape I'm in?
cough hack cough
Was it sixth grade that I wore a Yukata last?
I wore it in a play called Monkey Sake, when I played the part of a girl selling dango.
Dango! Dango! Would anyone like some dango? It'll give you lots of energy.

...I think it was a kimono, not a yukata.

Note: See Page 204

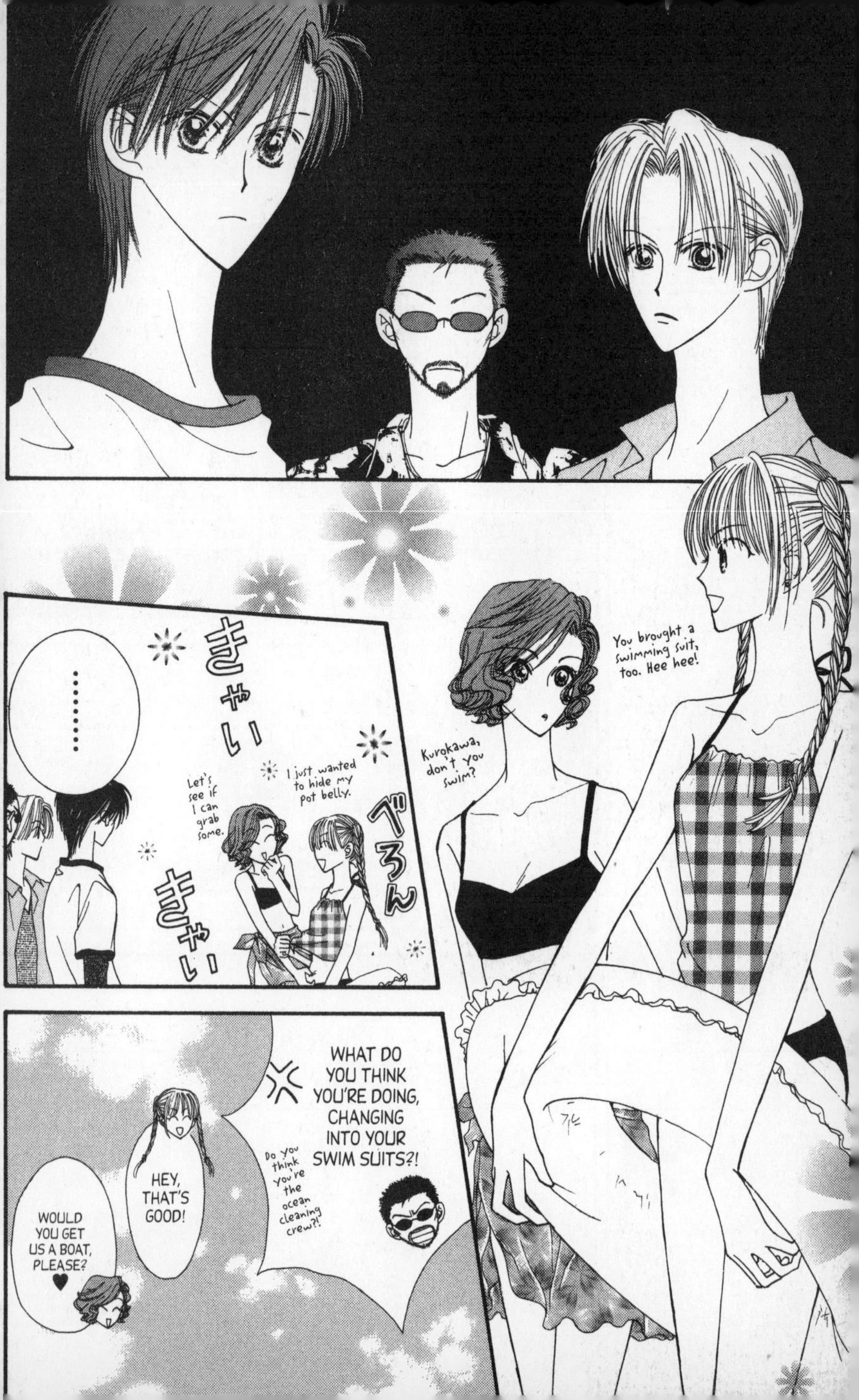
You brought a swimming suit, too. Hee hee!
Kurokawa, don't you swim?
べろん
I just wanted to hide my pot belly.
Let's see if I can grab some.
きゃいきゃい
......
WHAT DO YOU THINK YOU'RE DOING, CHANGING INTO YOUR SWIM SUITS?!
Do you think you're the ocean cleaning crew?!
HEY, THAT'S GOOD!
WOULD YOU GET US A BOAT, PLEASE? ♥

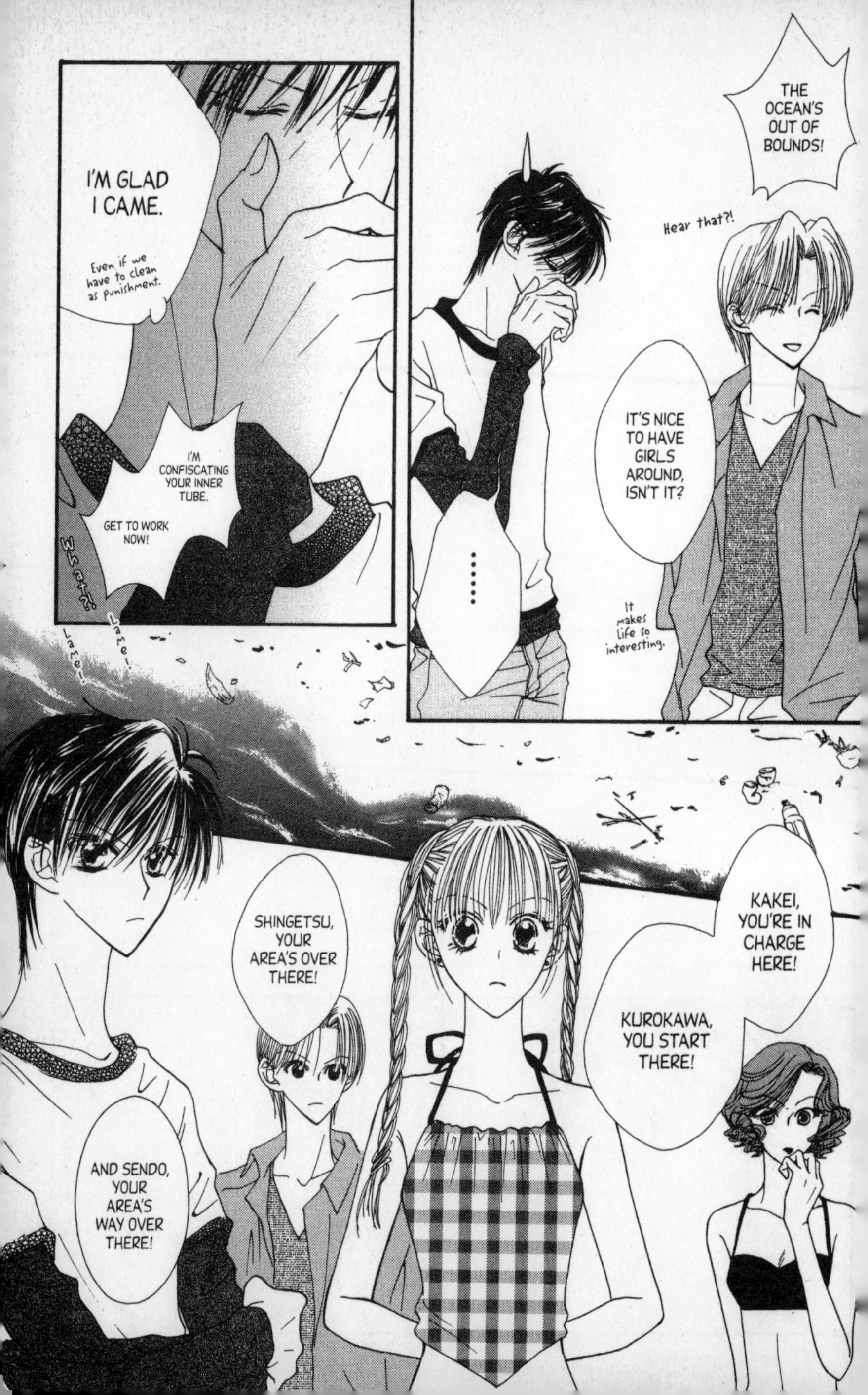
THE OCEAN'S OUT OF BOUNDS!
Hear that?!
IT'S NICE TO HAVE GIRLS AROUND, ISN'T IT?
It makes life so interesting.
......
I'M GLAD I CAME.
Even if we have to clean as punishment.
I'M CONFISCATING YOUR INNER TUBE.
GET TO WORK NOW!
What?!
Lame!
Lame!
KAKEI, YOU'RE IN CHARGE HERE!
KUROKAWA, YOU START THERE!
SHINGETSU, YOUR AREA'S OVER THERE!
AND SENDO, YOUR AREA'S WAY OVER THERE!

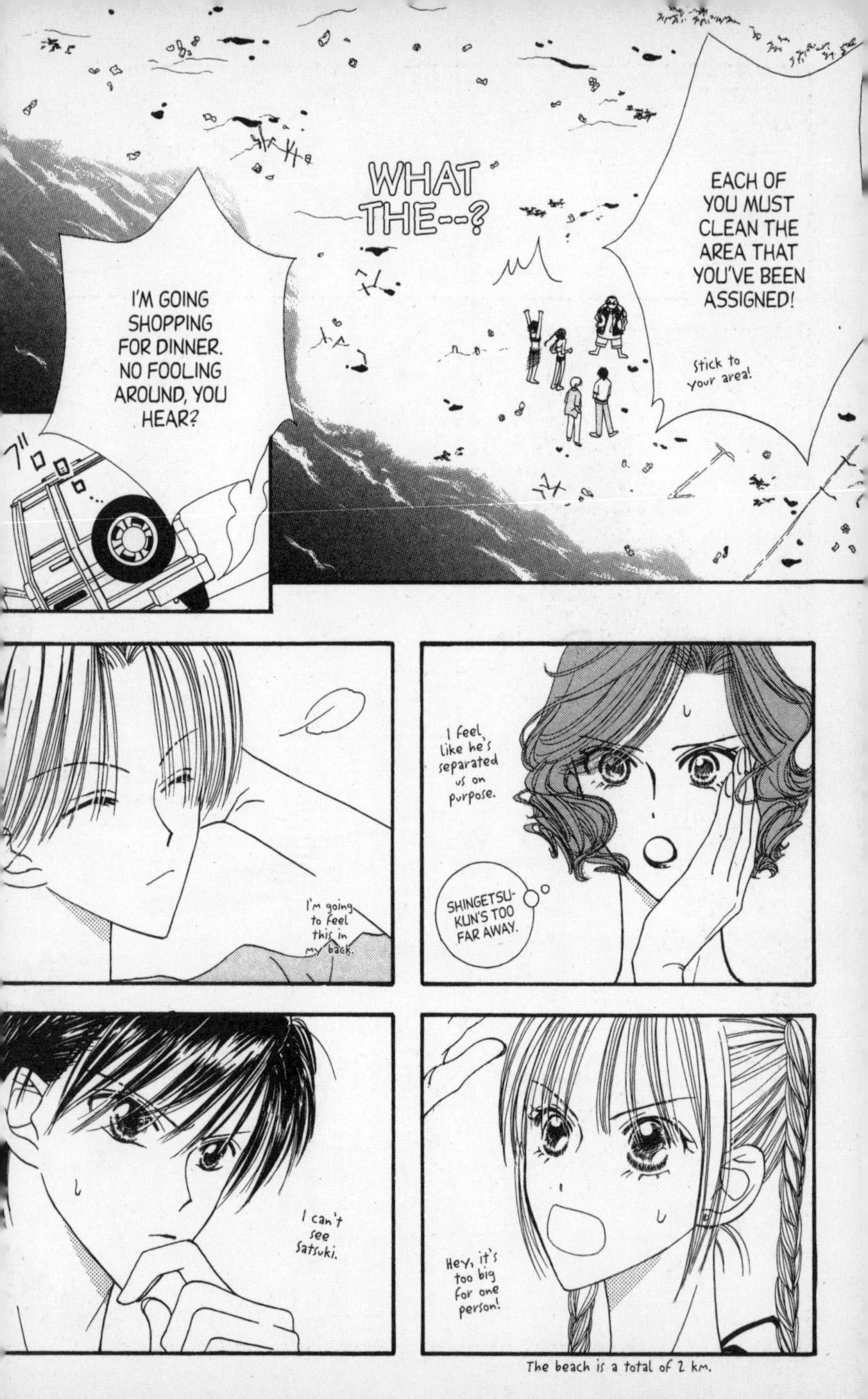
EACH OF YOU MUST CLEAN THE AREA THAT YOU'VE BEEN ASSIGNED!
Stick to your area!
WHAT THE--?
I'M GOING SHOPPING FOR DINNER. NO FOOLING AROUND, YOU HEAR?
I feel like he's separated us on purpose.
SHINGETSU-KUN'S TOO FAR AWAY.
I'm going to feel this in my back.
Hey, it's too big for one person!
I can't see Satsuki.
The beach is a total of 2 km.

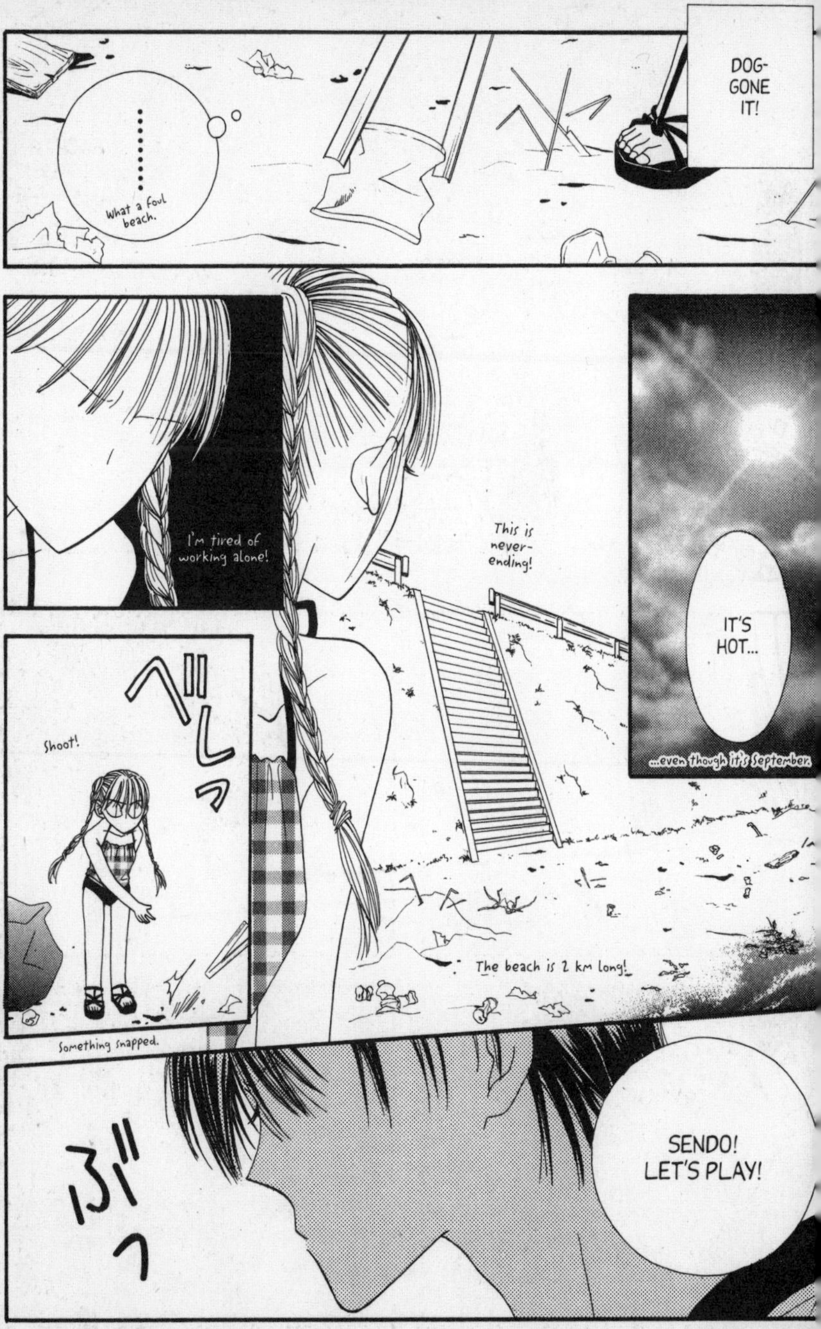
DOG-GONE IT!
......
What a foul beach.
IT'S HOT...
...even though it's September.
This is never-ending!
The beach is 2 km long!
I'm tired of working alone!
べしっ
Shoot!
Something snapped.
SENDO! LET'S PLAY!
ぶっ

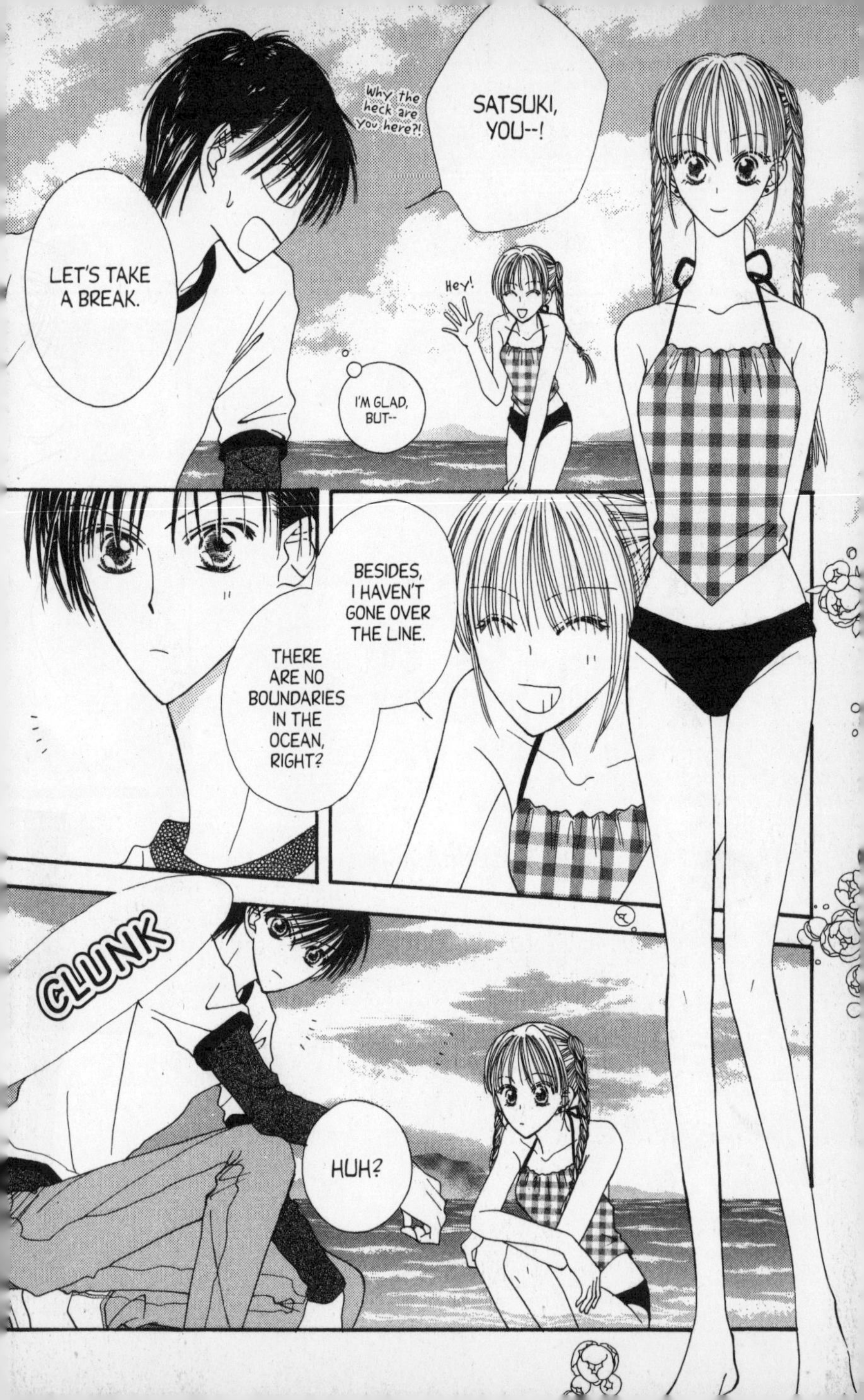
SATSUKI, YOU--!
Why the heck are you here?!
Hey!
I'M GLAD, BUT--
LET'S TAKE A BREAK.
BESIDES, I HAVEN'T GONE OVER THE LINE.
THERE ARE NO BOUNDARIES IN THE OCEAN, RIGHT?
CLUNK
HUH?

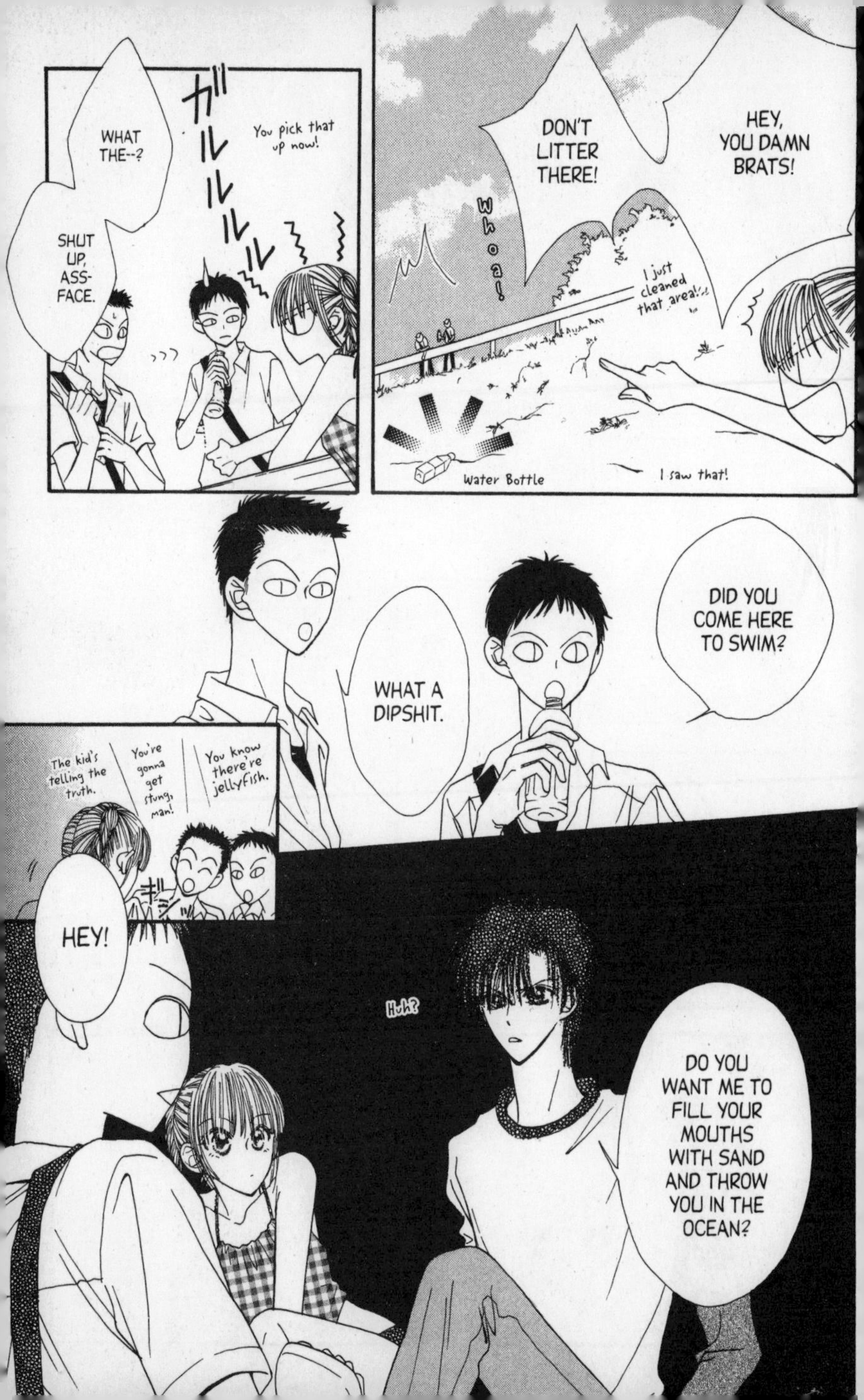
HEY, YOU DAMN BRATS!
DON'T LITTER THERE!
I just cleaned that area!
Whoa!
I saw that!
Water Bottle
You pick that up now!
ガルルルル
WHAT THE--?
SHUT UP, ASS-FACE.
DID YOU COME HERE TO SWIM?
WHAT A DIPSHIT.
You know there're jellyfish.
You're gonna get stung, man!
The kid's telling the truth.
DO YOU WANT ME TO FILL YOUR MOUTHS WITH SAND AND THROW YOU IN THE OCEAN?
Huh?
HEY!

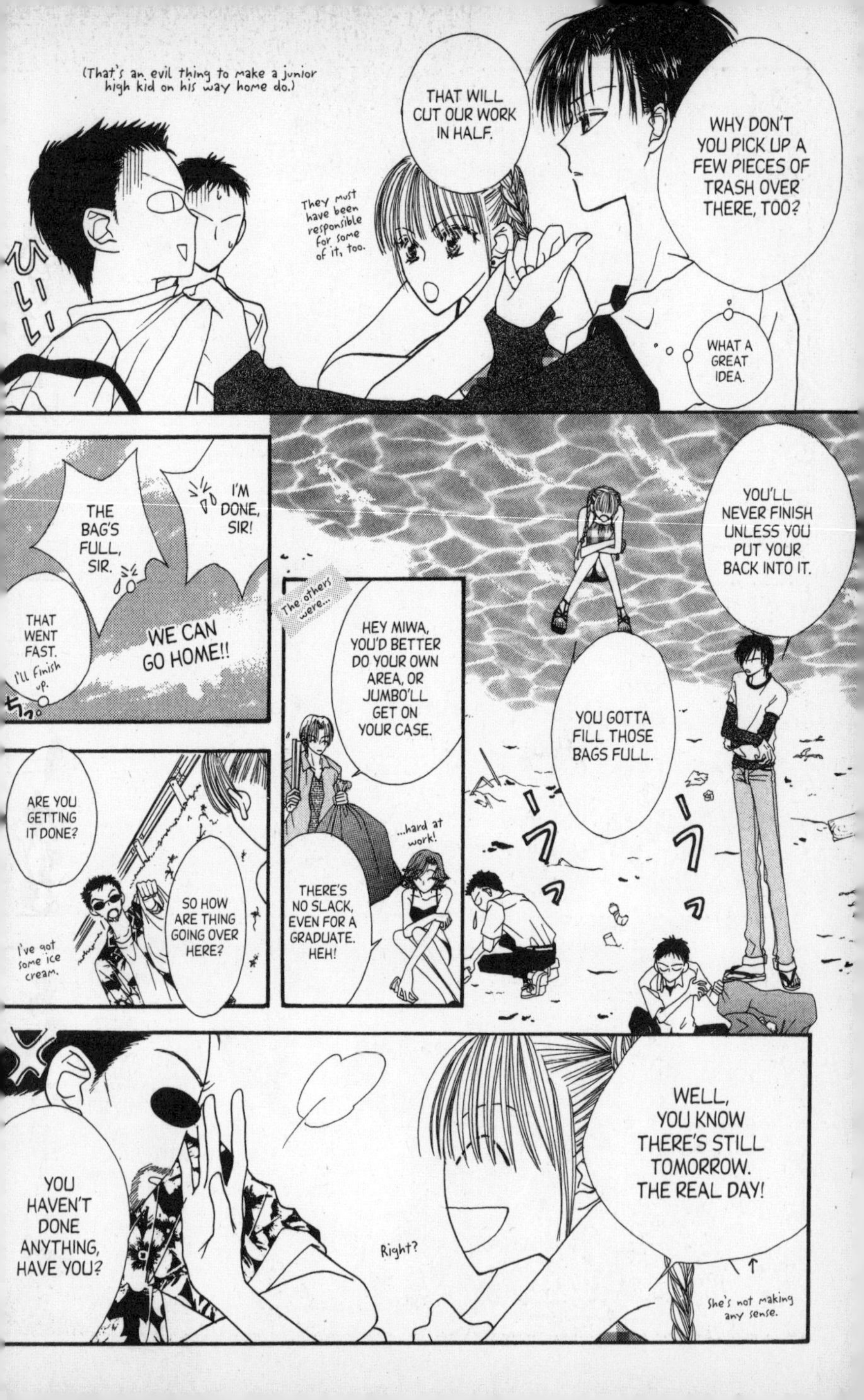
WHY DON'T YOU PICK UP A FEW PIECES OF TRASH OVER THERE, TOO?
WHAT A GREAT IDEA.
THAT WILL CUT OUR WORK IN HALF.
They must have been responsible for some of it, too.
(That's an evil thing to make a junior high kid on his way home do.)
YOU'LL NEVER FINISH UNLESS YOU PUT YOUR BACK INTO IT.
YOU GOTTA FILL THOSE BAGS FULL.
I'M DONE, SIR!
THE BAG'S FULL, SIR.
WE CAN GO HOME!!
THAT WENT FAST. I'll finish up.
The others were...
HEY MIWA, YOU'D BETTER DO YOUR OWN AREA, OR JUMBO'LL GET ON YOUR CASE.
...hard at work!
THERE'S NO SLACK, EVEN FOR A GRADUATE. HEH!
ARE YOU GETTING IT DONE?
SO HOW ARE THING GOING OVER HERE?
I've got some ice cream.
WELL, YOU KNOW THERE'S STILL TOMORROW. THE REAL DAY!
She's not making any sense.
Right?
YOU HAVEN'T DONE ANYTHING, HAVE YOU?

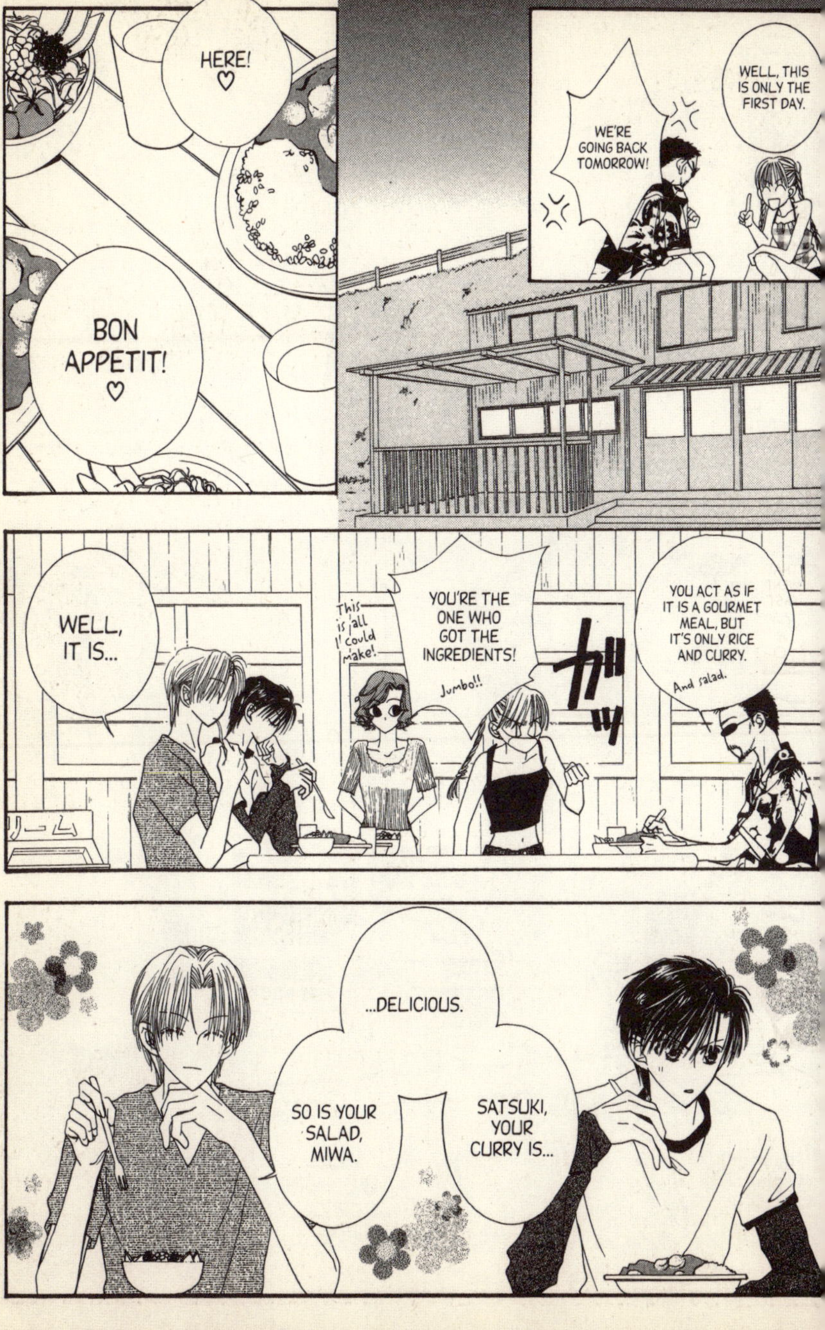
WELL, THIS IS ONLY THE FIRST DAY.
WE'RE GOING BACK TOMORROW!
HERE! ♡
BON APPETIT! ♡
YOU ACT AS IF IT IS A GOURMET MEAL, BUT IT'S ONLY RICE AND CURRY.
And salad.
YOU'RE THE ONE WHO GOT THE INGREDIENTS!
Jumbo!!
This is all I could make!
WELL, IT IS...
SATSUKI, YOUR CURRY IS...
...DELICIOUS.
SO IS YOUR SALAD, MIWA.

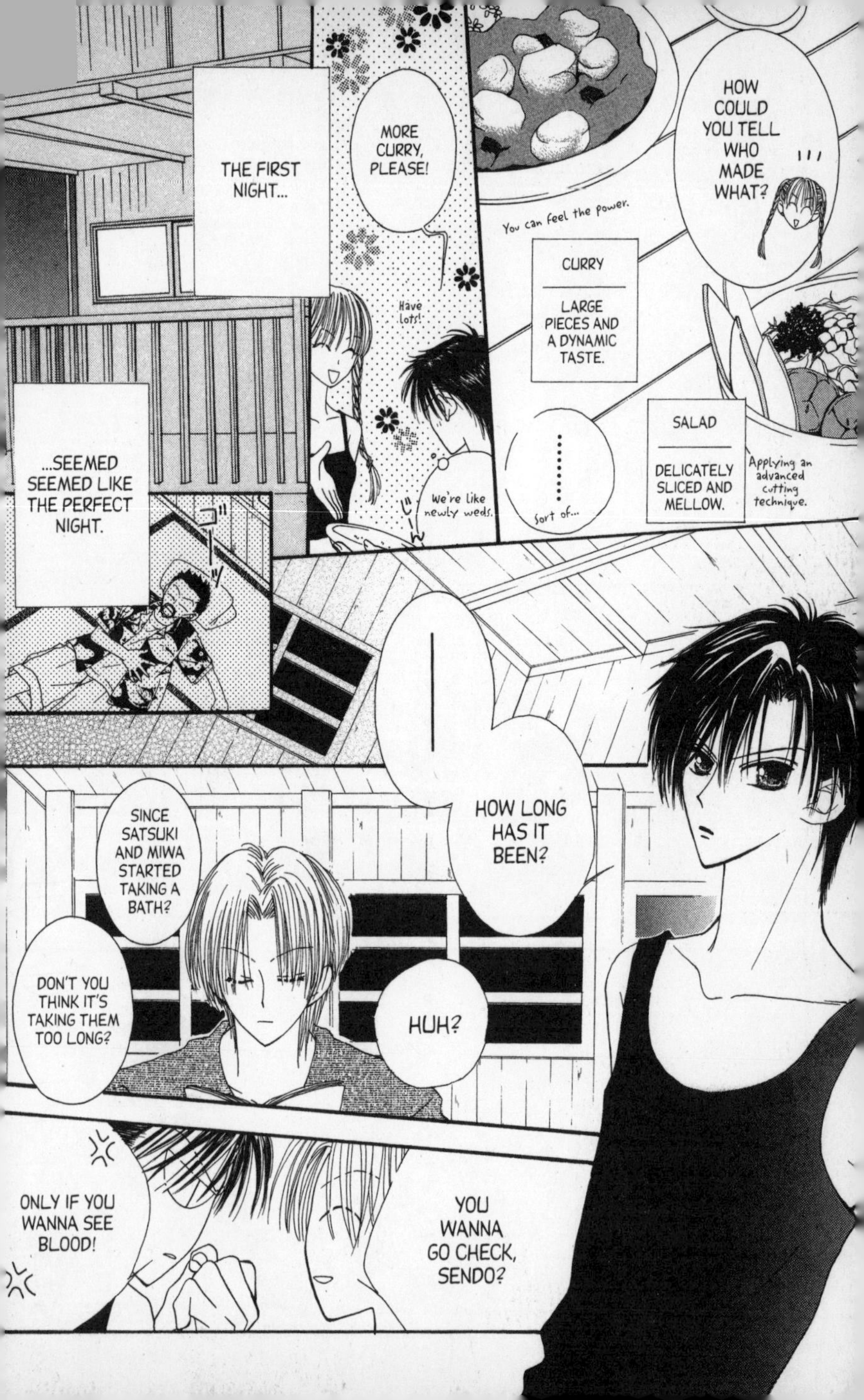
HOW COULD YOU TELL WHO MADE WHAT?
You can feel the power.
CURRY
LARGE PIECES AND A DYNAMIC TASTE.
SALAD
DELICATELY SLICED AND MELLOW.
Applying an advanced cutting technique.
......
Sort of...
MORE CURRY, PLEASE!
Have lots!
We're like newly weds.
THE FIRST NIGHT...
...SEEMED SEEMED LIKE THE PERFECT NIGHT.
HOW LONG HAS IT BEEN?
SINCE SATSUKI AND MIWA STARTED TAKING A BATH?
DON'T YOU THINK IT'S TAKING THEM TOO LONG?
HUH?
YOU WANNA GO CHECK, SENDO?
ONLY IF YOU WANNA SEE BLOOD!

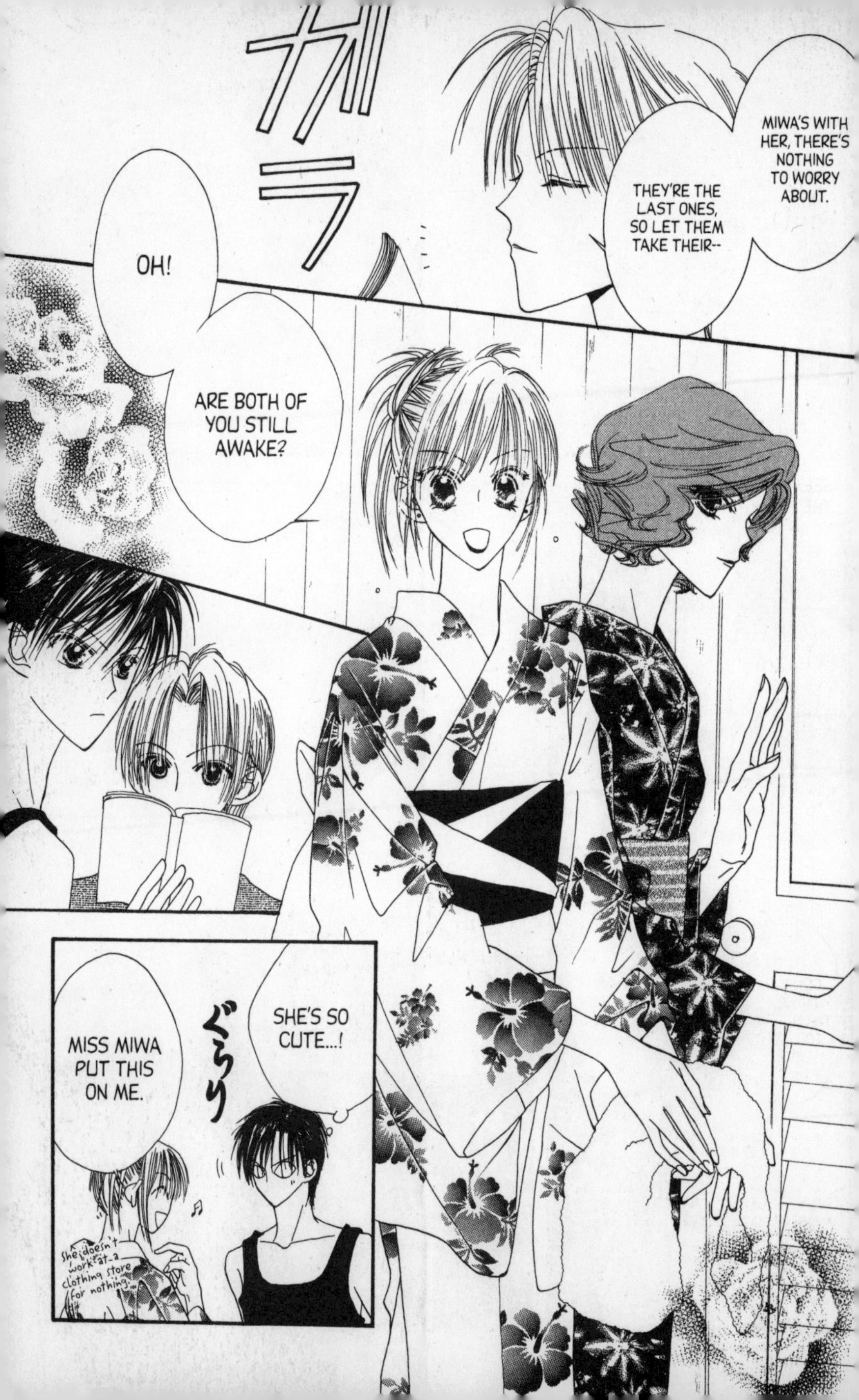
MIWA'S WITH HER, THERE'S NOTHING TO WORRY ABOUT.
THEY'RE THE LAST ONES, SO LET THEM TAKE THEIR--
ガラ
OH!
ARE BOTH OF YOU STILL AWAKE?
SHE'S SO CUTE...!
ぐらり
MISS MIWA PUT THIS ON ME.
She doesn't work at a clothing store for nothing.

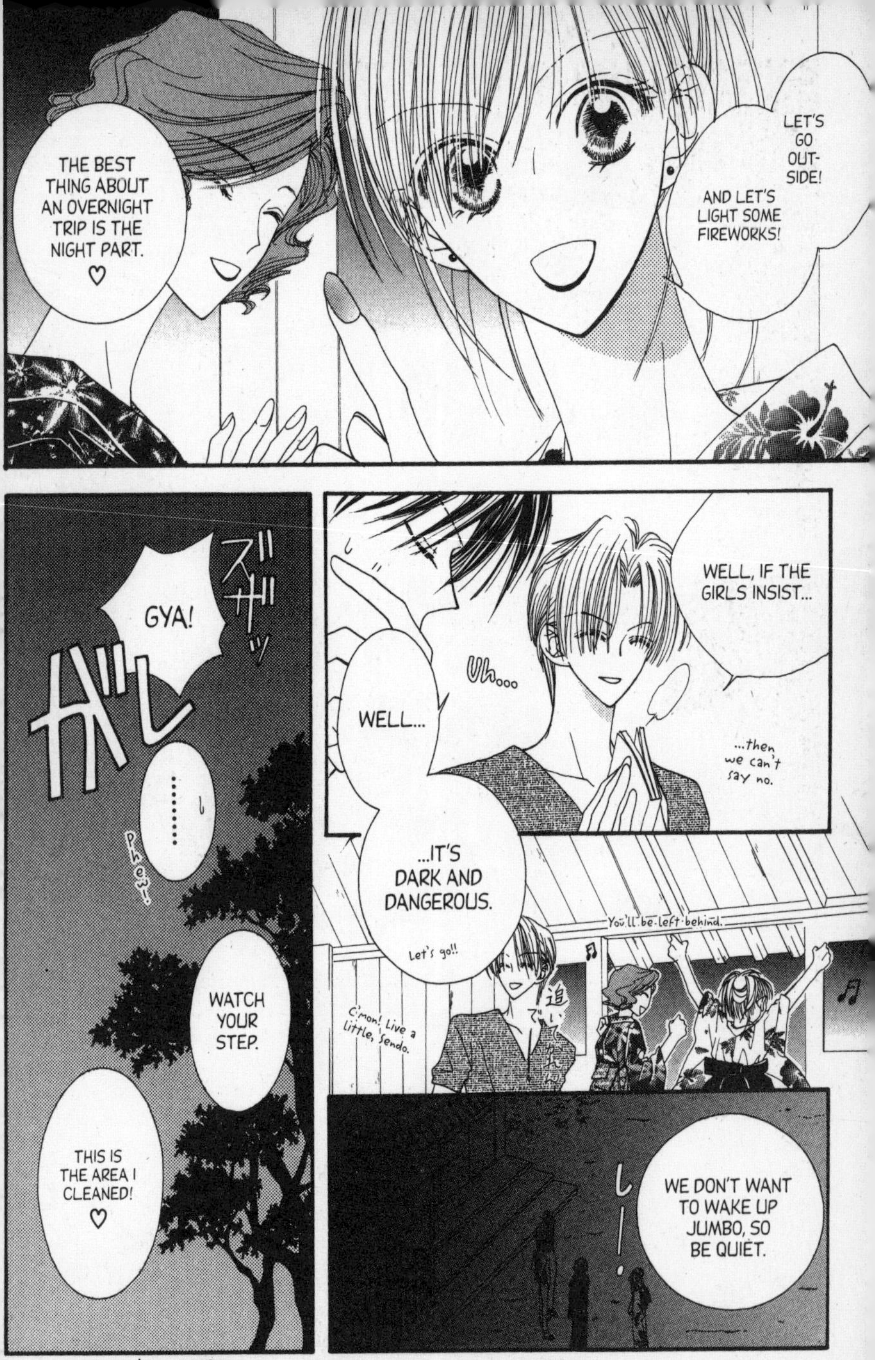
LET'S GO OUT-SIDE!
AND LET'S LIGHT SOME FIREWORKS!
THE BEST THING ABOUT AN OVERNIGHT TRIP IS THE NIGHT PART. ♡
WELL, IF THE GIRLS INSIST...
...then we can't say no.
Uh...
WELL...
...IT'S DARK AND DANGEROUS.
You'll be left behind.
Let's go!!
C'mon! Live a little, Sendo.
WE DON'T WANT TO WAKE UP JUMBO, SO BE QUIET.
GYA!
ズザッ
......
Phew!
WATCH YOUR STEP.
THIS IS THE AREA I CLEANED! ♡

Who said what?

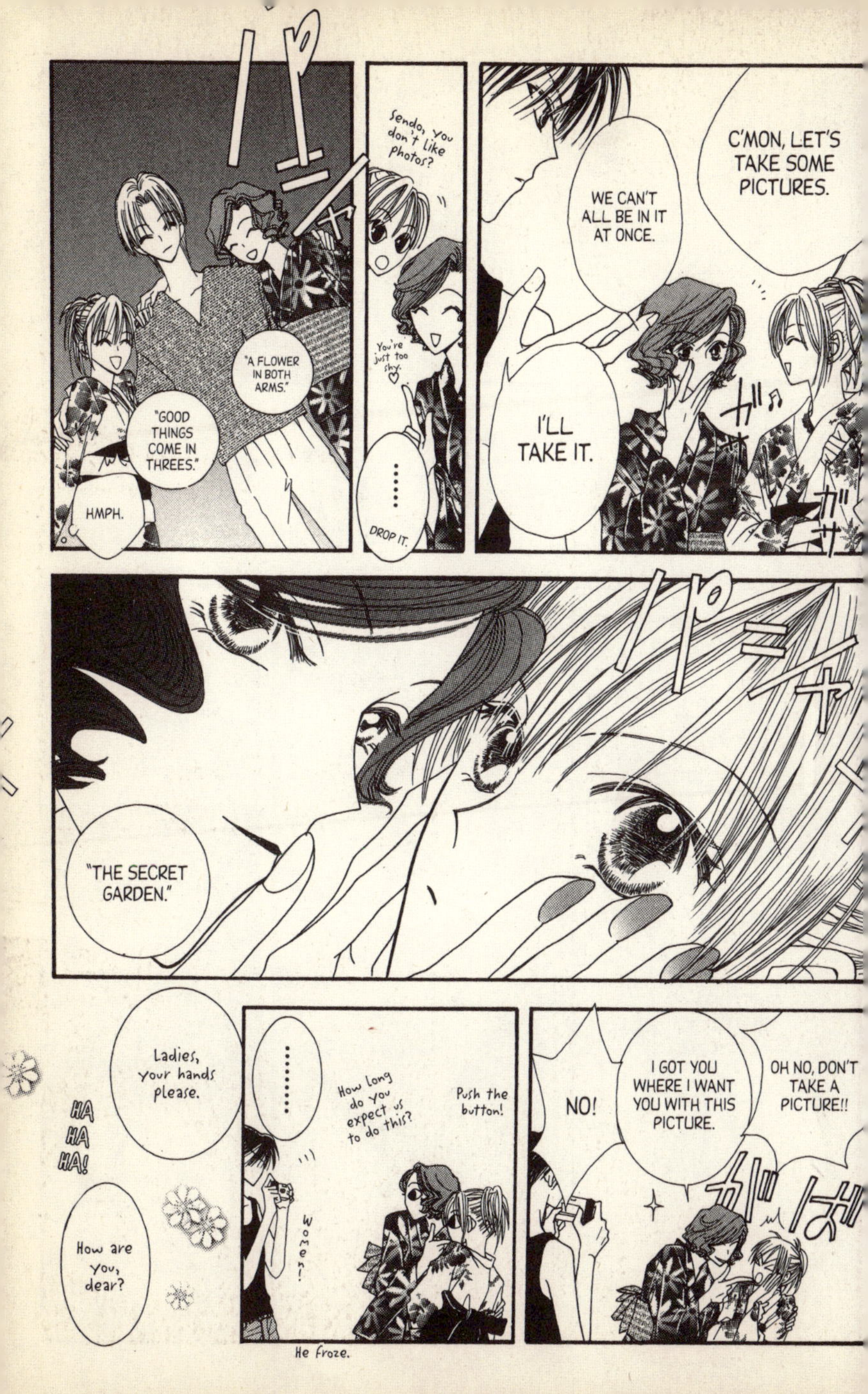
C'MON, LET'S TAKE SOME PICTURES.
WE CAN'T ALL BE IN IT AT ONCE.
I'LL TAKE IT.
Sendo, you don't like photos?
You're just too shy. ♡
......
DROP IT.
"A FLOWER IN BOTH ARMS."
"GOOD THINGS COME IN THREES."
HMPH.
"THE SECRET GARDEN."
OH NO, DON'T TAKE A PICTURE!!
I GOT YOU WHERE I WANT YOU WITH THIS PICTURE.
NO!
Push the button!
How long do you expect us to do this?
....
Women!
He froze.
Ladies, your hands please.
HA HA HA!
How are you, dear?

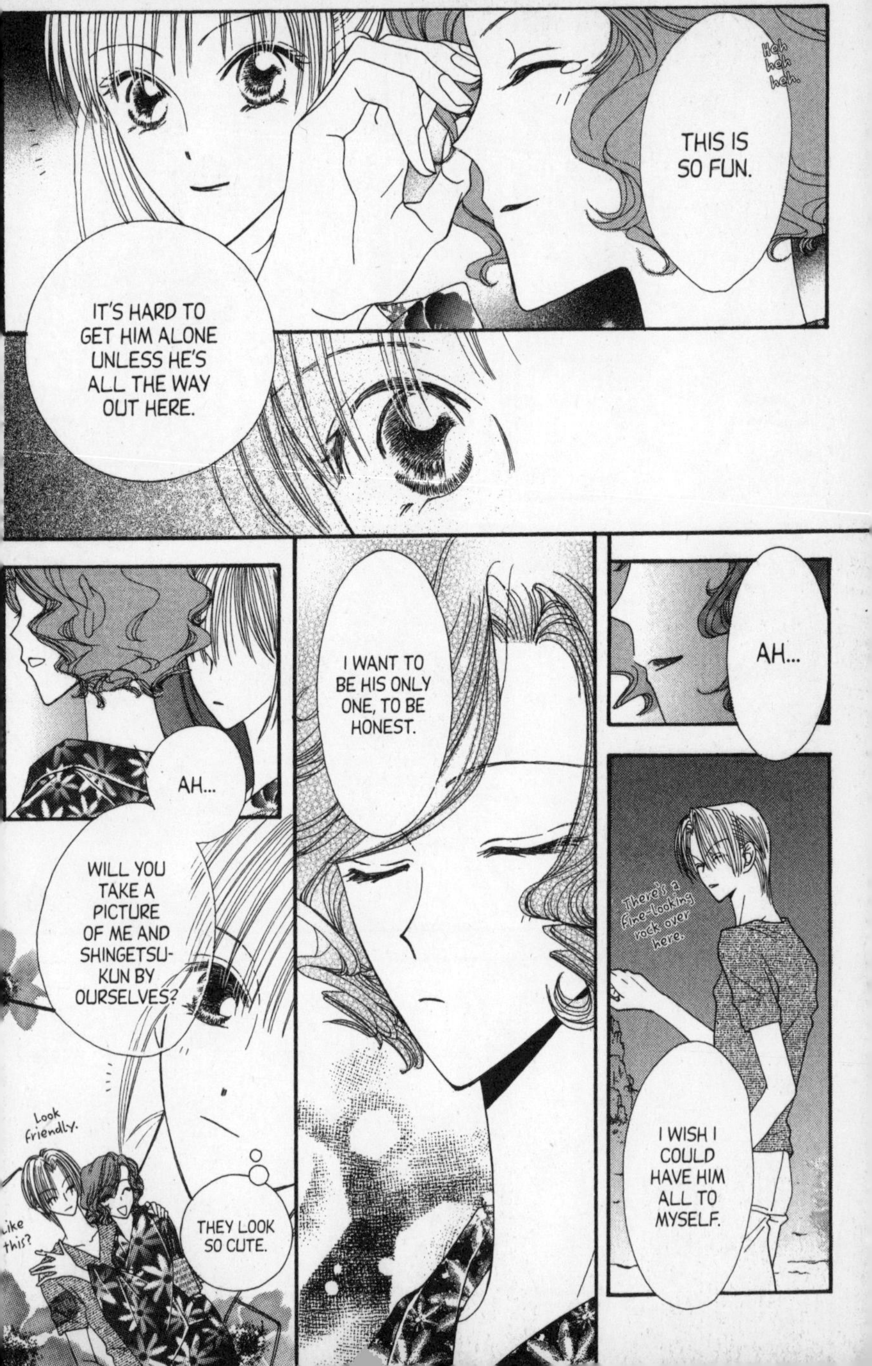
Heh heh heh.
THIS IS SO FUN.
IT'S HARD TO GET HIM ALONE UNLESS HE'S ALL THE WAY OUT HERE.
AH...
There's a fine-looking rock over here.
I WISH I COULD HAVE HIM ALL TO MYSELF.
I WANT TO BE HIS ONLY ONE, TO BE HONEST.
AH...
WILL YOU TAKE A PICTURE OF ME AND SHINGETSU-KUN BY OURSELVES?
Look friendly.
Like this?
THEY LOOK SO CUTE.

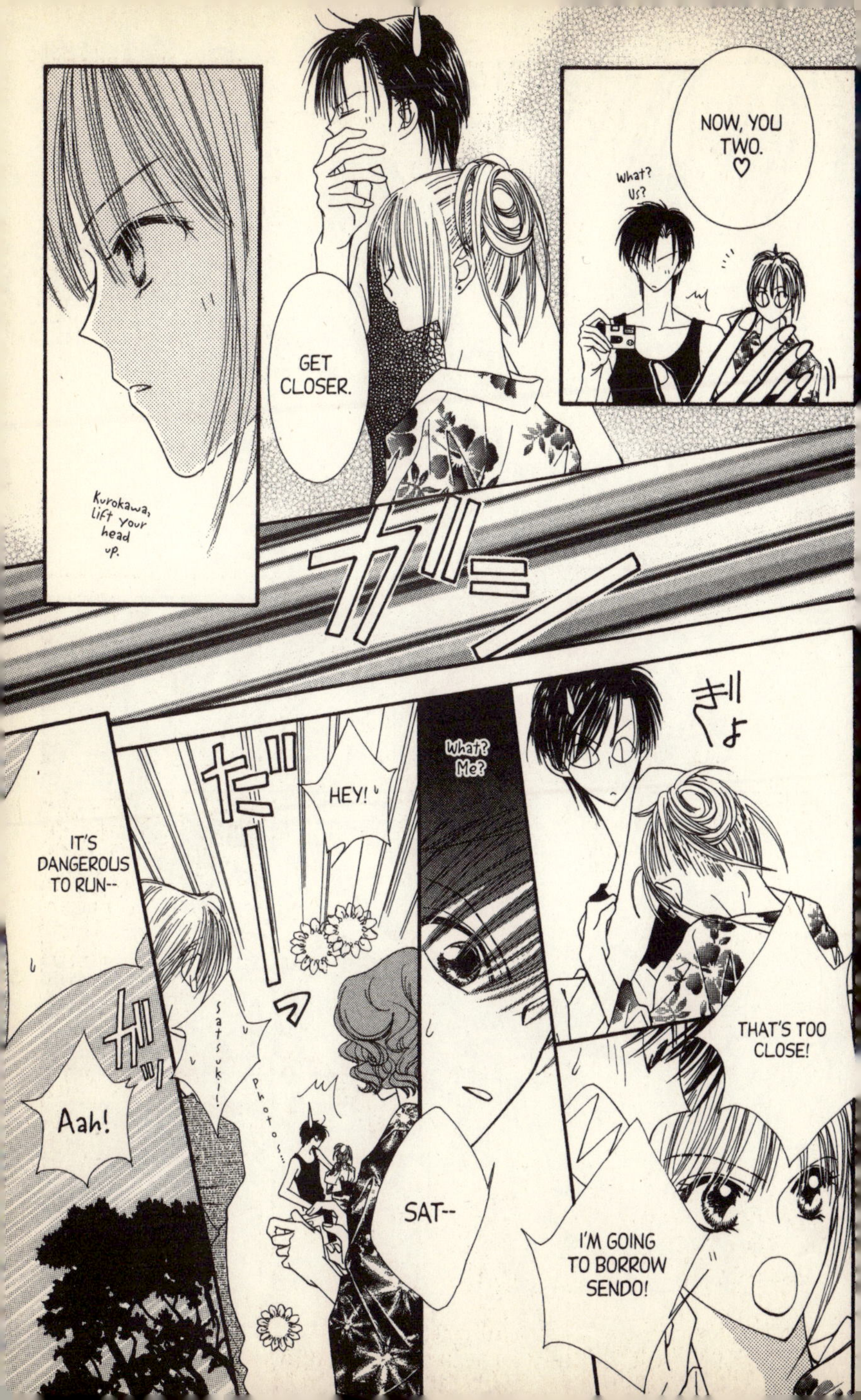
NOW, YOU TWO. ♡
What? Us?
GET CLOSER.
Kurokawa, lift your head up.
What? Me?
THAT'S TOO CLOSE!
I'M GOING TO BORROW SENDO!
SAT--
HEY!
IT'S DANGEROUS TO RUN--
Satsuki!
Photos...
Aah!

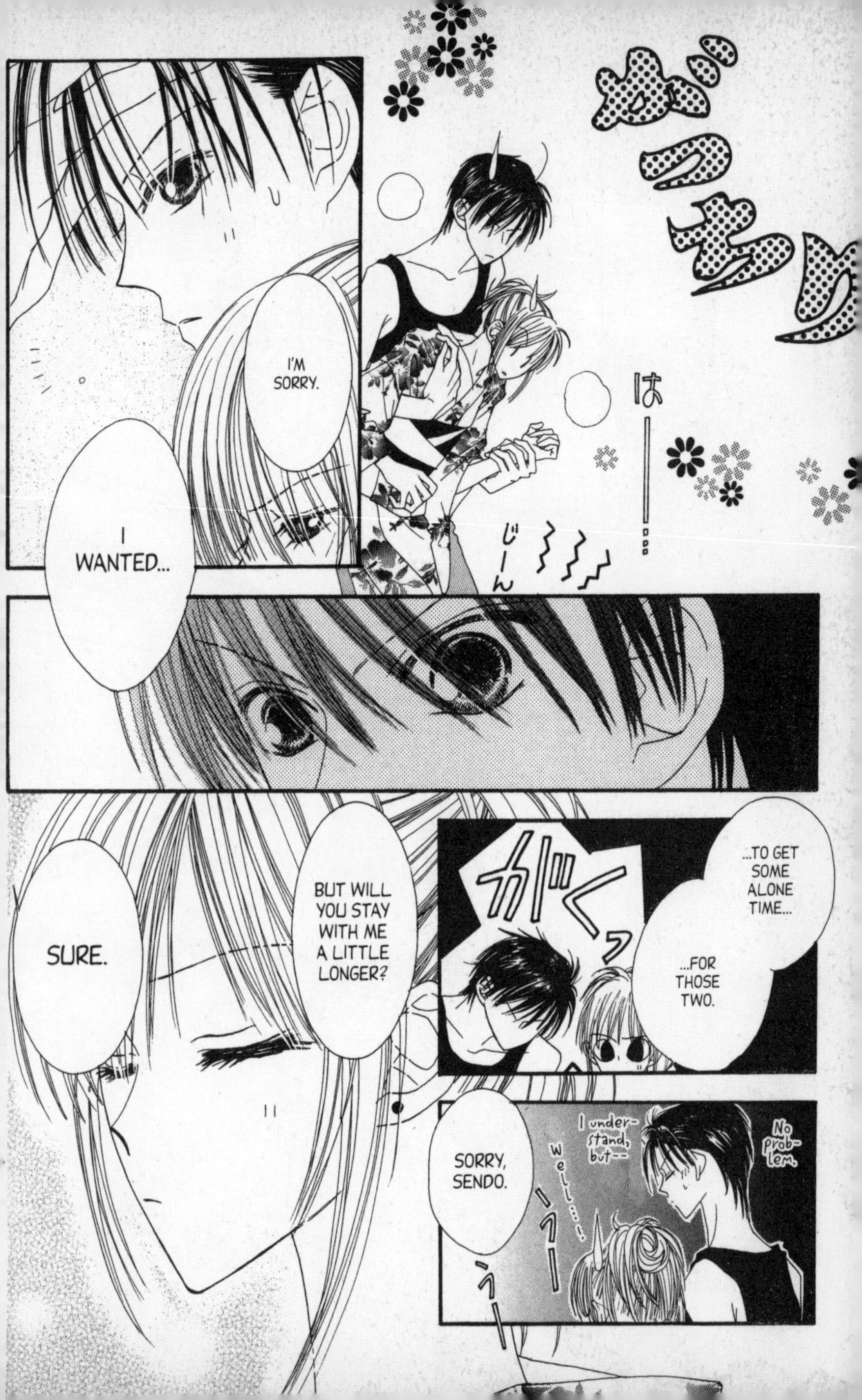
がっちり
はーー…
じーん
I'M SORRY.
I WANTED...
...TO GET SOME ALONE TIME...
...FOR THOSE TWO.
がくっ
No prob-lem.
I under-stand, but--
well...!
SORRY, SENDO.
BUT WILL YOU STAY WITH ME A LITTLE LONGER?
SURE.

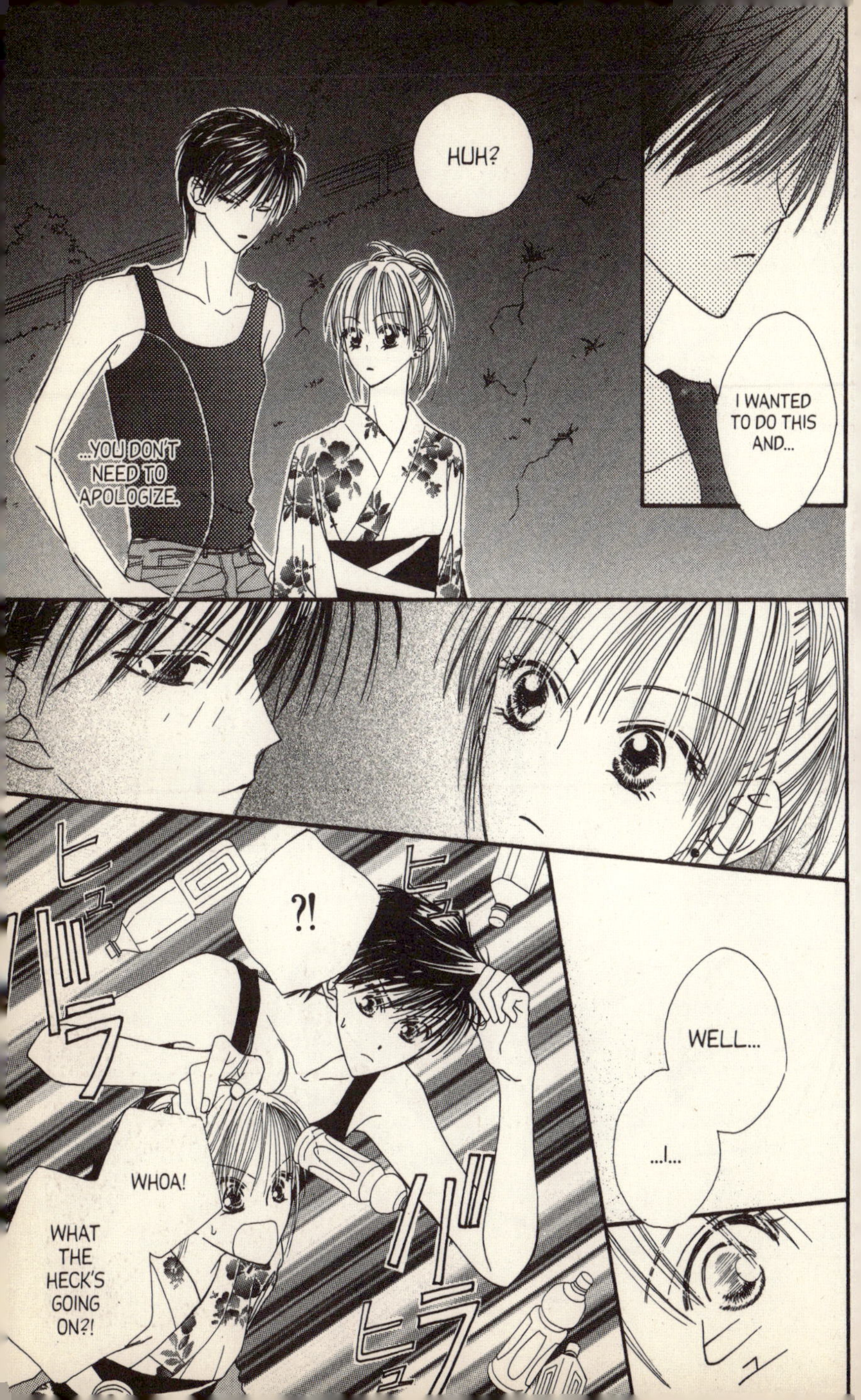
I WANTED TO DO THIS AND...
HUH?
...YOU DON'T NEED TO APOLOGIZE.
WELL...
...I...
?!
WHOA!
WHAT THE HECK'S GOING ON?!

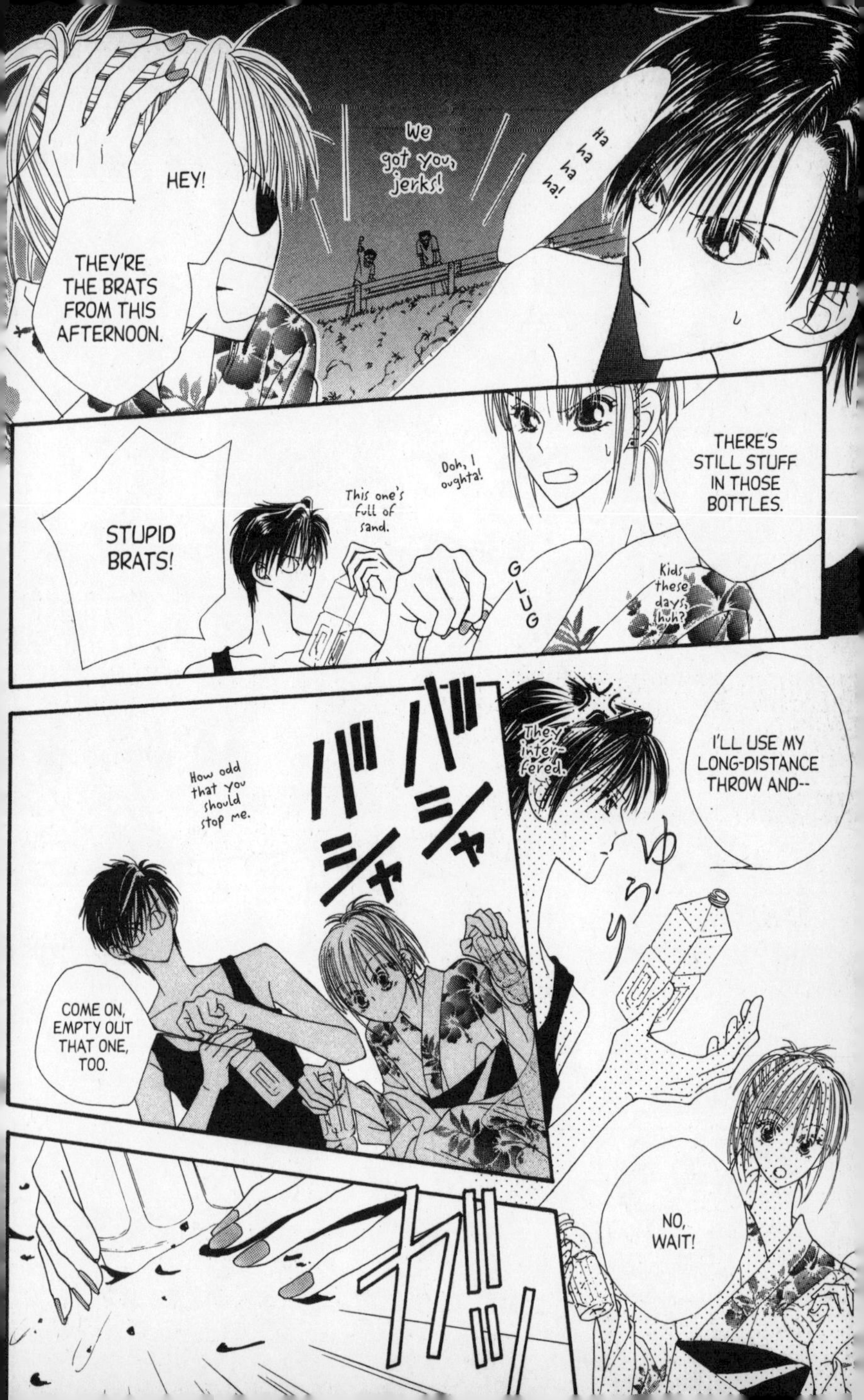
Ha ha ha ha!
We got you, jerks!
HEY!
THEY'RE THE BRATS FROM THIS AFTERNOON.
THERE'S STILL STUFF IN THOSE BOTTLES.
Kids these days, huh?
GLUG
Ooh, I oughta!
This one's full of sand.
STUPID BRATS!
I'LL USE MY LONG-DISTANCE THROW AND--
They interfered.
ゆらり
バシャ
バシャ
How odd that you should stop me.
COME ON, EMPTY OUT THAT ONE, TOO.
NO, WAIT!
ガッ

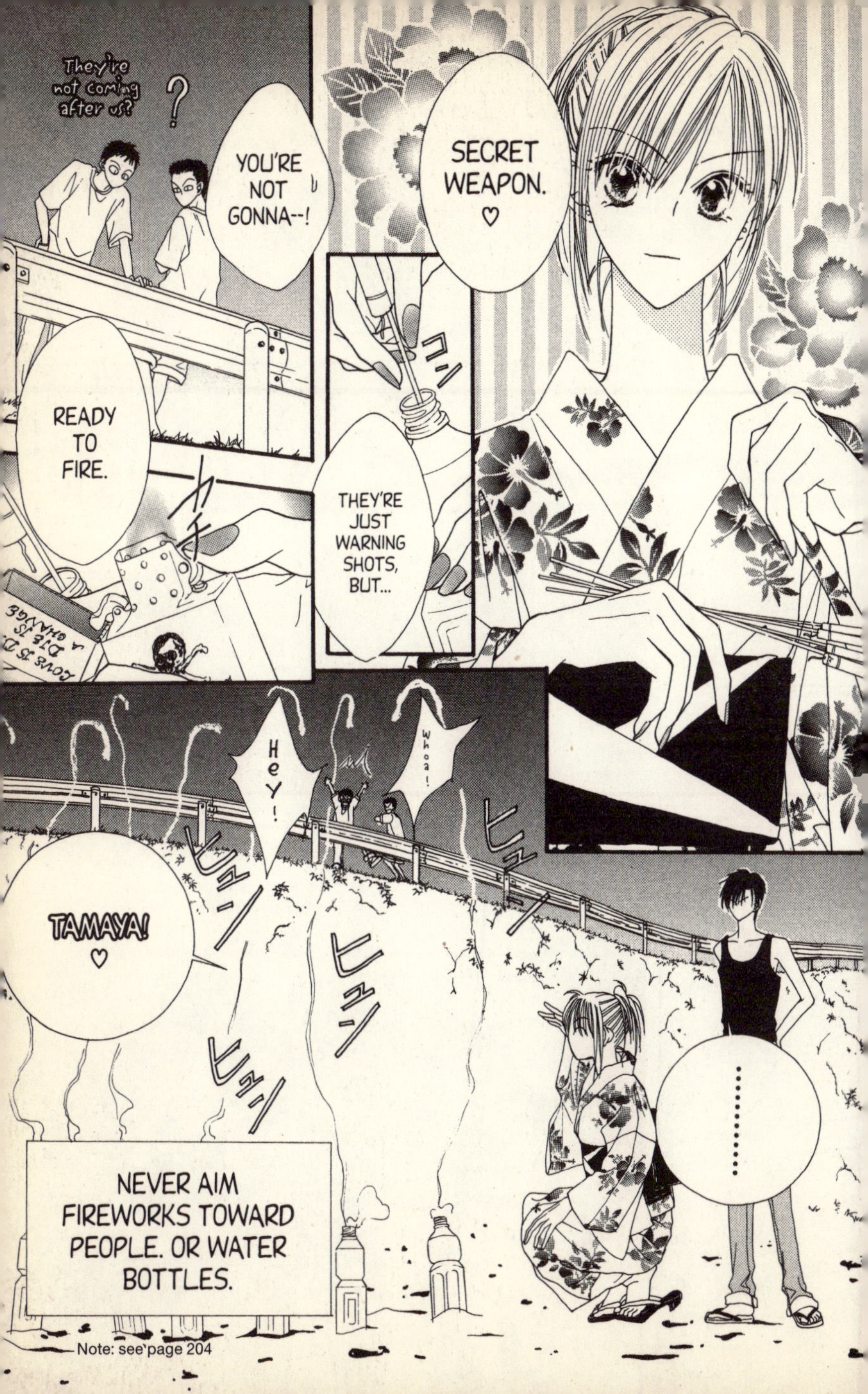

SECRET WEAPON. ♡
コン
THEY'RE JUST WARNING SHOTS, BUT...
They're not coming after us?
?
YOU'RE NOT GONNA--!
READY TO FIRE.
カチ
HeY!
Whoa!
ヒューン
ヒューン
TAMAYA! ♡
ヒュン
ヒュッ
......
NEVER AIM FIREWORKS TOWARD PEOPLE. OR WATER BOTTLES.

Note: see page 204

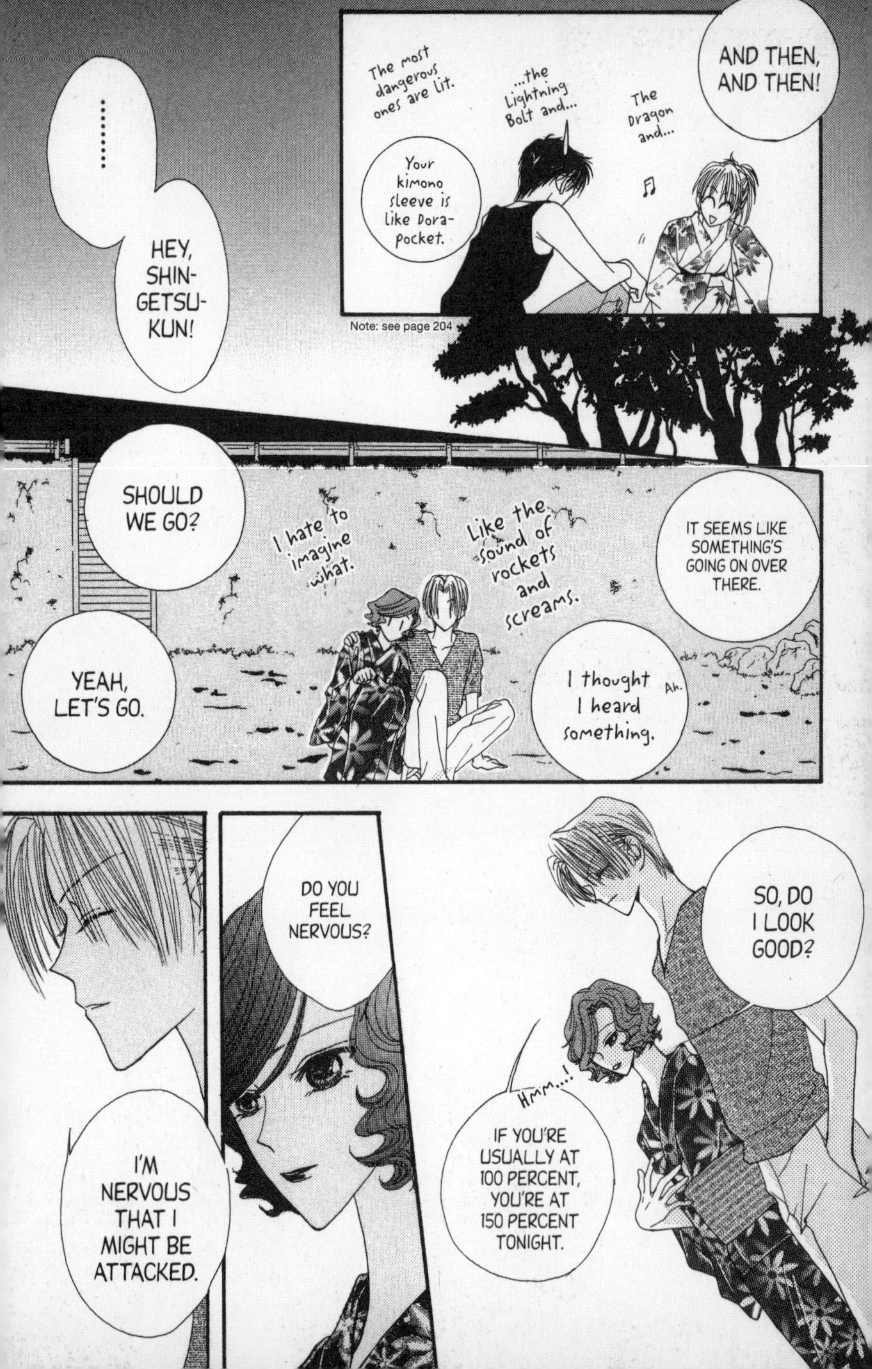
AND THEN, AND THEN!
The Dragon and...
...the Lightning Bolt and...
The most dangerous ones are lit.
Your kimono sleeve is like Dora-pocket.
Note: see page 204
......
HEY, SHIN-GETSU-KUN!
IT SEEMS LIKE SOMETHING'S GOING ON OVER THERE.
Ah.
I thought I heard something.
Like the sound of rockets and screams.
I hate to imagine what.
SHOULD WE GO?
YEAH, LET'S GO.
SO, DO I LOOK GOOD?
HMM...!
IF YOU'RE USUALLY AT 100 PERCENT, YOU'RE AT 150 PERCENT TONIGHT.
DO YOU FEEL NERVOUS?
I'M NERVOUS THAT I MIGHT BE ATTACKED.

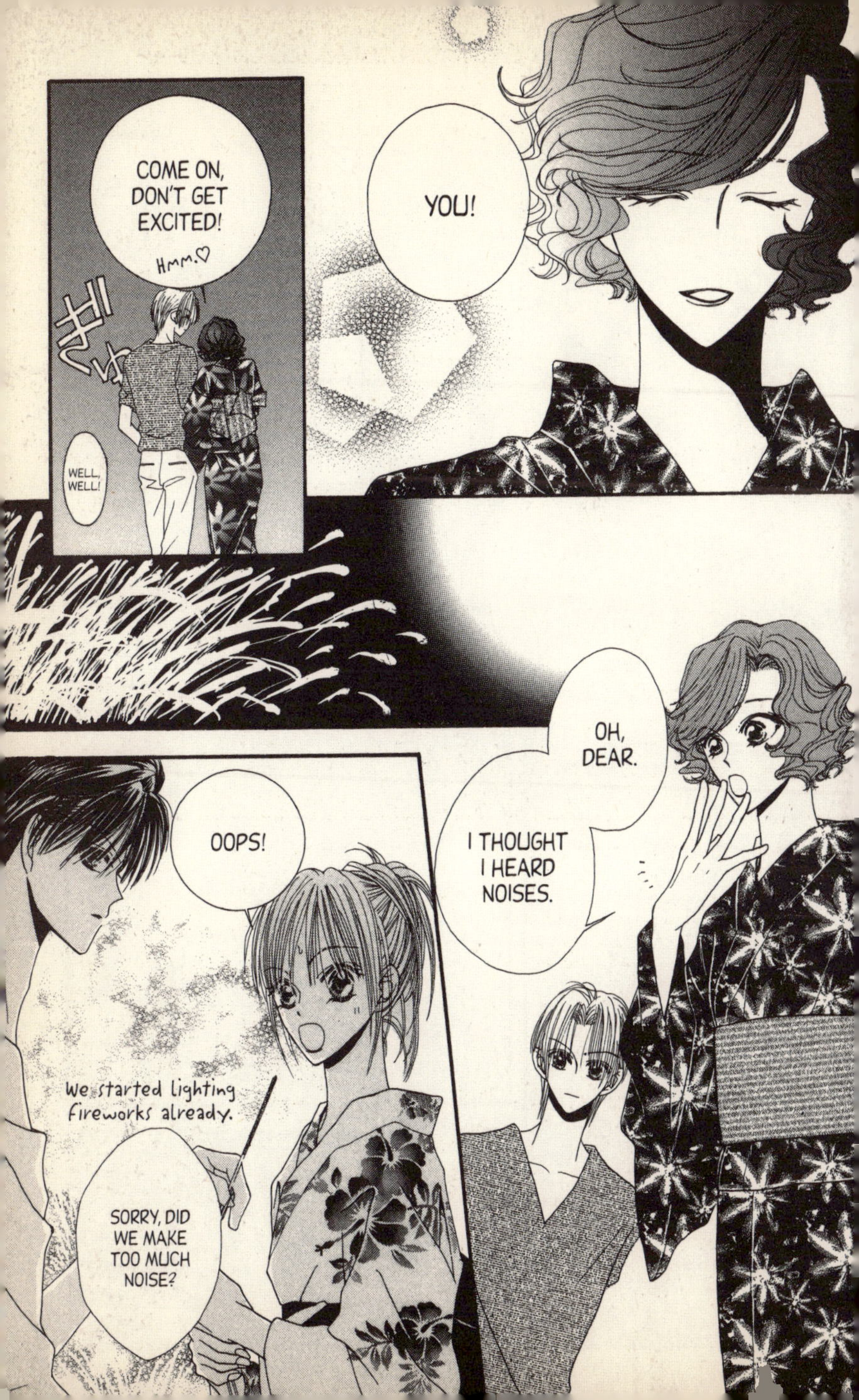
YOU!
COME ON, DON'T GET EXCITED!
Hmm.♡
WELL, WELL!
OH, DEAR.
I THOUGHT I HEARD NOISES.
OOPS!
We started lighting fireworks already.
SORRY, DID WE MAKE TOO MUCH NOISE?

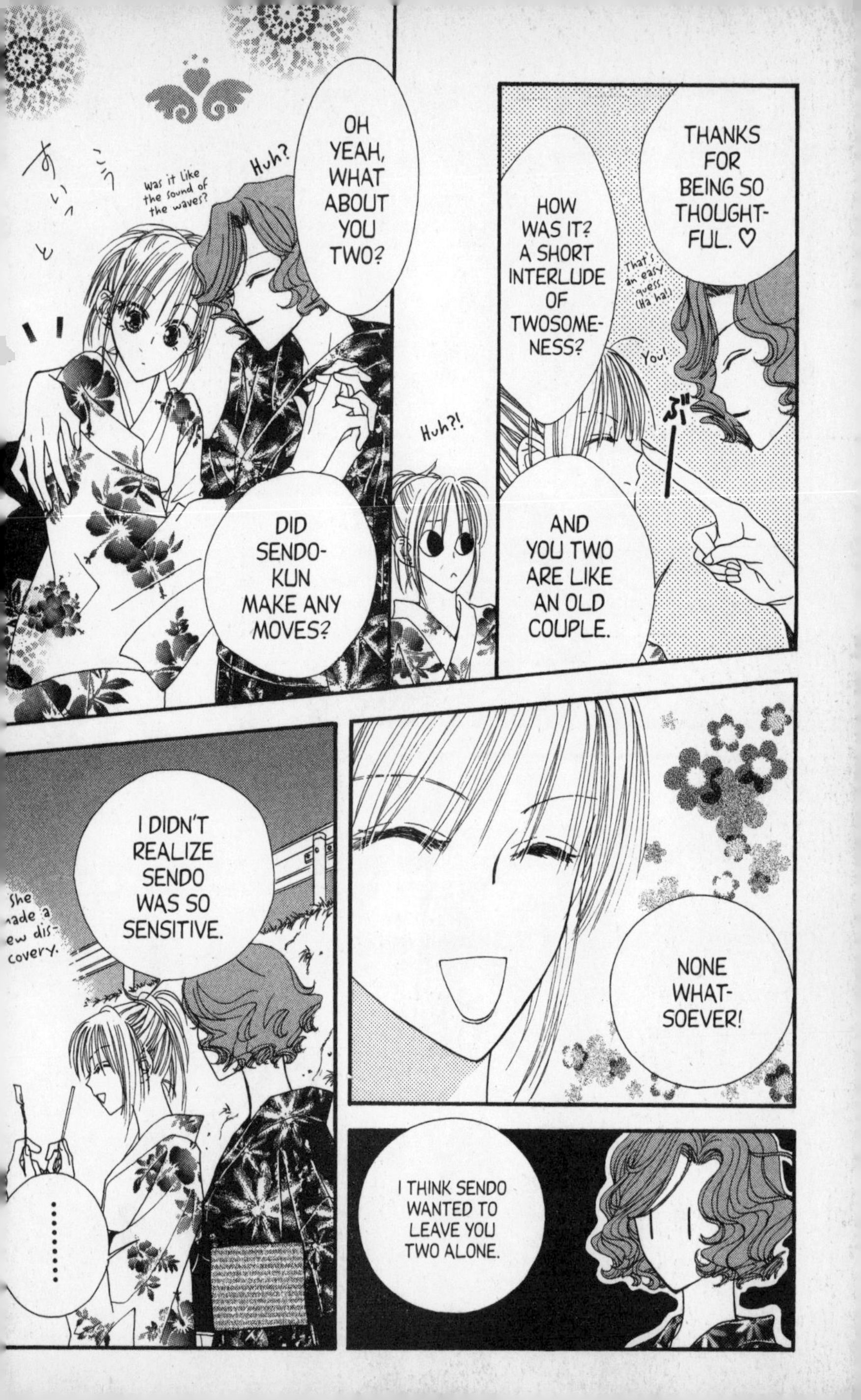
THANKS FOR BEING SO THOUGHTFUL. ♡
HOW WAS IT? A SHORT INTERLUDE OF TWOSOMENESS?
That's an easy guess. (Ha ha!)
You!
ぶー
AND YOU TWO ARE LIKE AN OLD COUPLE.
Huh?!
OH YEAH, WHAT ABOUT YOU TWO?
Huh?
Was it like the sound of the waves?
すいっと
DID SENDO-KUN MAKE ANY MOVES?
NONE WHATSOEVER!
I THINK SENDO WANTED TO LEAVE YOU TWO ALONE.
I DIDN'T REALIZE SENDO WAS SO SENSITIVE.
She
ade a
ew dis-
covery.
......

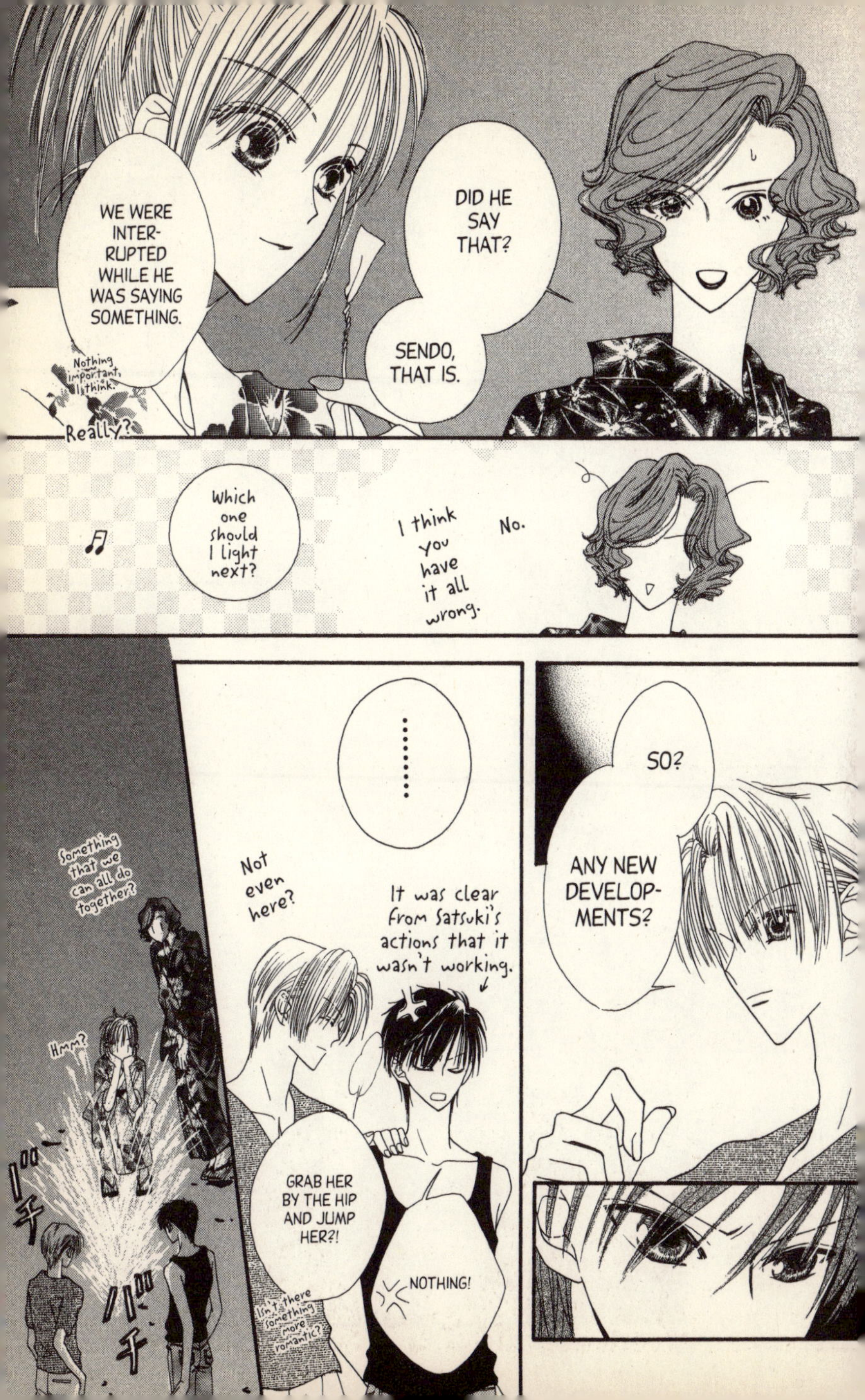
DID HE SAY THAT?
SENDO, THAT IS.
WE WERE INTER-RUPTED WHILE HE WAS SAYING SOMETHING.
Nothing important, I think.
Really?
No.
I think you have it all wrong.
Which one should I light next?
SO?
ANY NEW DEVELOP-MENTS?
......
Not even here?
It was clear from Satsuki's actions that it wasn't working.
GRAB HER BY THE HIP AND JUMP HER?!
NOTHING!
Isn't there something more romantic?
Something that we can all do together?
Hmm?

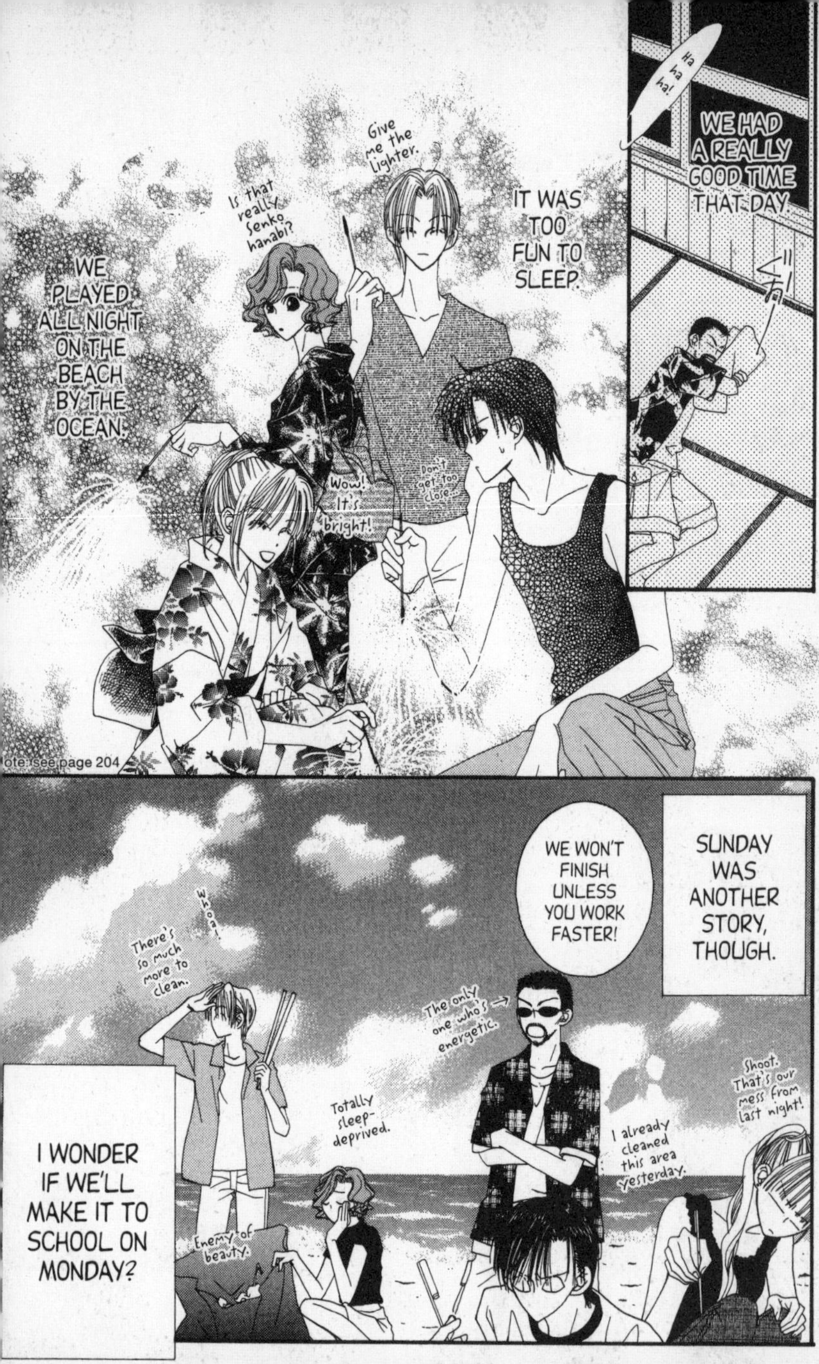
Ha ha ha!
WE HAD A REALLY GOOD TIME THAT DAY.
IT WAS TOO FUN TO SLEEP.
Give me the lighter.
Is that really Senko hanabi?
WE PLAYED ALL NIGHT ON THE BEACH BY THE OCEAN.
Don't get too close...
Wow! It's bright!
SUNDAY WAS ANOTHER STORY, THOUGH.
WE WON'T FINISH UNLESS YOU WORK FASTER!
Shoot. That's our mess from last night!
I already cleaned this area yesterday.
The only one who's energetic. →
Whoa!
There's so much more to clean.
Totally sleep-deprived.
Enemy of beauty.
I WONDER IF WE'LL MAKE IT TO SCHOOL ON MONDAY?

ote: see page 204

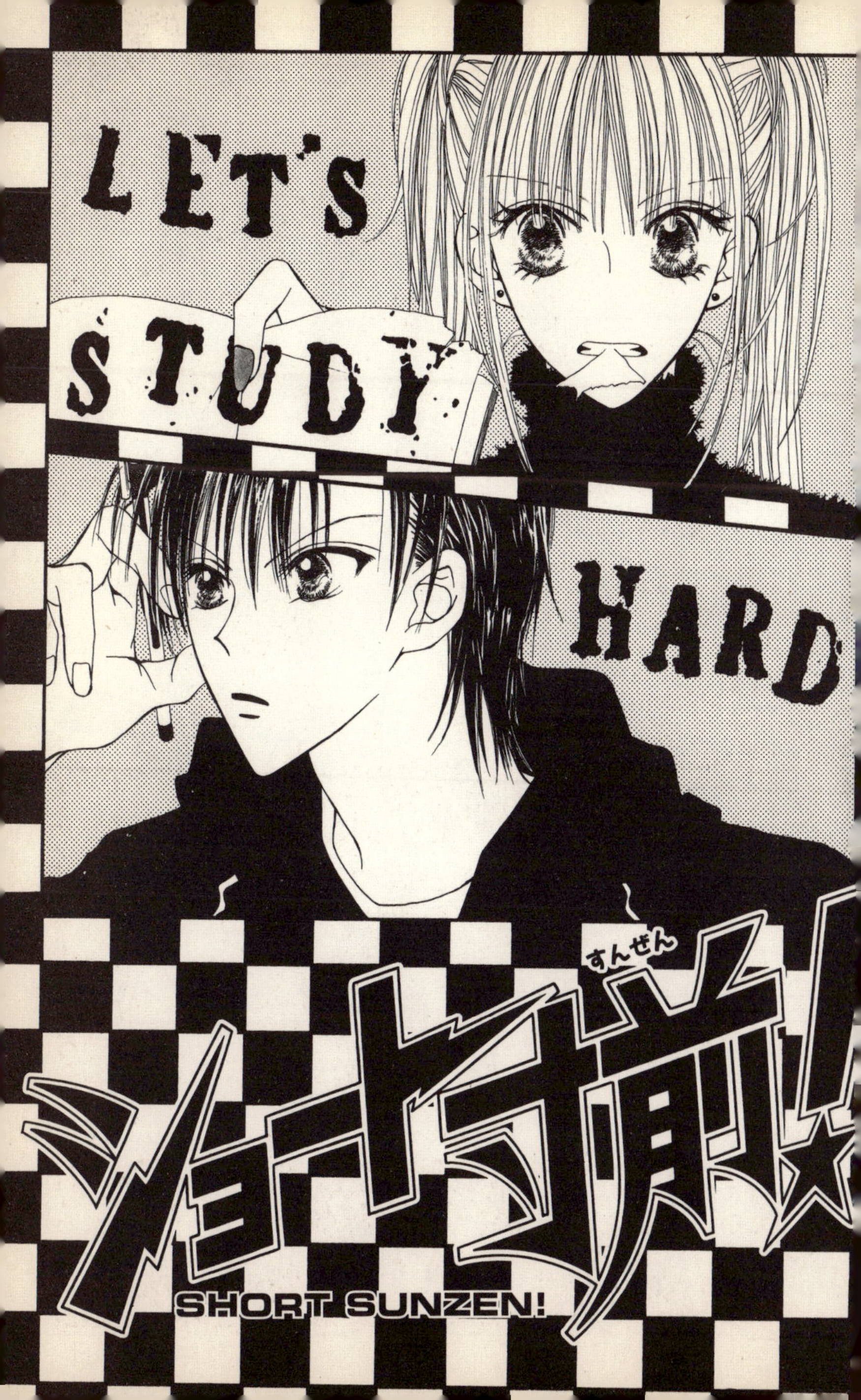
LET'S STUDY HARD
すんぜん
ショート寸前!
SHORT SUNZEN!

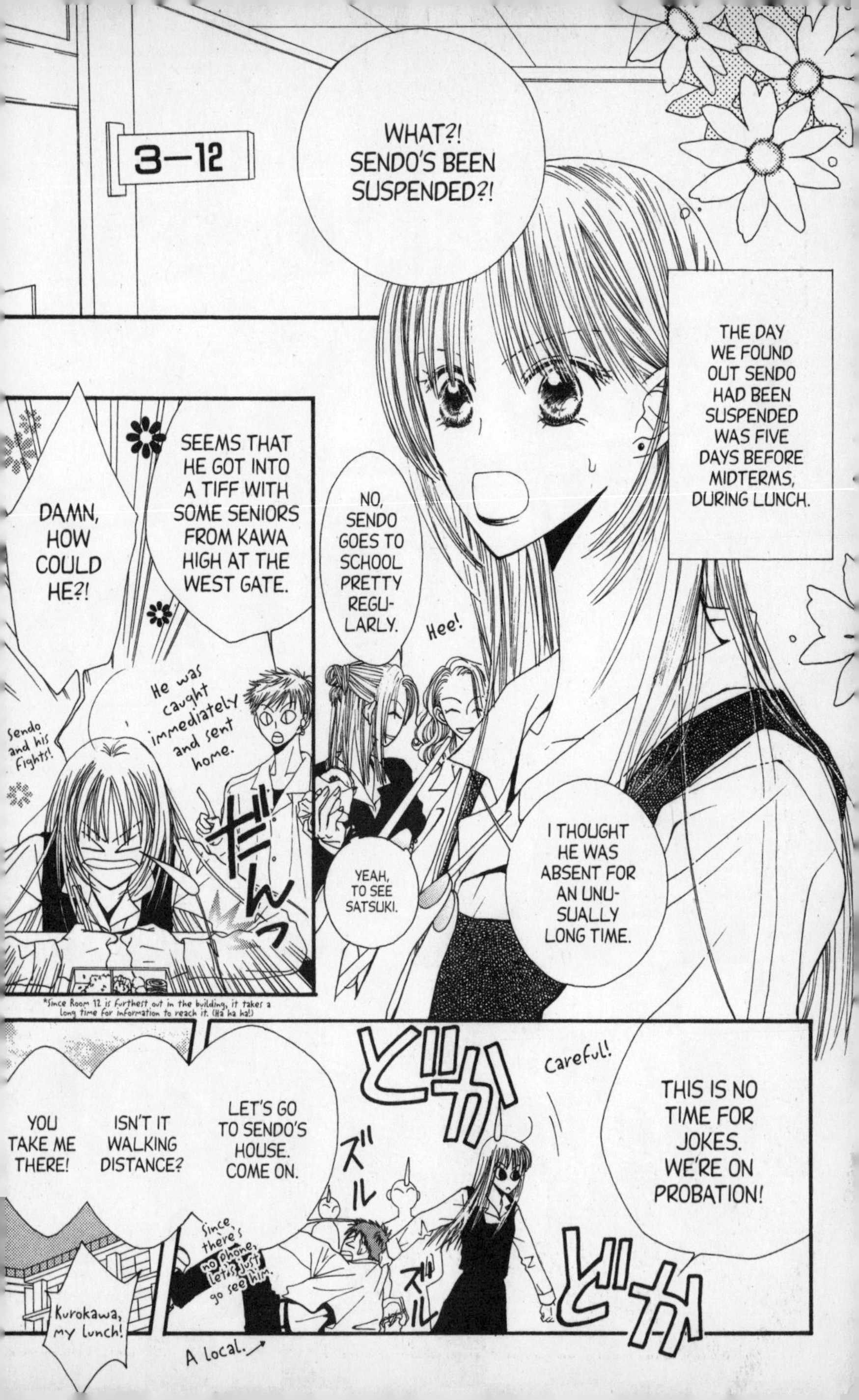
3—12
WHAT?! SENDO'S BEEN SUSPENDED?!
THE DAY WE FOUND OUT SENDO HAD BEEN SUSPENDED WAS FIVE DAYS BEFORE MIDTERMS, DURING LUNCH.
I THOUGHT HE WAS ABSENT FOR AN UNUSUALLY LONG TIME.
NO, SENDO GOES TO SCHOOL PRETTY REGULARLY.
Hee!
YEAH, TO SEE SATSUKI.
SEEMS THAT HE GOT INTO A TIFF WITH SOME SENIORS FROM KAWA HIGH AT THE WEST GATE.
DAMN, HOW COULD HE?!
He was caught immediately and sent home.
Sendo and his fights!
だんっ
*Since Room 12 is furthest out in the building, it takes a long time for information to reach it. (Ha ha ha!)
THIS IS NO TIME FOR JOKES. WE'RE ON PROBATION!
Careful!
どか
ズル
LET'S GO TO SENDO'S HOUSE. COME ON.
ISN'T IT WALKING DISTANCE?
YOU TAKE ME THERE!
Since there's no phone, let's just go see him.
ズル
どか
Kurokawa, my lunch!
A local.

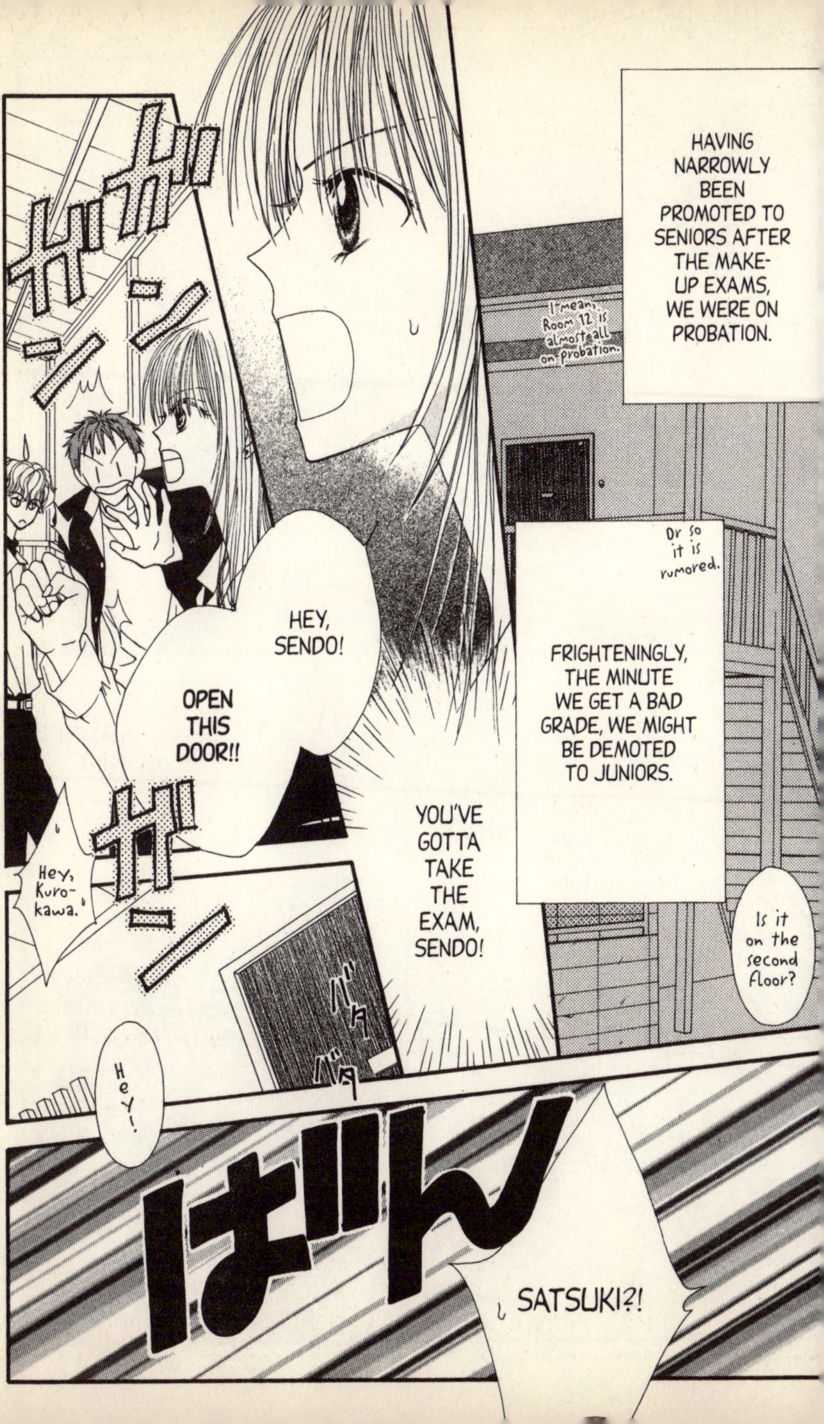
HAVING NARROWLY BEEN PROMOTED TO SENIORS AFTER THE MAKE-UP EXAMS, WE WERE ON PROBATION.
I mean, Room 12 is almost all on probation.
Or so it is rumored.
FRIGHTENINGLY, THE MINUTE WE GET A BAD GRADE, WE MIGHT BE DEMOTED TO JUNIORS.
Is it on the second floor?
YOU'VE GOTTA TAKE THE EXAM, SENDO!
HEY, SENDO!
OPEN THIS DOOR!!
Hey, Kuro-kawa.
バタ
バタ
Hey!
SATSUKI?!

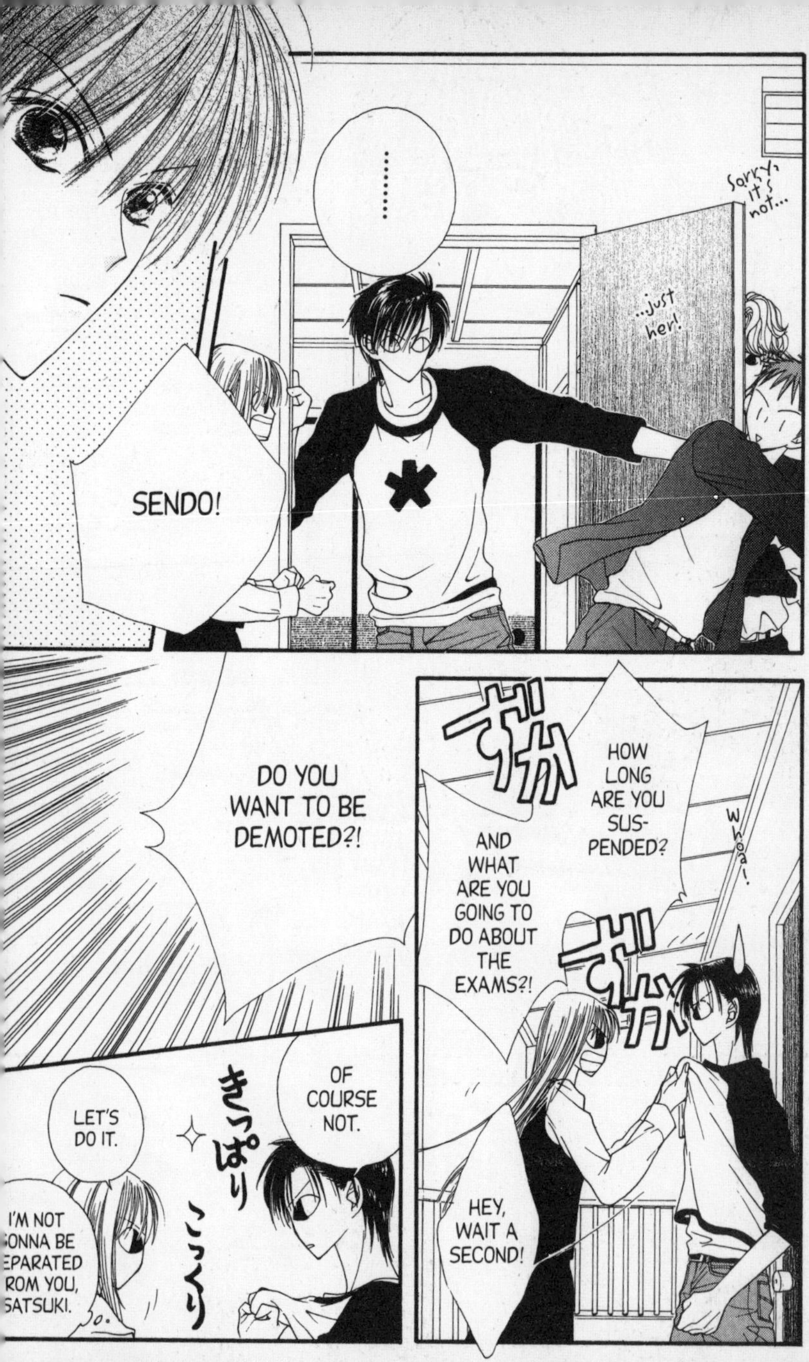
Sorry, it's not...
...just her!
......
SENDO!
ずか
HOW LONG ARE YOU SUS-PENDED?
Whoa!
AND WHAT ARE YOU GOING TO DO ABOUT THE EXAMS?!
ずか
HEY, WAIT A SECOND!
DO YOU WANT TO BE DEMOTED?!
OF COURSE NOT.
きっぱり
LET'S DO IT.
こっくり
I'M NOT ONNA BE EPARATED ROM YOU, ATSUKI.

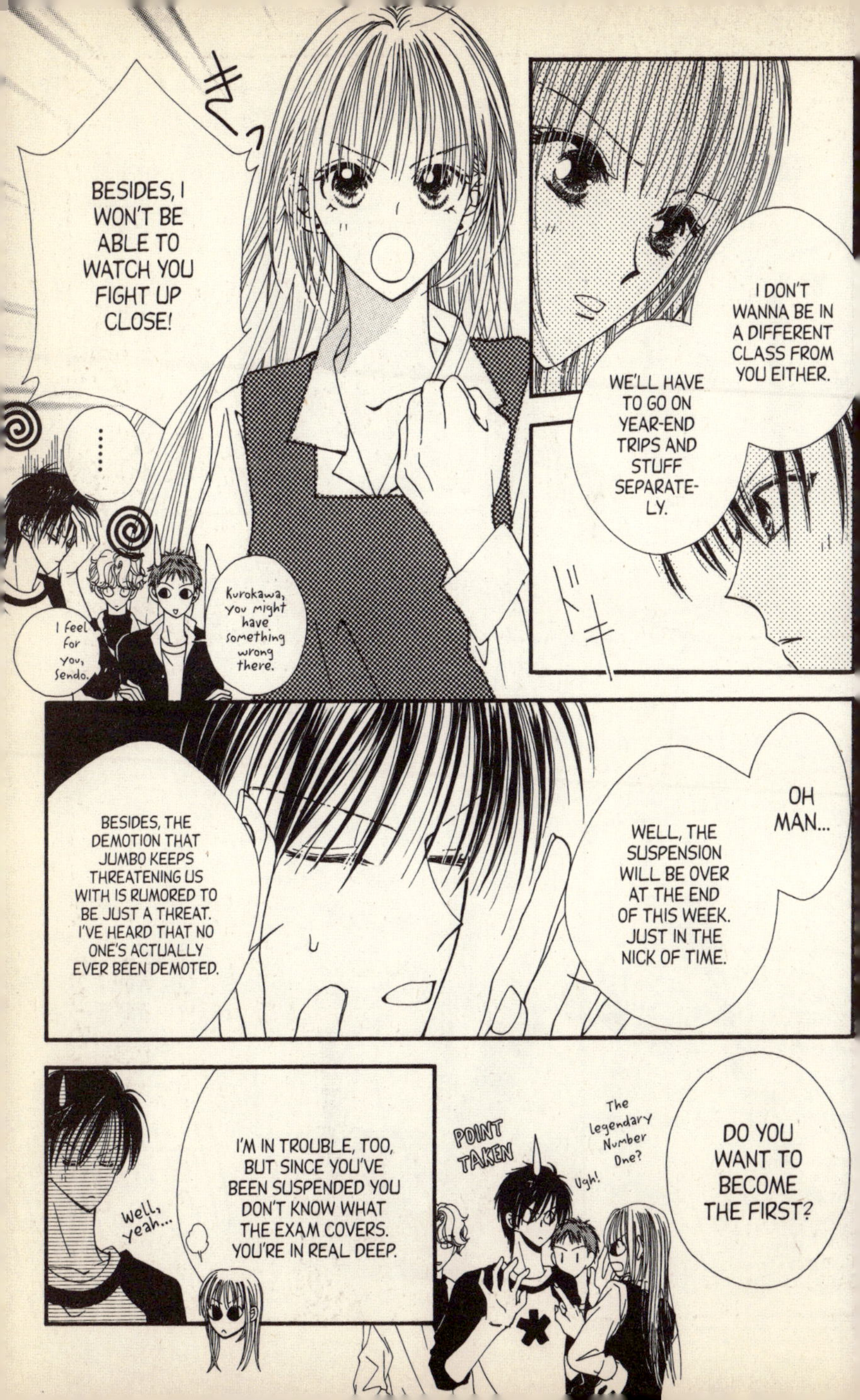
I DON'T WANNA BE IN A DIFFERENT CLASS FROM YOU EITHER.
WE'LL HAVE TO GO ON YEAR-END TRIPS AND STUFF SEPARATE-LY.
ドキ
きっ
BESIDES, I WON'T BE ABLE TO WATCH YOU FIGHT UP CLOSE!
......
Kurokawa, you might have something wrong there.
I feel for you, Sendo.
OH MAN...
WELL, THE SUSPENSION WILL BE OVER AT THE END OF THIS WEEK. JUST IN THE NICK OF TIME.
BESIDES, THE DEMOTION THAT JUMBO KEEPS THREATENING US WITH IS RUMORED TO BE JUST A THREAT. I'VE HEARD THAT NO ONE'S ACTUALLY EVER BEEN DEMOTED.
DO YOU WANT TO BECOME THE FIRST?
The legendary Number One?
Ugh!
POINT TAKEN
I'M IN TROUBLE, TOO, BUT SINCE YOU'VE BEEN SUSPENDED YOU DON'T KNOW WHAT THE EXAM COVERS. YOU'RE IN REAL DEEP.
Well, yeah...

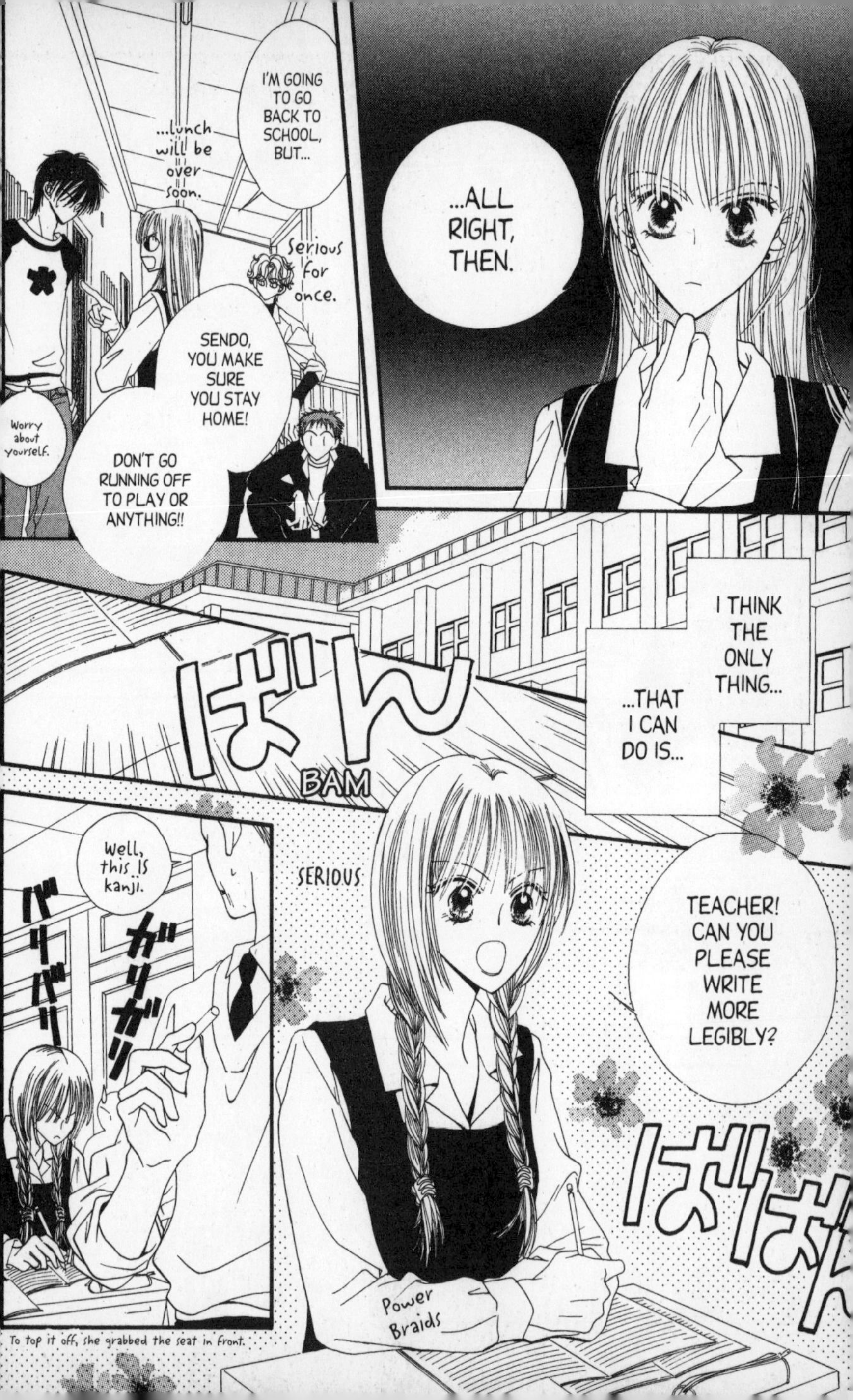
...ALL RIGHT, THEN.
I'M GOING TO GO BACK TO SCHOOL, BUT...
...lunch will be over soon.
Serious for once.
SENDO, YOU MAKE SURE YOU STAY HOME!
DON'T GO RUNNING OFF TO PLAY OR ANYTHING!!
Worry about yourself.
I THINK THE ONLY THING...
...THAT I CAN DO IS...
ばん
BAM
TEACHER! CAN YOU PLEASE WRITE MORE LEGIBLY?
ぱぱん
SERIOUS
Power Braids
Well, this IS kanji.
ガリガリ
バリバリ
To top it off, she grabbed the seat in front.

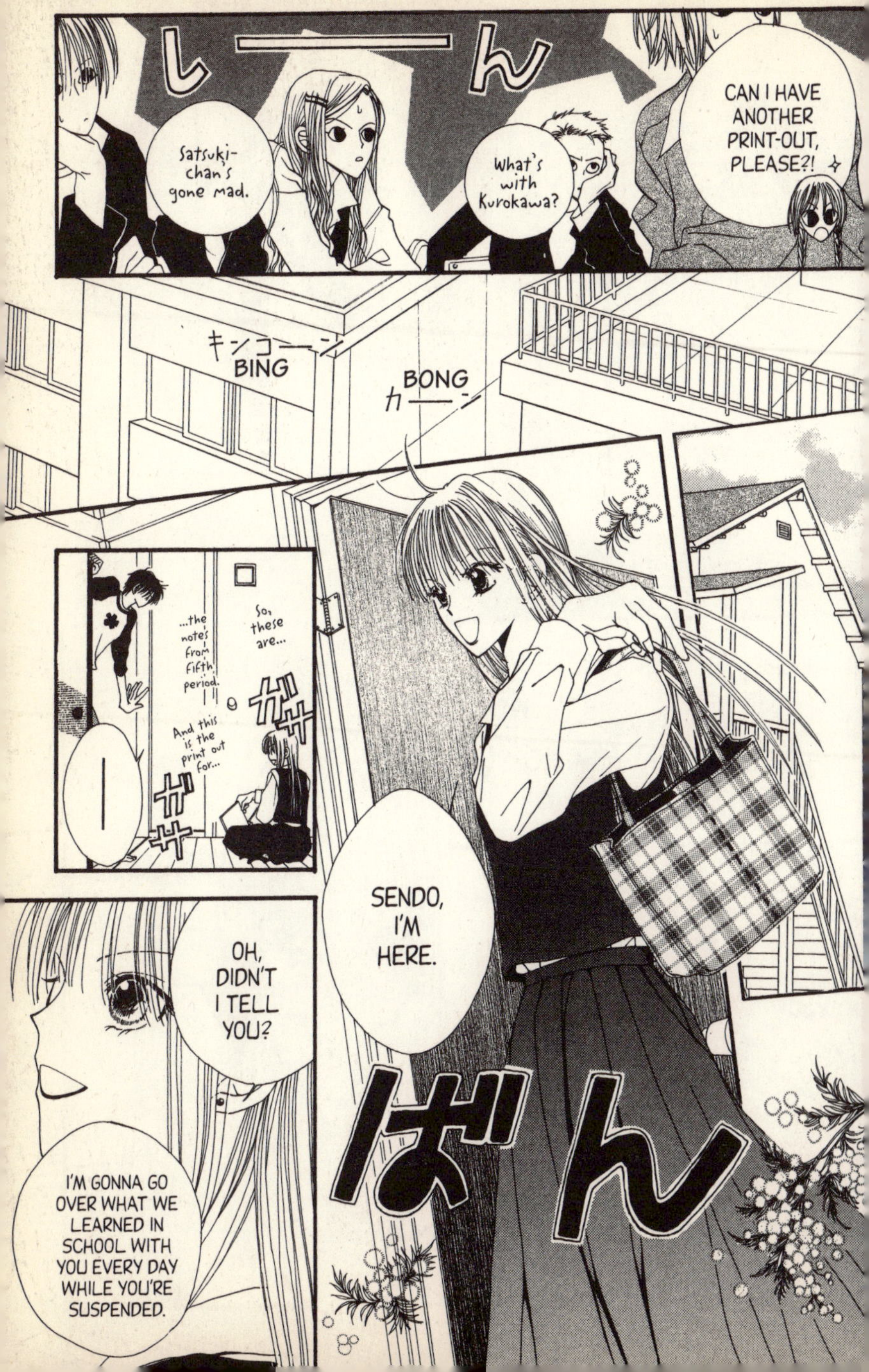
CAN I HAVE ANOTHER PRINT-OUT, PLEASE?!
しーーーん
What's with Kurokawa?
Satsuki-chan's gone mad.
キンコーン
BING
カーン
BONG
SENDO, I'M HERE.
ばん
So, these are...
...the note's from fifth period.
ガサガサ
And this is the print out for...
ガサ
OH, DIDN'T I TELL YOU?
I'M GONNA GO OVER WHAT WE LEARNED IN SCHOOL WITH YOU EVERY DAY WHILE YOU'RE SUSPENDED.

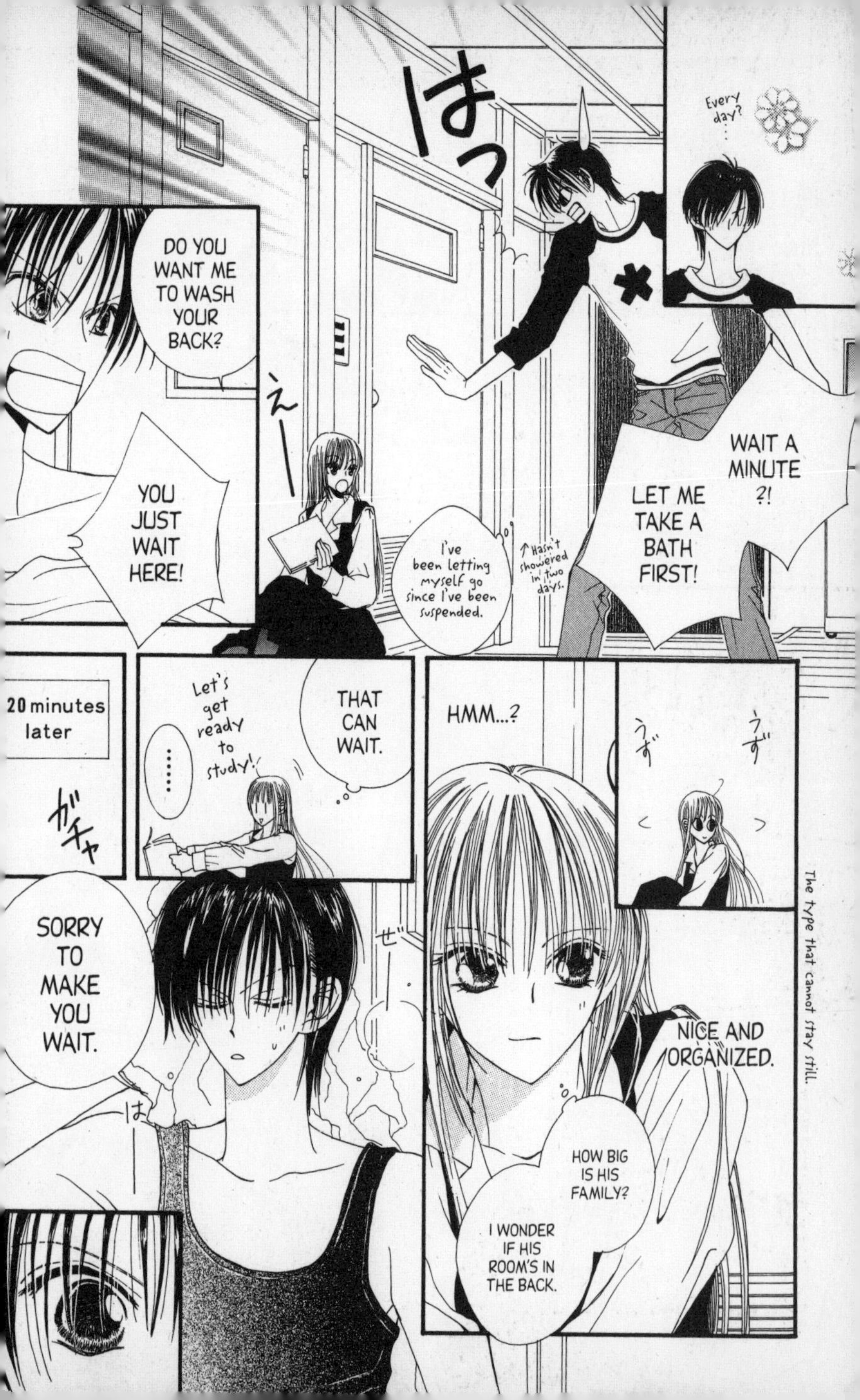
Every day? ...
はっ
WAIT A MINUTE ?!
LET ME TAKE A BATH FIRST!
↑Hasn't showered in two days.
I've been letting myself go since I've been suspended.
えー
DO YOU WANT ME TO WASH YOUR BACK?
YOU JUST WAIT HERE!
うず
うず
HMM...?
THAT CAN WAIT.
Let's get ready to study!
......
20 minutes later
ガチャ
The type that cannot stay still.
NICE AND ORGANIZED.
HOW BIG IS HIS FAMILY?
I WONDER IF HIS ROOM'S IN THE BACK.
ぜー
SORRY TO MAKE YOU WAIT.
はー

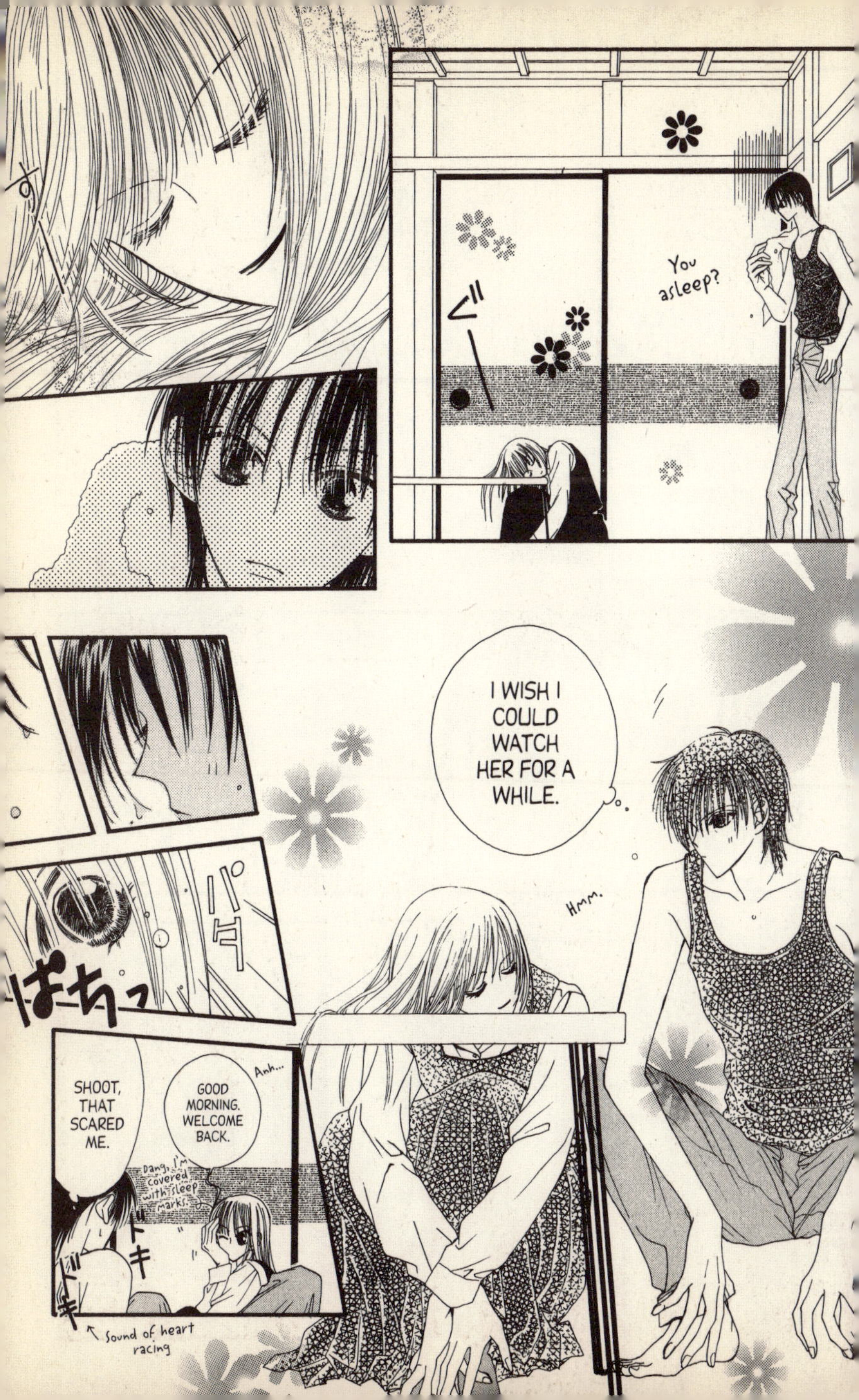
You asleep?
すー
I WISH I COULD WATCH HER FOR A WHILE.
Hmm.
パタ
ぱちっ
Anh...
GOOD MORNING. WELCOME BACK.
Dang, I'm covered with sleep marks.
SHOOT, THAT SCARED ME.
ドキ
ドキ
Sound of heart racing

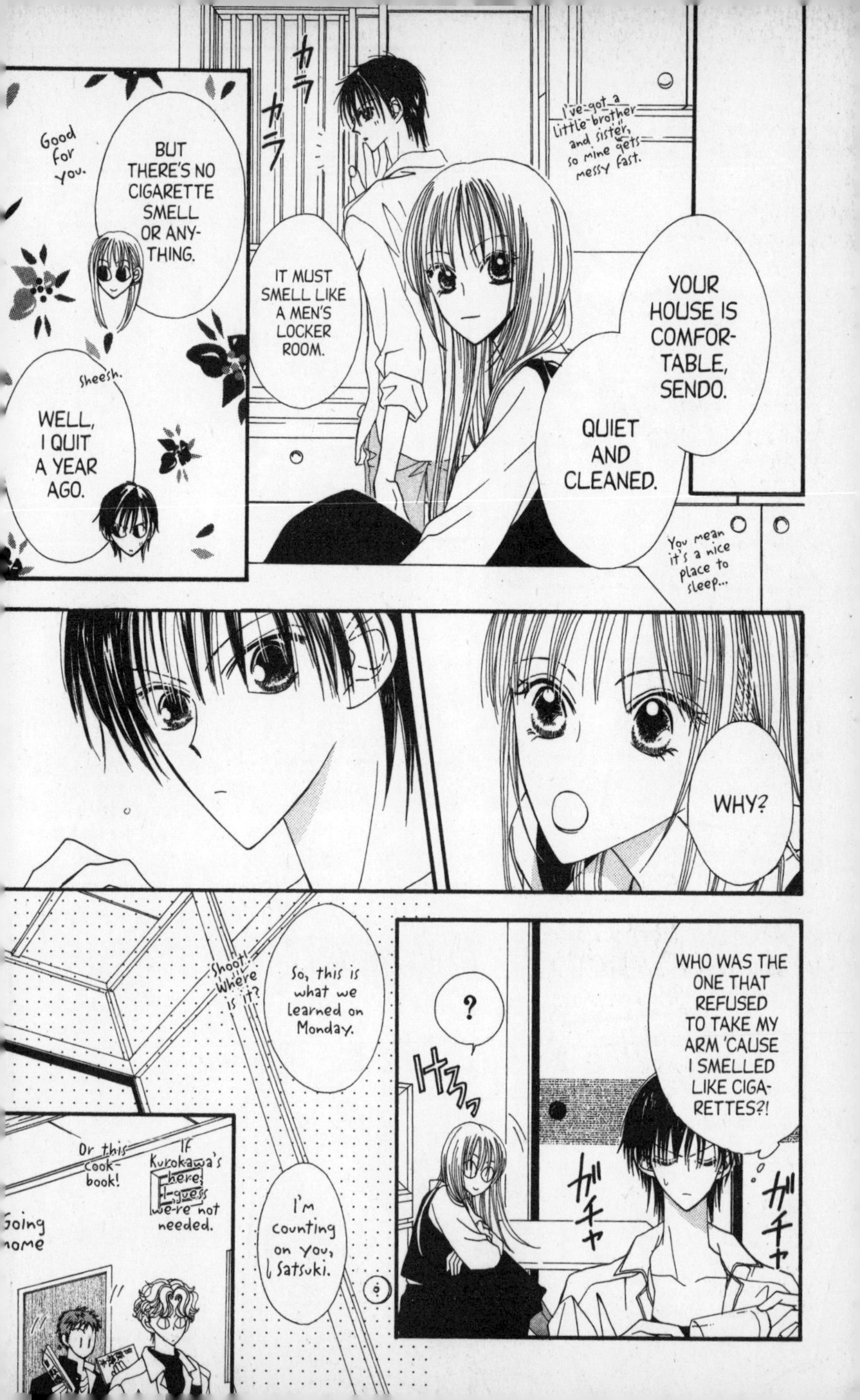
カラ
カラ
I've got a little brother and sister, so mine gets messy fast.
YOUR HOUSE IS COMFORTABLE, SENDO.
QUIET AND CLEANED.
You mean it's a nice place to sleep...
IT MUST SMELL LIKE A MEN'S LOCKER ROOM.
BUT THERE'S NO CIGARETTE SMELL OR ANYTHING.
Good for you.
WELL, I QUIT A YEAR AGO.
Sheesh.
WHY?
WHO WAS THE ONE THAT REFUSED TO TAKE MY ARM 'CAUSE I SMELLED LIKE CIGARETTES?!
ガチャ
ガチャ
?
けろっ
So, this is what we learned on Monday.
Shoot! Where is it?
I'm counting on you, Satsuki.
If Kurokawa's here, I guess we're not needed.
Or this cookbook!
Going home

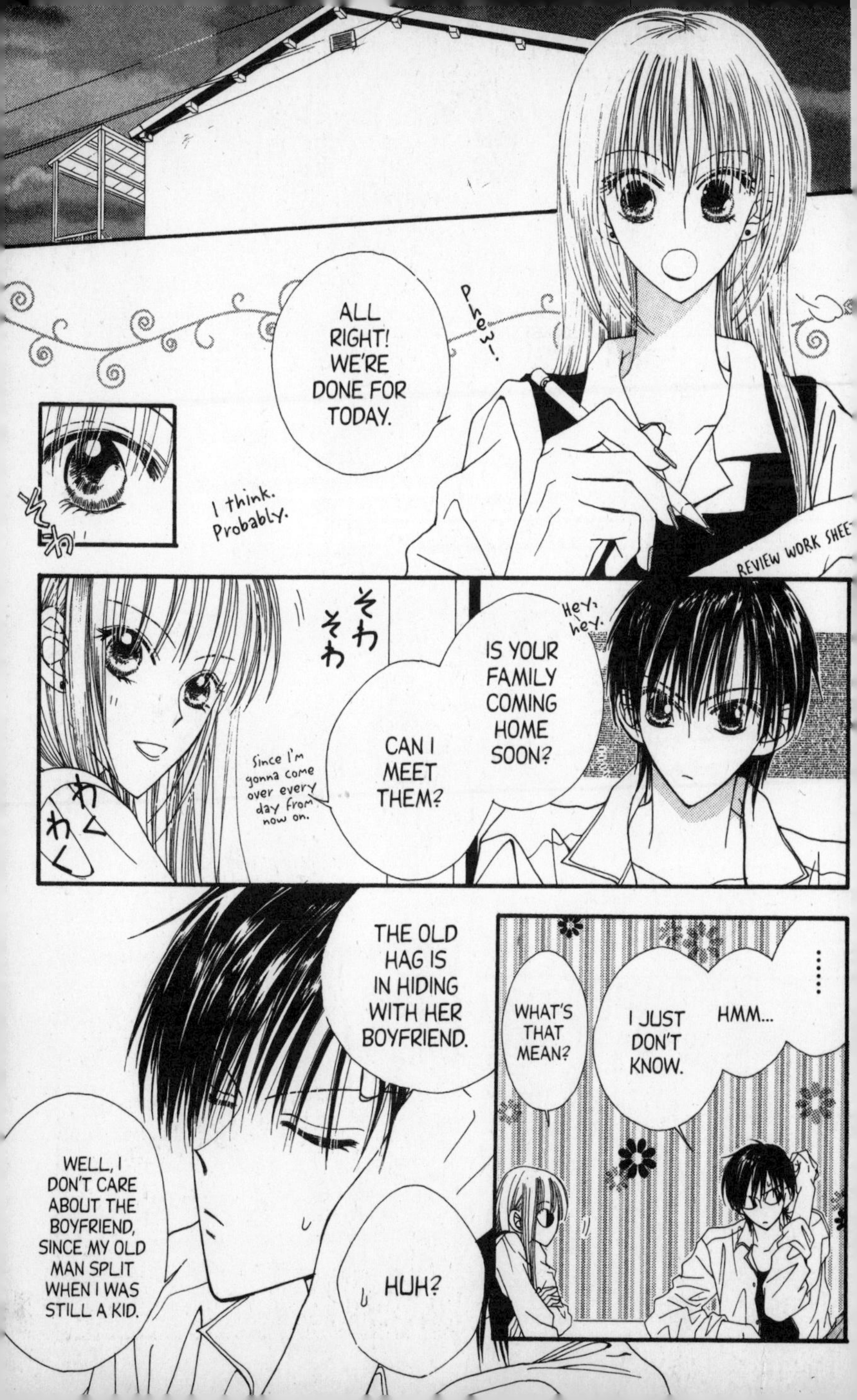

Phew!
ALL RIGHT! WE'RE DONE FOR TODAY.
REVIEW WORK SHEE-
I think. Probably.
Hey, hey.
IS YOUR FAMILY COMING HOME SOON?
CAN I MEET THEM?
Since I'm gonna come over every day from now on.
そわそわ
わくわく
THE OLD HAG IS IN HIDING WITH HER BOYFRIEND.
HMM...
......
I JUST DON'T KNOW.
WHAT'S THAT MEAN?
WELL, I DON'T CARE ABOUT THE BOYFRIEND, SINCE MY OLD MAN SPLIT WHEN I WAS STILL A KID.
HUH?

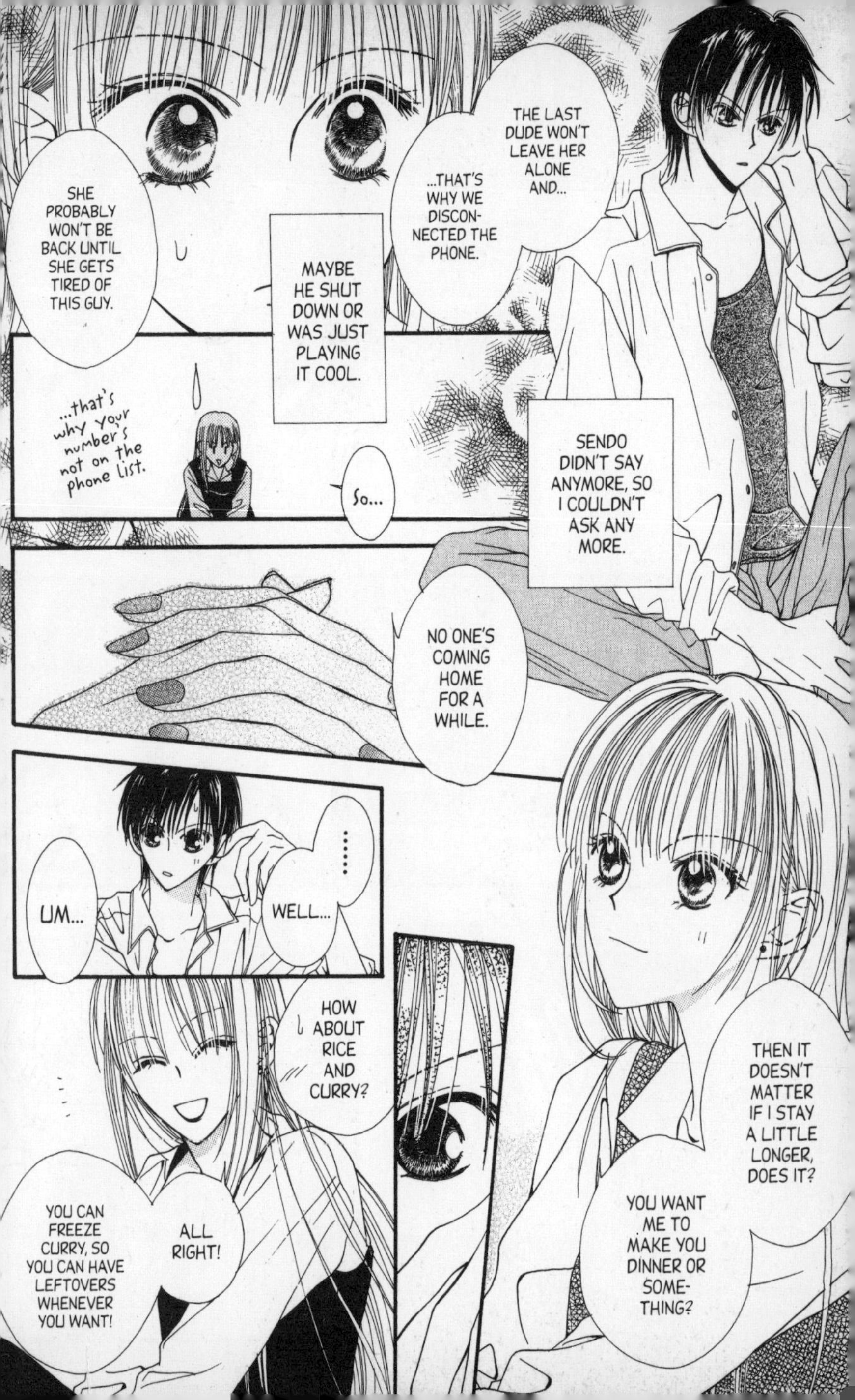

THE LAST DUDE WON'T LEAVE HER ALONE AND...
...THAT'S WHY WE DISCONNECTED THE PHONE.
SHE PROBABLY WON'T BE BACK UNTIL SHE GETS TIRED OF THIS GUY.
MAYBE HE SHUT DOWN OR WAS JUST PLAYING IT COOL.
So...
...that's why your number's not on the phone list.
SENDO DIDN'T SAY ANYMORE, SO I COULDN'T ASK ANY MORE.
NO ONE'S COMING HOME FOR A WHILE.
......
WELL...
UM...
THEN IT DOESN'T MATTER IF I STAY A LITTLE LONGER, DOES IT?
YOU WANT ME TO MAKE YOU DINNER OR SOMETHING?
HOW ABOUT RICE AND CURRY?
ALL RIGHT!
YOU CAN FREEZE CURRY, SO YOU CAN HAVE LEFTOVERS WHENEVER YOU WANT!

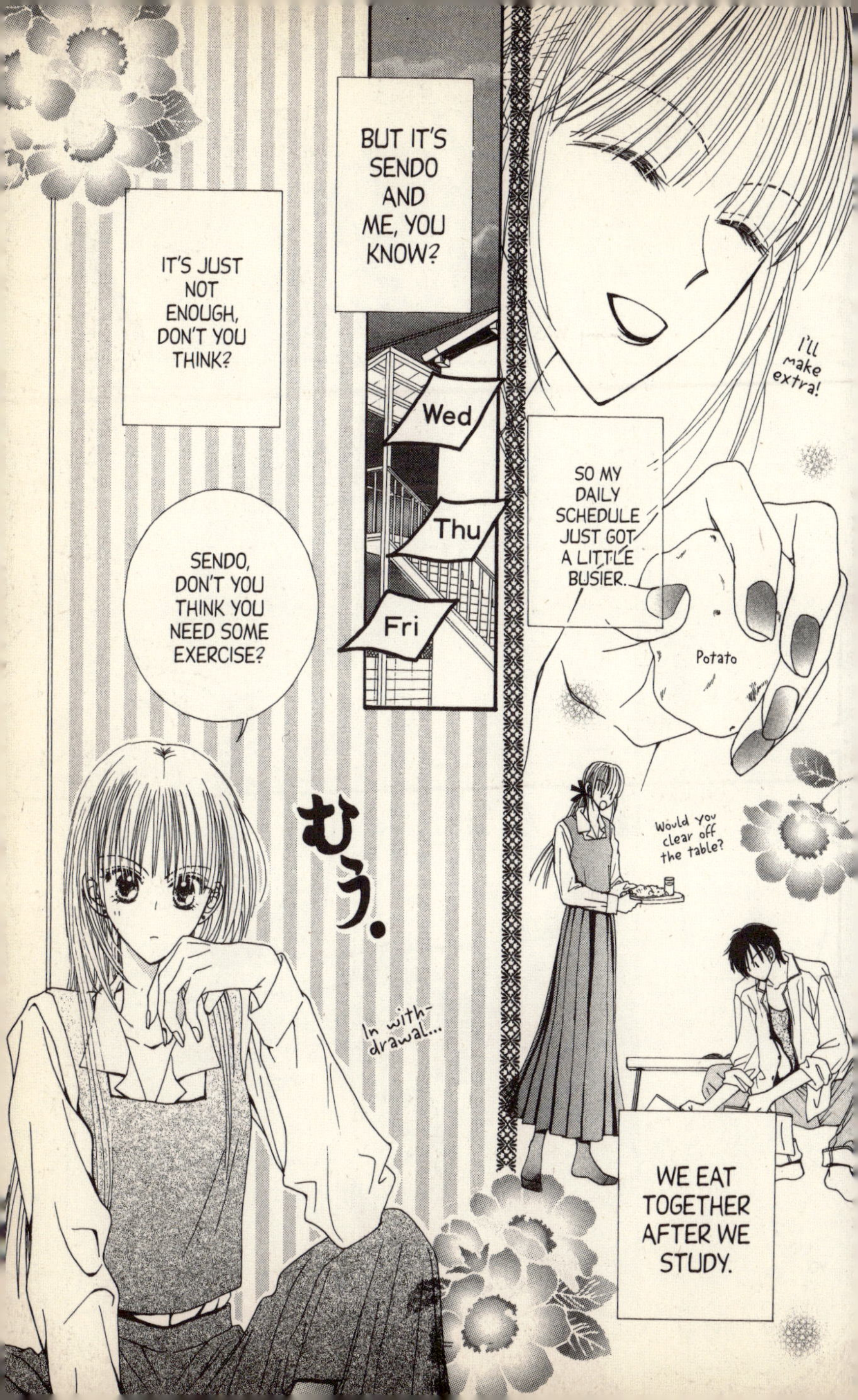
I'll make extra!
SO MY DAILY SCHEDULE JUST GOT A LITTLE BUSIER.
Potato
Would you clear off the table?
WE EAT TOGETHER AFTER WE STUDY.
BUT IT'S SENDO AND ME, YOU KNOW?
Wed
Thu
Fri
IT'S JUST NOT ENOUGH, DON'T YOU THINK?
SENDO, DON'T YOU THINK YOU NEED SOME EXERCISE?
むう.
In with-drawal...

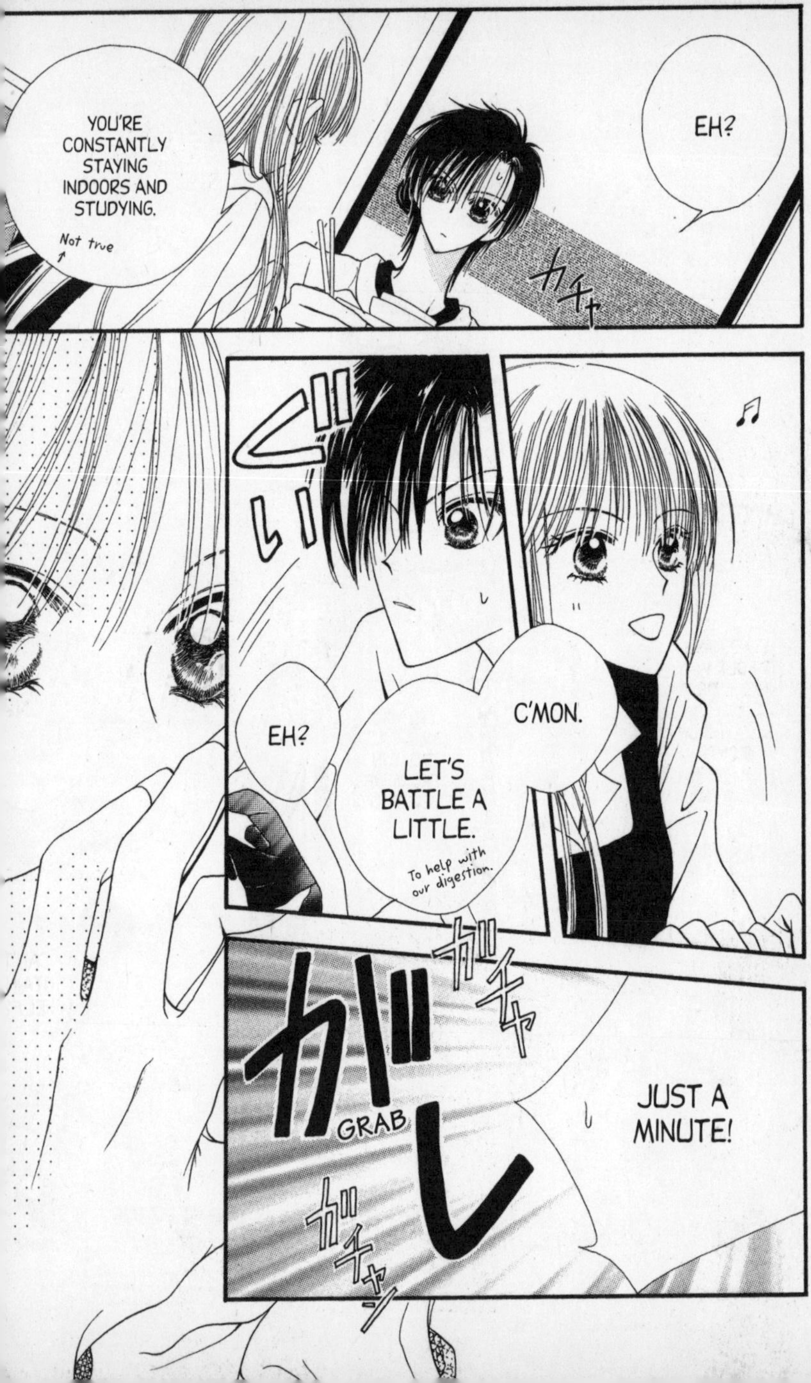
EH?
カチャ
YOU'RE CONSTANTLY STAYING INDOORS AND STUDYING.
Not true ↑
ぐい
C'MON.
LET'S BATTLE A LITTLE.
To help with our digestion.
EH?
JUST A MINUTE!
ガチャ
がし
GRAB
ガチャン

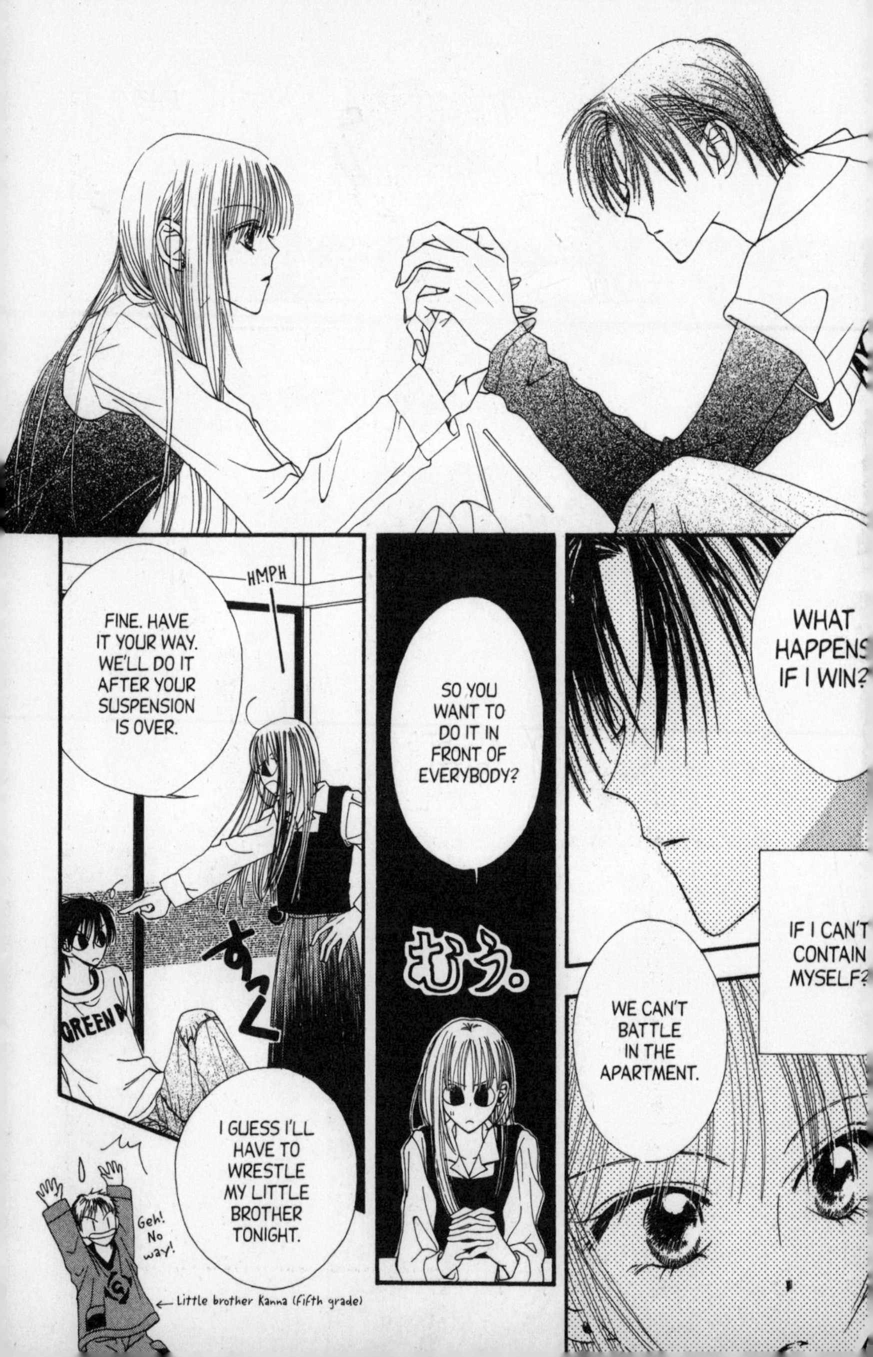

WHAT HAPPENS IF I WIN?
IF I CAN'T CONTAIN MYSELF?
WE CAN'T BATTLE IN THE APARTMENT.
SO YOU WANT TO DO IT IN FRONT OF EVERYBODY?
むう。
HMPH
FINE. HAVE IT YOUR WAY. WE'LL DO IT AFTER YOUR SUSPENSION IS OVER.
すっく
I GUESS I'LL HAVE TO WRESTLE MY LITTLE BROTHER TONIGHT.
Geh! No way!
← Little brother Kanna (fifth grade)

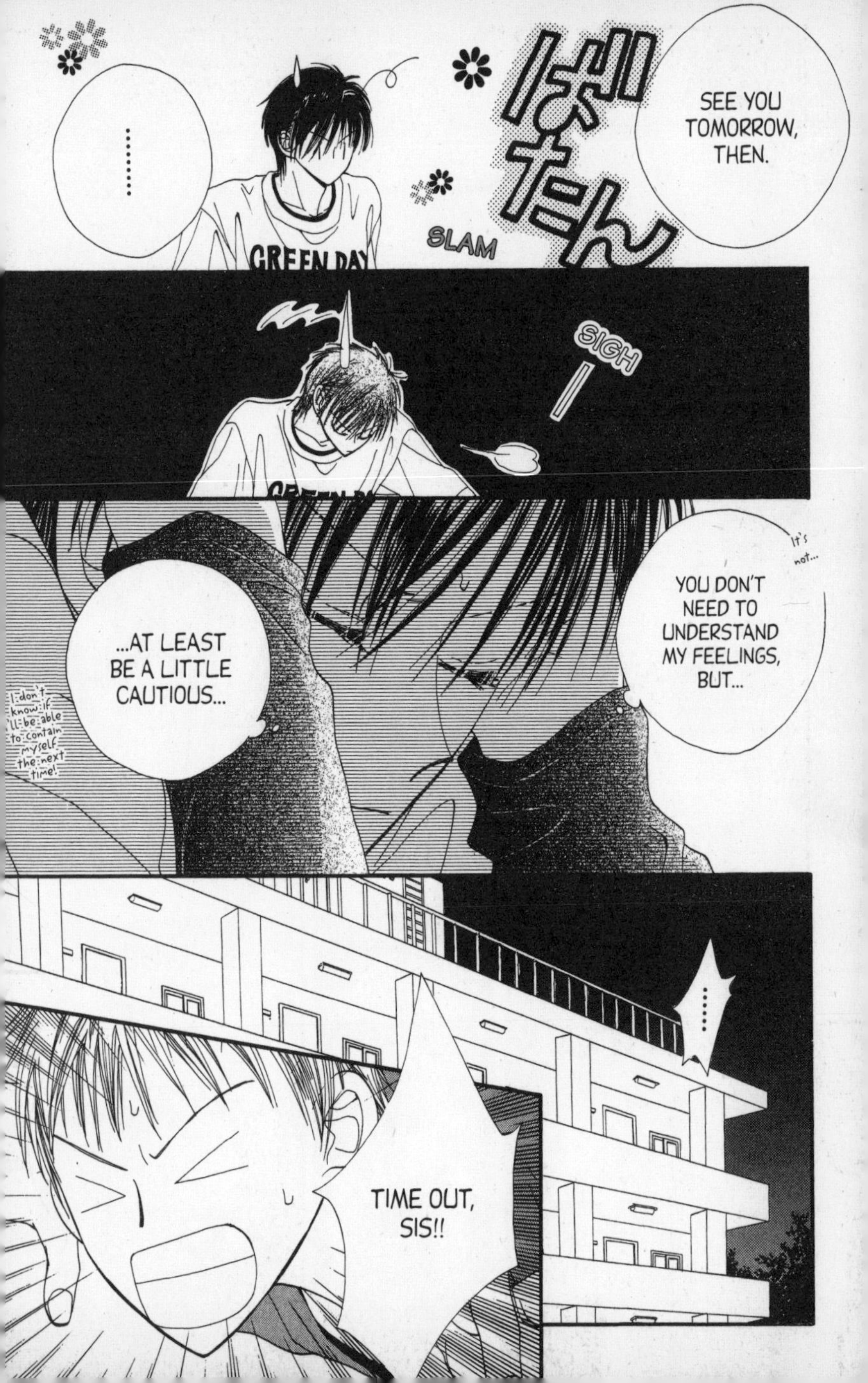
SEE YOU TOMORROW, THEN.
ばたん
SLAM
......
SIGH
It's not...
YOU DON'T NEED TO UNDERSTAND MY FEELINGS, BUT...
...AT LEAST BE A LITTLE CAUTIOUS...
I don't know if I'll be able to contain myself the next time!
......
TIME OUT, SIS!!

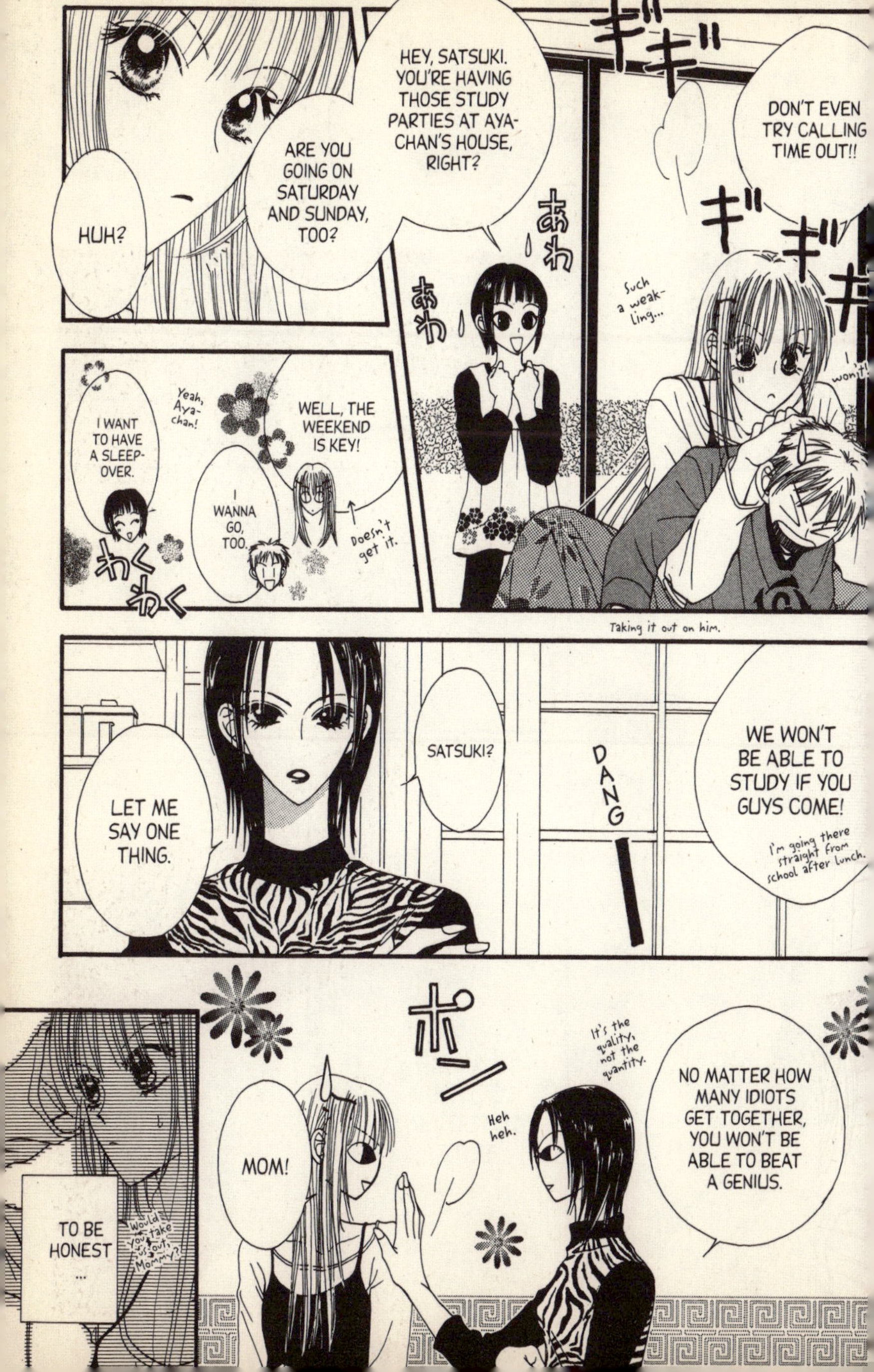
ギギ
DON'T EVEN TRY CALLING TIME OUT!!
ギギギ
I won't!
Such a weak-ling...
Taking it out on him.
HEY, SATSUKI. YOU'RE HAVING THOSE STUDY PARTIES AT AYA-CHAN'S HOUSE, RIGHT?
あわあわ
ARE YOU GOING ON SATURDAY AND SUNDAY, TOO?
HUH?
WELL, THE WEEKEND IS KEY!
Doesn't get it.
Yeah, Aya-chan!
I WANT TO HAVE A SLEEP-OVER.
I WANNA GO, TOO.
わくわく
WE WON'T BE ABLE TO STUDY IF YOU GUYS COME!
I'm going there straight from school after lunch.
DANG
SATSUKI?
LET ME SAY ONE THING.
NO MATTER HOW MANY IDIOTS GET TOGETHER, YOU WON'T BE ABLE TO BEAT A GENIUS.
It's the quality, not the quantity.
Heh heh.
ポー
MOM!
Would you take us out, Mommy?
TO BE HONEST ...

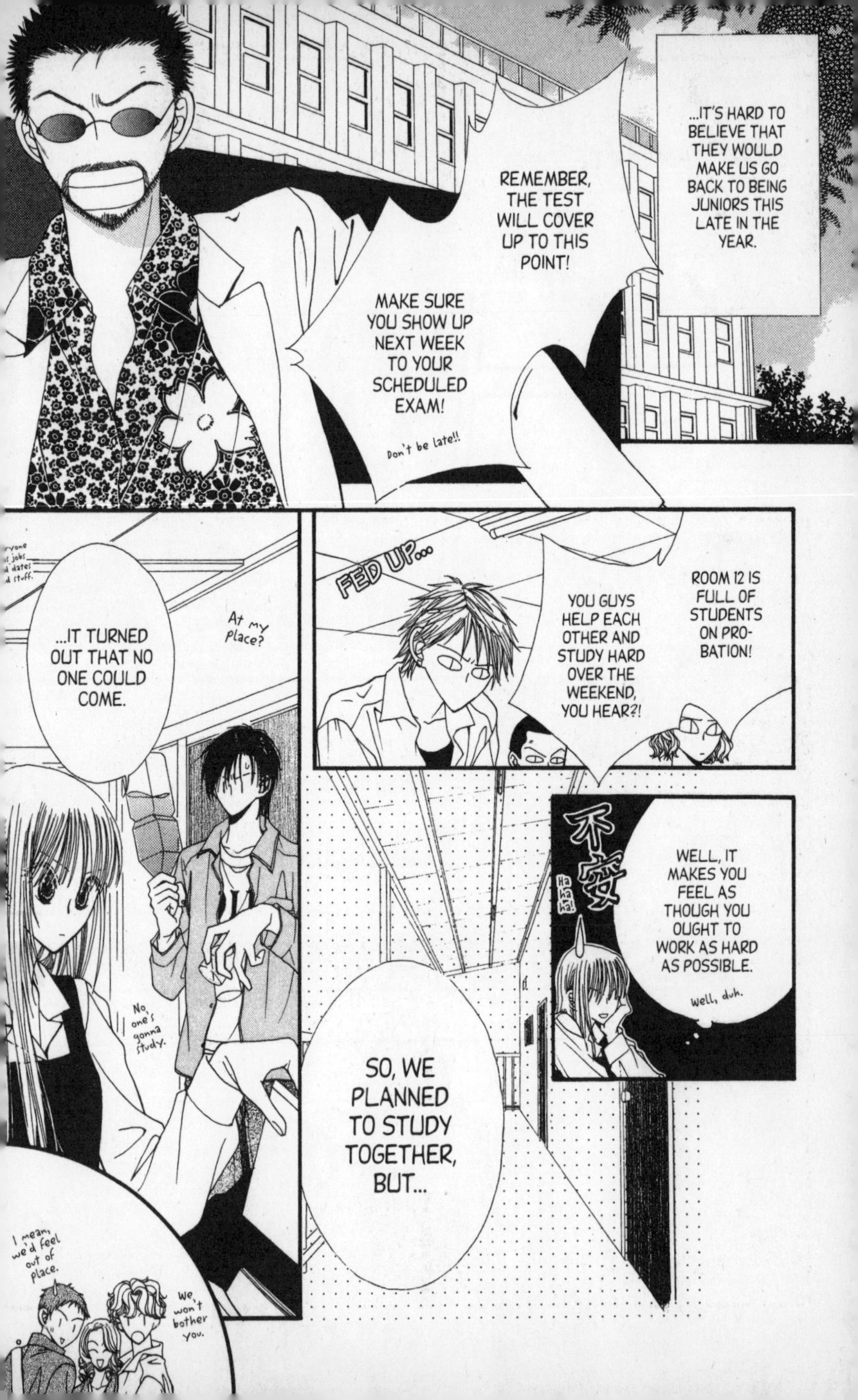

...IT'S HARD TO BELIEVE THAT THEY WOULD MAKE US GO BACK TO BEING JUNIORS THIS LATE IN THE YEAR.
REMEMBER, THE TEST WILL COVER UP TO THIS POINT!
MAKE SURE YOU SHOW UP NEXT WEEK TO YOUR SCHEDULED EXAM!
Don't be late!!
ROOM 12 IS FULL OF STUDENTS ON PRO-BATION!
YOU GUYS HELP EACH OTHER AND STUDY HARD OVER THE WEEKEND, YOU HEAR?!
FED UP...
不安
Ha ha ha!
WELL, IT MAKES YOU FEEL AS THOUGH YOU OUGHT TO WORK AS HARD AS POSSIBLE.
Well, duh.
SO, WE PLANNED TO STUDY TOGETHER, BUT...
...IT TURNED OUT THAT NO ONE COULD COME.
At my place?
No one's gonna study.
We, won't bother you.
I mean, we'd feel out of place.

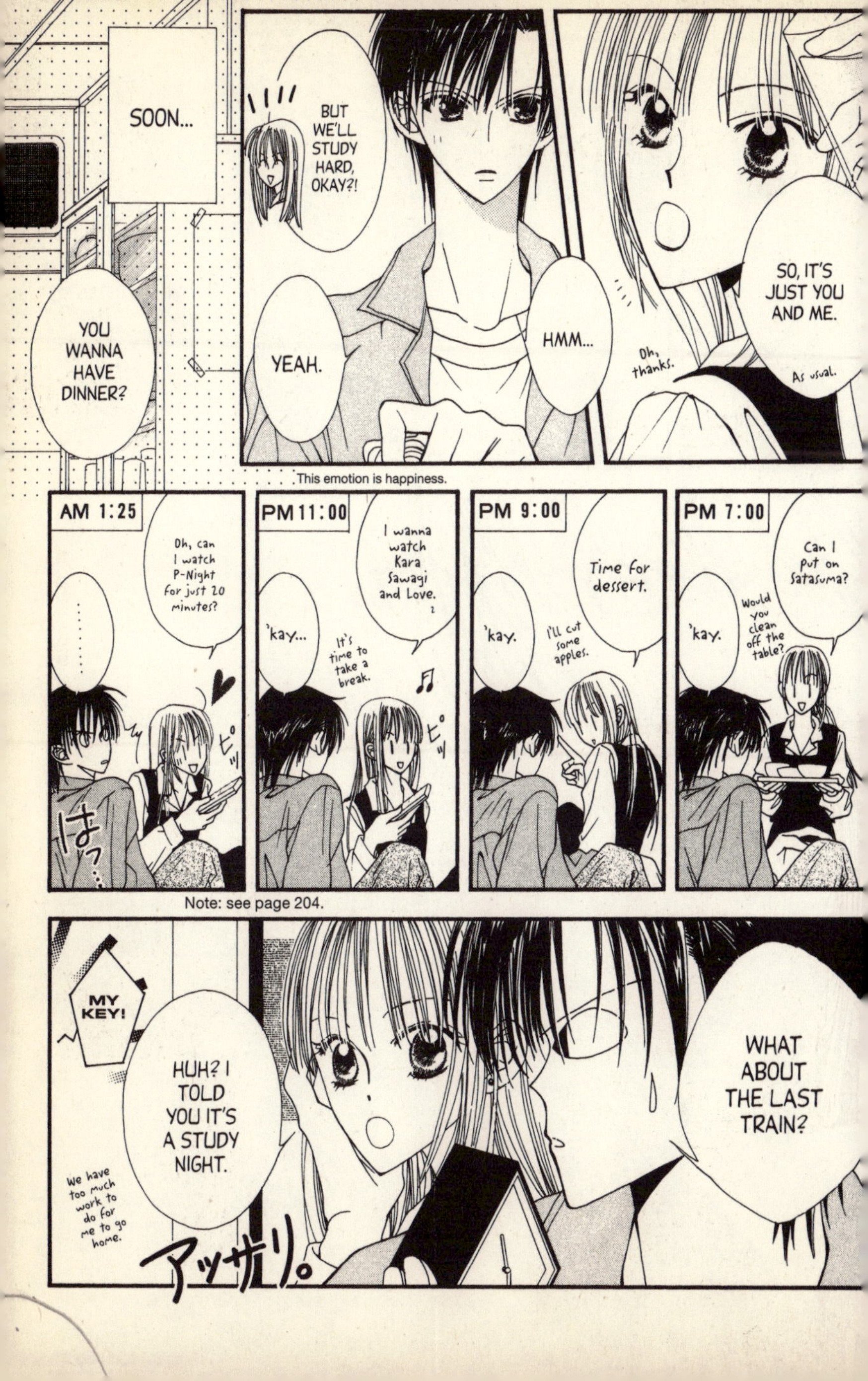
SO, IT'S JUST YOU AND ME.
As usual.
Oh, thanks.
HMM...
BUT WE'LL STUDY HARD, OKAY?!
YEAH.
SOON...
YOU WANNA HAVE DINNER?
This emotion is happiness.
PM 7:00
Can I put on Satasuma?
Would you clean off the table?
'kay.
PM 9:00
Time for dessert.
I'll cut some apples.
'kay.
PM 11:00
I wanna watch Kara Sawagi and Love.[2]
It's time to take a break.
'kay...
ピッ
AM 1:25
Oh, can I watch P-Night for just 20 minutes?
......
ピッ
はっ…
WHAT ABOUT THE LAST TRAIN?
HUH? I TOLD YOU IT'S A STUDY NIGHT.
We have too much work to do for me to go home.
MY KEY!
アッサリ。
Note: see page 204.

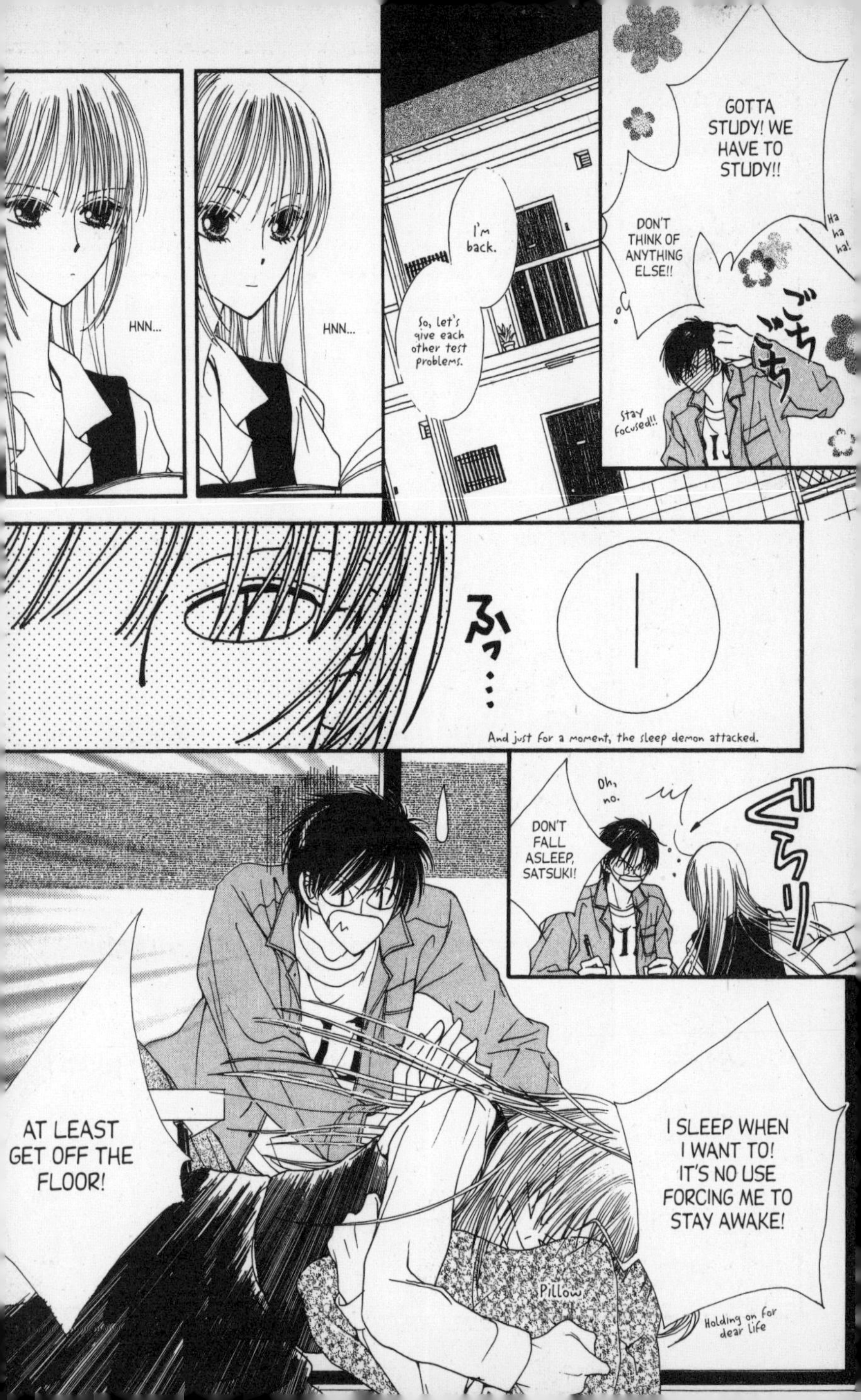
GOTTA STUDY! WE HAVE TO STUDY!!
Ha ha ha!
DON'T THINK OF ANYTHING ELSE!!
ごちごち
Stay focused!!
I'm back.
So, let's give each other test problems.
HNN...
HNN...
And just for a moment, the sleep demon attacked.
ふっ…
Oh, no.
DON'T FALL ASLEEP, SATSUKI!
I SLEEP WHEN I WANT TO! IT'S NO USE FORCING ME TO STAY AWAKE!
Pillow
Holding on for dear life
AT LEAST GET OFF THE FLOOR!

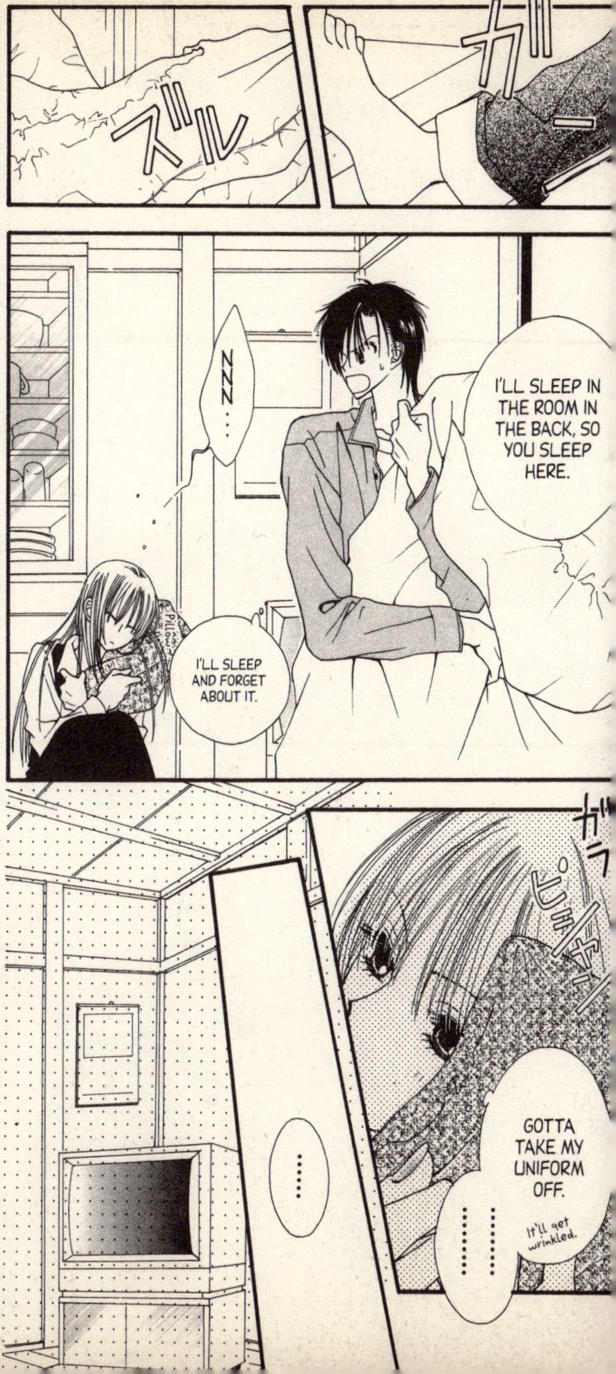
ガー
ズル
I'LL SLEEP IN THE ROOM IN THE BACK, SO YOU SLEEP HERE.
NNN...
Pillow
I'LL SLEEP AND FORGET ABOUT IT.
ガラ
GOTTA TAKE MY UNIFORM OFF.
It'll get wrinkled.
......
......

WARDROBE

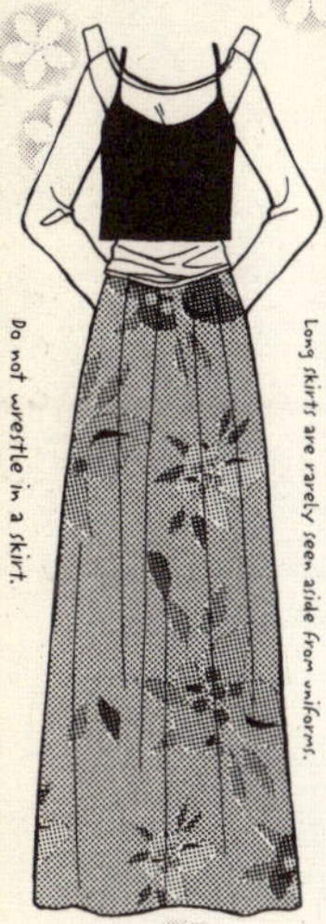
Long skirts are rarely seen aside from uniforms.
Do not wrestle in a skirt.

I played tag wearing a tight skirt, and ripped the side of the skirt all the way open. That was in grade school. I don't remember changing my clothes. I wonder what I wore the rest of the day?

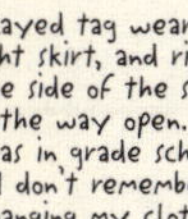

I started off with images of small flowers. How did I end up with this? But I think maybe this is okay now. I'm far from sexy normally...but leopard print in light pink could be very cute. (I wouldn't wear it, but...)

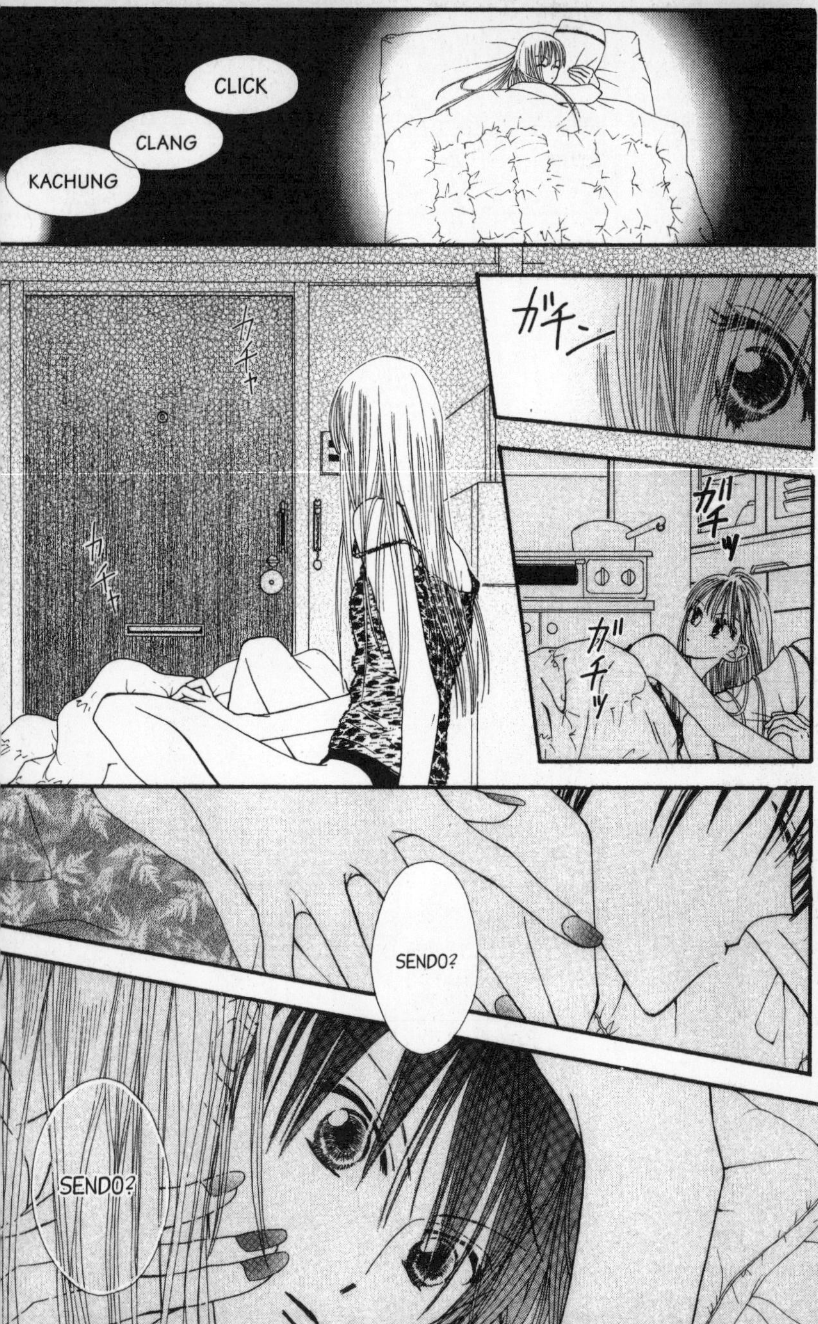
CLICK
CLANG
KACHUNG
ガチン
ガチッ
ガチッ
カチャ
カチャ
SENDO?
SENDO?

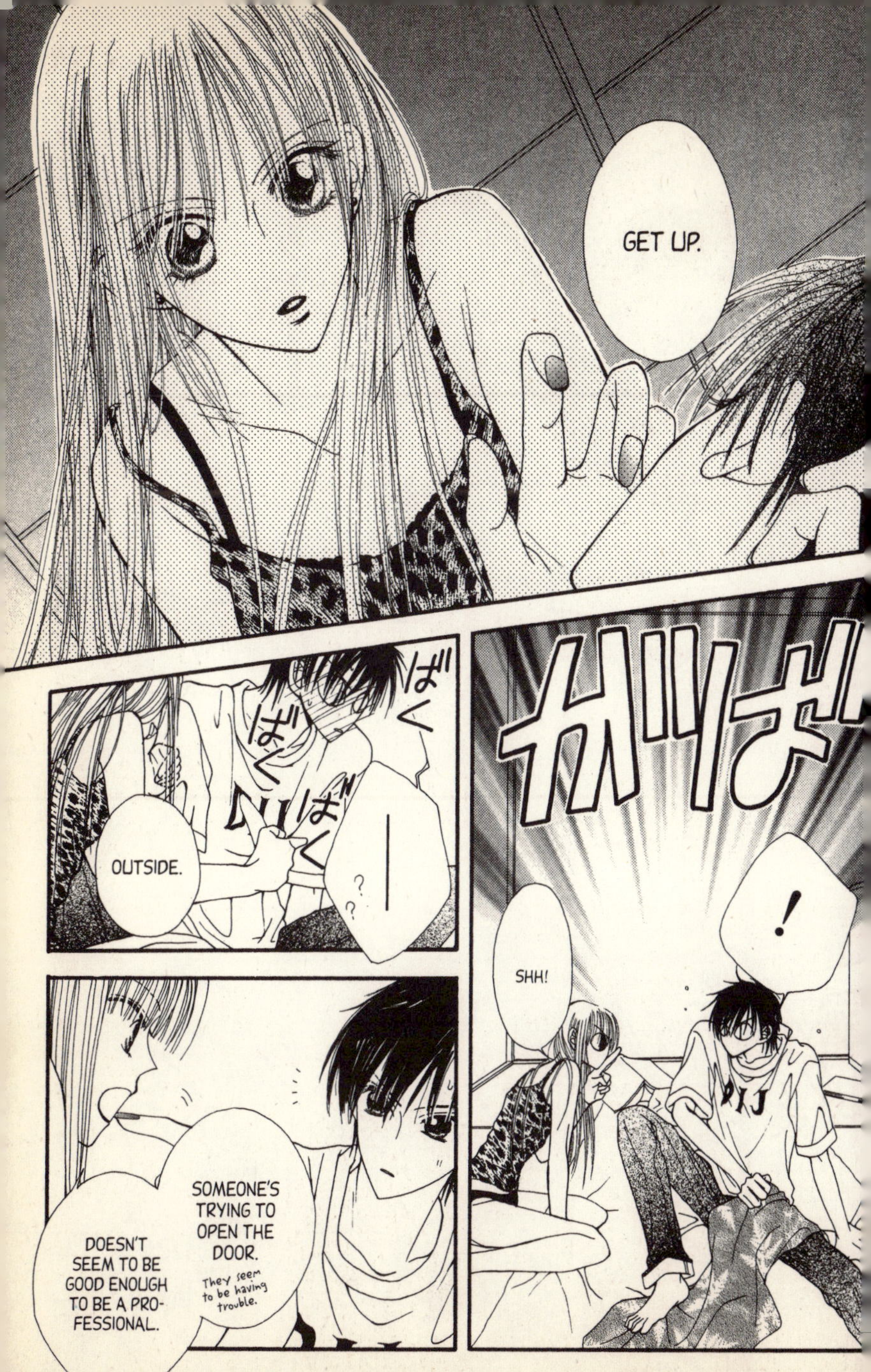
GET UP.
!
SHH!
ばく
ばく
ばく
—
? ?
OUTSIDE.
SOMEONE'S TRYING TO OPEN THE DOOR.
They seem to be having trouble.
DOESN'T SEEM TO BE GOOD ENOUGH TO BE A PRO-FESSIONAL.

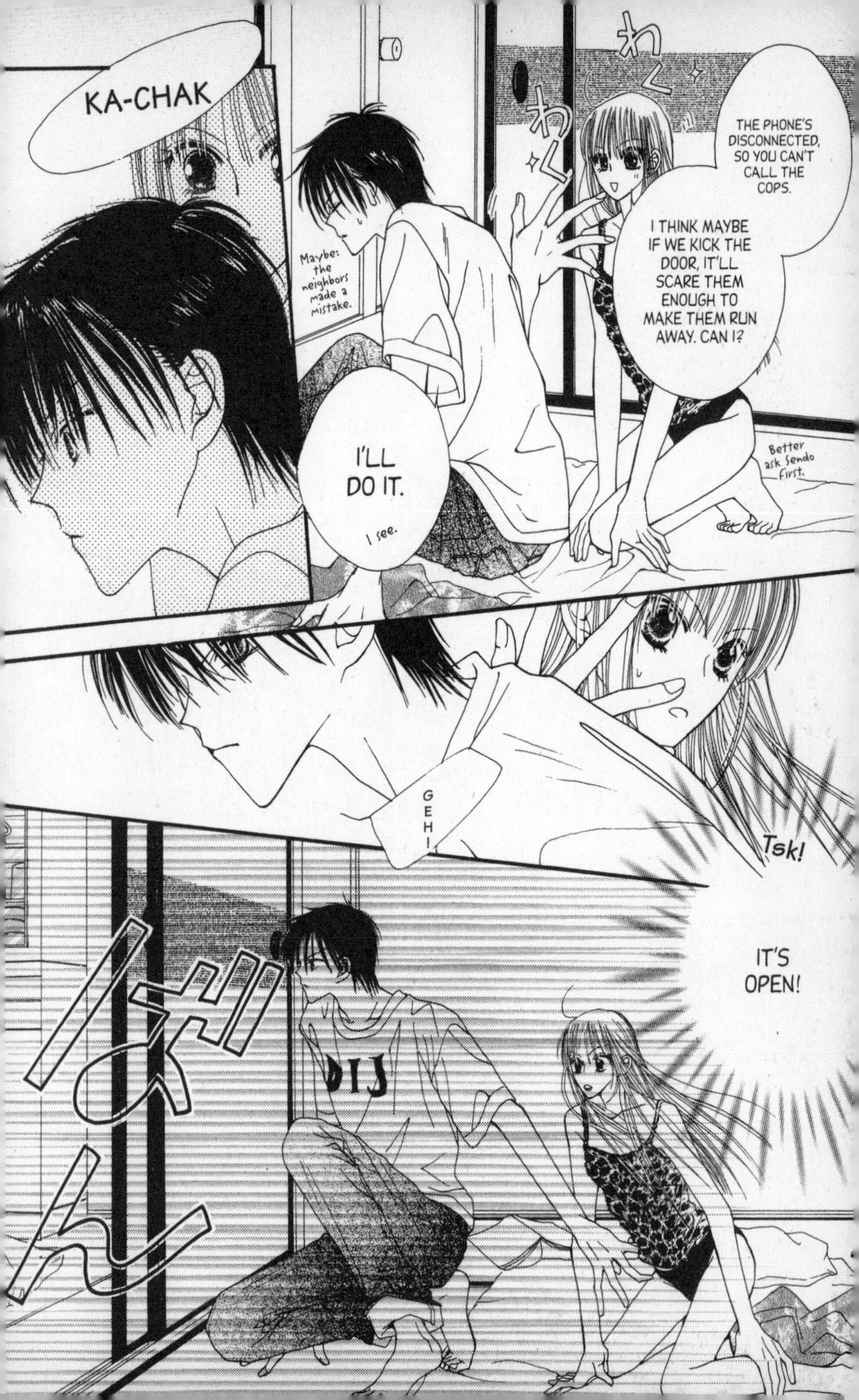
わくわく
THE PHONE'S DISCONNECTED, SO YOU CAN'T CALL THE COPS.
I THINK MAYBE IF WE KICK THE DOOR, IT'LL SCARE THEM ENOUGH TO MAKE THEM RUN AWAY. CAN I?
Better ask Sendo first.
Maybe: the neighbors made a mistake.
KA-CHAK
I'LL DO IT.
I see.
GEHI!
Tsk!
IT'S OPEN!

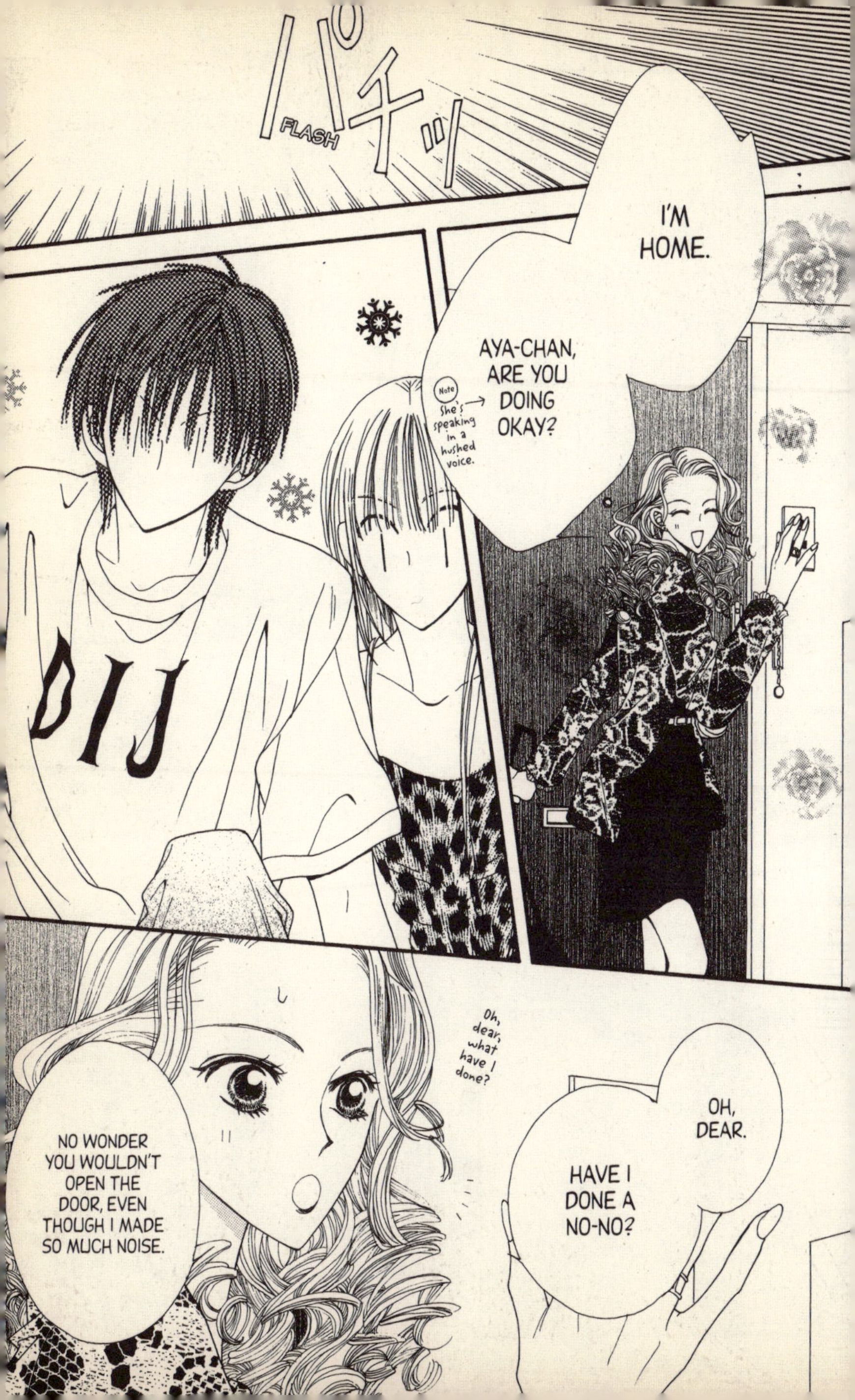
FLASH
I'M HOME.
AYA-CHAN, ARE YOU DOING OKAY?
Note She's speaking in a hushed voice.
OH, DEAR.
HAVE I DONE A NO-NO?
Oh, dear, what have I done?
NO WONDER YOU WOULDN'T OPEN THE DOOR, EVEN THOUGH I MADE SO MUCH NOISE.

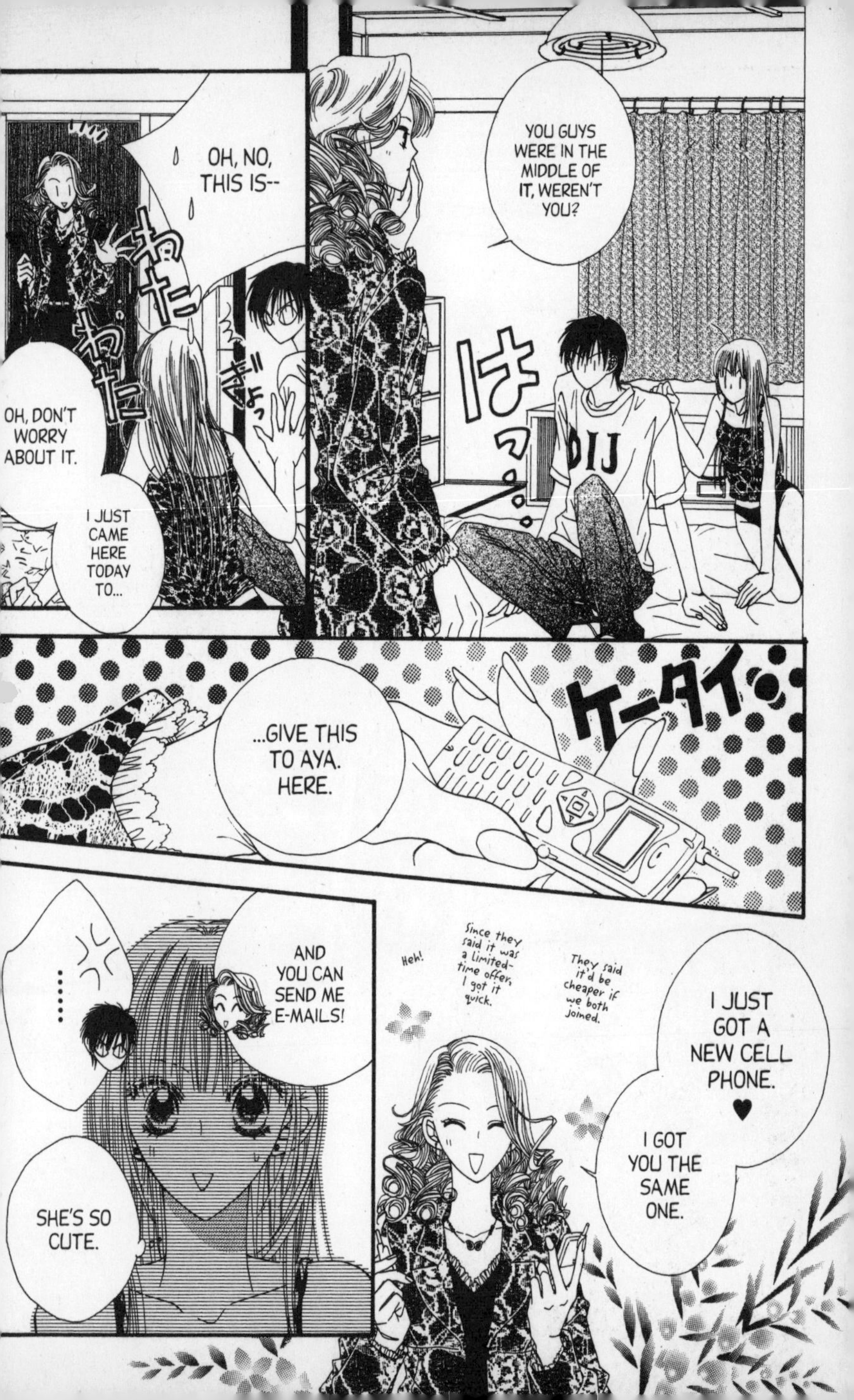
YOU GUYS WERE IN THE MIDDLE OF IT, WEREN'T YOU?
はっ
OH, NO, THIS IS--
わたわた
ぎょっ
OH, DON'T WORRY ABOUT IT.
I JUST CAME HERE TODAY TO...
ケータイ
...GIVE THIS TO AYA. HERE.
I JUST GOT A NEW CELL PHONE. ♥
I GOT YOU THE SAME ONE.
They said it'd be cheaper if we both joined.
Since they said it was a limited-time offer, I got it quick.
Heh!
AND YOU CAN SEND ME E-MAILS!
......
SHE'S SO CUTE.

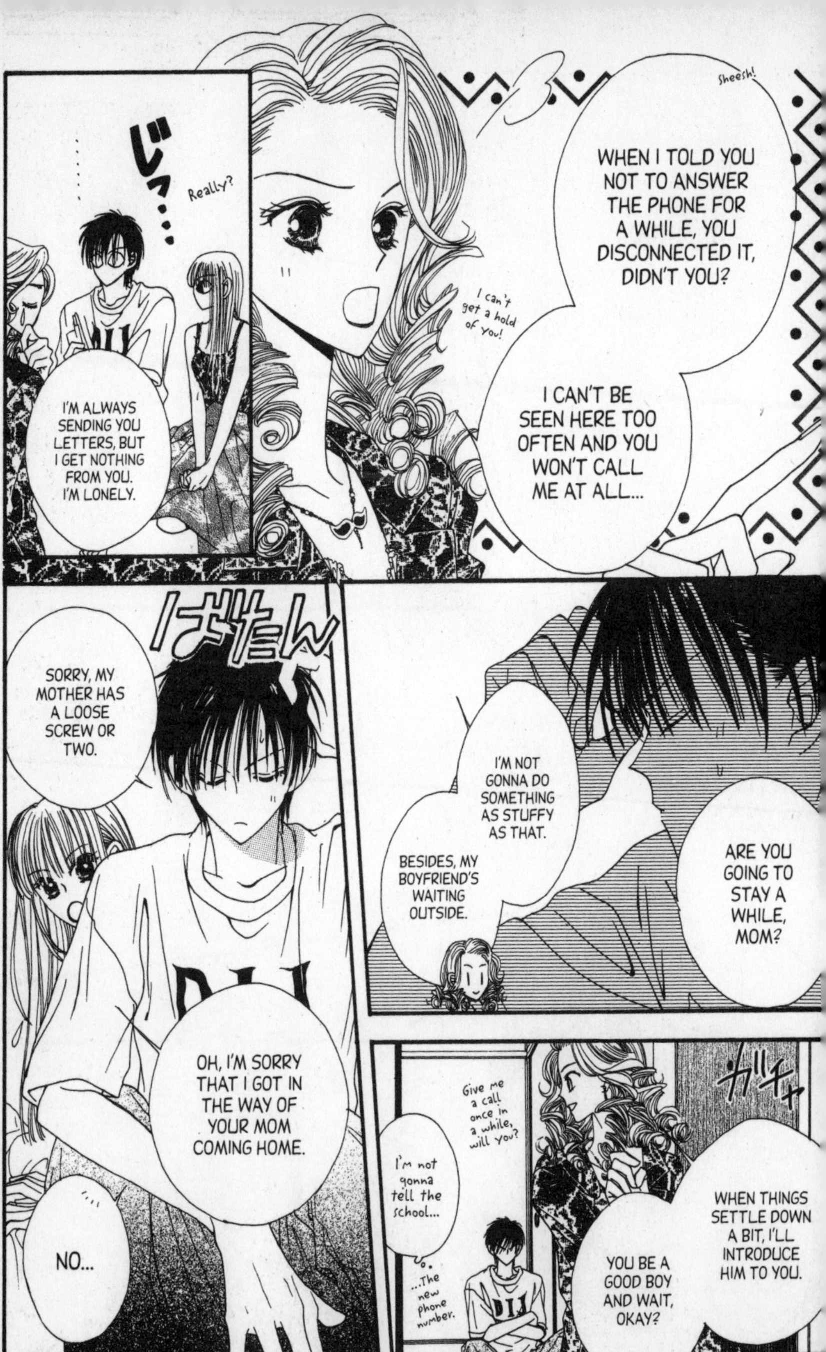

Sheesh!
WHEN I TOLD YOU NOT TO ANSWER THE PHONE FOR A WHILE, YOU DISCONNECTED IT, DIDN'T YOU?
I can't get a hold of you!
I CAN'T BE SEEN HERE TOO OFTEN AND YOU WON'T CALL ME AT ALL...
Really?
......
I'M ALWAYS SENDING YOU LETTERS, BUT I GET NOTHING FROM YOU. I'M LONELY.
ARE YOU GOING TO STAY A WHILE, MOM?
I'M NOT GONNA DO SOMETHING AS STUFFY AS THAT.
BESIDES, MY BOYFRIEND'S WAITING OUTSIDE.
ガチャ
WHEN THINGS SETTLE DOWN A BIT, I'LL INTRODUCE HIM TO YOU.
YOU BE A GOOD BOY AND WAIT, OKAY?
Give me a call once in a while, will you?
I'm not gonna tell the school...
...The new phone number.
ぱたん
SORRY, MY MOTHER HAS A LOOSE SCREW OR TWO.
OH, I'M SORRY THAT I GOT IN THE WAY OF YOUR MOM COMING HOME.
NO...

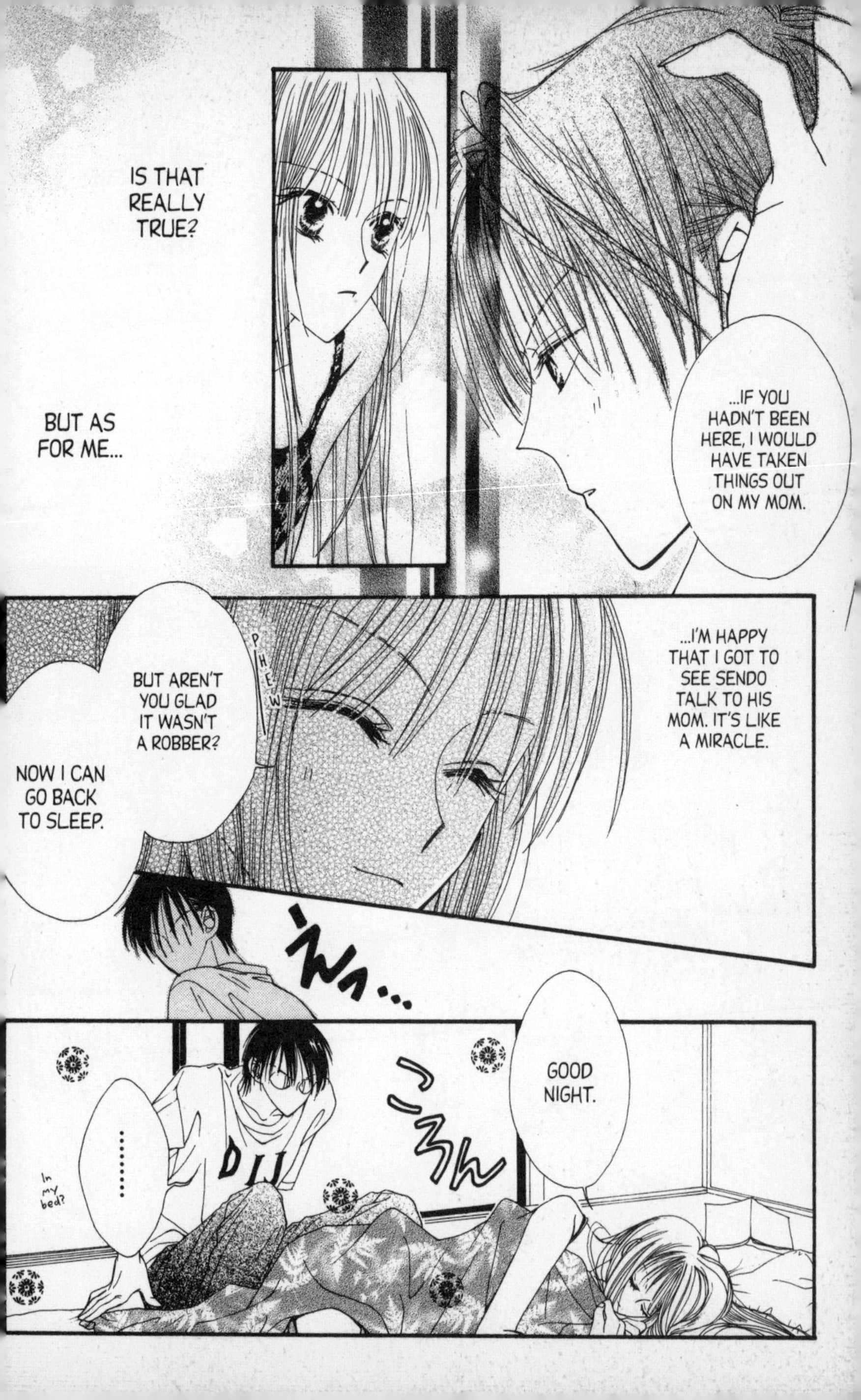

...IF YOU HADN'T BEEN HERE, I WOULD HAVE TAKEN THINGS OUT ON MY MOM.
IS THAT REALLY TRUE?
BUT AS FOR ME...
...I'M HAPPY THAT I GOT TO SEE SENDO TALK TO HIS MOM. IT'S LIKE A MIRACLE.
PHEW
BUT AREN'T YOU GLAD IT WASN'T A ROBBER?
NOW I CAN GO BACK TO SLEEP.
GOOD NIGHT.
ころん
......
In my bed?

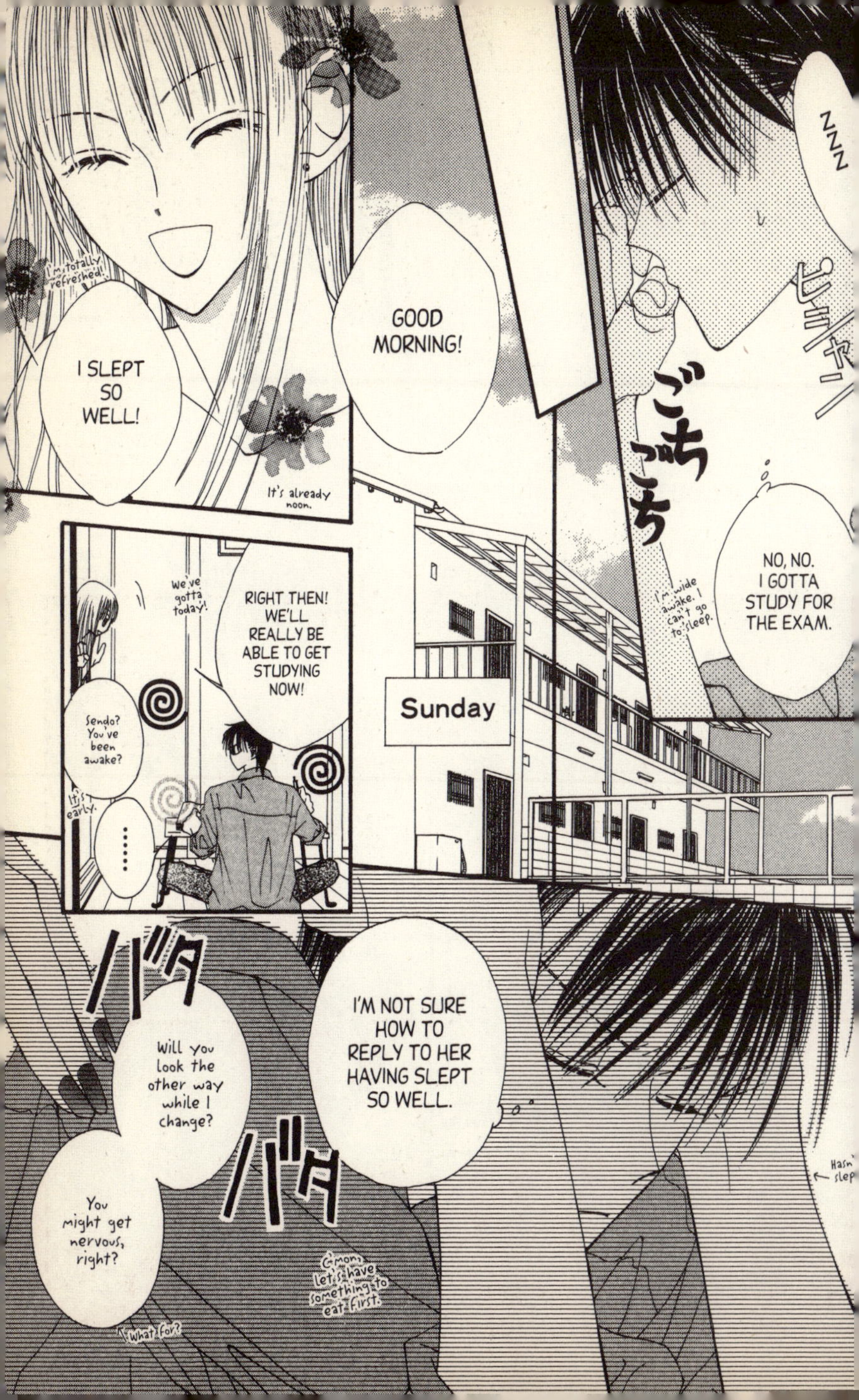
ZZZ
ごち ごち
NO, NO. I GOTTA STUDY FOR THE EXAM.
I'm wide awake. I can't go to sleep.
Sunday
GOOD MORNING!
I SLEPT SO WELL!
I'm totally refreshed!
It's already noon.
RIGHT THEN! WE'LL REALLY BE ABLE TO GET STUDYING NOW!
We've gotta today!
Sendo? You've been awake?
It's early.
......
I'M NOT SURE HOW TO REPLY TO HER HAVING SLEPT SO WELL.
バタ
Will you look the other way while I change?
バタ
You might get nervous, right?
What for?
C'mon, let's have something to eat first.

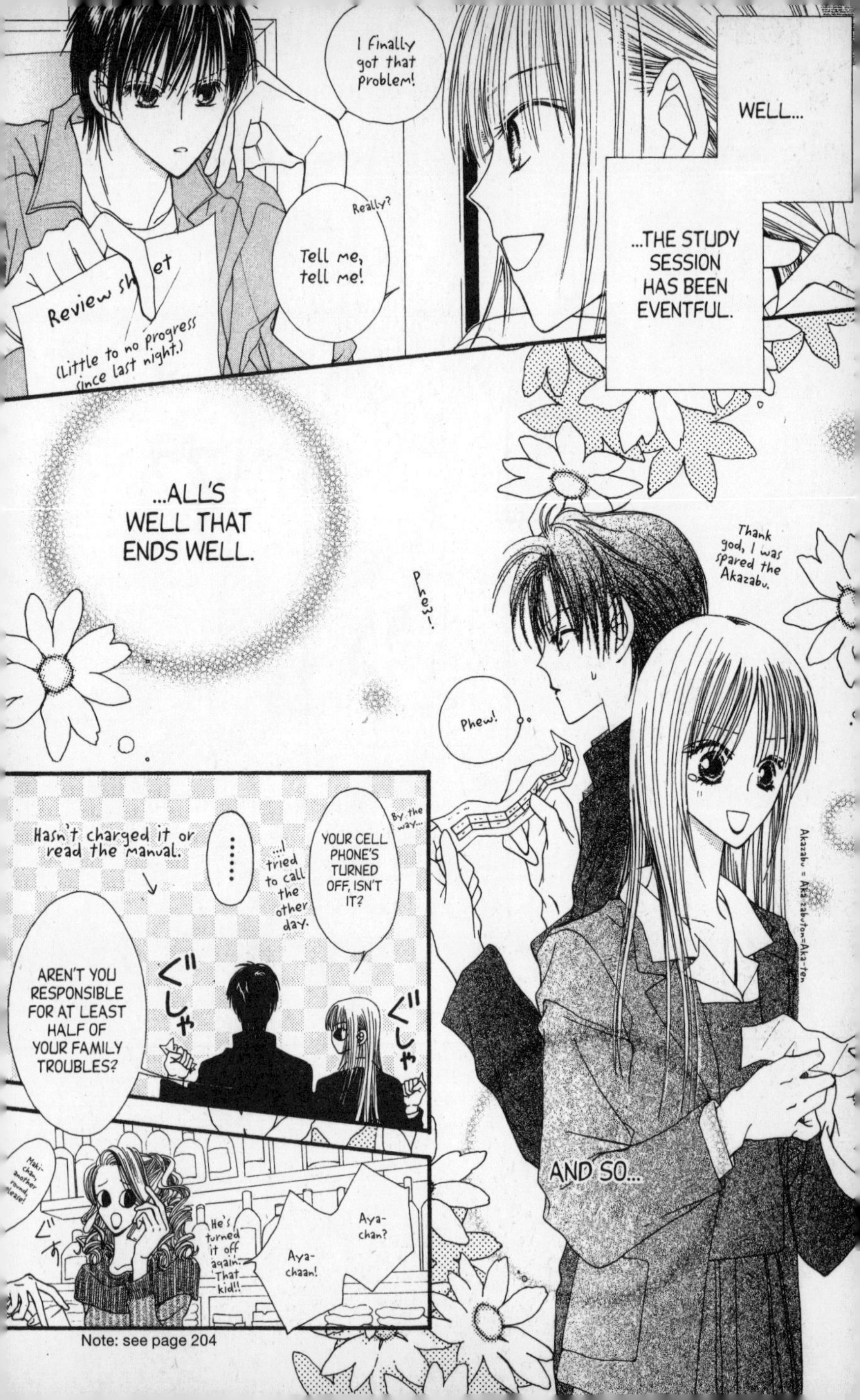
WELL...
...THE STUDY SESSION HAS BEEN EVENTFUL.
I finally got that problem!
Really?
Tell me, tell me!
Review sheet
(Little to no progress since last night.)
Thank god, I was spared the Akazabu.
Phew!
...ALL'S WELL THAT ENDS WELL.
Phew!
Akazabu = Aka-zabuton=Aka-ten
AND SO...
By the way...
YOUR CELL PHONE'S TURNED OFF, ISN'T IT?
...I tried to call the other day.
......
Hasn't charged it or read the manual.
ぐしゃ
ぐしゃ
AREN'T YOU RESPONSIBLE FOR AT LEAST HALF OF YOUR FAMILY TROUBLES?
Aya-chan?
Aya-chaan!
He's turned it off again. That kid!!
Maki-chan, another round, please!

Note: see page 204

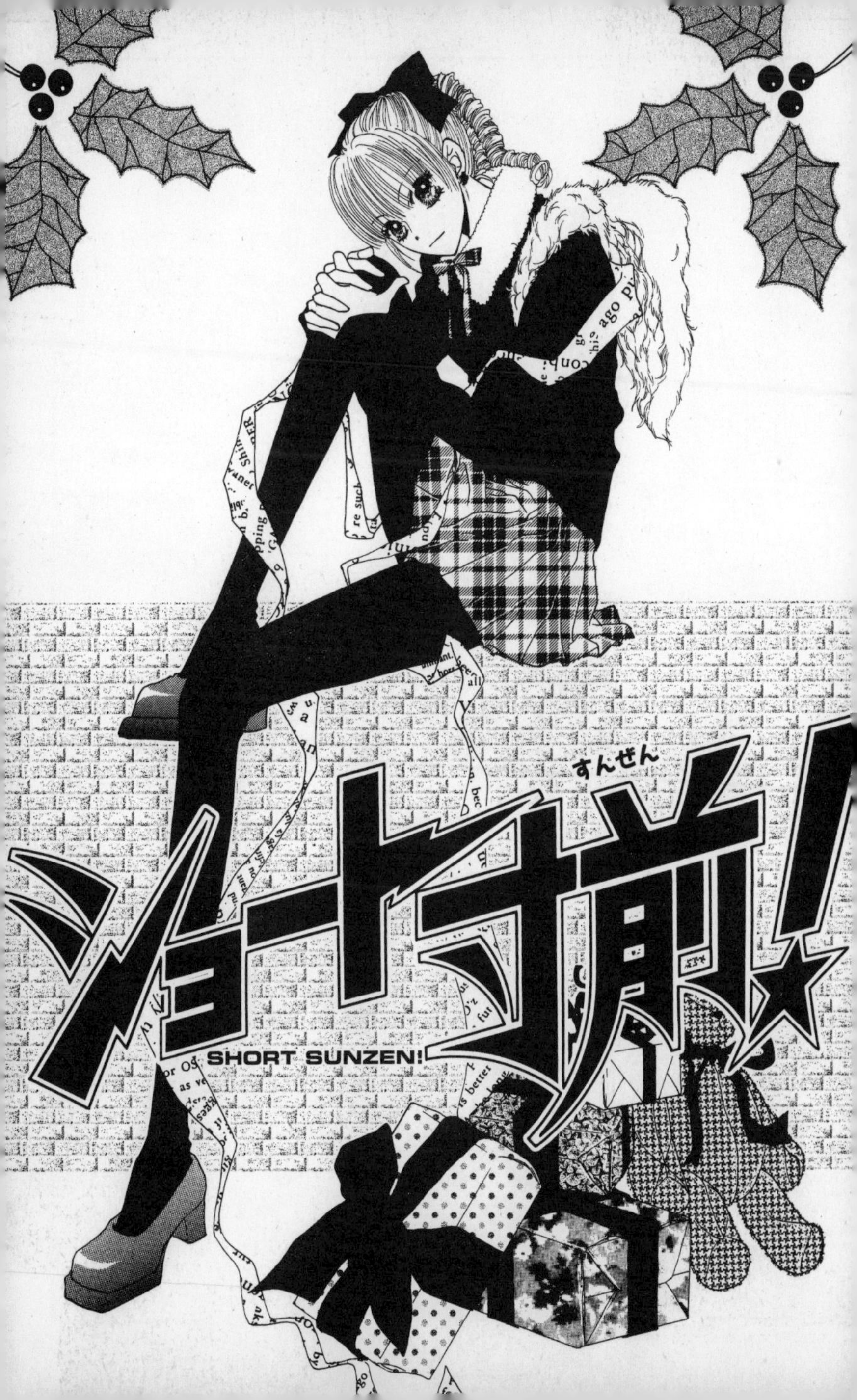
すんぜん
ショート寸前!
SHORT SUNZEN!

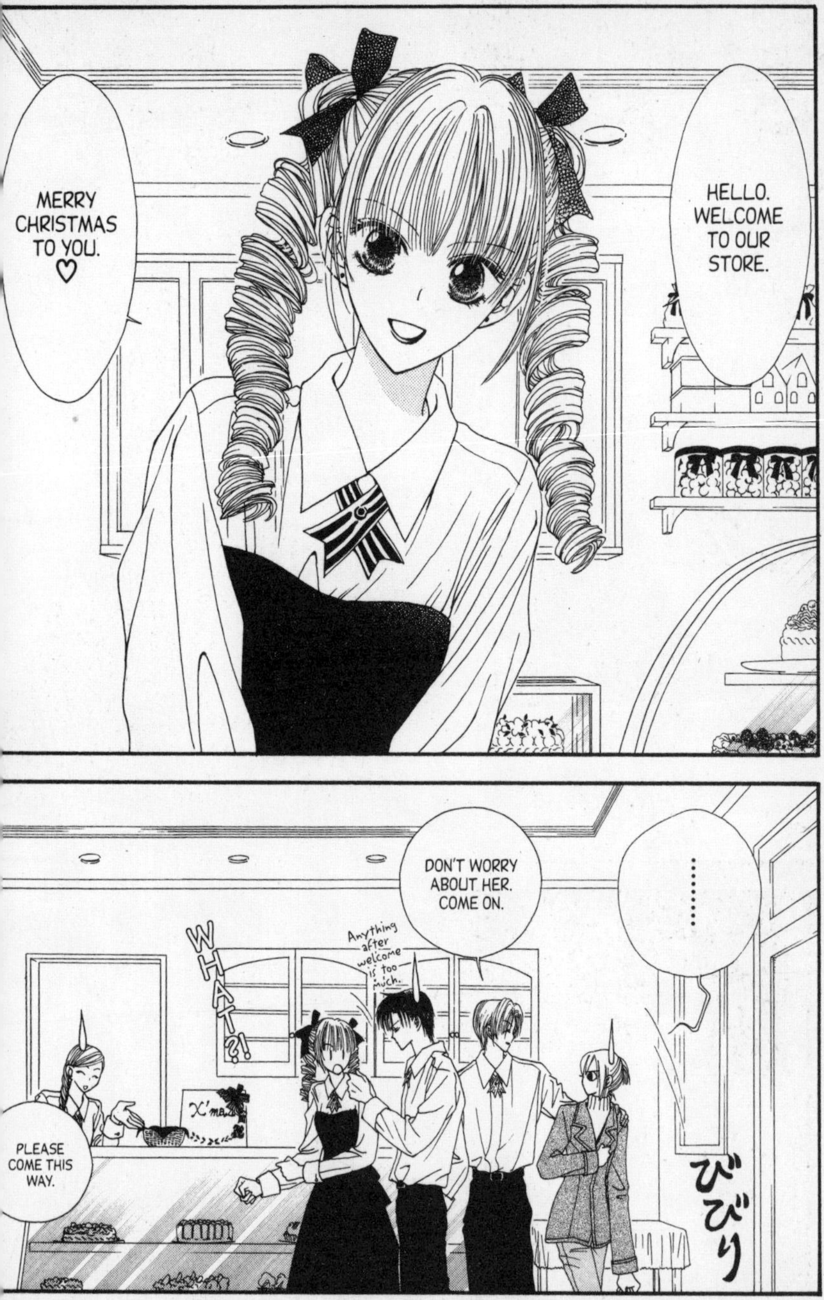
HELLO. WELCOME TO OUR STORE.
MERRY CHRISTMAS TO YOU. ♡
……
びびり
DON'T WORRY ABOUT HER. COME ON.
Anything after welcome is too much.
WHAT?!
X'mas
PLEASE COME THIS WAY.

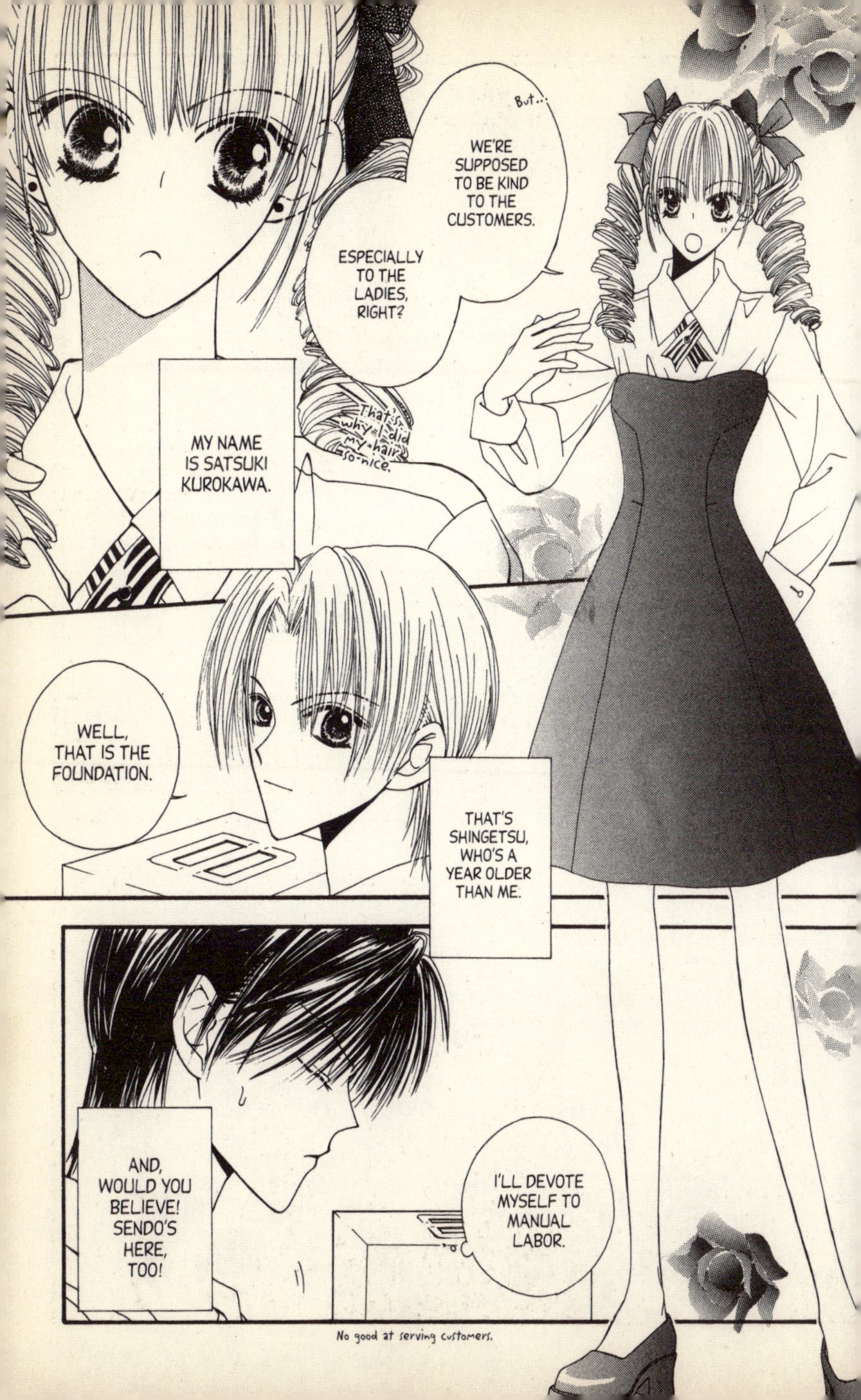
But...
WE'RE SUPPOSED TO BE KIND TO THE CUSTOMERS.
ESPECIALLY TO THE LADIES, RIGHT?
That's why I did my hair so nice.
MY NAME IS SATSUKI KUROKAWA.
THAT'S SHINGETSU, WHO'S A YEAR OLDER THAN ME.
WELL, THAT IS THE FOUNDATION.
AND, WOULD YOU BELIEVE! SENDO'S HERE, TOO!
I'LL DEVOTE MYSELF TO MANUAL LABOR.
No good at serving customers.

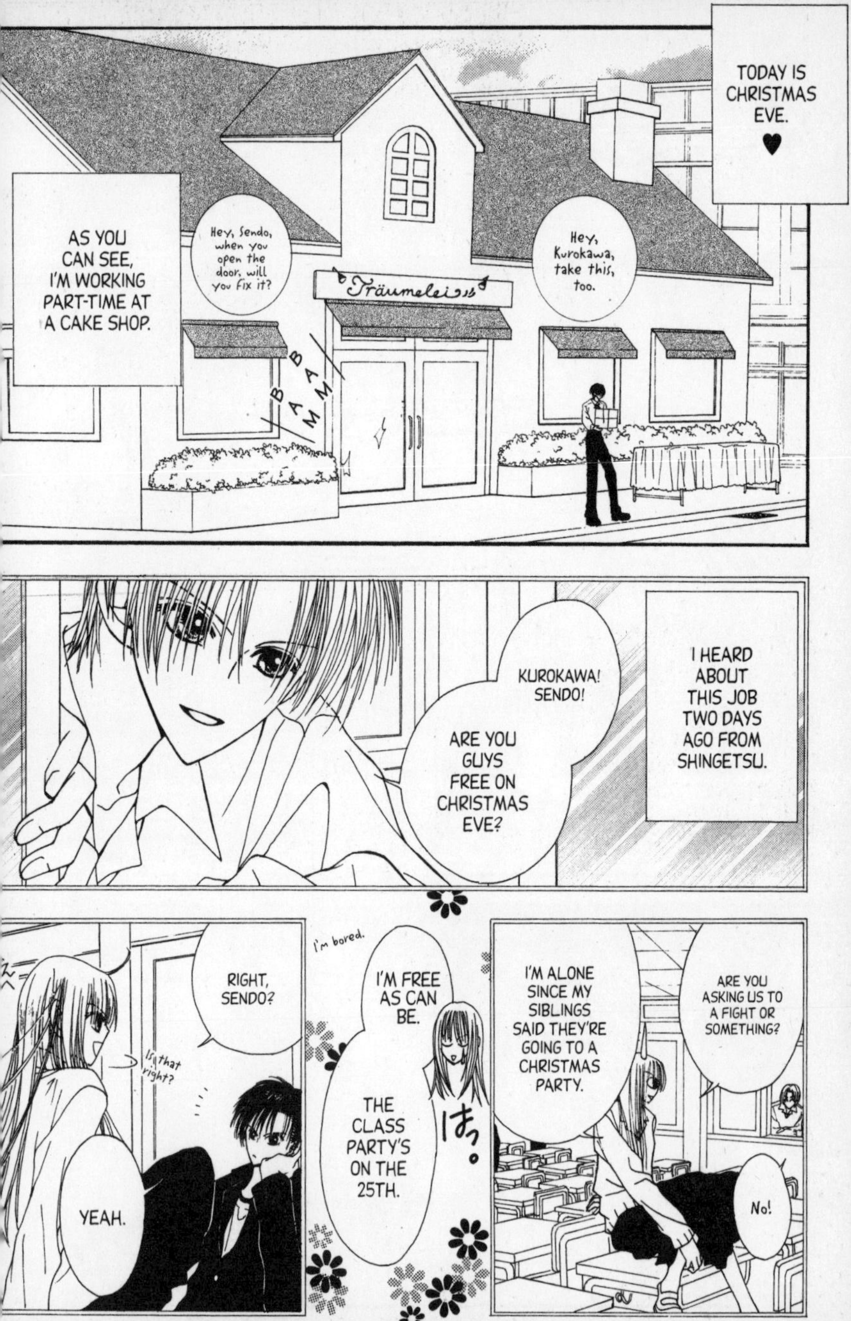
TODAY IS CHRISTMAS EVE. ♥
Hey, Kurokawa, take this, too.
Träumelei
Hey, Sendo, when you open the door, will you fix it?
BAMM
AS YOU CAN SEE, I'M WORKING PART-TIME AT A CAKE SHOP.
I HEARD ABOUT THIS JOB TWO DAYS AGO FROM SHINGETSU.
KUROKAWA! SENDO!
ARE YOU GUYS FREE ON CHRISTMAS EVE?
ARE YOU ASKING US TO A FIGHT OR SOMETHING?
No!
I'M ALONE SINCE MY SIBLINGS SAID THEY'RE GOING TO A CHRISTMAS PARTY.
I'm bored.
I'M FREE AS CAN BE.
THE CLASS PARTY'S ON THE 25TH.
はっ
RIGHT, SENDO?
Is that right?
YEAH.

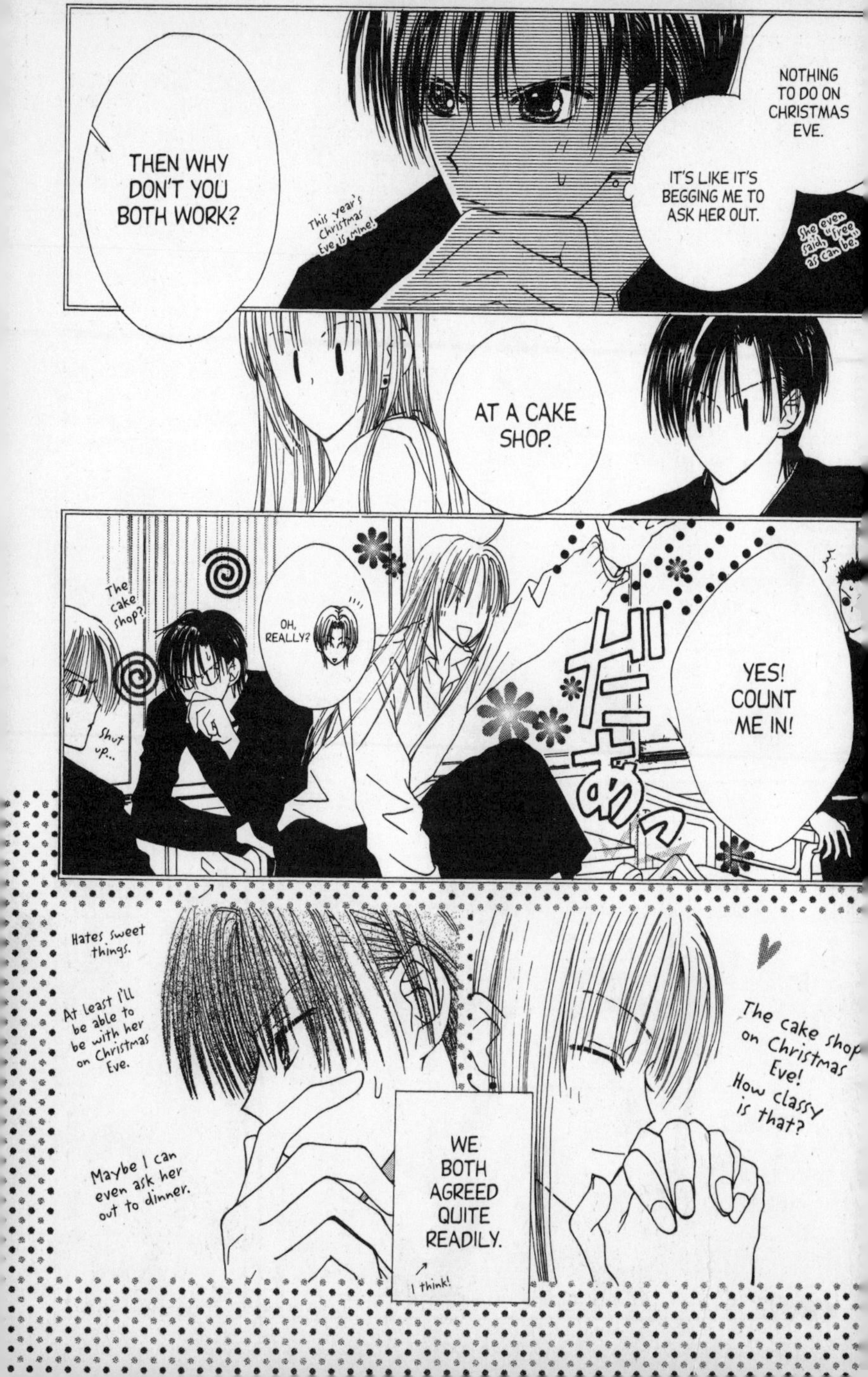

NOTHING TO DO ON CHRISTMAS EVE.
IT'S LIKE IT'S BEGGING ME TO ASK HER OUT.
She even said, "free as can be."
This year's Christmas Eve is mine!
THEN WHY DON'T YOU BOTH WORK?
AT A CAKE SHOP.
YES! COUNT ME IN!
だーあっ
OH, REALLY?
The cake shop?
Shut up...
The cake shop on Christmas Eve! How classy is that?
WE BOTH AGREED QUITE READILY.
I think!
Hates sweet things.
At least I'll be able to be with her on Christmas Eve.
Maybe I can even ask her out to dinner.

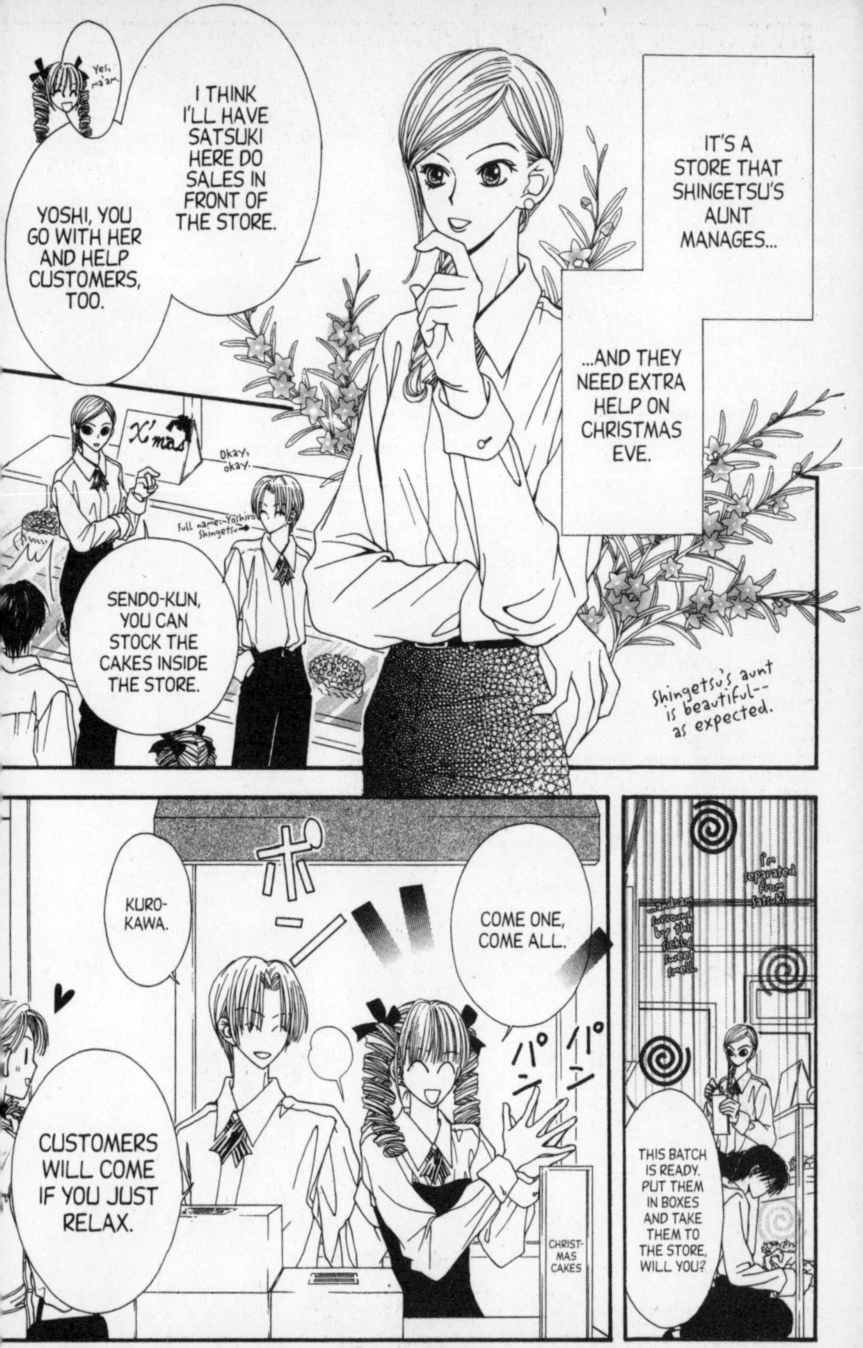
IT'S A STORE THAT SHINGETSU'S AUNT MANAGES...
...AND THEY NEED EXTRA HELP ON CHRISTMAS EVE.
I THINK I'LL HAVE SATSUKI HERE DO SALES IN FRONT OF THE STORE.
Yes, ma'am.
YOSHI, YOU GO WITH HER AND HELP CUSTOMERS, TOO.
Shingetsu's aunt is beautiful-- as expected.
X'mas
Okay, okay.
Full name:-Yoshiro Shingetsu
SENDO-KUN, YOU CAN STOCK THE CAKES INSIDE THE STORE.
I'm separated from Satsuki...
...and am surrounded by this sickly sweet smell.
THIS BATCH IS READY. PUT THEM IN BOXES AND TAKE THEM TO THE STORE, WILL YOU?
パン パン
COME ONE, COME ALL.
ポー
KURO-KAWA.
CUSTOMERS WILL COME IF YOU JUST RELAX.
CHRIST-MAS CAKES

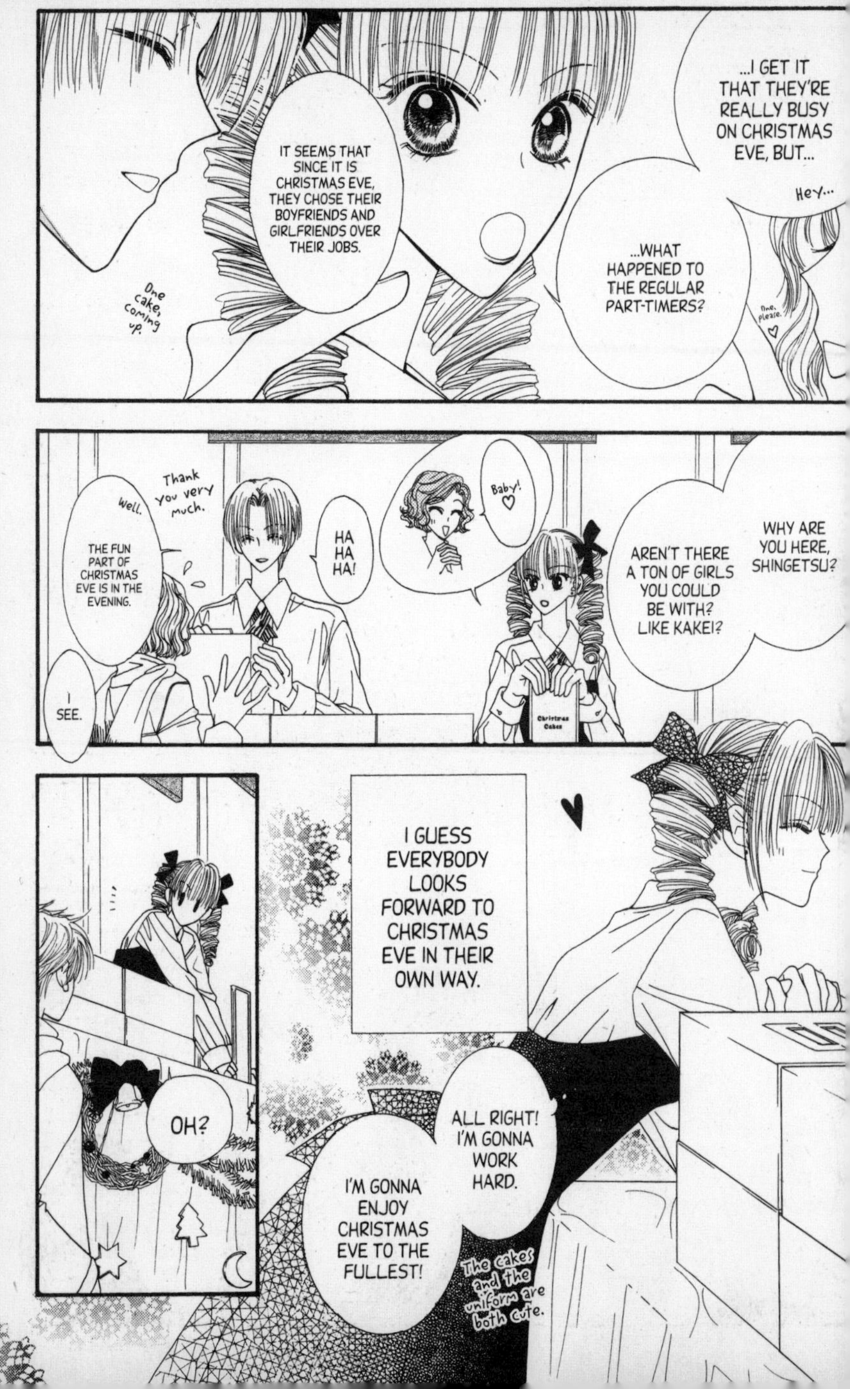
...I GET IT THAT THEY'RE REALLY BUSY ON CHRISTMAS EVE, BUT...
Hey...
One, please. ♡
...WHAT HAPPENED TO THE REGULAR PART-TIMERS?
IT SEEMS THAT SINCE IT IS CHRISTMAS EVE, THEY CHOSE THEIR BOYFRIENDS AND GIRLFRIENDS OVER THEIR JOBS.
One cake, coming up.
WHY ARE YOU HERE, SHINGETSU?
AREN'T THERE A TON OF GIRLS YOU COULD BE WITH? LIKE KAKEI?
Christmas Cakes
Baby! ♡
HA HA HA!
Thank you very much.
Well.
THE FUN PART OF CHRISTMAS EVE IS IN THE EVENING.
I SEE.
I GUESS EVERYBODY LOOKS FORWARD TO CHRISTMAS EVE IN THEIR OWN WAY.
ALL RIGHT! I'M GONNA WORK HARD.
I'M GONNA ENJOY CHRISTMAS EVE TO THE FULLEST!
The cakes and the uniform are both cute.
OH?

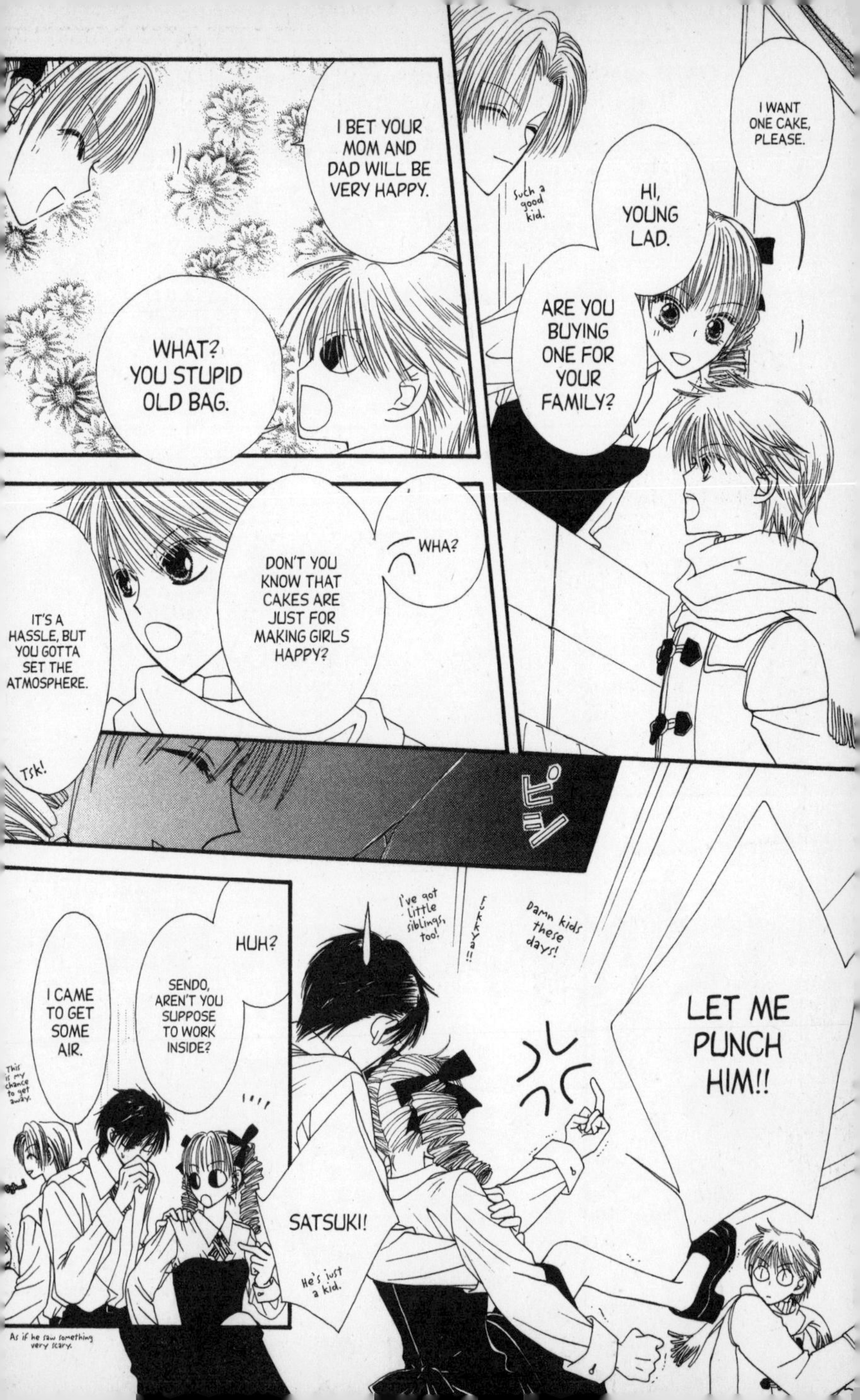

I WANT ONE CAKE, PLEASE.
HI, YOUNG LAD.
Such a good kid.
ARE YOU BUYING ONE FOR YOUR FAMILY?
I BET YOUR MOM AND DAD WILL BE VERY HAPPY.
WHAT? YOU STUPID OLD BAG.
WHA?
DON'T YOU KNOW THAT CAKES ARE JUST FOR MAKING GIRLS HAPPY?
IT'S A HASSLE, BUT YOU GOTTA SET THE ATMOSPHERE.
ピシ
Tsk!
LET ME PUNCH HIM!!
Damn kids these days!
Fukkya!!
I've got little siblings, too!
SATSUKI!
He's just a kid.
HUH?
SENDO, AREN'T YOU SUPPOSE TO WORK INSIDE?
I CAME TO GET SOME AIR.
This is my chance to get away.
As if he saw something very scary.

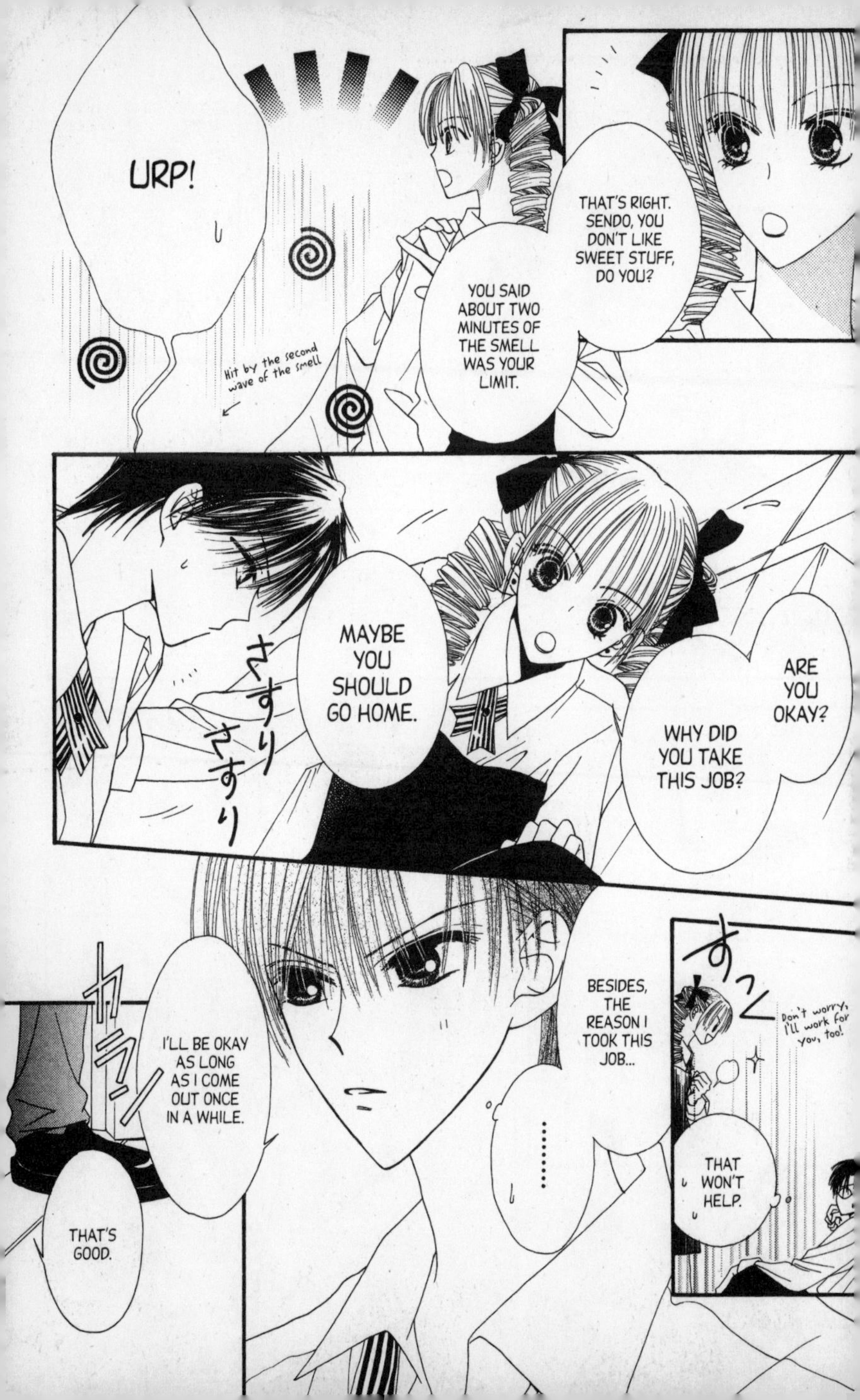
THAT'S RIGHT. SENDO, YOU DON'T LIKE SWEET STUFF, DO YOU?
YOU SAID ABOUT TWO MINUTES OF THE SMELL WAS YOUR LIMIT.
URP!
Hit by the second wave of the smell
ARE YOU OKAY?
WHY DID YOU TAKE THIS JOB?
MAYBE YOU SHOULD GO HOME.
さすり さすり
すっく
Don't worry, I'll work for you, too!
THAT WON'T HELP.
BESIDES, THE REASON I TOOK THIS JOB...
....
I'LL BE OKAY AS LONG AS I COME OUT ONCE IN A WHILE.
THAT'S GOOD.

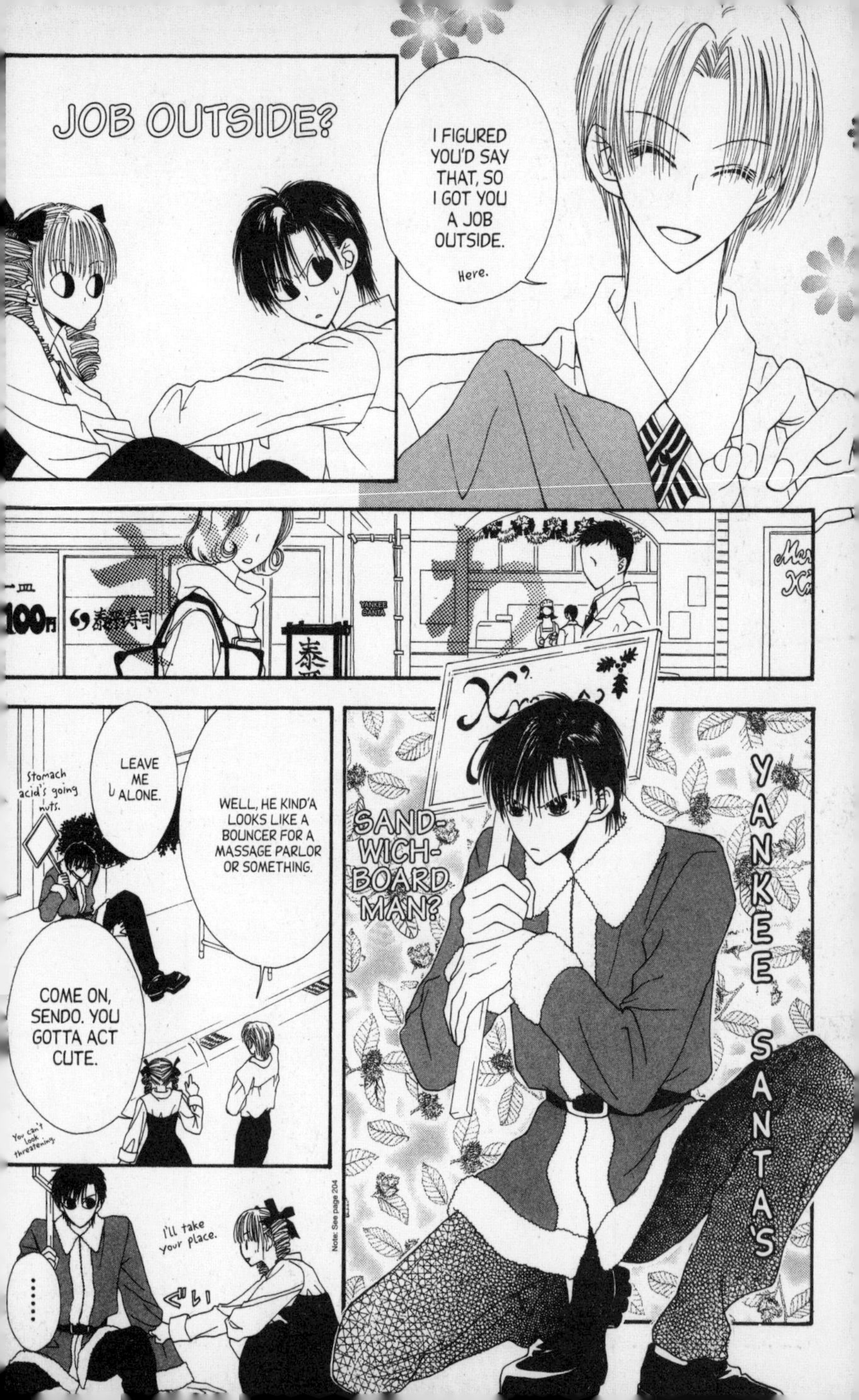
I FIGURED YOU'D SAY THAT, SO I GOT YOU A JOB OUTSIDE.
Here.
JOB OUTSIDE?
100円
YANKEE SANTA
YANKEE SANTA'S
SAND-WICH-BOARD MAN?
WELL, HE KIND'A LOOKS LIKE A BOUNCER FOR A MASSAGE PARLOR OR SOMETHING.
LEAVE ME ALONE.
Stomach acid's going nuts.
COME ON, SENDO. YOU GOTTA ACT CUTE.
You can't look threatening.
I'll take your place.
ぐい
......
Note: See page 204

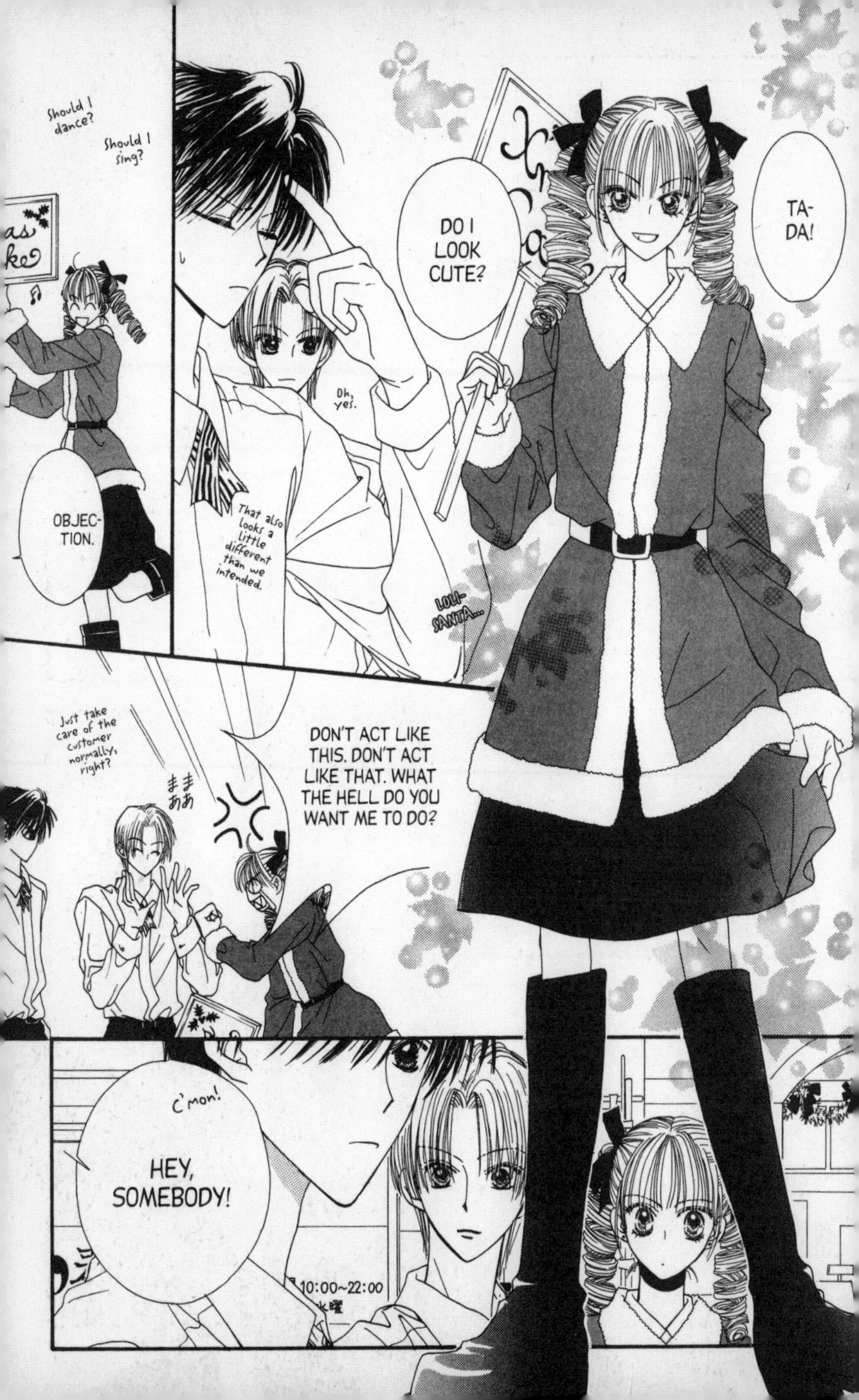
TA-DA!
DO I LOOK CUTE?
LOLI-SANTA...
Oh, yes.
That also looks a little different than we intended.
Should I dance?
Should I sing?
OBJECTION.
DON'T ACT LIKE THIS. DON'T ACT LIKE THAT. WHAT THE HELL DO YOU WANT ME TO DO?
まあまあ
Just take care of the customer normally, right?
C'mon!
HEY, SOMEBODY!
10:00~22:00
水曜

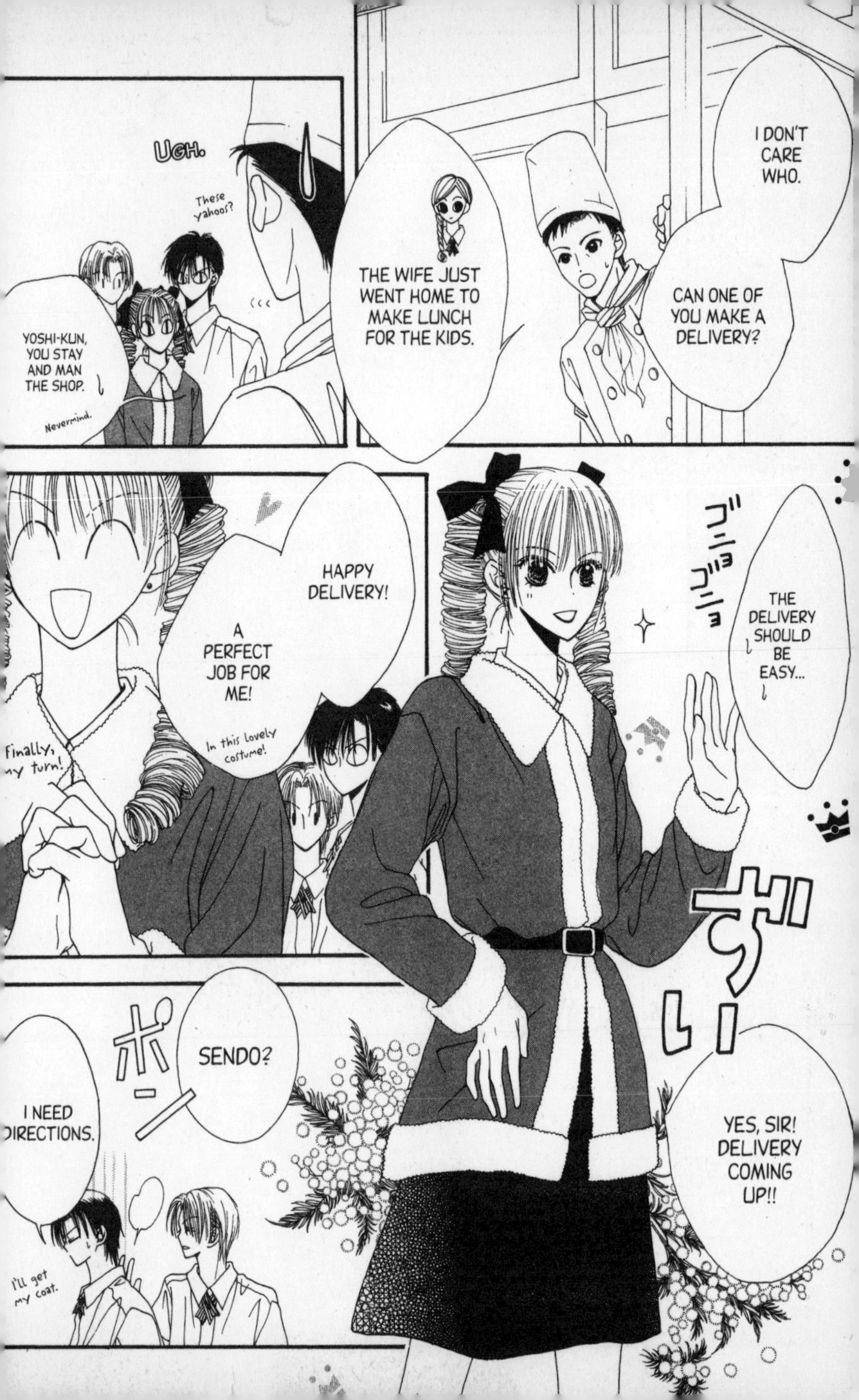
I DON'T CARE WHO.
CAN ONE OF YOU MAKE A DELIVERY?
THE WIFE JUST WENT HOME TO MAKE LUNCH FOR THE KIDS.
UGH.
These yahoos?
YOSHI-KUN, YOU STAY AND MAN THE SHOP.
Nevermind.
ゴニョゴニョ
THE DELIVERY SHOULD BE EASY...
HAPPY DELIVERY!
A PERFECT JOB FOR ME!
In this lovely costume!
Finally, my turn!
ずい
YES, SIR! DELIVERY COMING UP!!
SENDO?
ポーン
I NEED DIRECTIONS.
I'll get my coat.

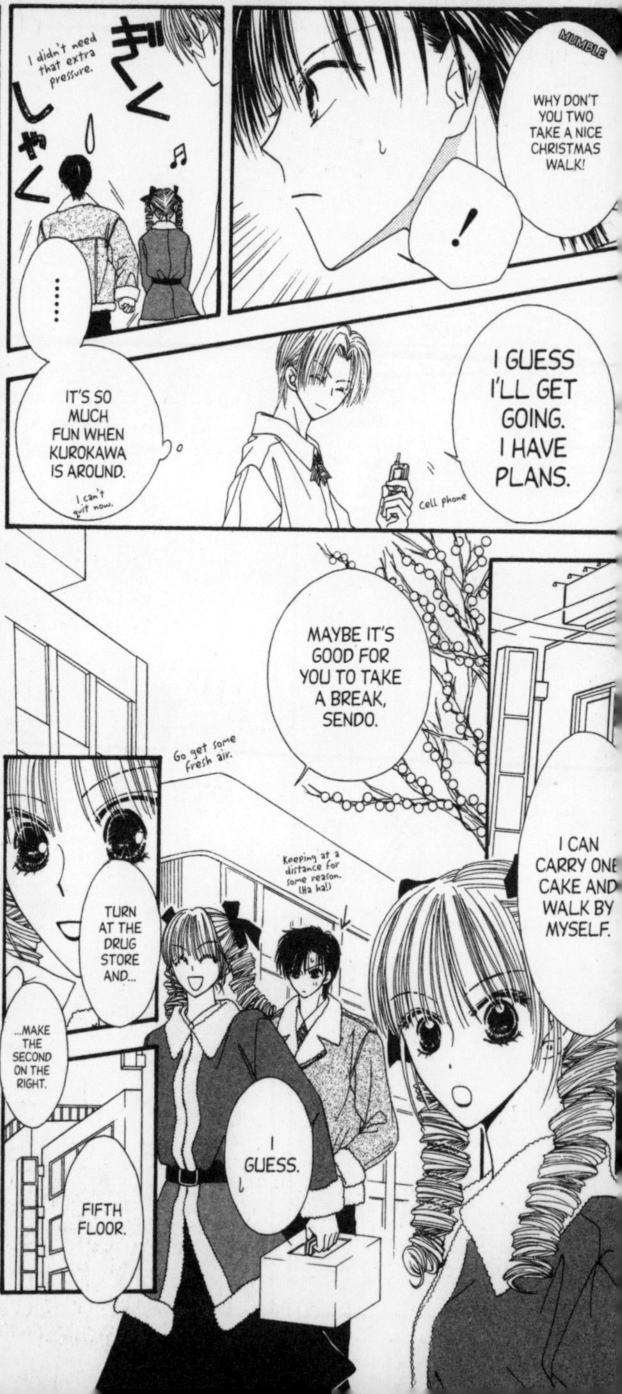
MUMBLE
WHY DON'T YOU TWO TAKE A NICE CHRISTMAS WALK!
!
ぎくしゃく
I didn't need that extra pressure.
......
I GUESS I'LL GET GOING. I HAVE PLANS.
Cell phone
IT'S SO MUCH FUN WHEN KUROKAWA IS AROUND.
I can't quit now.
MAYBE IT'S GOOD FOR YOU TO TAKE A BREAK, SENDO.
Go get some fresh air.
I CAN CARRY ONE CAKE AND WALK BY MYSELF.
Keeping at a distance for some reason. (Ha ha!)
I GUESS.
TURN AT THE DRUG STORE AND...
...MAKE THE SECOND ON THE RIGHT.
FIFTH FLOOR.

WARDROBE

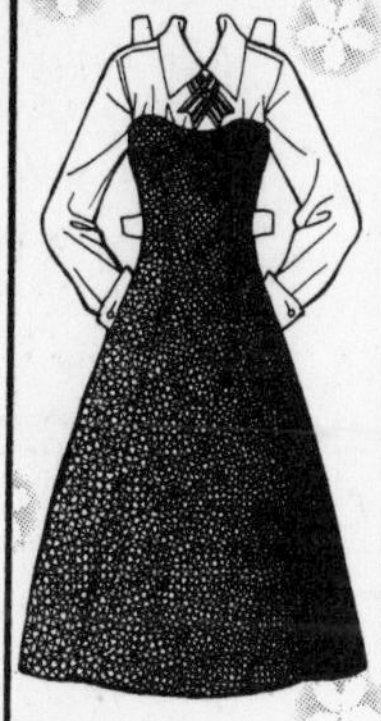

Cleaning these must be a hassle. I had to wear a uniform covered in oil and onions at a takoyaki shop. My jeans were torn, my hands died pink from the pickled ginger and cleaning the grill made burnt food fly into my face. I spent my 19th and 20th years covered in oil and full of burns. But the food was good! I think I ate the most around this time. I remember going to three restaurants to eat dinner after work and eating 26 pieces of cake in one hour at all-you-can-eat cake shops.

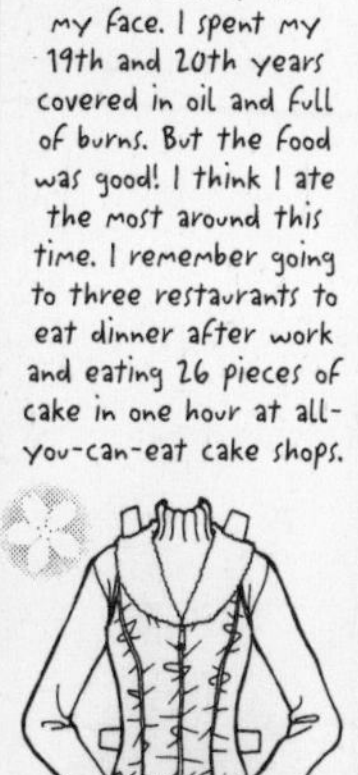

Being out on the town on Christmas Eve is so much fun. You can see window displays that are set up only for Christmas Eve.

But all you see is couples.♪

Note: see page 204

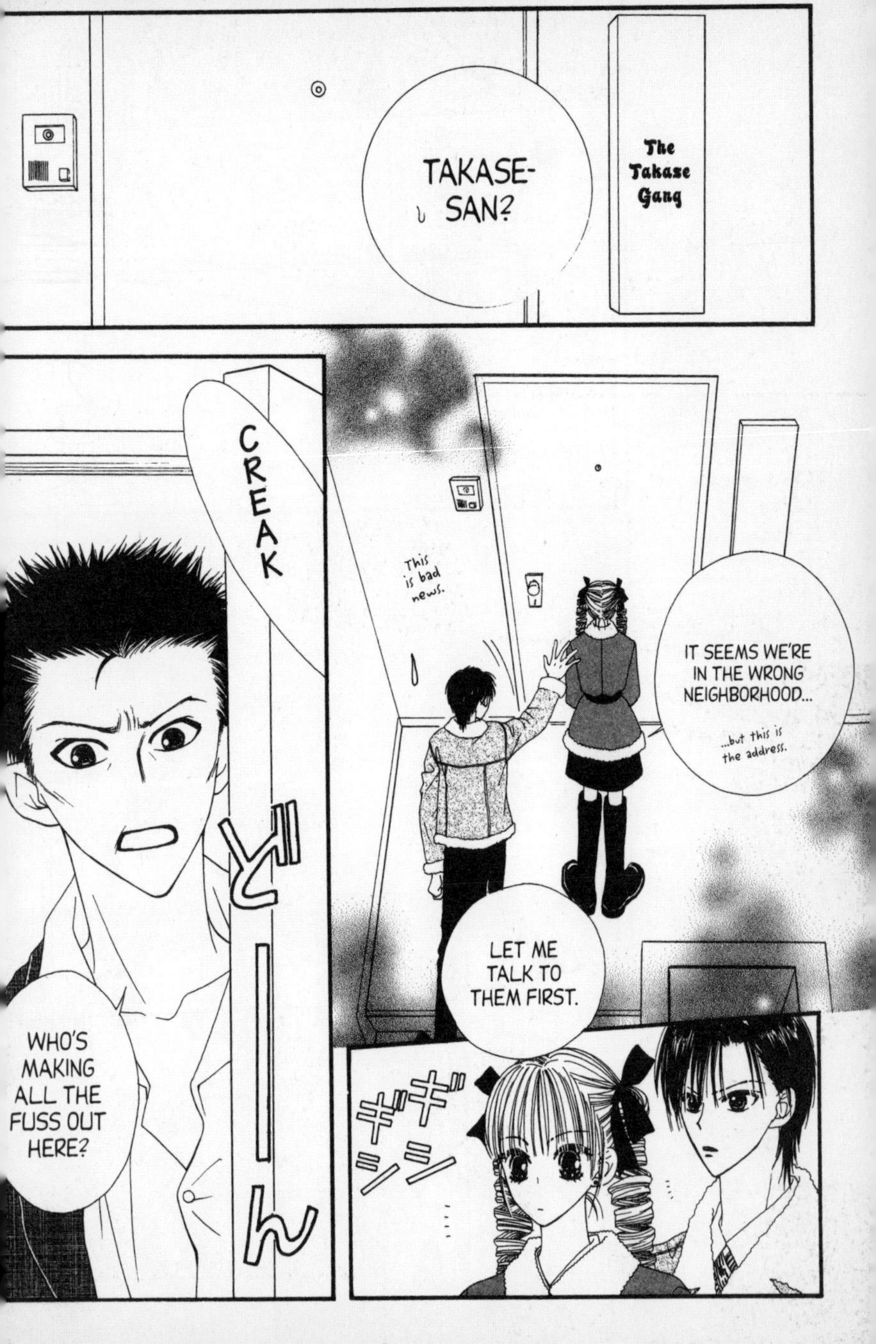
The Takase Gang
TAKASE-SAN?
IT SEEMS WE'RE IN THE WRONG NEIGHBORHOOD...
...but this is the address.
This is bad news.
LET ME TALK TO THEM FIRST.
ギシギシ
CREAK
どーん
WHO'S MAKING ALL THE FUSS OUT HERE?

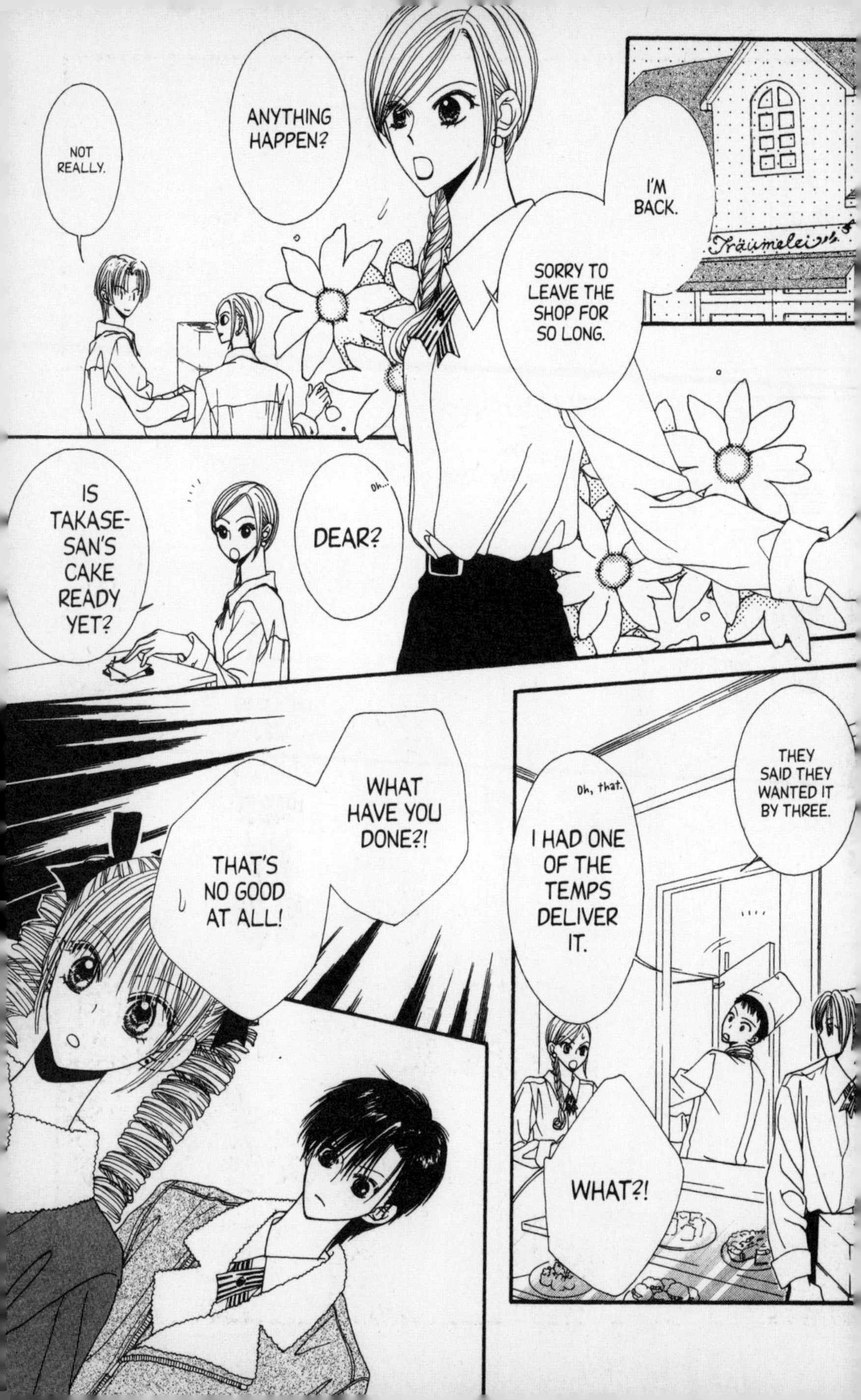
Träumelei
I'M BACK.
SORRY TO LEAVE THE SHOP FOR SO LONG.
ANYTHING HAPPEN?
NOT REALLY.
Oh...
DEAR?
IS TAKASE-SAN'S CAKE READY YET?
THEY SAID THEY WANTED IT BY THREE.
Oh, that.
I HAD ONE OF THE TEMPS DELIVER IT.
WHAT?!
WHAT HAVE YOU DONE?!
THAT'S NO GOOD AT ALL!

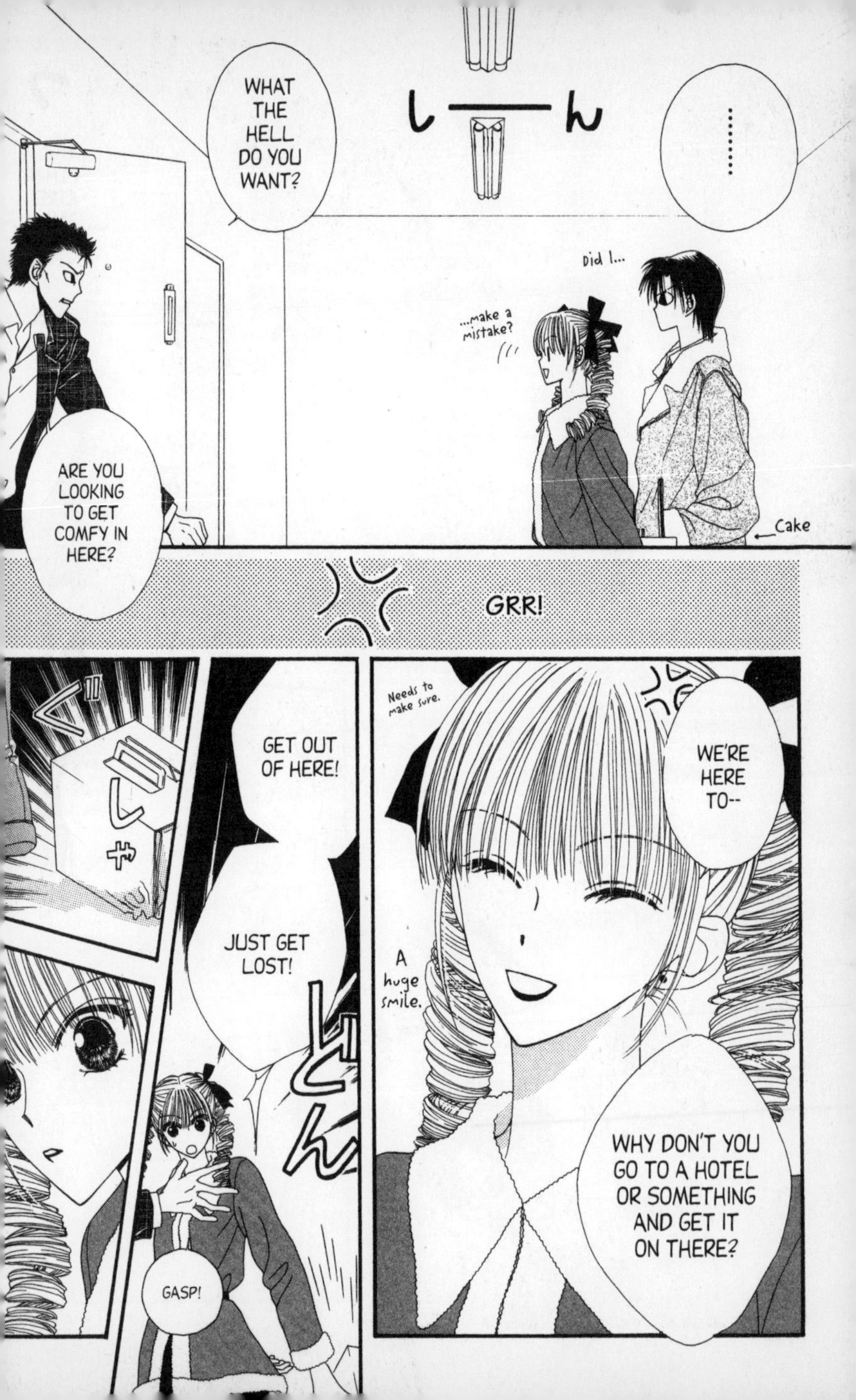
......
しーーん
Did I...
...make a mistake?
Cake
WHAT THE HELL DO YOU WANT?
ARE YOU LOOKING TO GET COMFY IN HERE?
GRR!
Needs to make sure.
WE'RE HERE TO--
A huge smile.
WHY DON'T YOU GO TO A HOTEL OR SOMETHING AND GET IT ON THERE?
GET OUT OF HERE!
JUST GET LOST!
GASP!

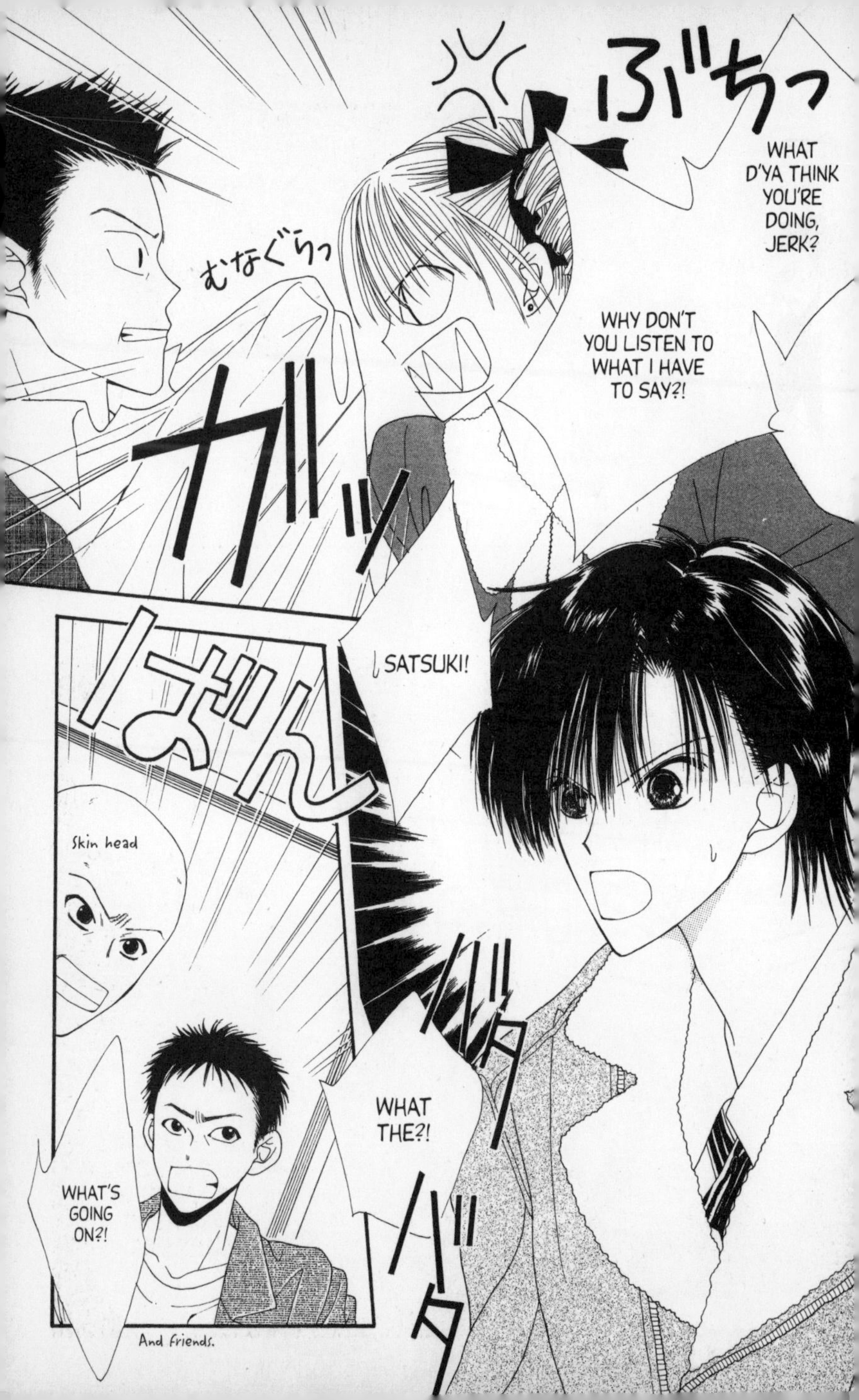
ぶちっ
WHAT D'YA THINK YOU'RE DOING, JERK?
WHY DON'T YOU LISTEN TO WHAT I HAVE TO SAY?!
むなぐらっ
ガッ
SATSUKI!
バタ
バタ
ばん
Skin head
WHAT THE?!
WHAT'S GOING ON?!
And friends.

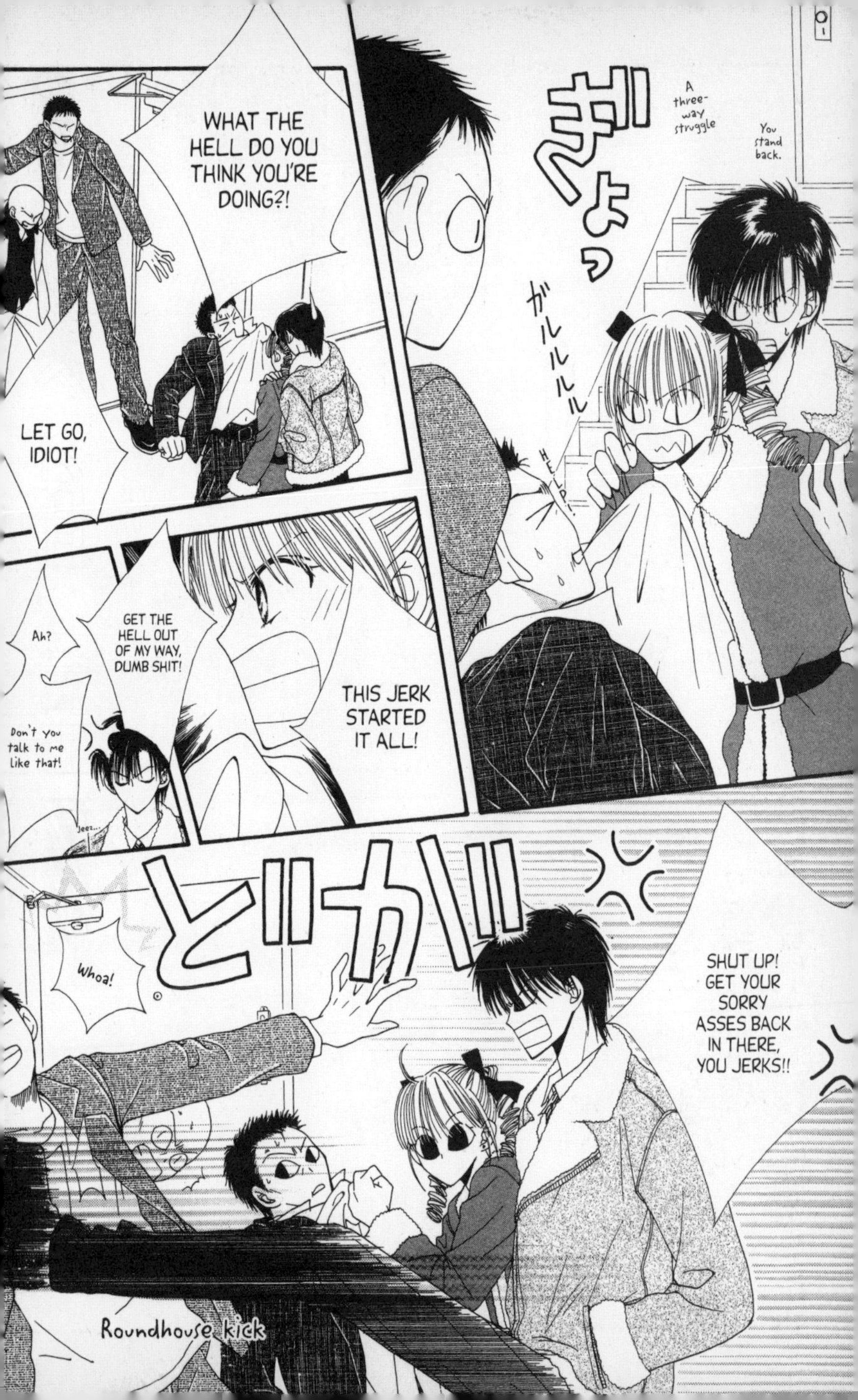
ぎょっ
A three-way struggle
You stand back.
ガルルルル
HELP!
WHAT THE HELL DO YOU THINK YOU'RE DOING?!
LET GO, IDIOT!
THIS JERK STARTED IT ALL!
GET THE HELL OUT OF MY WAY, DUMB SHIT!
Ah?
Don't you talk to me like that!
Jeez...
どかッ
SHUT UP! GET YOUR SORRY ASSES BACK IN THERE, YOU JERKS!!
Whoa!
Roundhouse kick

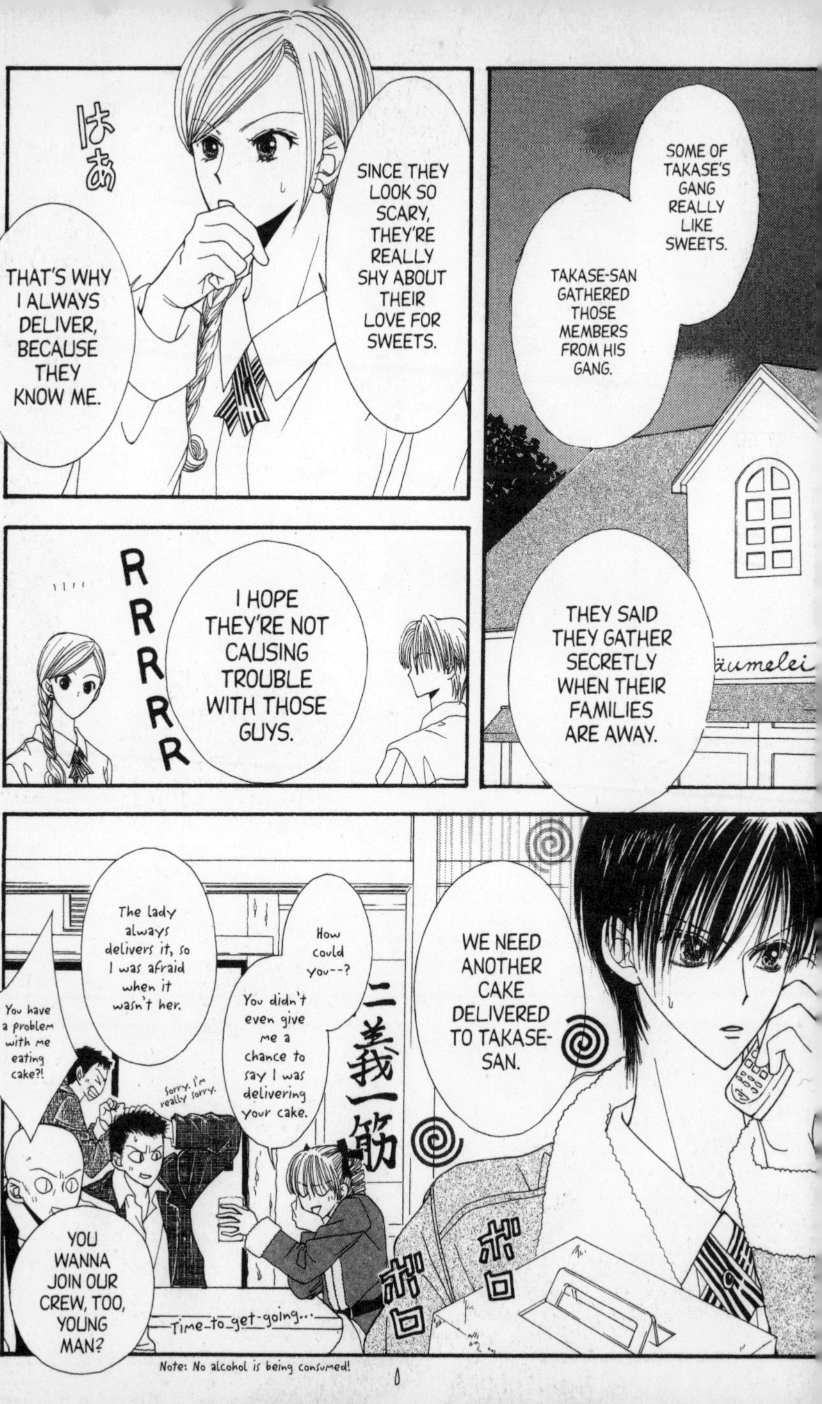
SOME OF TAKASE'S GANG REALLY LIKE SWEETS.
TAKASE-SAN GATHERED THOSE MEMBERS FROM HIS GANG.
THEY SAID THEY GATHER SECRETLY WHEN THEIR FAMILIES ARE AWAY.
はあ
SINCE THEY LOOK SO SCARY, THEY'RE REALLY SHY ABOUT THEIR LOVE FOR SWEETS.
THAT'S WHY I ALWAYS DELIVER, BECAUSE THEY KNOW ME.
I HOPE THEY'RE NOT CAUSING TROUBLE WITH THOSE GUYS.
RRRRR
WE NEED ANOTHER CAKE DELIVERED TO TAKASE-SAN.
ボロ
ボロ
二義一筋
How could you--?
You didn't even give me a chance to say I was delivering your cake.
The lady always delivers it, so I was afraid when it wasn't her.
You have a problem with me eating cake?!
Sorry. I'm really sorry.
YOU WANNA JOIN OUR CREW, TOO, YOUNG MAN?
Time-to-get-going...

Note: No alcohol is being consumed!

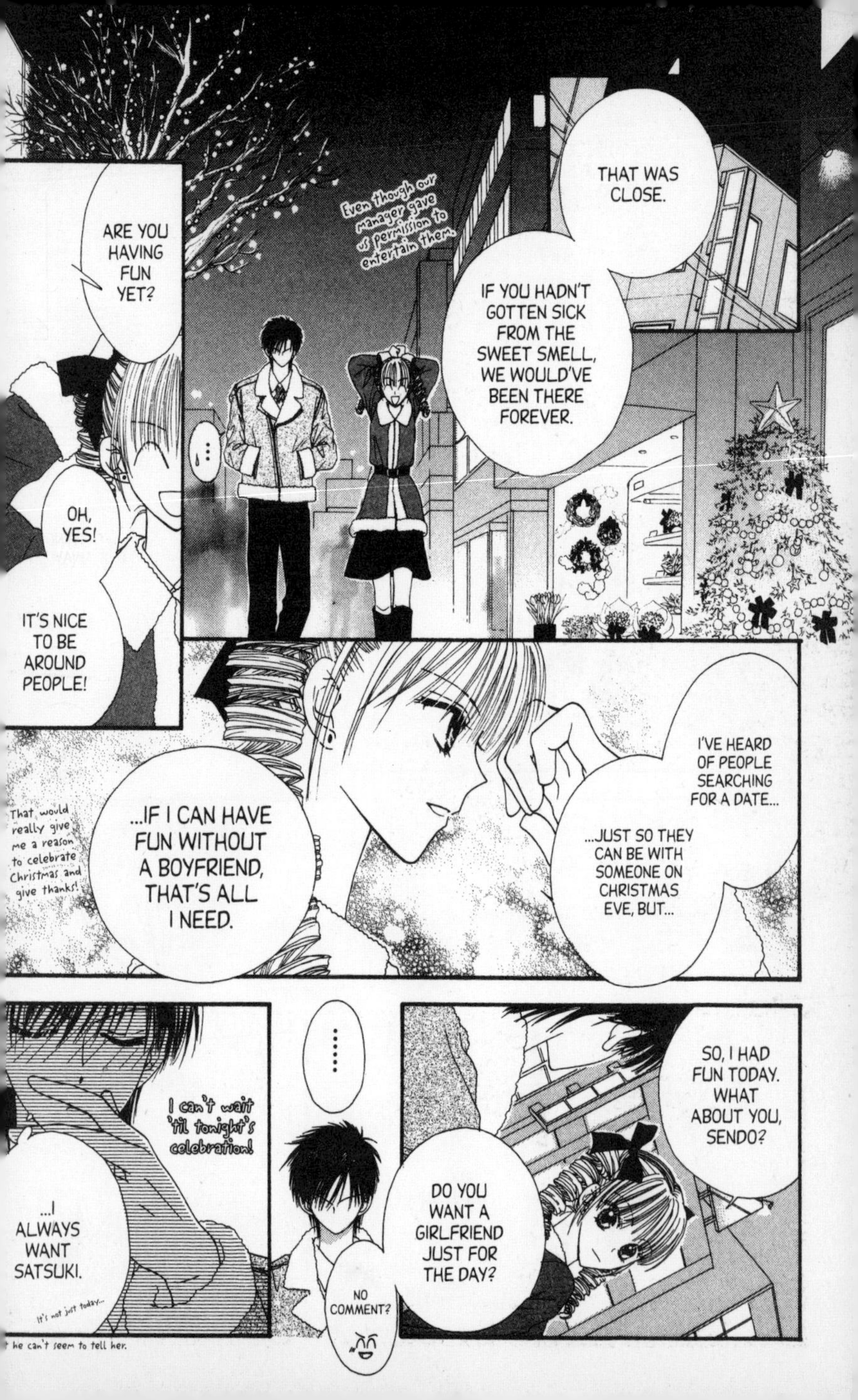
THAT WAS CLOSE.
IF YOU HADN'T GOTTEN SICK FROM THE SWEET SMELL, WE WOULD'VE BEEN THERE FOREVER.
Even though our manager gave us permission to entertain them.
...
ARE YOU HAVING FUN YET?
OH, YES!
IT'S NICE TO BE AROUND PEOPLE!
I'VE HEARD OF PEOPLE SEARCHING FOR A DATE...
...JUST SO THEY CAN BE WITH SOMEONE ON CHRISTMAS EVE, BUT...
...IF I CAN HAVE FUN WITHOUT A BOYFRIEND, THAT'S ALL I NEED.
That would really give me a reason to celebrate Christmas and give thanks!
SO, I HAD FUN TODAY. WHAT ABOUT YOU, SENDO?
DO YOU WANT A GIRLFRIEND JUST FOR THE DAY?
NO COMMENT?
......
I can't wait 'til tonight's celebration!
...I ALWAYS WANT SATSUKI.
It's not just today...
t he can't seem to tell her.

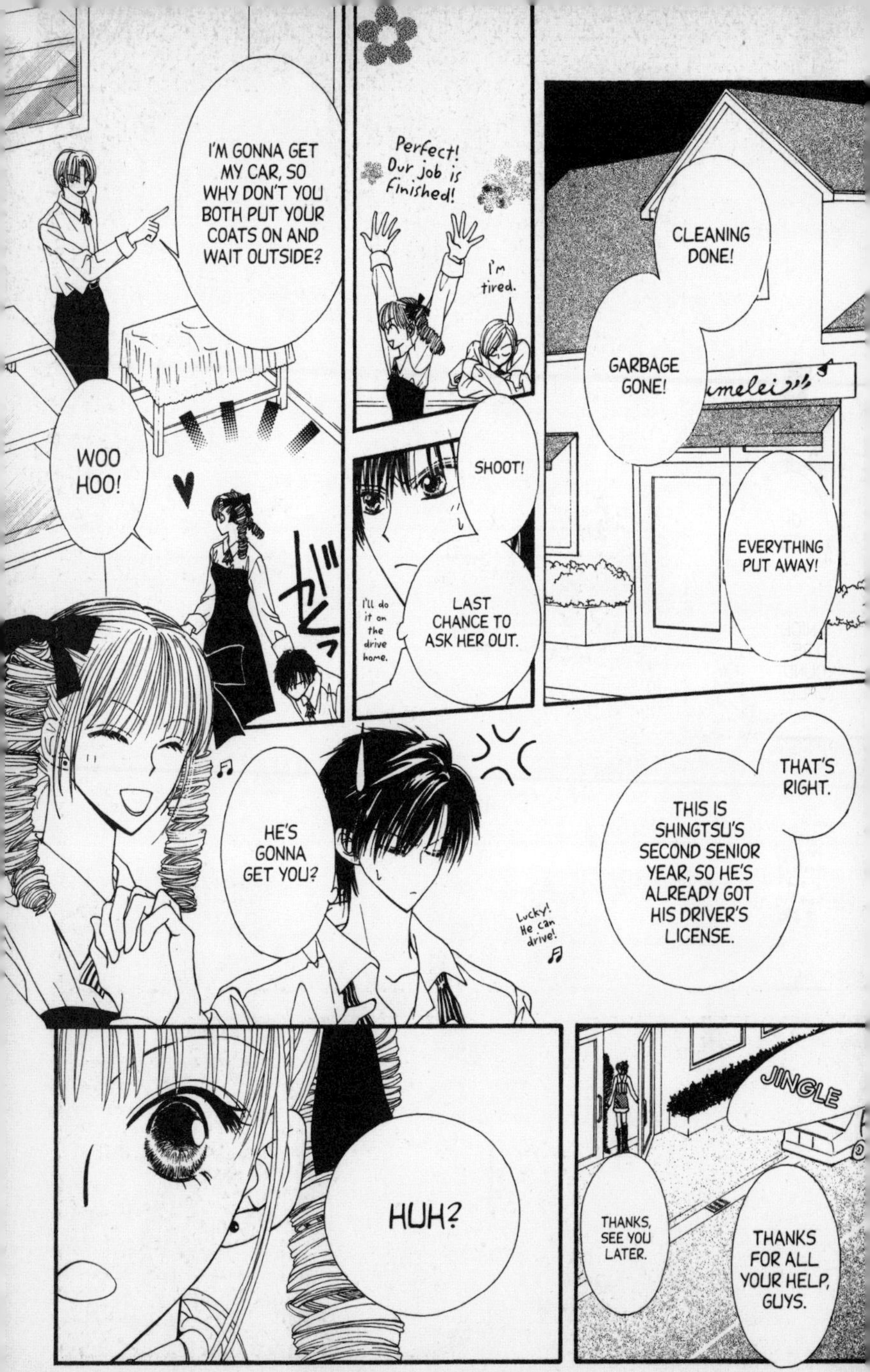

CLEANING DONE!
GARBAGE GONE!
EVERYTHING PUT AWAY!
Perfect! Our job is finished!
I'm tired.
SHOOT!
LAST CHANCE TO ASK HER OUT.
I'll do it on the drive home.
I'M GONNA GET MY CAR, SO WHY DON'T YOU BOTH PUT YOUR COATS ON AND WAIT OUTSIDE?
WOO HOO!
THAT'S RIGHT.
THIS IS SHINGTSU'S SECOND SENIOR YEAR, SO HE'S ALREADY GOT HIS DRIVER'S LICENSE.
Lucky! He can drive!
HE'S GONNA GET YOU?
JINGLE
THANKS FOR ALL YOUR HELP, GUYS.
THANKS, SEE YOU LATER.
HUH?

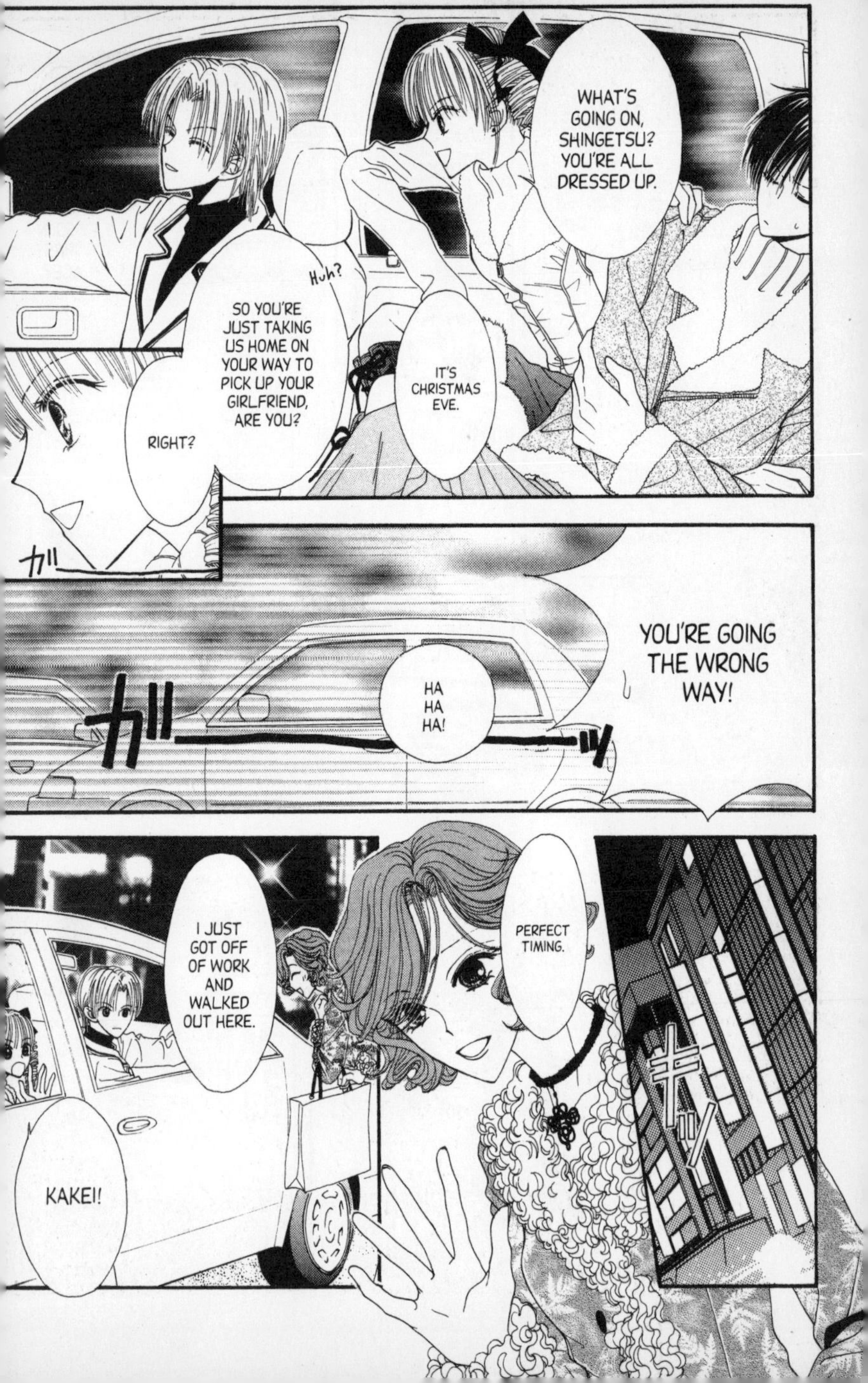
WHAT'S GOING ON, SHINGETSU? YOU'RE ALL DRESSED UP.
IT'S CHRISTMAS EVE.
Huh?
SO YOU'RE JUST TAKING US HOME ON YOUR WAY TO PICK UP YOUR GIRLFRIEND, ARE YOU?
RIGHT?
YOU'RE GOING THE WRONG WAY!
HA HA HA!
PERFECT TIMING.
I JUST GOT OFF OF WORK AND WALKED OUT HERE.
KAKEI!

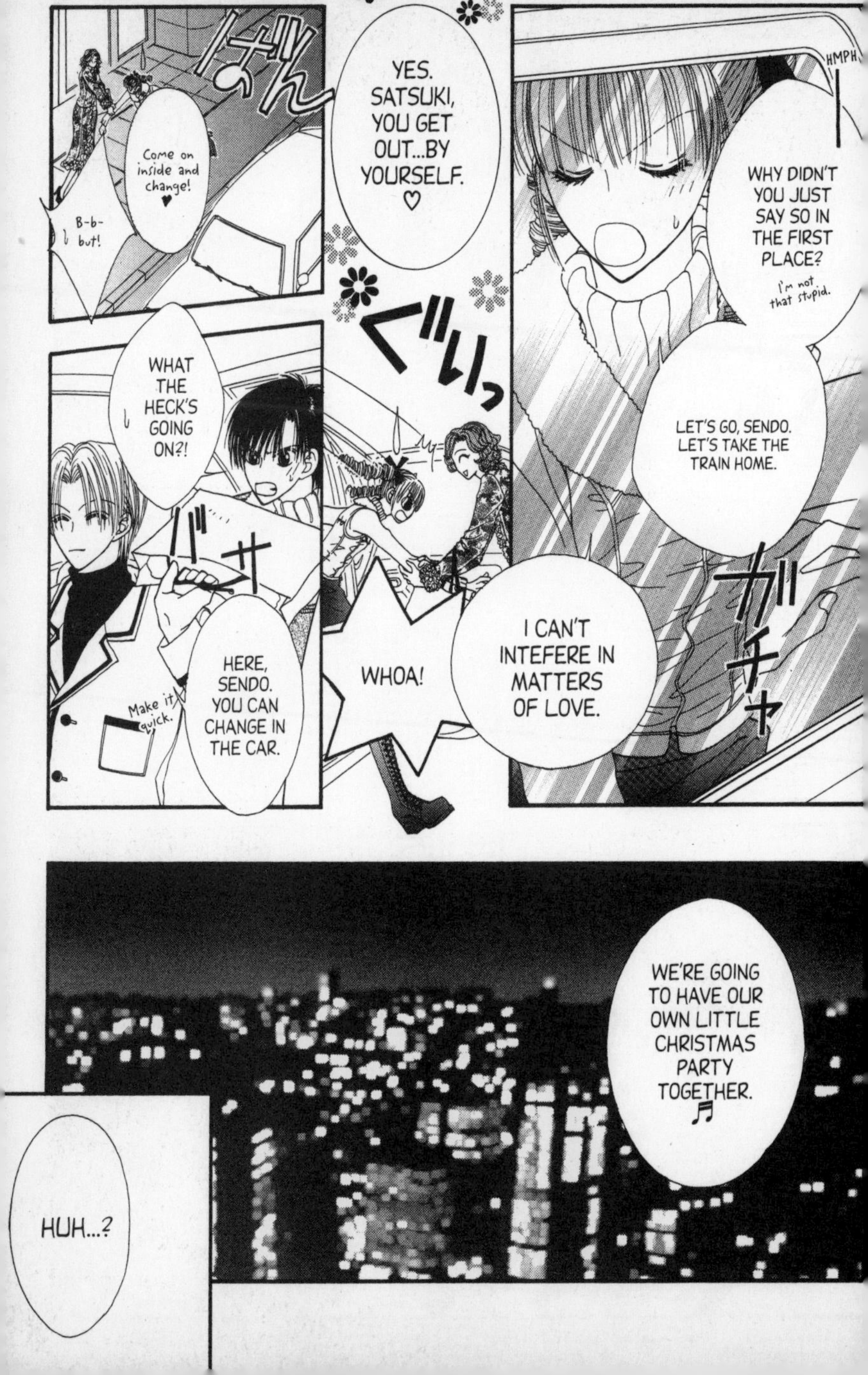
HMPH
WHY DIDN'T YOU JUST SAY SO IN THE FIRST PLACE?
I'm not that stupid.
LET'S GO, SENDO. LET'S TAKE THE TRAIN HOME.
ガチャ
YES. SATSUKI, YOU GET OUT...BY YOURSELF. ♡
はん
Come on inside and change! ♥
B-b-but!
ぐいっ
I CAN'T INTEFERE IN MATTERS OF LOVE.
WHOA!
バサ
HERE, SENDO. YOU CAN CHANGE IN THE CAR.
Make it quick.
WHAT THE HECK'S GOING ON?!
WE'RE GOING TO HAVE OUR OWN LITTLE CHRISTMAS PARTY TOGETHER. ♬
HUH...?

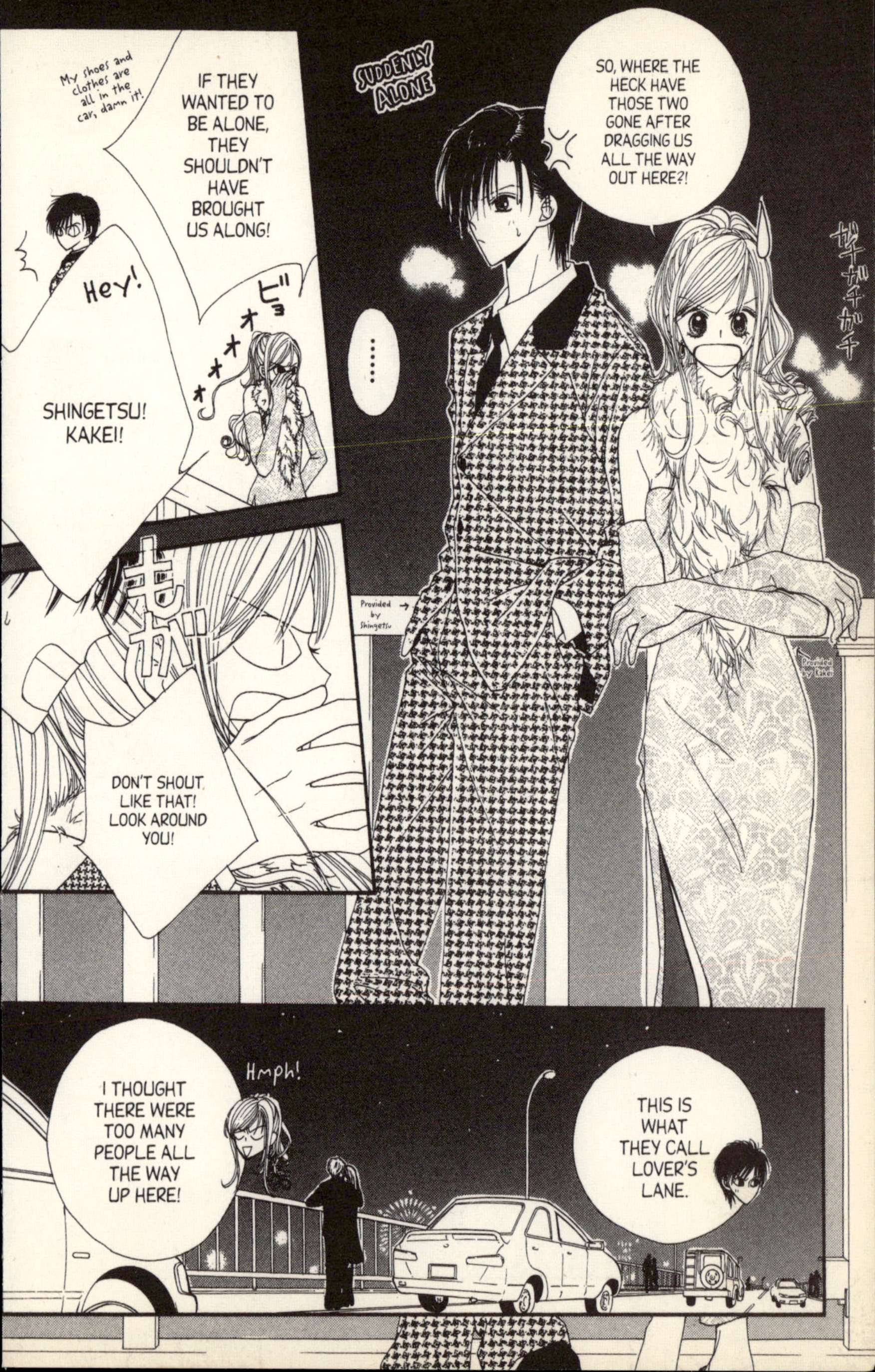
SUDDENLY ALONE
SO, WHERE THE HECK HAVE THOSE TWO GONE AFTER DRAGGING US ALL THE WAY OUT HERE?!
......
IF THEY WANTED TO BE ALONE, THEY SHOULDN'T HAVE BROUGHT US ALONG!
My shoes and clothes are all in the car, damn it!
Hey!
SHINGETSU! KAKEI!
DON'T SHOUT LIKE THAT! LOOK AROUND YOU!
Provided by Shingetsu
THIS IS WHAT THEY CALL LOVER'S LANE.
I THOUGHT THERE WERE TOO MANY PEOPLE ALL THE WAY UP HERE!
Hmph!

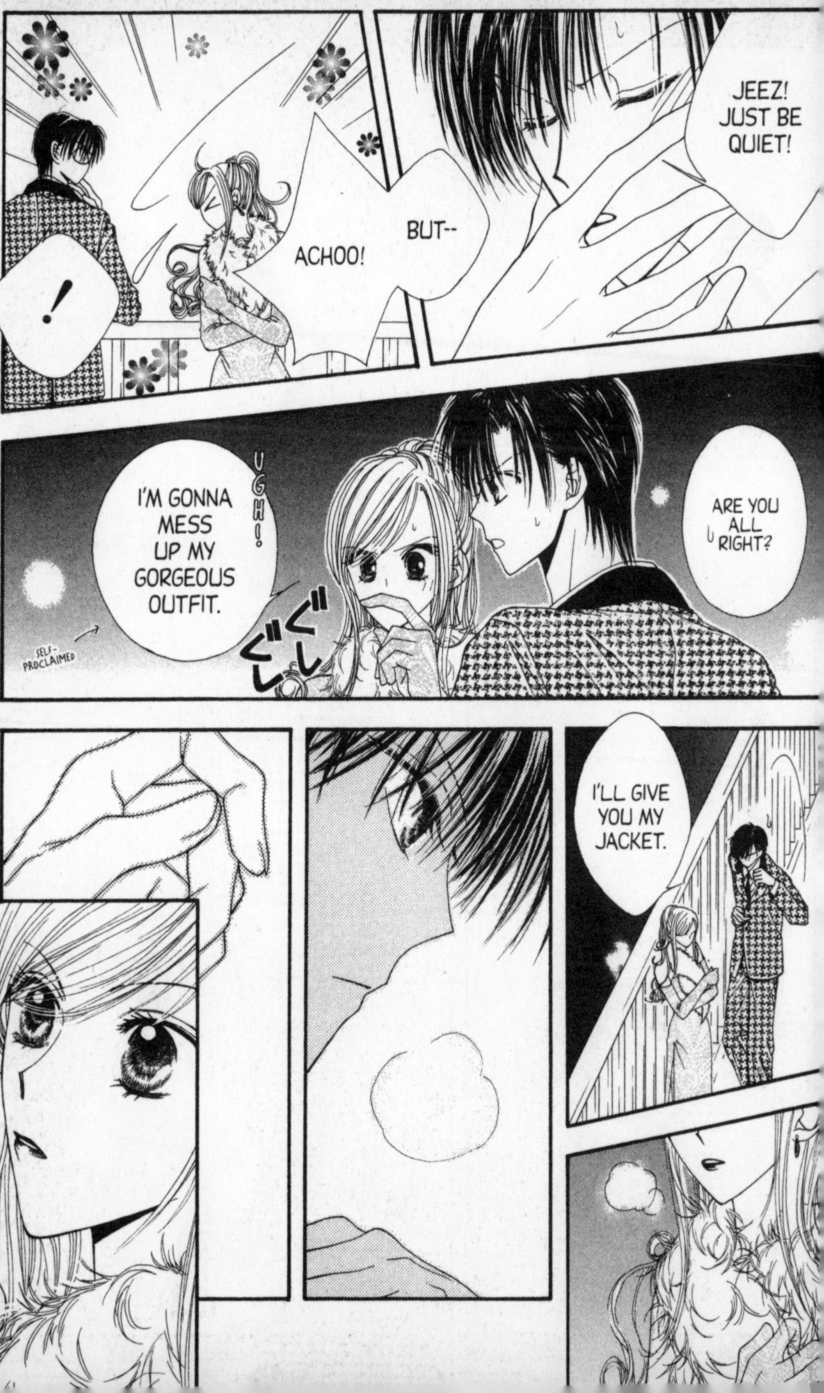
JEEZ! JUST BE QUIET!
BUT--
ACHOO!
!
ARE YOU ALL RIGHT?
I'M GONNA MESS UP MY GORGEOUS OUTFIT.
UGH!
SELF-PROCLAIMED
I'LL GIVE YOU MY JACKET.

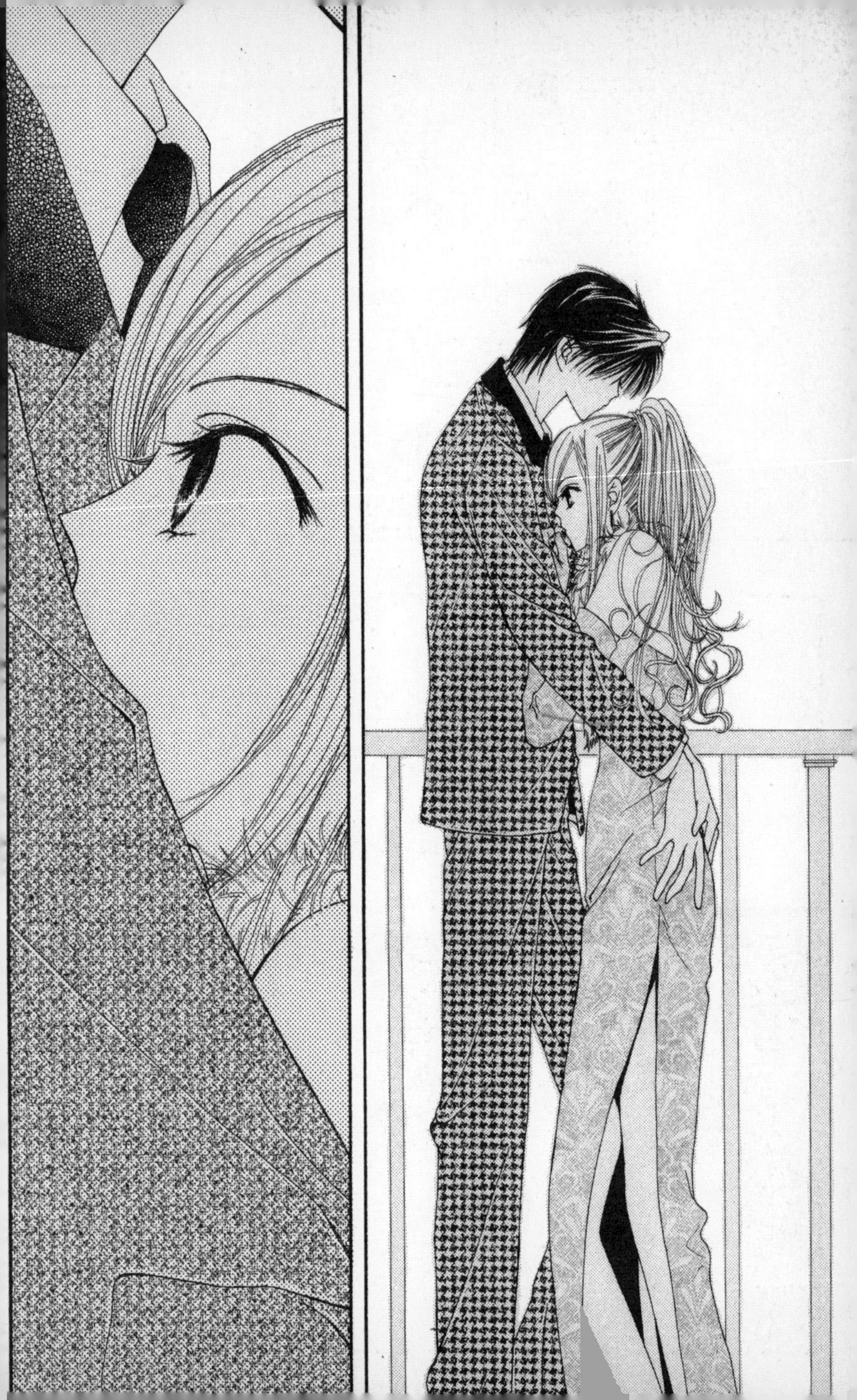

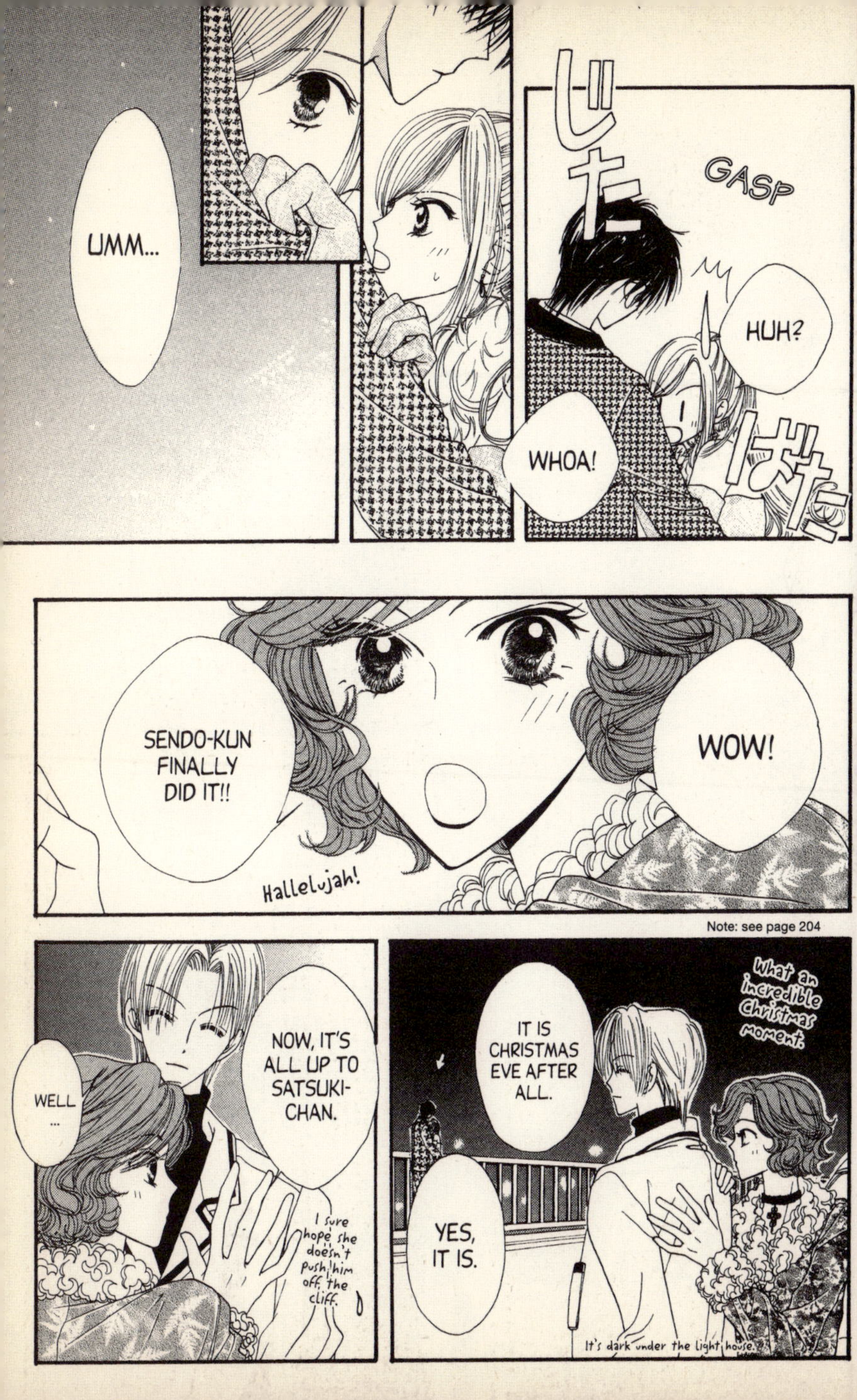
じた
GASP
HUH?
WHOA!
ばた
UMM...
WOW!
SENDO-KUN FINALLY DID IT!!
Hallelujah!
What an incredible Christmas moment.
IT IS CHRISTMAS EVE AFTER ALL.
YES, IT IS.
It's dark under the light house.
NOW, IT'S ALL UP TO SATSUKI-CHAN.
WELL ...
I sure hope she doesn't push him off the cliff.

Note: see page 204

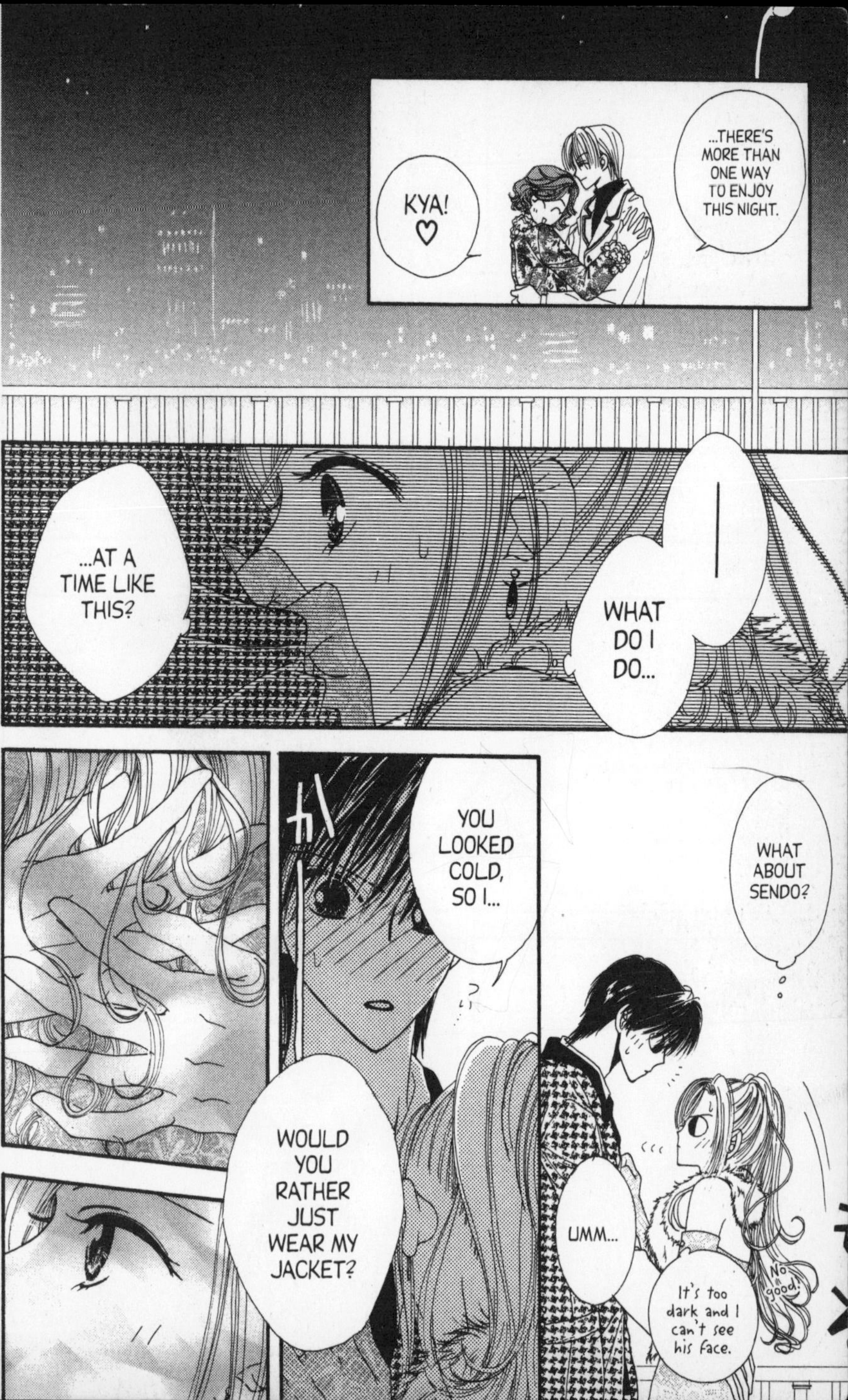

...THERE'S MORE THAN ONE WAY TO ENJOY THIS NIGHT.
KYA! ♡
WHAT DO I DO...
...AT A TIME LIKE THIS?
WHAT ABOUT SENDO?
No good!
UMM...
It's too dark and I can't see his face.
YOU LOOKED COLD, SO I...
WOULD YOU RATHER JUST WEAR MY JACKET?

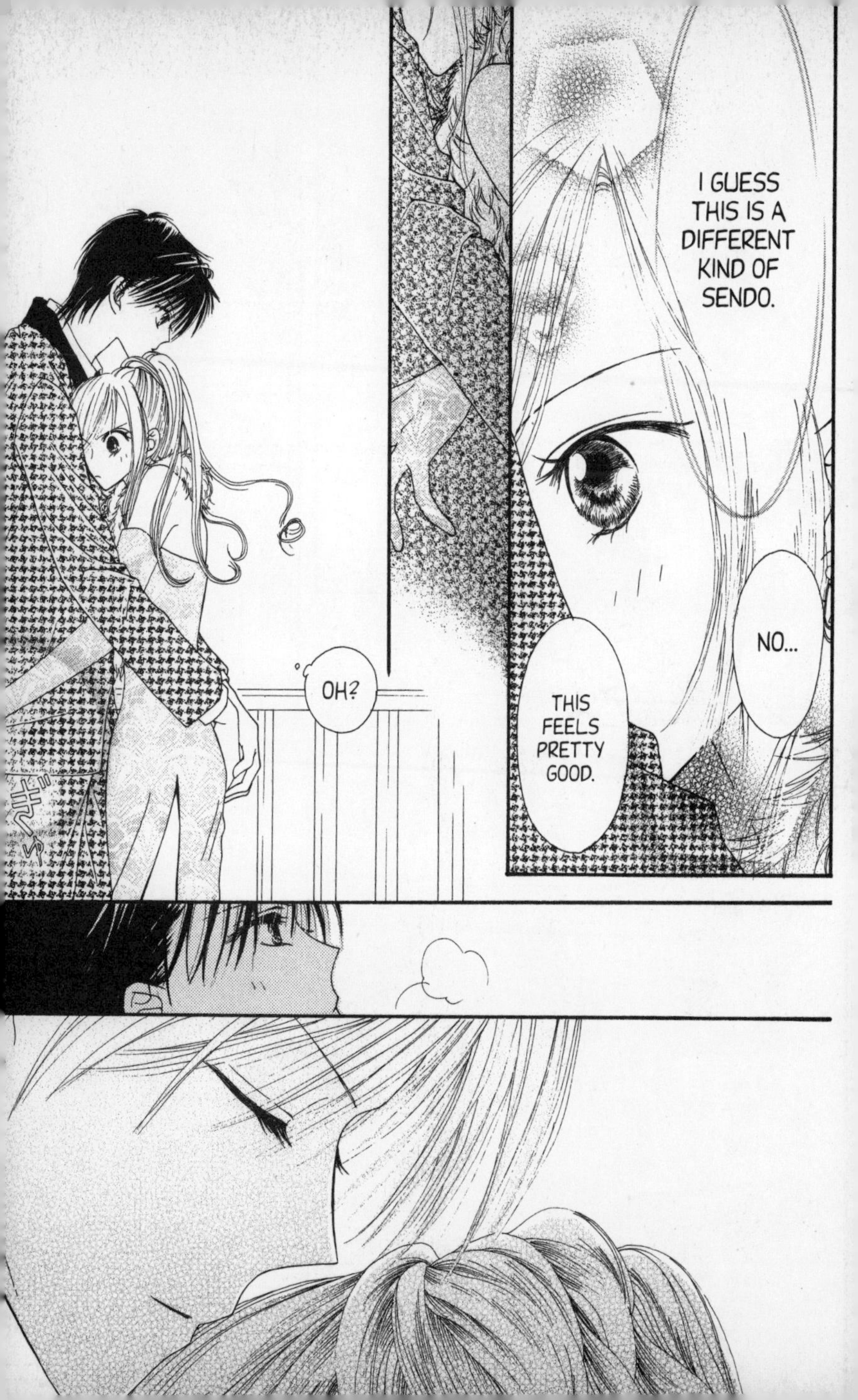
I GUESS THIS IS A DIFFERENT KIND OF SENDO.
NO...
THIS FEELS PRETTY GOOD.
OH?
ぎゅ

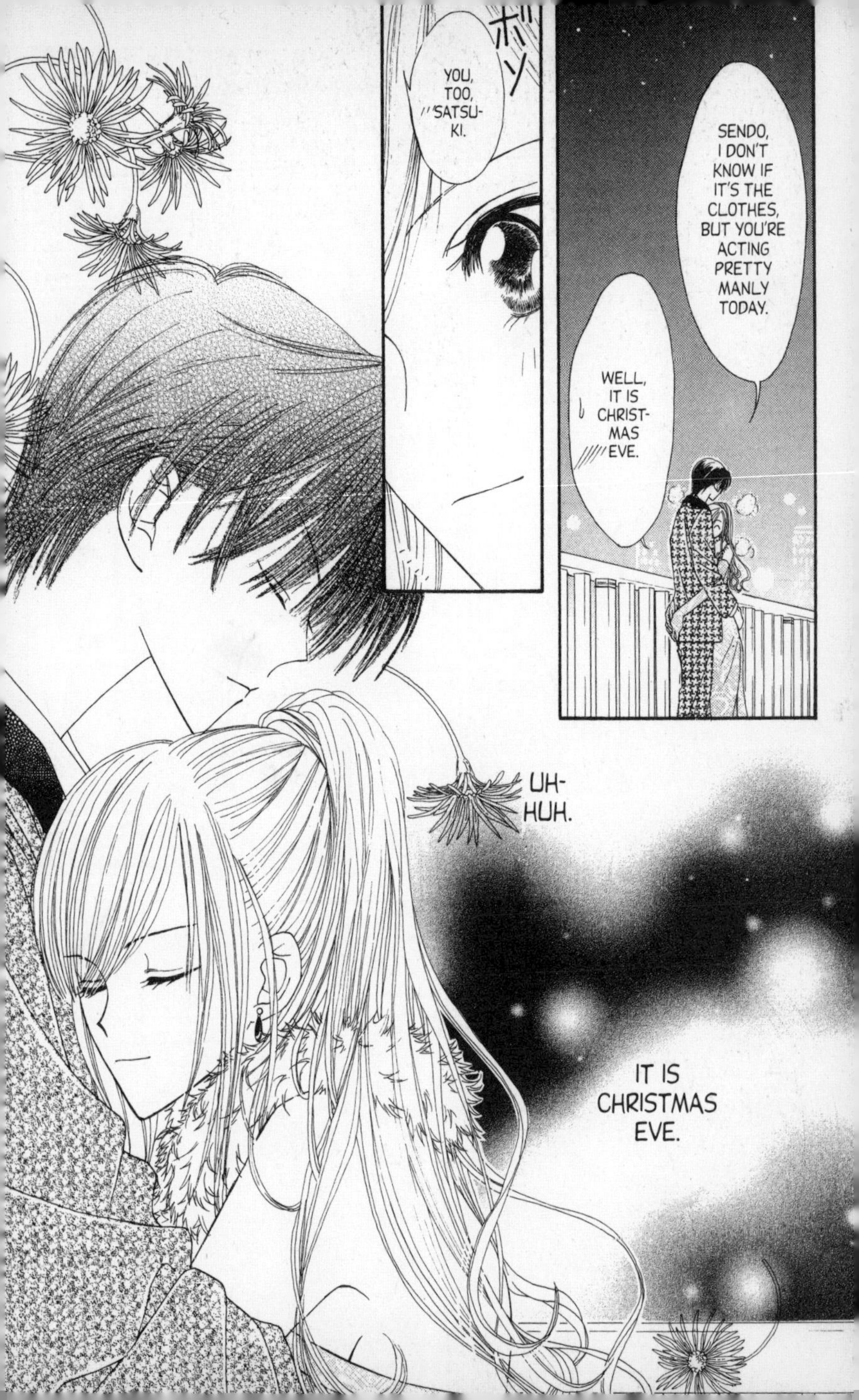
SENDO, I DON'T KNOW IF IT'S THE CLOTHES, BUT YOU'RE ACTING PRETTY MANLY TODAY.
WELL, IT IS CHRISTMAS EVE.
ボソ
YOU, TOO, SATSUKI.
UH-HUH.
IT IS CHRISTMAS EVE.

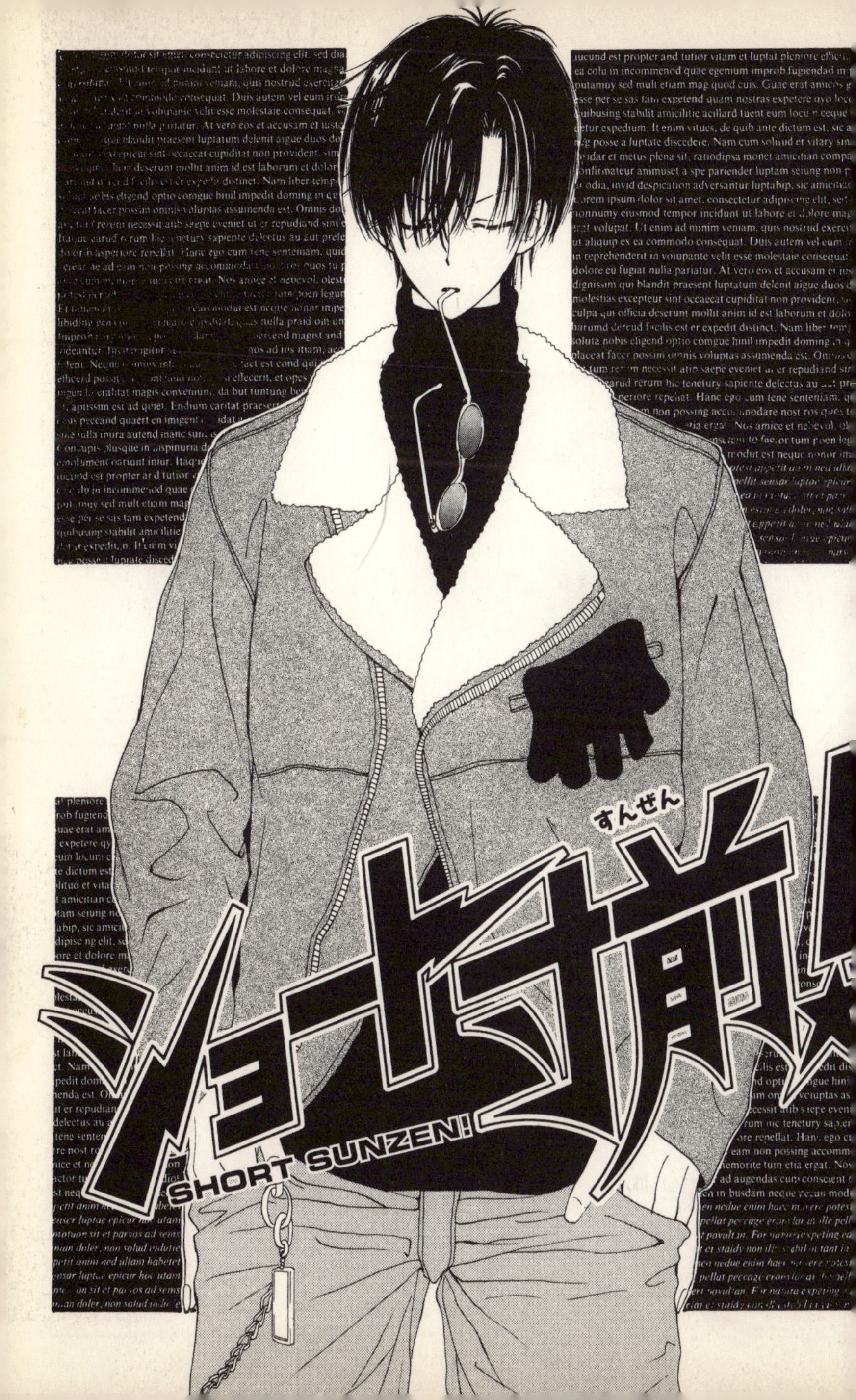
すんぜん
ショート寸前!
SHORT SUNZEN!

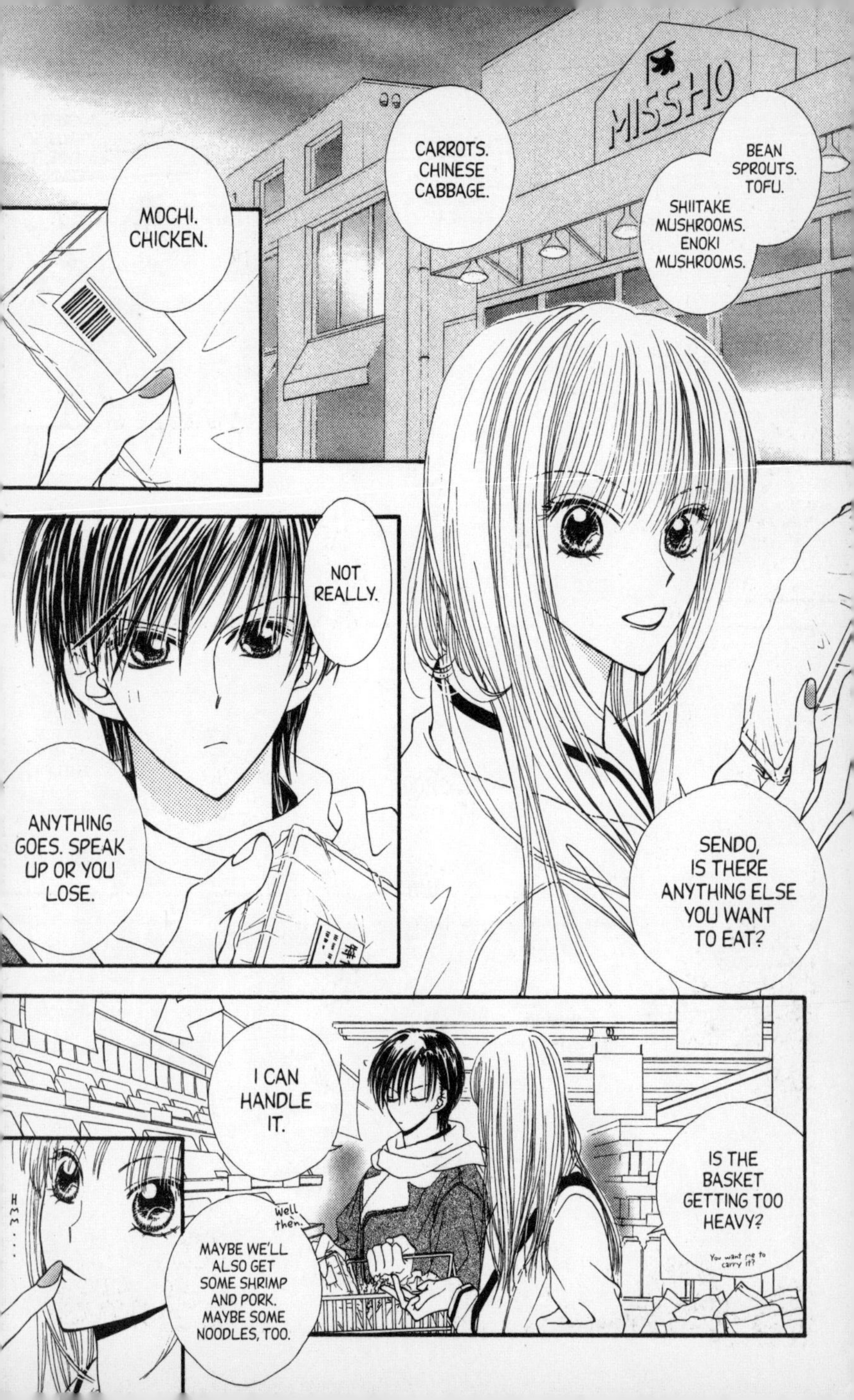
BEAN SPROUTS. TOFU.
SHIITAKE MUSHROOMS. ENOKI MUSHROOMS.
CARROTS. CHINESE CABBAGE.
MISSHO
MOCHI. CHICKEN.
SENDO, IS THERE ANYTHING ELSE YOU WANT TO EAT?
NOT REALLY.
ANYTHING GOES. SPEAK UP OR YOU LOSE.
IS THE BASKET GETTING TOO HEAVY?
You want me to carry it?
I CAN HANDLE IT.
Well then.
HMM...
MAYBE WE'LL ALSO GET SOME SHRIMP AND PORK. MAYBE SOME NOODLES, TOO.

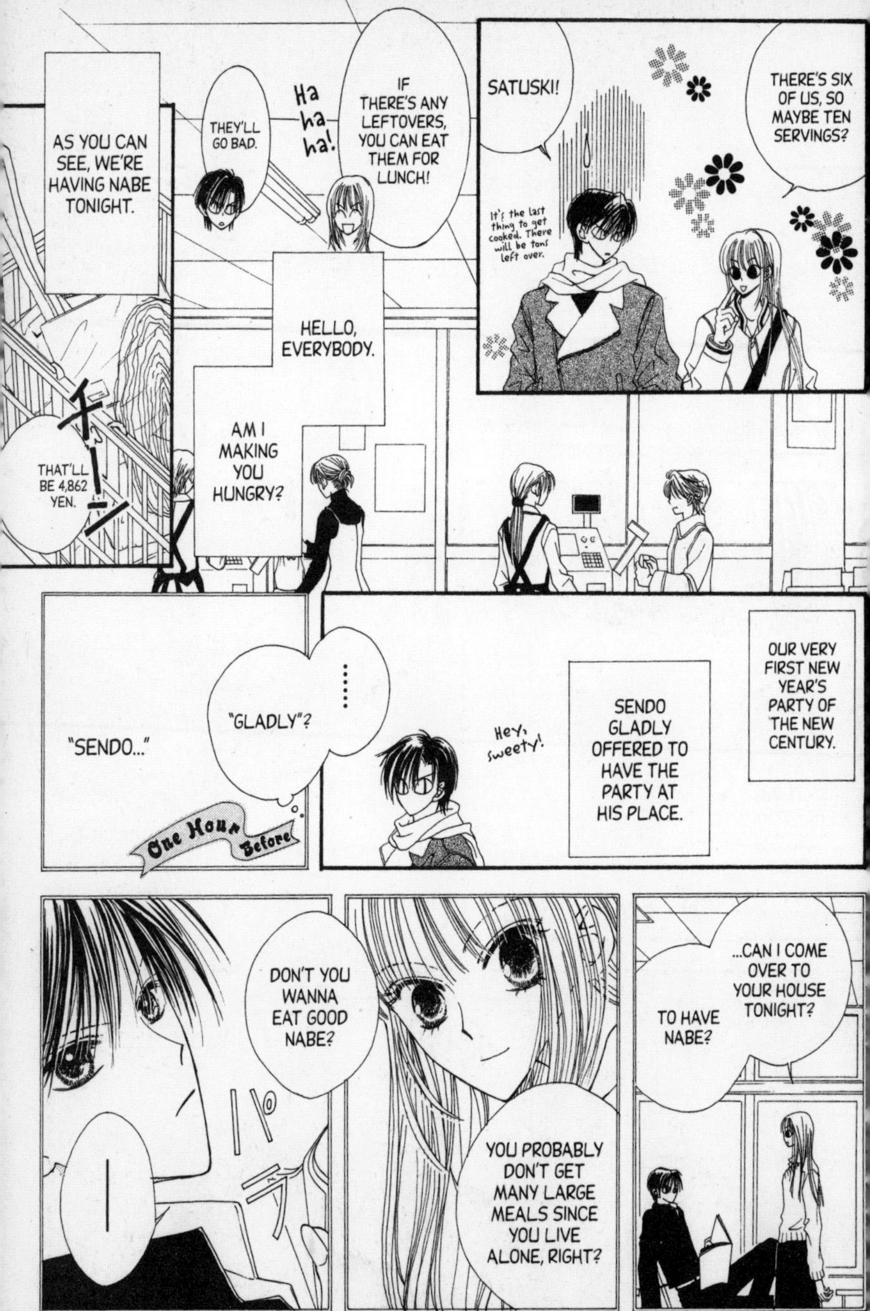
THERE'S SIX OF US, SO MAYBE TEN SERVINGS?
SATUSKI!
It's the last thing to get cooked. There will be tons left over.
IF THERE'S ANY LEFTOVERS, YOU CAN EAT THEM FOR LUNCH!
Ha ha ha!
THEY'LL GO BAD.
AS YOU CAN SEE, WE'RE HAVING NABE TONIGHT.
HELLO, EVERYBODY.
AM I MAKING YOU HUNGRY?
THAT'LL BE 4,862 YEN.
OUR VERY FIRST NEW YEAR'S PARTY OF THE NEW CENTURY.
SENDO GLADLY OFFERED TO HAVE THE PARTY AT HIS PLACE.
Hey, sweety!
......
"GLADLY"?
"SENDO..."
One Hour Before
...CAN I COME OVER TO YOUR HOUSE TONIGHT?
TO HAVE NABE?
DON'T YOU WANNA EAT GOOD NABE?
YOU PROBABLY DON'T GET MANY LARGE MEALS SINCE YOU LIVE ALONE, RIGHT?

Note: see page 204

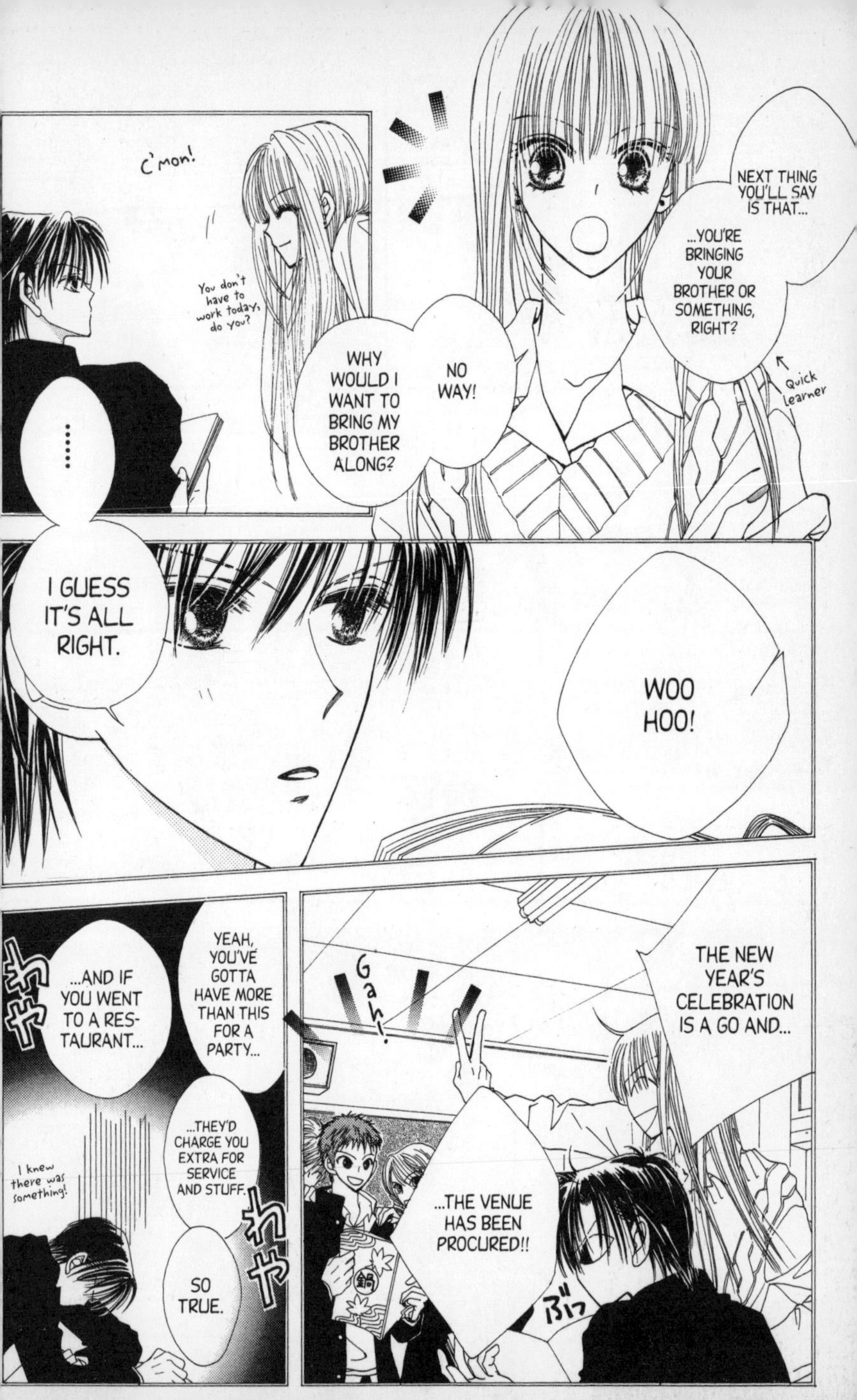
NEXT THING YOU'LL SAY IS THAT...
...YOU'RE BRINGING YOUR BROTHER OR SOMETHING, RIGHT?
Quick learner
NO WAY!
WHY WOULD I WANT TO BRING MY BROTHER ALONG?
C'mon!
You don't have to work today, do you?
......
I GUESS IT'S ALL RIGHT.
WOO HOO!
THE NEW YEAR'S CELEBRATION IS A GO AND...
Gah!
...THE VENUE HAS BEEN PROCURED!!
ぶっ
YEAH, YOU'VE GOTTA HAVE MORE THAN THIS FOR A PARTY...
...AND IF YOU WENT TO A RES-TAURANT...
わや
...THEY'D CHARGE YOU EXTRA FOR SERVICE AND STUFF.
わや
SO TRUE.
I knew there was something!

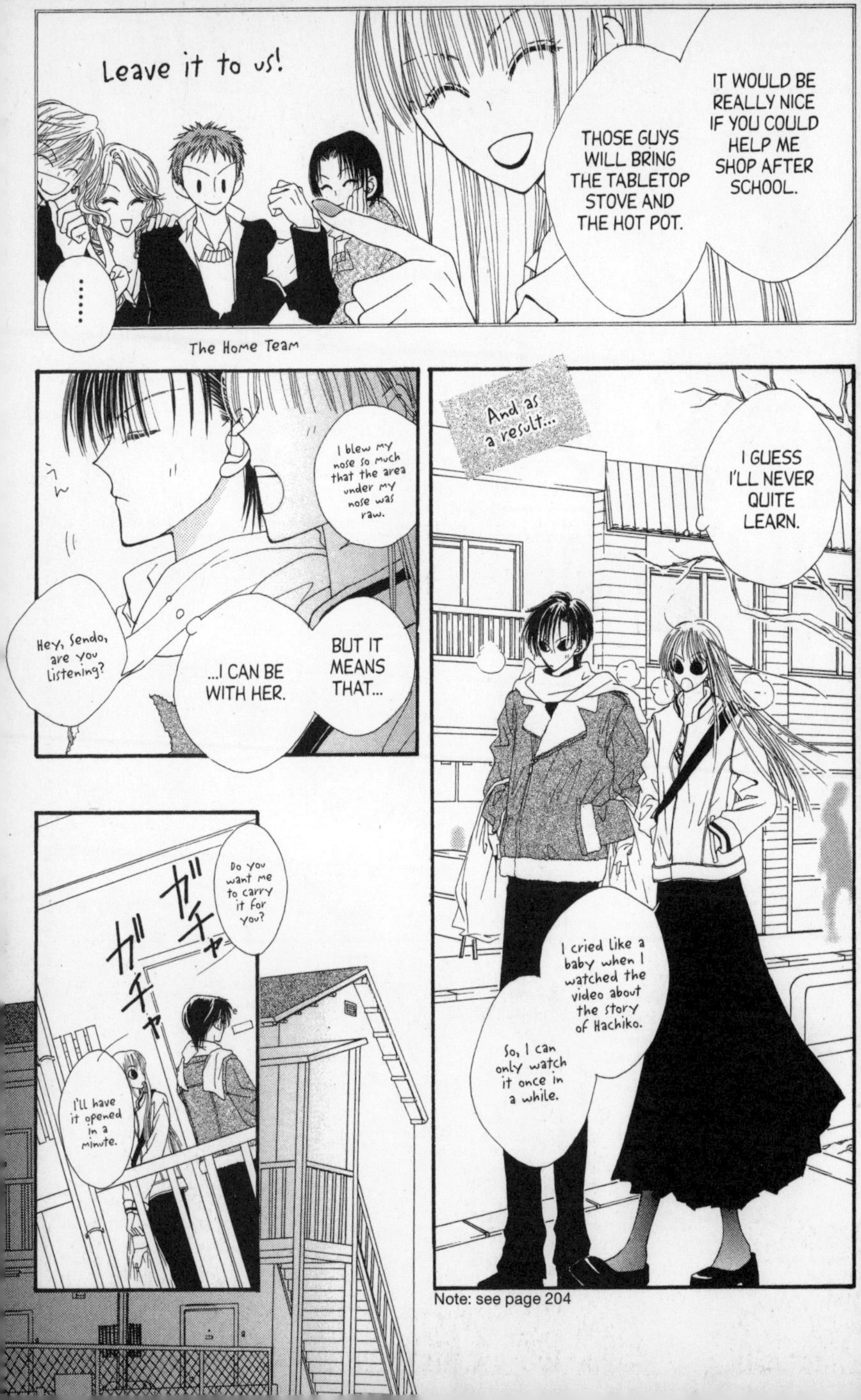
IT WOULD BE REALLY NICE IF YOU COULD HELP ME SHOP AFTER SCHOOL.
THOSE GUYS WILL BRING THE TABLETOP STOVE AND THE HOT POT.
Leave it to us!
......
The Home Team
And as a result...
I GUESS I'LL NEVER QUITE LEARN.
I cried like a baby when I watched the video about the story of Hachiko.
So, I can only watch it once in a while.
I blew my nose so much that the area under my nose was raw.
BUT IT MEANS THAT...
...I CAN BE WITH HER.
Hey, Sendo, are you listening?
Do you want me to carry it for you?
ガチャ
ガチャ
I'll have it opened in a minute.

Note: see page 204

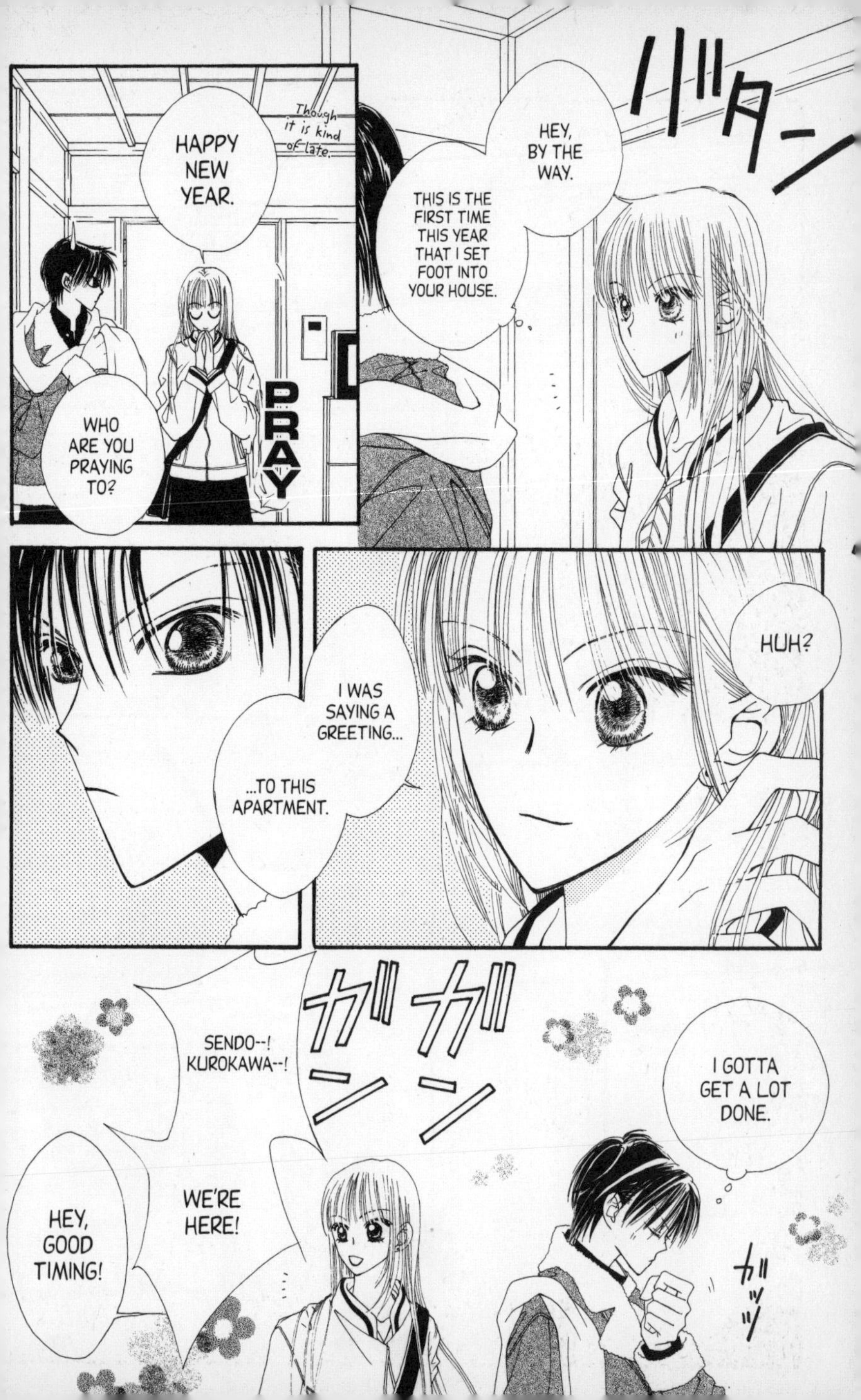
バターン
HEY, BY THE WAY.
THIS IS THE FIRST TIME THIS YEAR THAT I SET FOOT INTO YOUR HOUSE.
Though it is kind of late.
HAPPY NEW YEAR.
PRAY
WHO ARE YOU PRAYING TO?
HUH?
I WAS SAYING A GREETING...
...TO THIS APARTMENT.
I GOTTA GET A LOT DONE.
ガッツ
ガーン ガーン
SENDO--! KUROKAWA--!
WE'RE HERE!
HEY, GOOD TIMING!

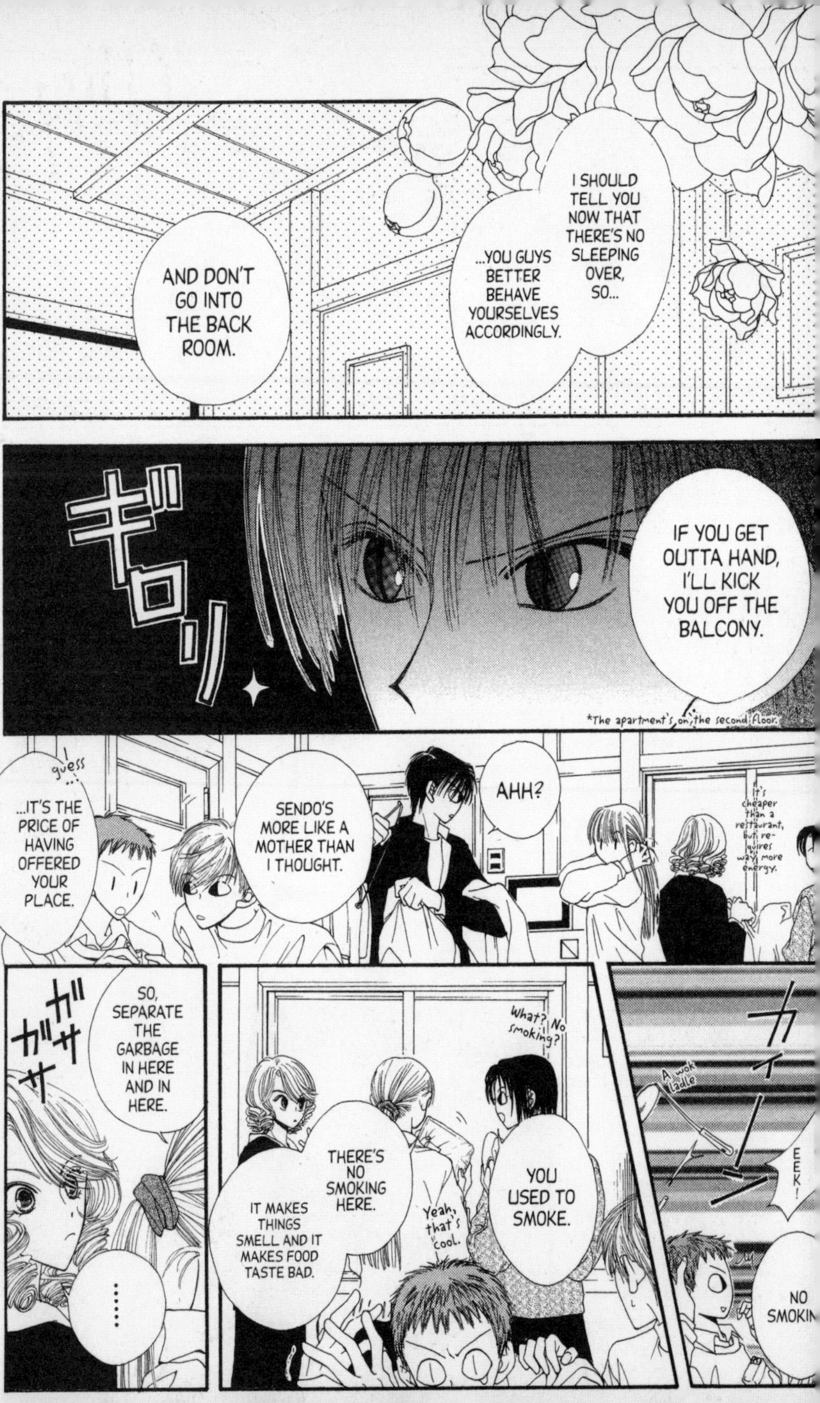
I SHOULD TELL YOU NOW THAT THERE'S NO SLEEPING OVER, SO...
...YOU GUYS BETTER BEHAVE YOURSELVES ACCORDINGLY.
AND DON'T GO INTO THE BACK ROOM.
IF YOU GET OUTTA HAND, I'LL KICK YOU OFF THE BALCONY.
ギロリ
*The apartment's on the second floor.
It's cheaper than a restaurant, but requires way more energy.
AHH?
SENDO'S MORE LIKE A MOTHER THAN I THOUGHT.
I guess...
...IT'S THE PRICE OF HAVING OFFERED YOUR PLACE.
カイーン
A wok ladle
EEK!
NO SMOKIN
What?! No smoking?!
YOU USED TO SMOKE.
Yeah, that's cool.
THERE'S NO SMOKING HERE.
IT MAKES THINGS SMELL AND IT MAKES FOOD TASTE BAD.
ガサガサ
SO, SEPARATE THE GARBAGE IN HERE AND IN HERE.
......

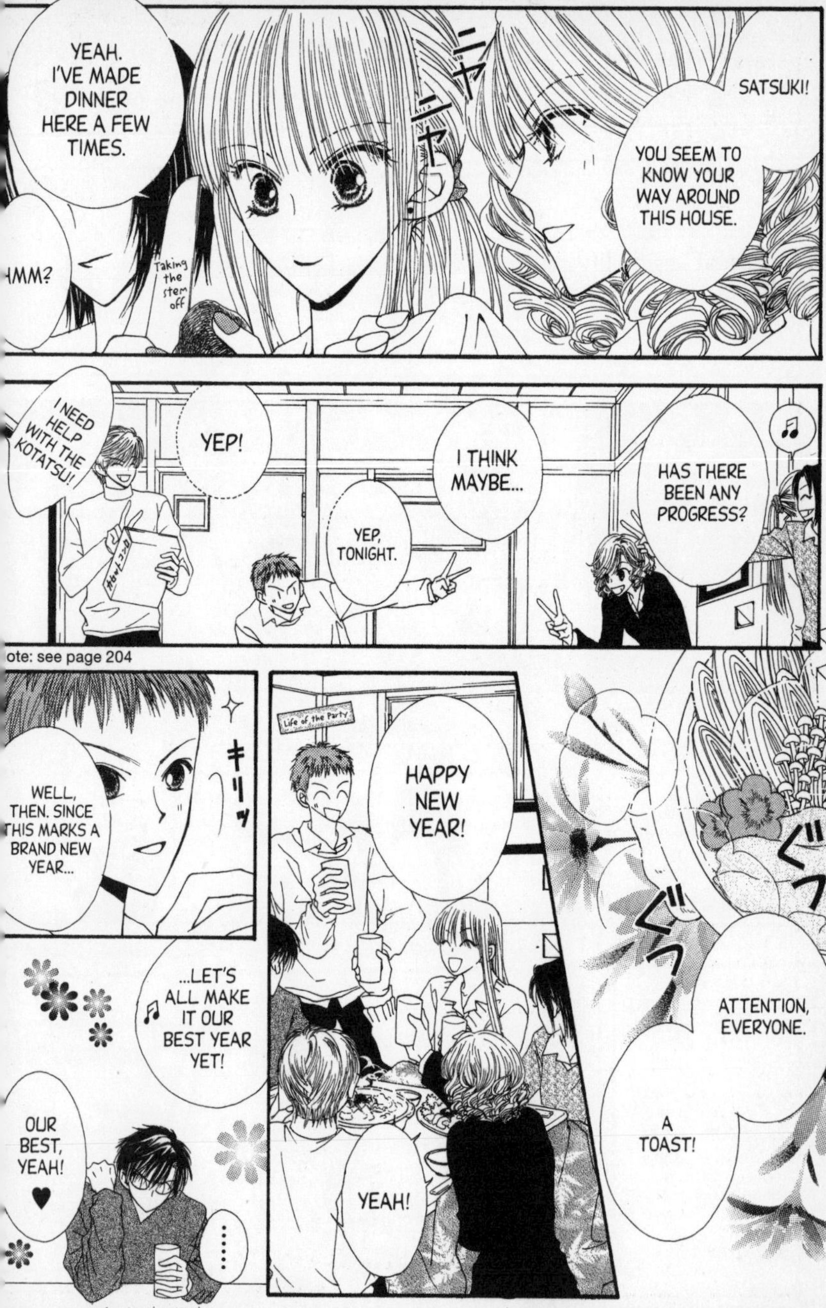
SATSUKI!
YOU SEEM TO KNOW YOUR WAY AROUND THIS HOUSE.
HMM?
Taking the stem off
YEAH. I'VE MADE DINNER HERE A FEW TIMES.
HAS THERE BEEN ANY PROGRESS?
I THINK MAYBE...
YEP, TONIGHT.
YEP!
I NEED HELP WITH THE KOTATSU!
ote: see page 204
ATTENTION, EVERYONE.
A TOAST!
WELL, THEN. SINCE THIS MARKS A BRAND NEW YEAR...
...LET'S ALL MAKE IT OUR BEST YEAR YET!
Life of the Party
HAPPY NEW YEAR!
YEAH!
OUR BEST, YEAH!
......
So not paying attention.

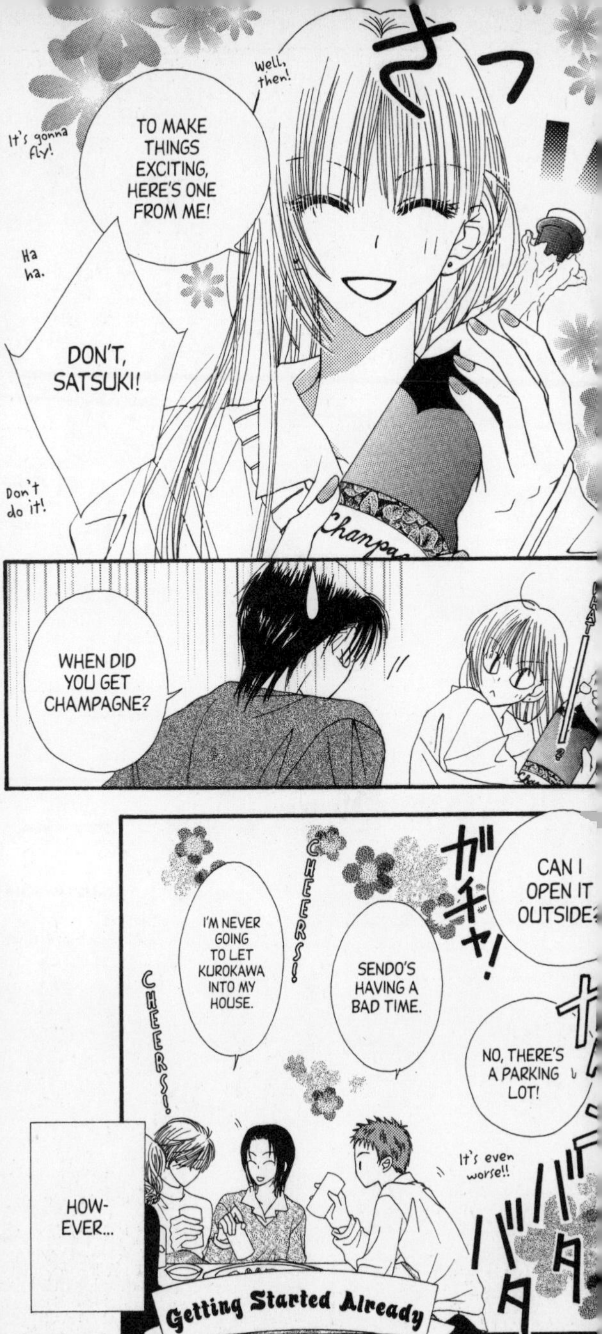

さっ
Well, then!
TO MAKE THINGS EXCITING, HERE'S ONE FROM ME!
It's gonna fly!
Ha ha.
DON'T, SATSUKI!
Don't do it!
WHEN DID YOU GET CHAMPAGNE?
ガチャ!
CAN I OPEN IT OUTSIDE?
NO, THERE'S A PARKING LOT!
バタバタ
It's even worse!!
SENDO'S HAVING A BAD TIME.
CHEERS!
I'M NEVER GOING TO LET KUROKAWA INTO MY HOUSE.
CHEERS!
HOW-EVER...
Getting Started Already

WARDROBE

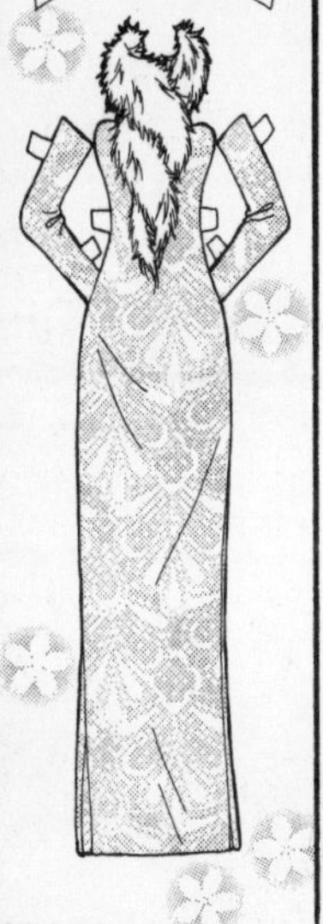

On Christmas Eve, this dress would be too cold!

I remember being out with a friend on Christmas Eve some years ago, and being afraid of static electricity! No matter what we touched--like walls, fingers, our faces--we would get a shock. When I complained that, "I wouldn't even be able to kiss a boyfriend on Christmas Eve like this," my friend answered, "You shouldn't say things you don't mean."

Satsuki and Sendo were lucky. They didn't get electrocuted! (Just you wait!)

On Christmas Eve '00, I had cake with a friend at Abeno (where there isn't a crowd), had dinner and went out drinking. Everything was delicious. ♥

Ninety-five percent of customers in the restaurants were couples. I didn't care. I had fun anyway!

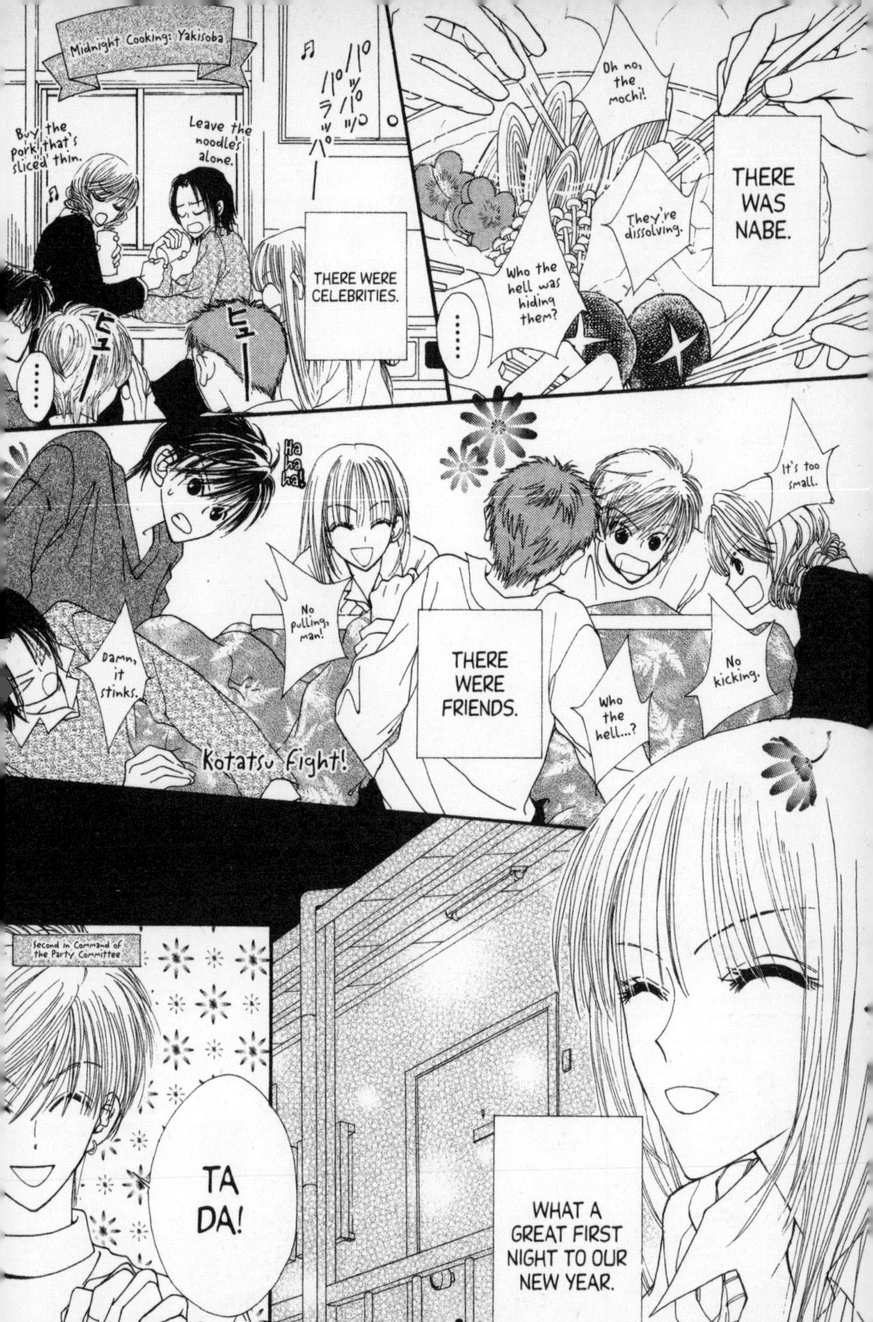
Oh no, the mochi!
THERE WAS NABE.
They're dissolving.
Who the hell was hiding them?
......
Midnight Cooking: Yakisoba
Leave the noodles alone.
Buy the pork that's sliced thin.
THERE WERE CELEBRITIES.
ヒュー
ヒュー
......
It's too small.
No kicking.
Who the hell...?
THERE WERE FRIENDS.
No pulling, man!
Ha ha ha!
Damn, it stinks.
Kotatsu fight!
WHAT A GREAT FIRST NIGHT TO OUR NEW YEAR.
Second in Command of the Party Committee
TA DA!

Note: see page 204

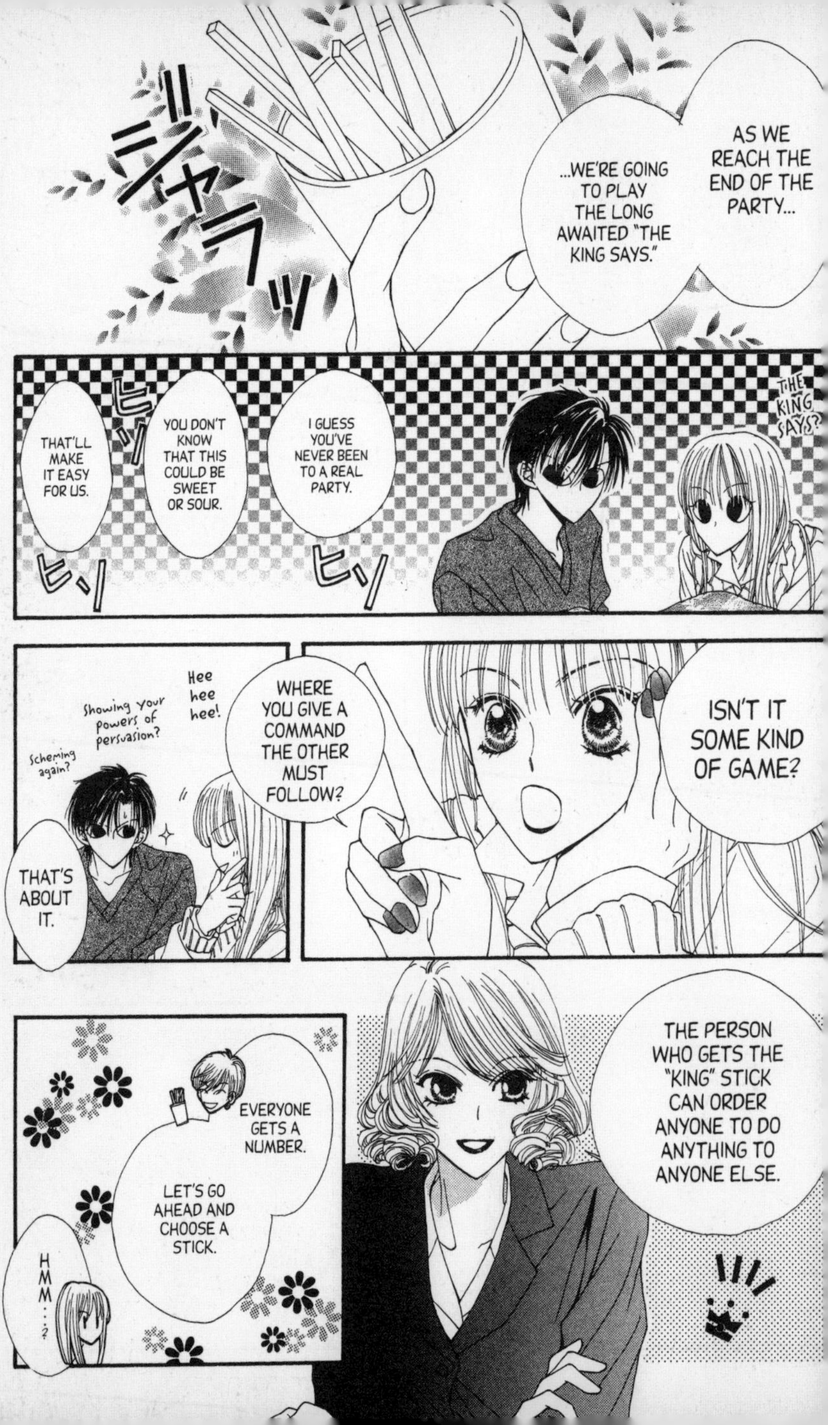
AS WE REACH THE END OF THE PARTY...
...WE'RE GOING TO PLAY THE LONG AWAITED "THE KING SAYS."
ジャラッ
THE KING SAYS?
I GUESS YOU'VE NEVER BEEN TO A REAL PARTY.
ヒソ
YOU DON'T KNOW THAT THIS COULD BE SWEET OR SOUR.
ヒソ
THAT'LL MAKE IT EASY FOR US.
ヒソ
ISN'T IT SOME KIND OF GAME?
WHERE YOU GIVE A COMMAND THE OTHER MUST FOLLOW?
Hee hee hee!
Showing your powers of persuasion?
Scheming again?
THAT'S ABOUT IT.
THE PERSON WHO GETS THE "KING" STICK CAN ORDER ANYONE TO DO ANYTHING TO ANYONE ELSE.
EVERYONE GETS A NUMBER.
LET'S GO AHEAD AND CHOOSE A STICK.
HMM...?

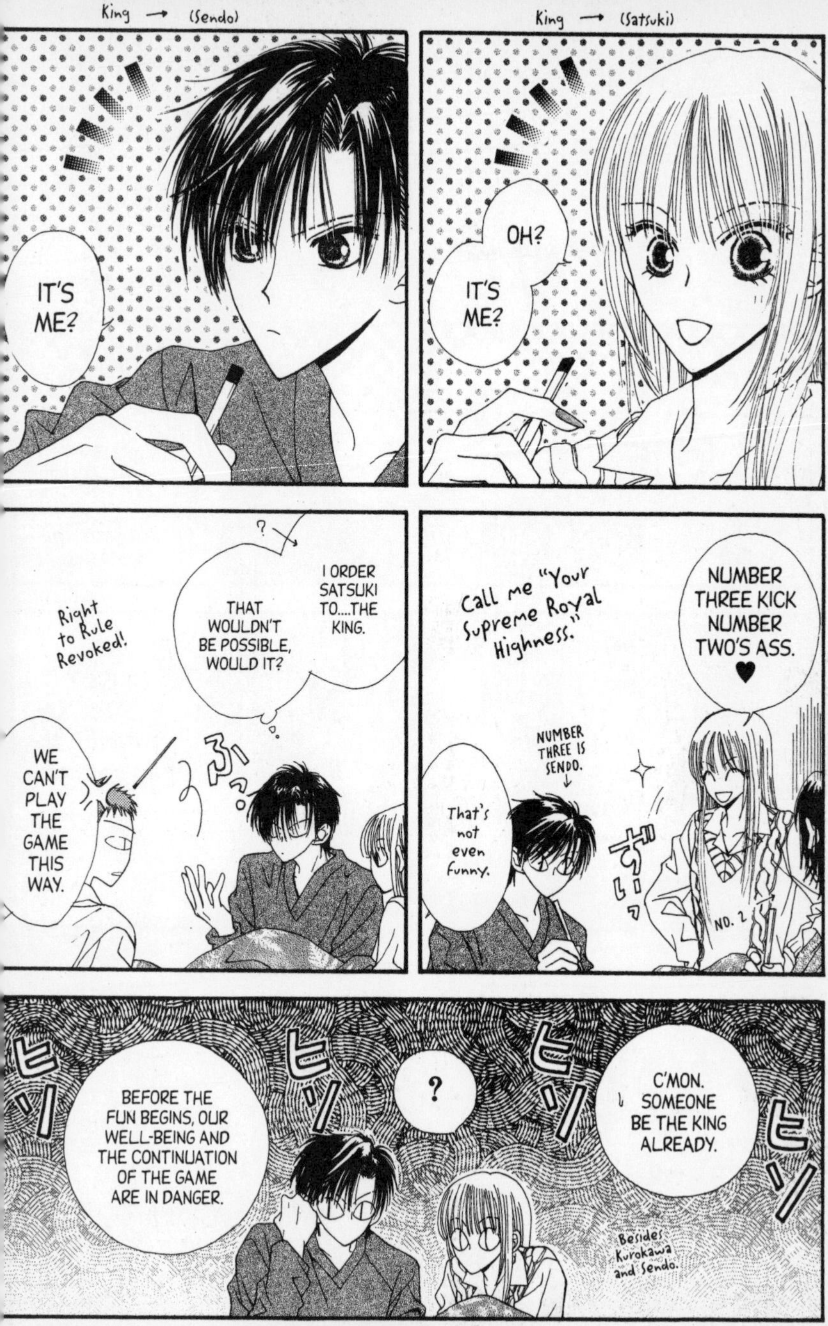
King → (Satsuki)
OH?
IT'S ME?
King → (Sendo)
IT'S ME?
NUMBER THREE KICK NUMBER TWO'S ASS. ♥
Call me "Your Supreme Royal Highness."
NUMBER THREE IS SENDO.
That's not even funny.
NO. 2
I ORDER SATSUKI TO....THE KING.
THAT WOULDN'T BE POSSIBLE, WOULD IT?
Right to Rule Revoked!
ふっ
WE CAN'T PLAY THE GAME THIS WAY.
ヒソ
C'MON. SOMEONE BE THE KING ALREADY.
Besides Kurokawa and Sendo.
ヒソ
?
ヒソ
BEFORE THE FUN BEGINS, OUR WELL-BEING AND THE CONTINUATION OF THE GAME ARE IN DANGER.
ヒソ

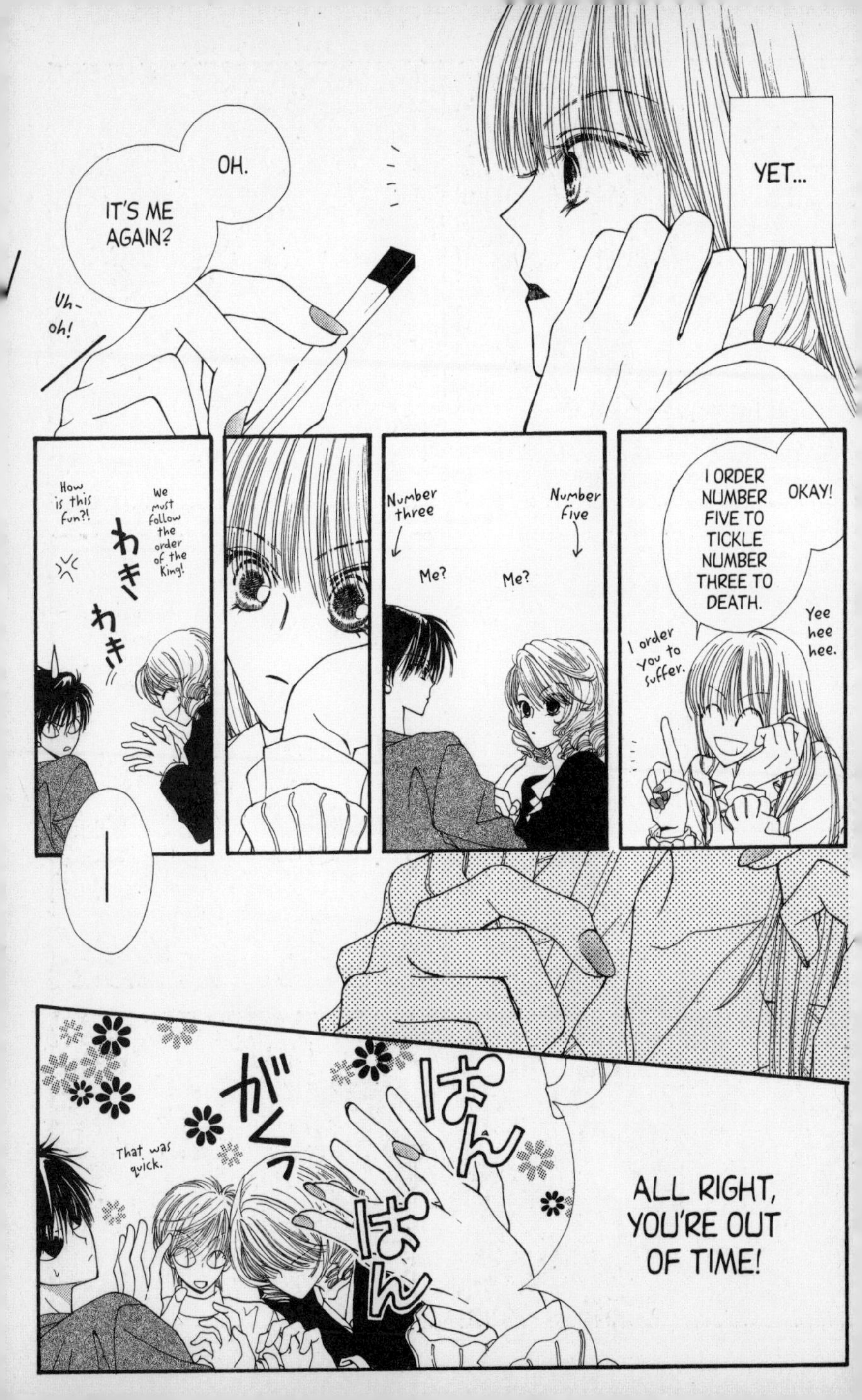

YET...
OH.
IT'S ME AGAIN?
Uh-oh!
OKAY!
I ORDER NUMBER FIVE TO TICKLE NUMBER THREE TO DEATH.
Yee hee hee.
I order you to suffer.
Number five
Me?
Number three
Me?
We must follow the order of the King!
わき
わき
How is this fun?!
ー
ALL RIGHT, YOU'RE OUT OF TIME!
ぱん
ぱん
がくっ
That was quick.

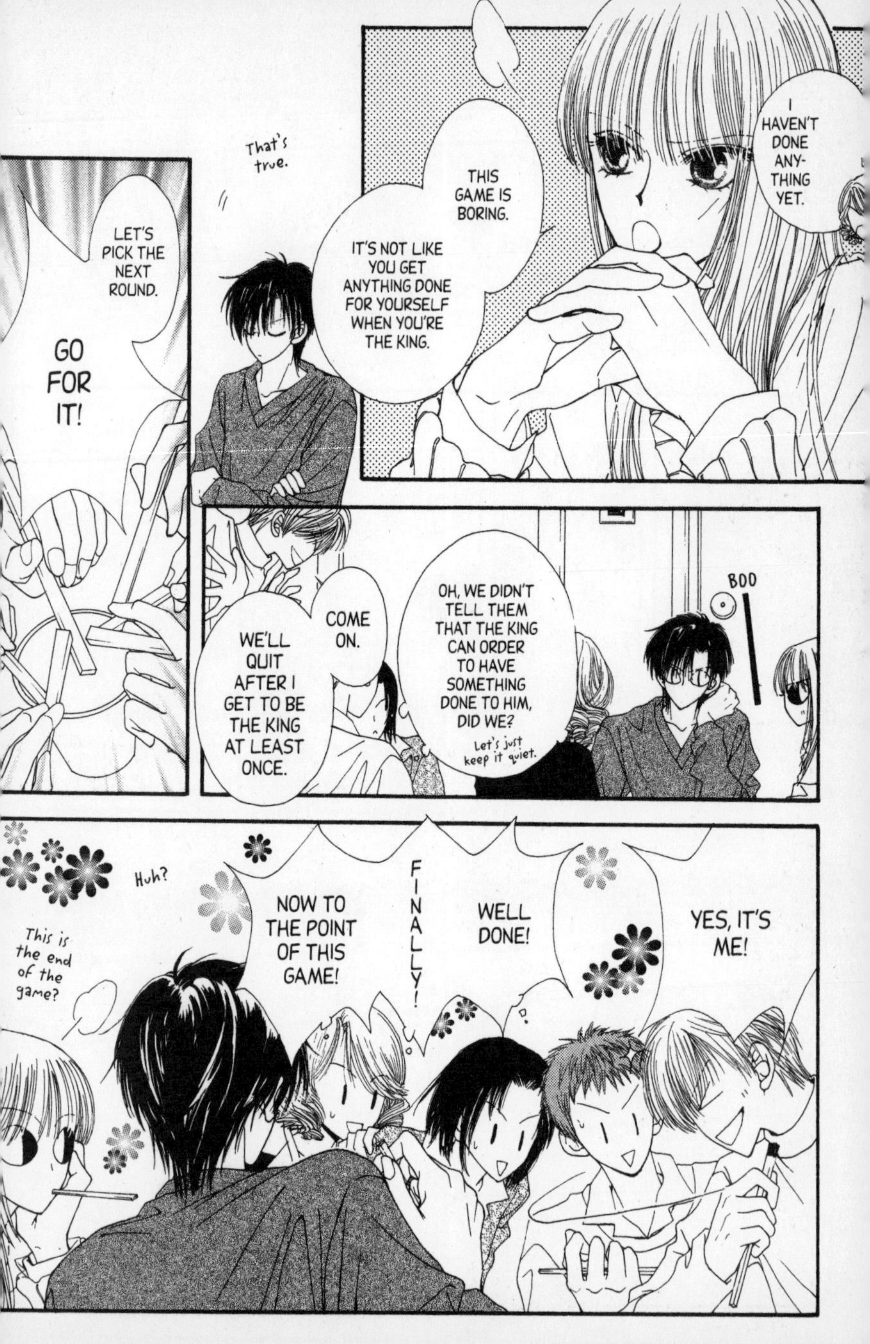
I HAVEN'T DONE ANYTHING YET.
THIS GAME IS BORING.
IT'S NOT LIKE YOU GET ANYTHING DONE FOR YOURSELF WHEN YOU'RE THE KING.
That's true.
BOO
OH, WE DIDN'T TELL THEM THAT THE KING CAN ORDER TO HAVE SOMETHING DONE TO HIM, DID WE?
Let's just keep it quiet.
COME ON.
WE'LL QUIT AFTER I GET TO BE THE KING AT LEAST ONCE.
LET'S PICK THE NEXT ROUND.
GO FOR IT!
YES, IT'S ME!
WELL DONE!
FINALLY!
NOW TO THE POINT OF THIS GAME!
Huh?
This is the end of the game?

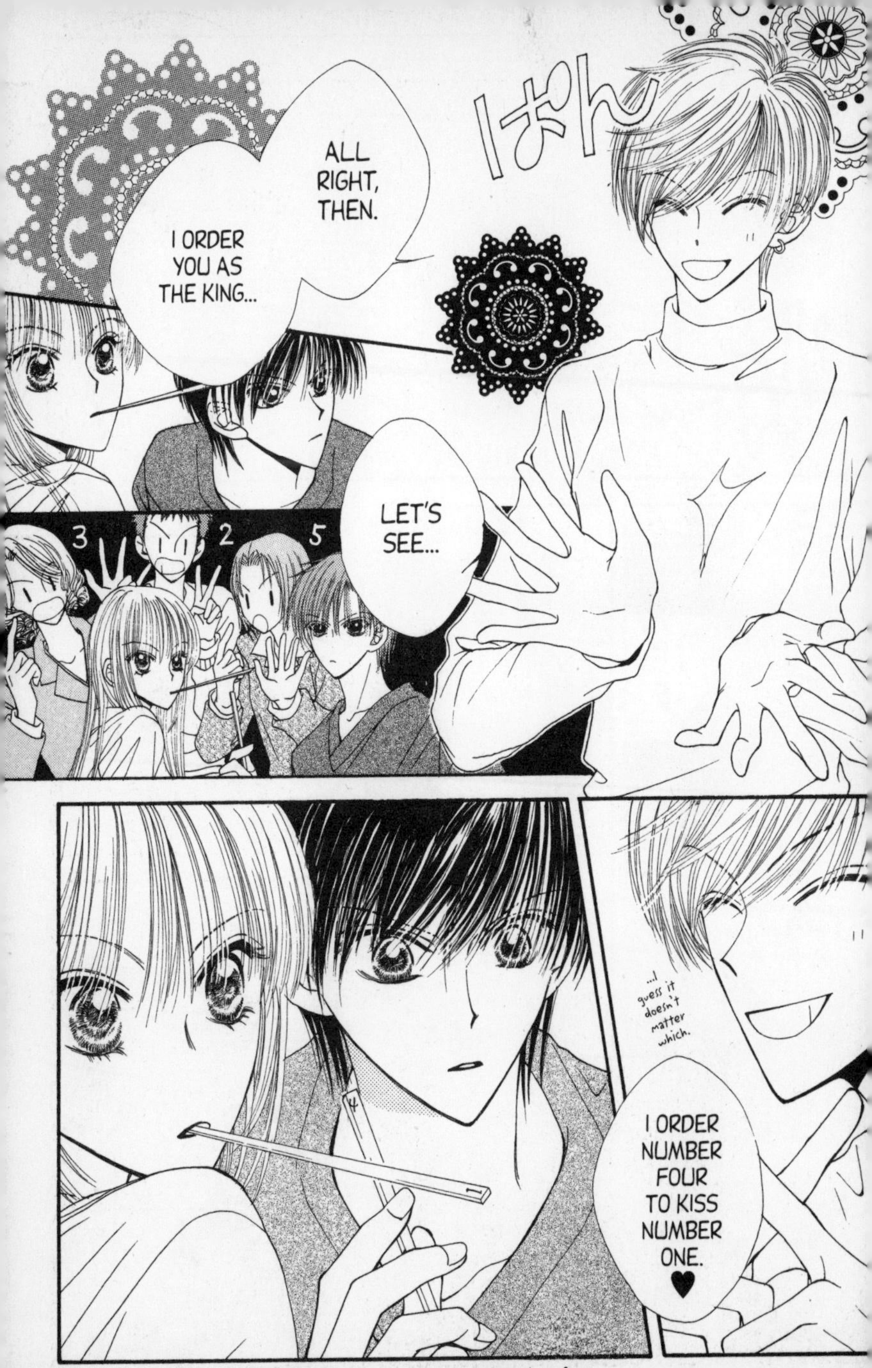
ぱん
ALL RIGHT, THEN.
I ORDER YOU AS THE KING...
LET'S SEE...
5
2
3
...I guess it doesn't matter which.
I ORDER NUMBER FOUR TO KISS NUMBER ONE. ♥
4

Number one ↗ ↖ Number four

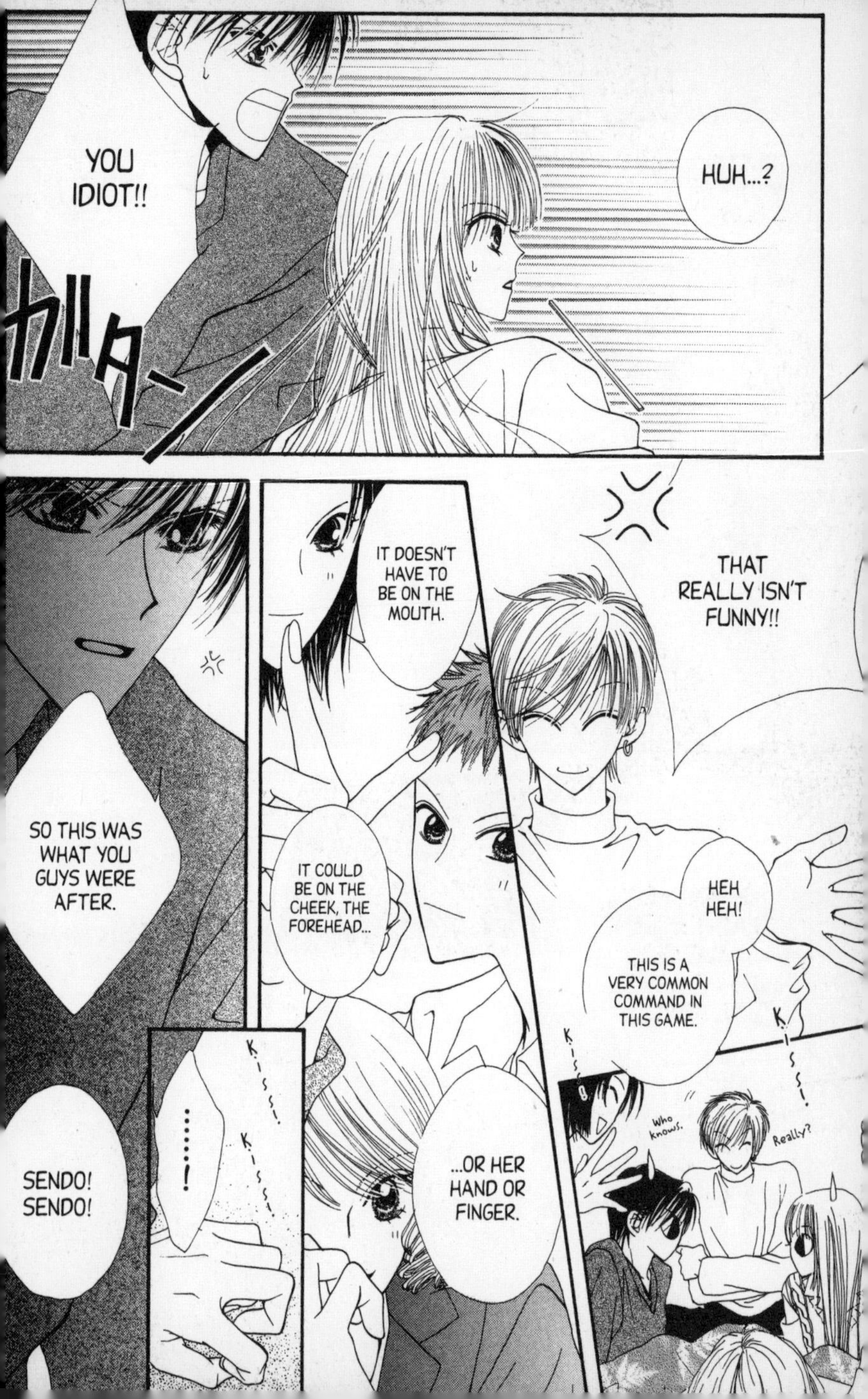
HUH...?
YOU IDIOT!!
THAT REALLY ISN'T FUNNY!!
HEH HEH!
THIS IS A VERY COMMON COMMAND IN THIS GAME.
IT DOESN'T HAVE TO BE ON THE MOUTH.
IT COULD BE ON THE CHEEK, THE FOREHEAD...
...OR HER HAND OR FINGER.
KISS!
KISS!
Who knows.
Really?
SO THIS WAS WHAT YOU GUYS WERE AFTER.
KISS!
KISS!
......!
SENDO! SENDO!

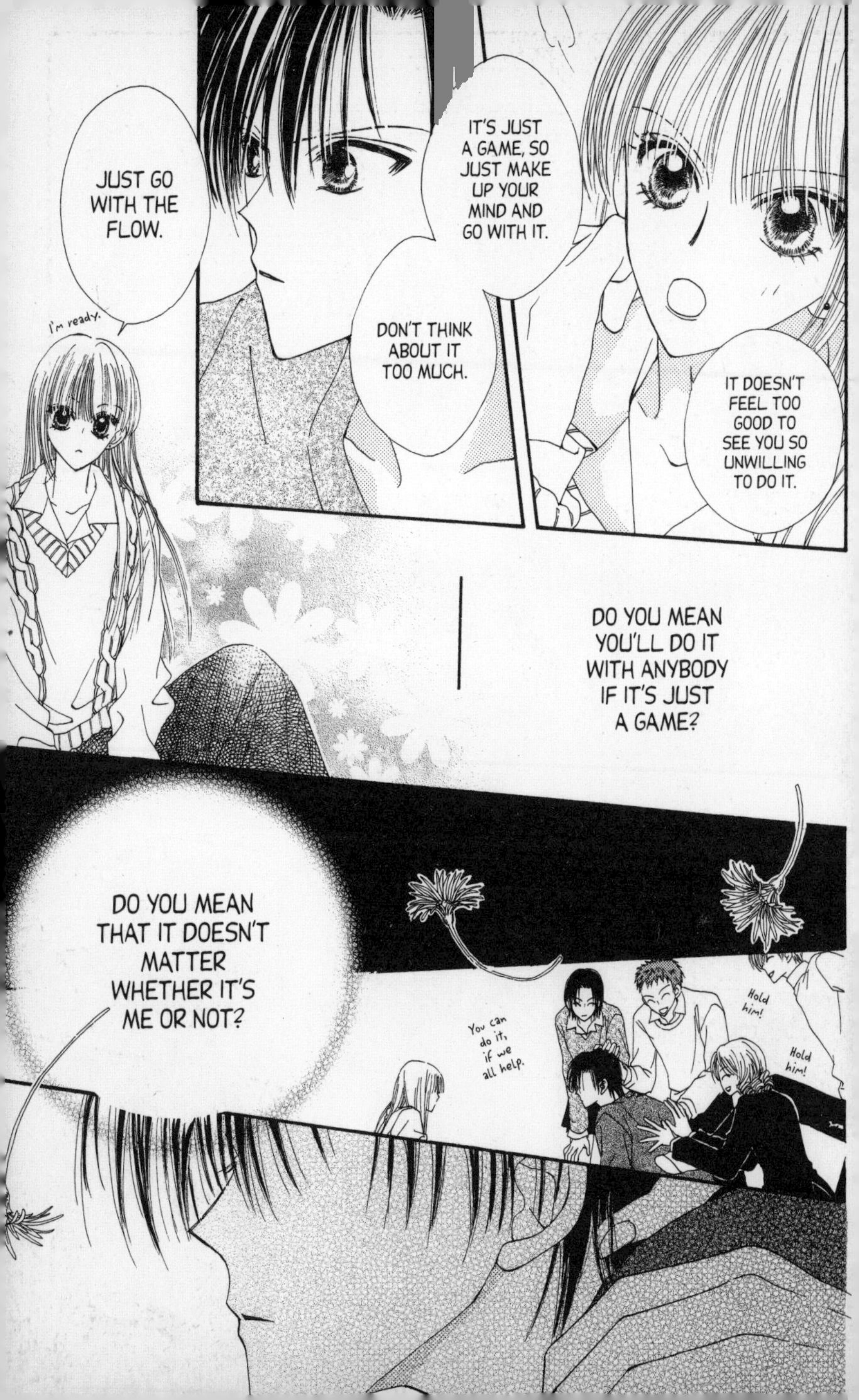

IT DOESN'T FEEL TOO GOOD TO SEE YOU SO UNWILLING TO DO IT.
IT'S JUST A GAME, SO JUST MAKE UP YOUR MIND AND GO WITH IT.
DON'T THINK ABOUT IT TOO MUCH.
JUST GO WITH THE FLOW.
I'm ready.
DO YOU MEAN YOU'LL DO IT WITH ANYBODY IF IT'S JUST A GAME?
Hold him!
Hold him!
You can do it, if we all help.
DO YOU MEAN THAT IT DOESN'T MATTER WHETHER IT'S ME OR NOT?

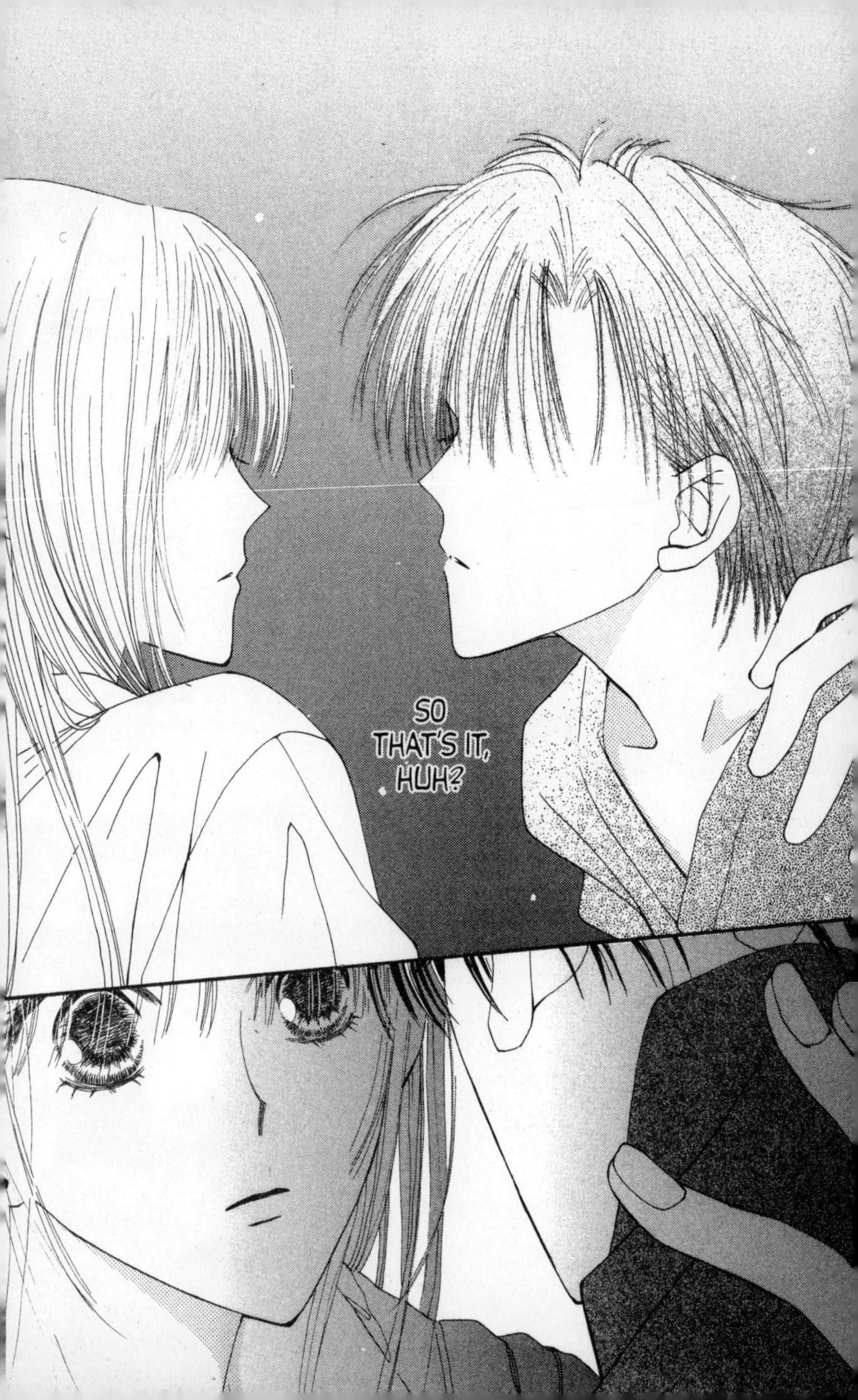
SO THAT'S IT, HUH?

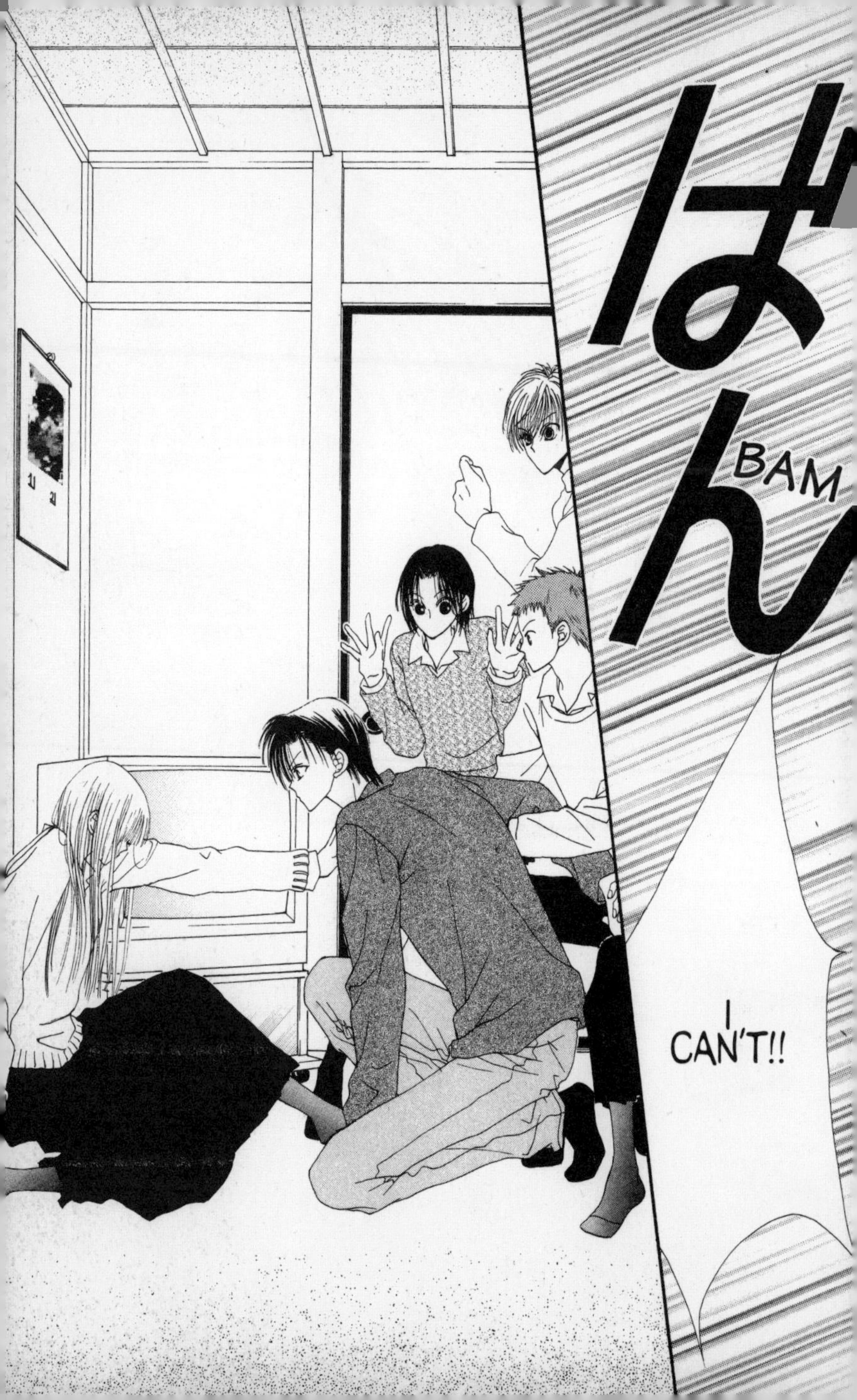
ばん
BAM
I CAN'T!!

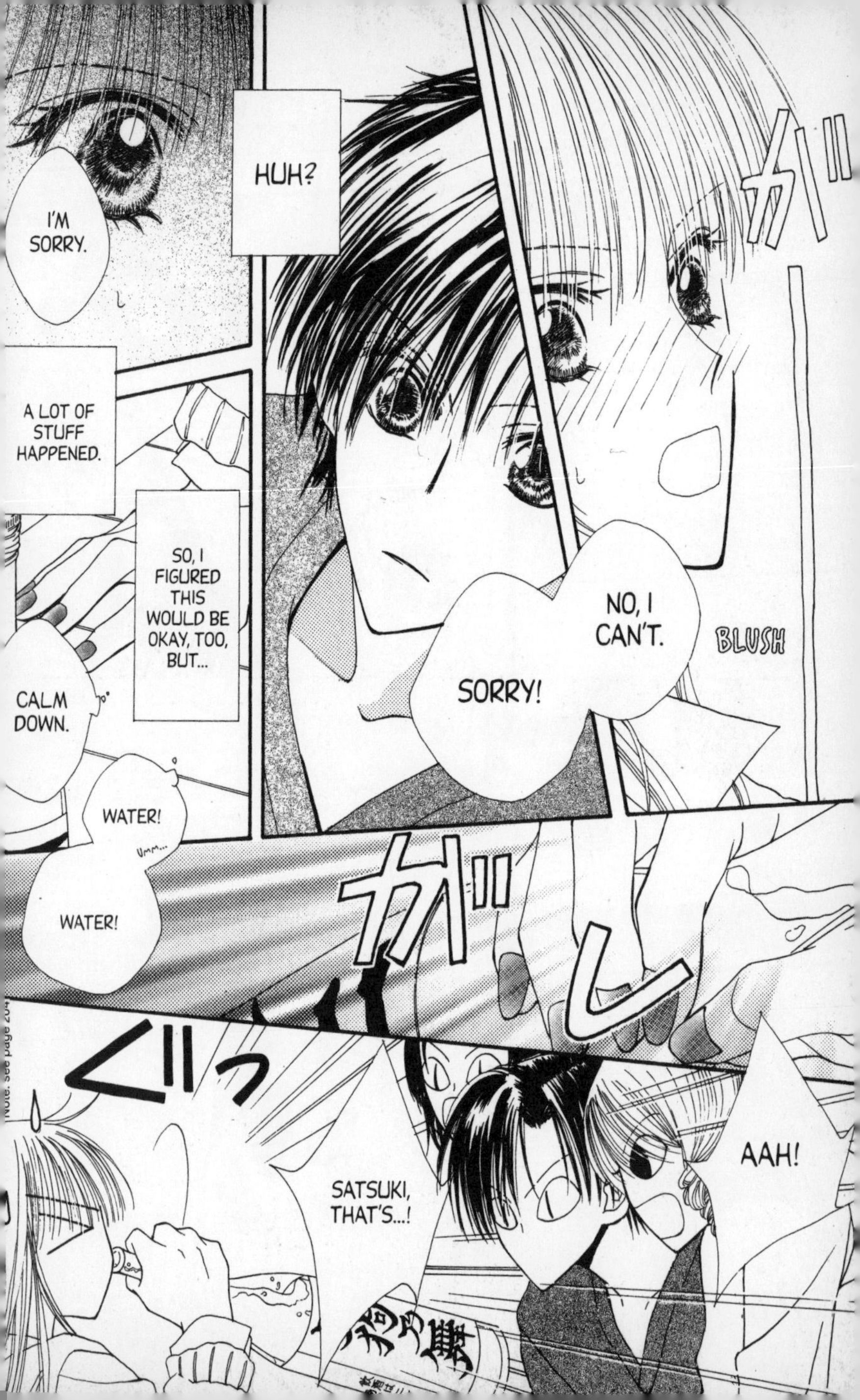
ガッ
NO, I CAN'T.
SORRY!
BLUSH
HUH?
I'M SORRY.
A LOT OF STUFF HAPPENED.
SO, I FIGURED THIS WOULD BE OKAY, TOO, BUT...
CALM DOWN.
WATER!
UMM...
WATER!
ガシ
AAH!
SATSUKI, THAT'S...!
ぐいっ

Note: see page 204

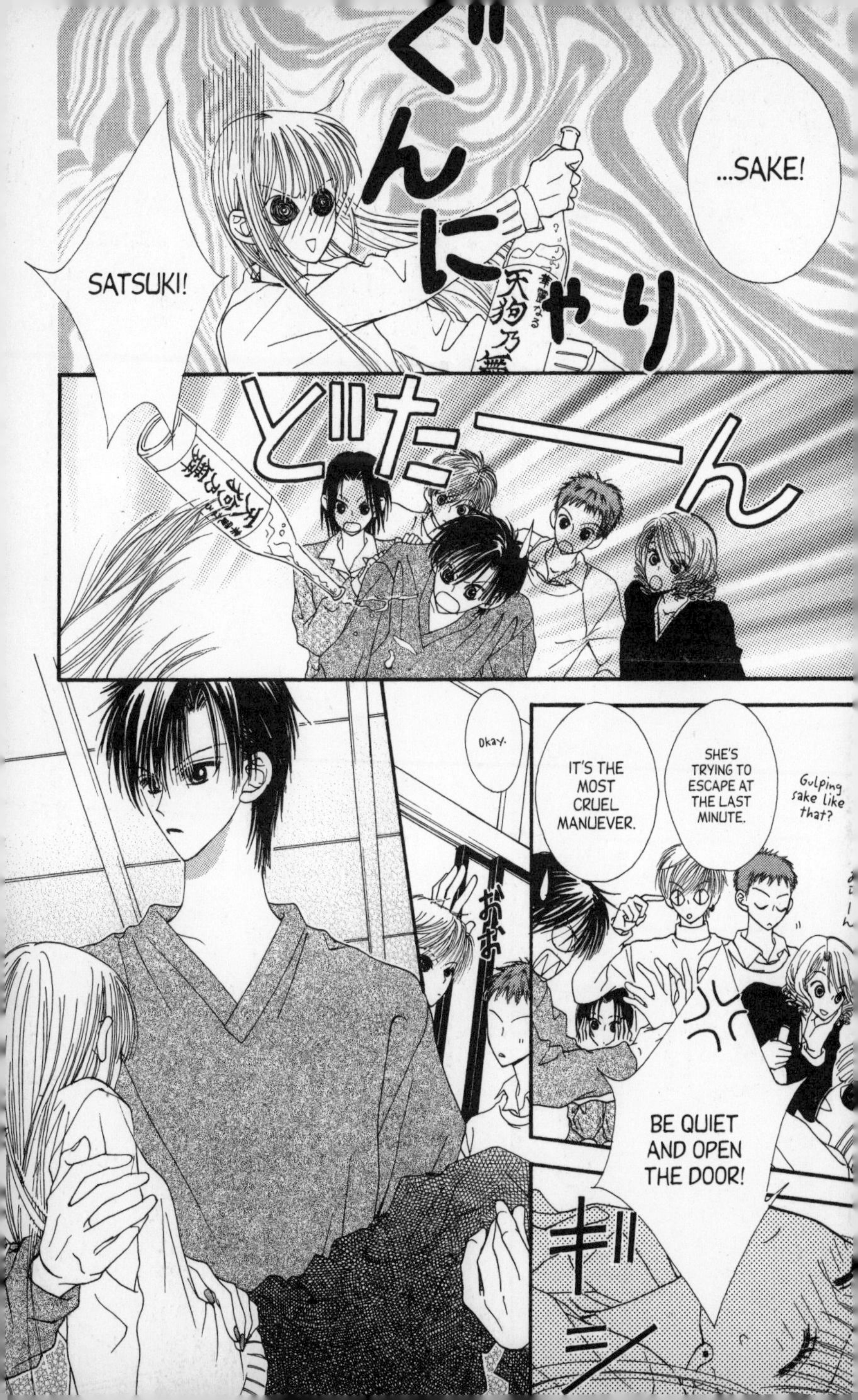
...SAKE!
ぐんにゃり
SATSUKI!
華麗なる
天狗乃舞
どたーーん
Gulping sake like that?
SHE'S TRYING TO ESCAPE AT THE LAST MINUTE.
IT'S THE MOST CRUEL MANUEVER.
BE QUIET AND OPEN THE DOOR!
Okay.

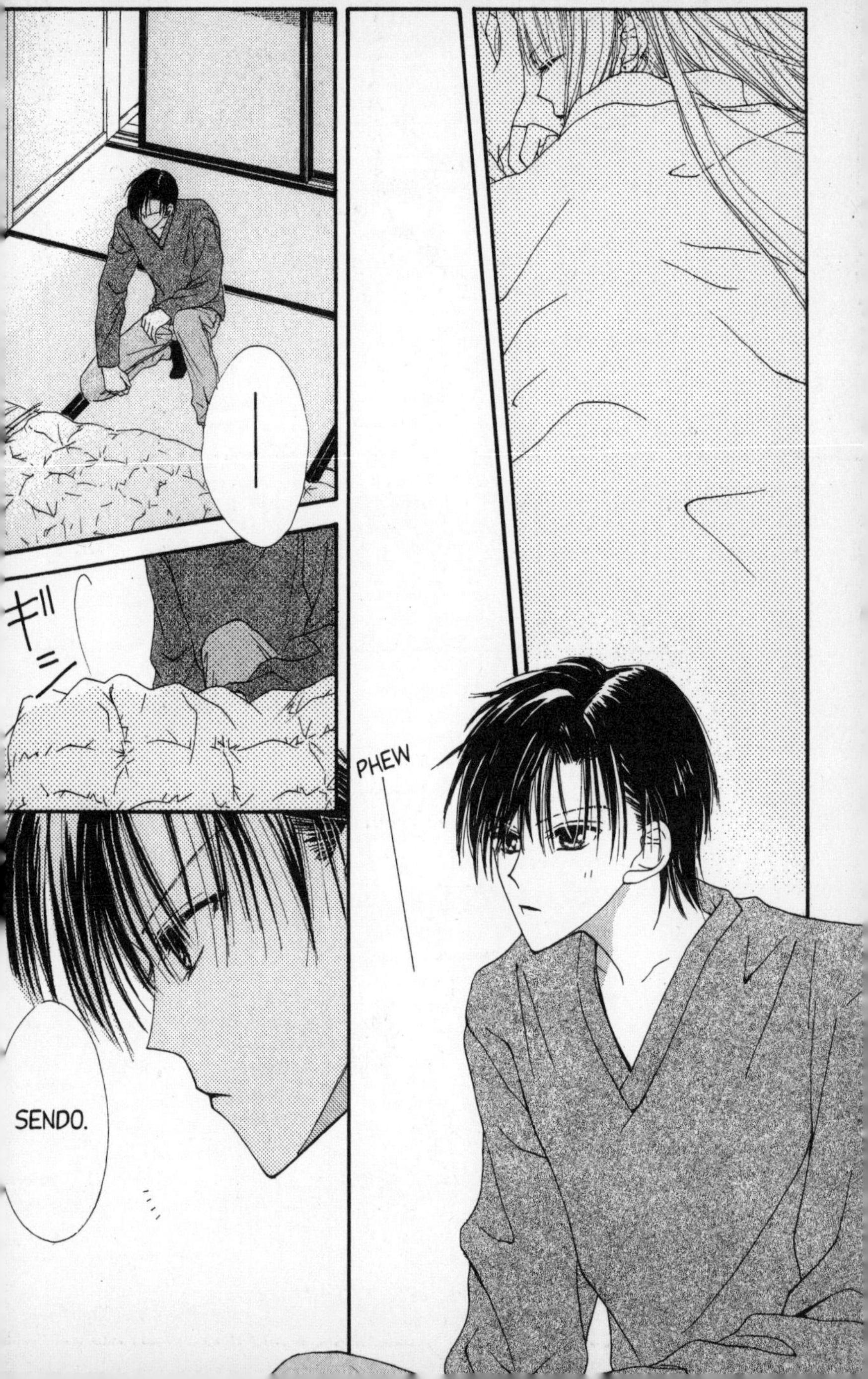
PHEW
ギリ
SENDO.

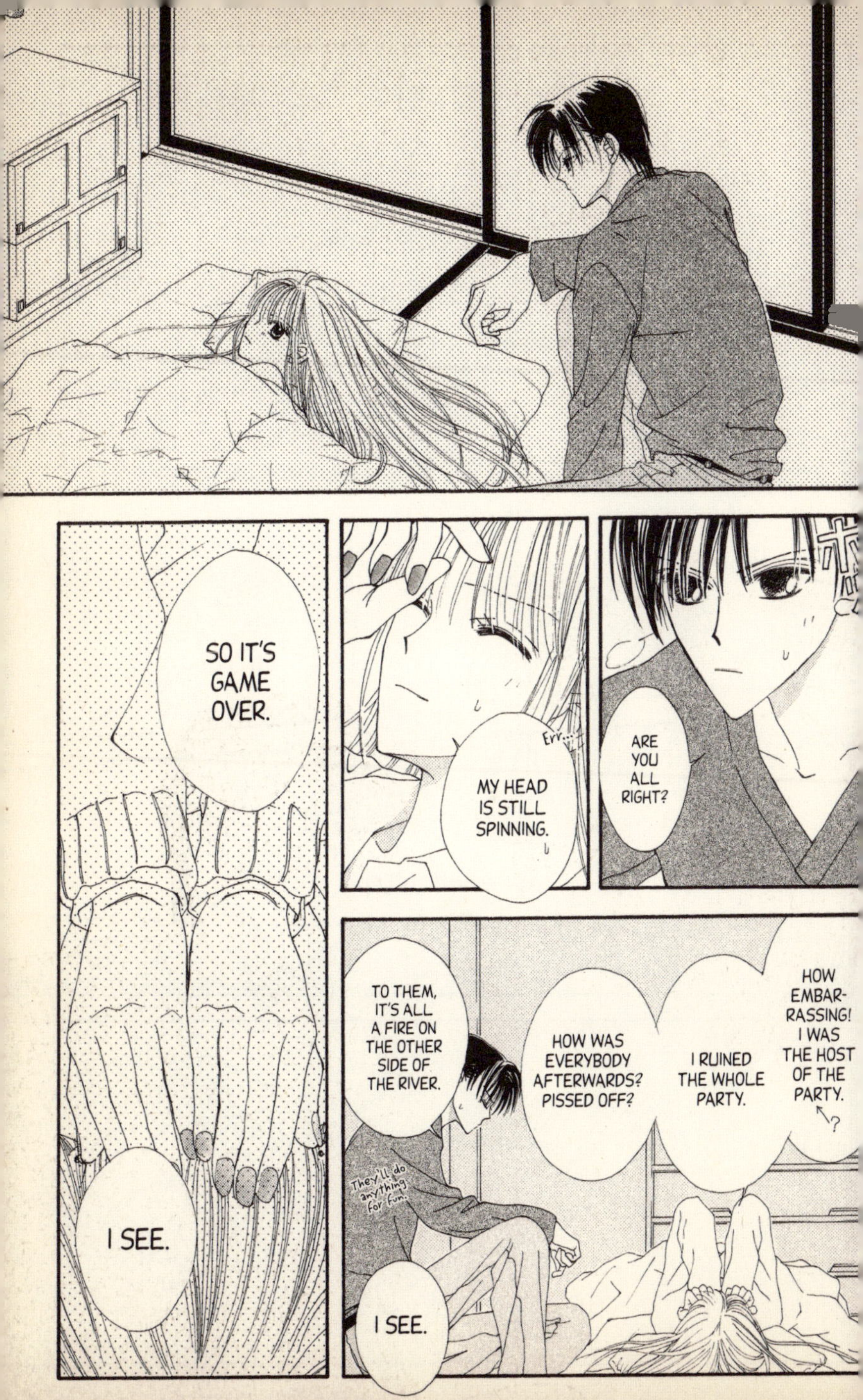
ARE YOU ALL RIGHT?
Err...
MY HEAD IS STILL SPINNING.
HOW EMBARRASSING! I WAS THE HOST OF THE PARTY.
?
I RUINED THE WHOLE PARTY.
HOW WAS EVERYBODY AFTERWARDS? PISSED OFF?
TO THEM, IT'S ALL A FIRE ON THE OTHER SIDE OF THE RIVER.
They'll do anything for fun.
I SEE.
SO IT'S GAME OVER.
I SEE.

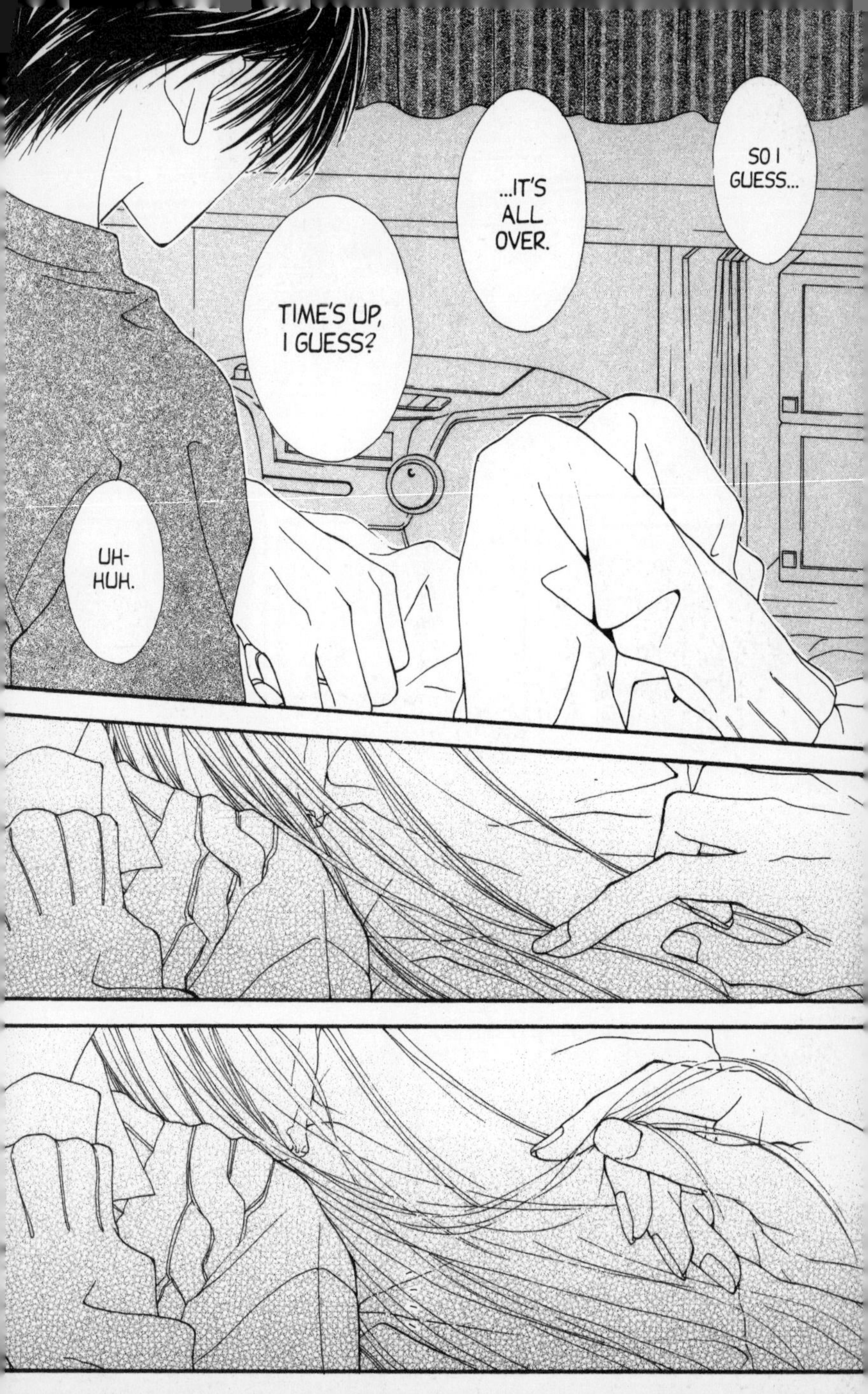
SO I GUESS...
...IT'S ALL OVER.
TIME'S UP, I GUESS?
UH-HUH.

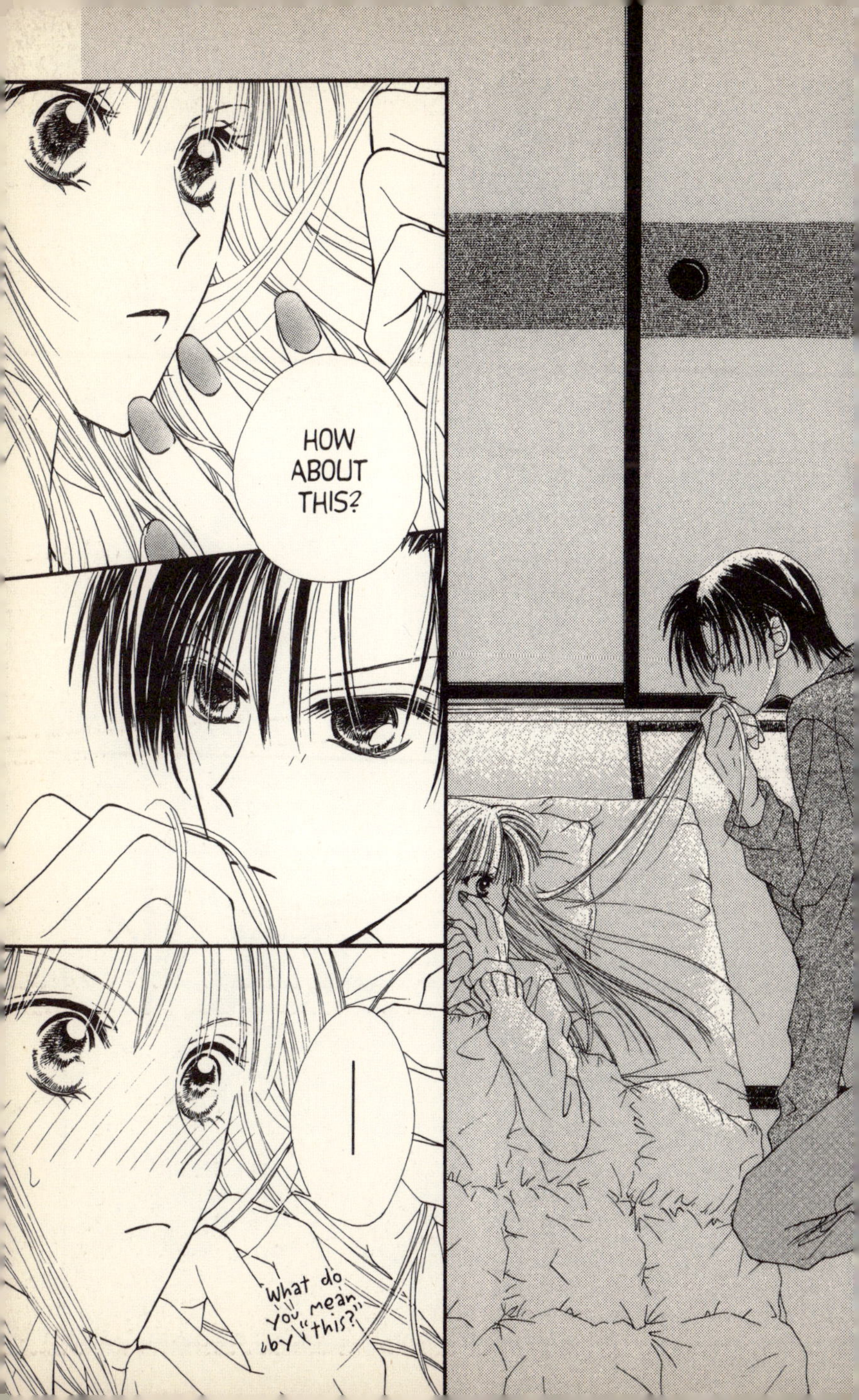
HOW ABOUT THIS?
What do you mean by "this?"

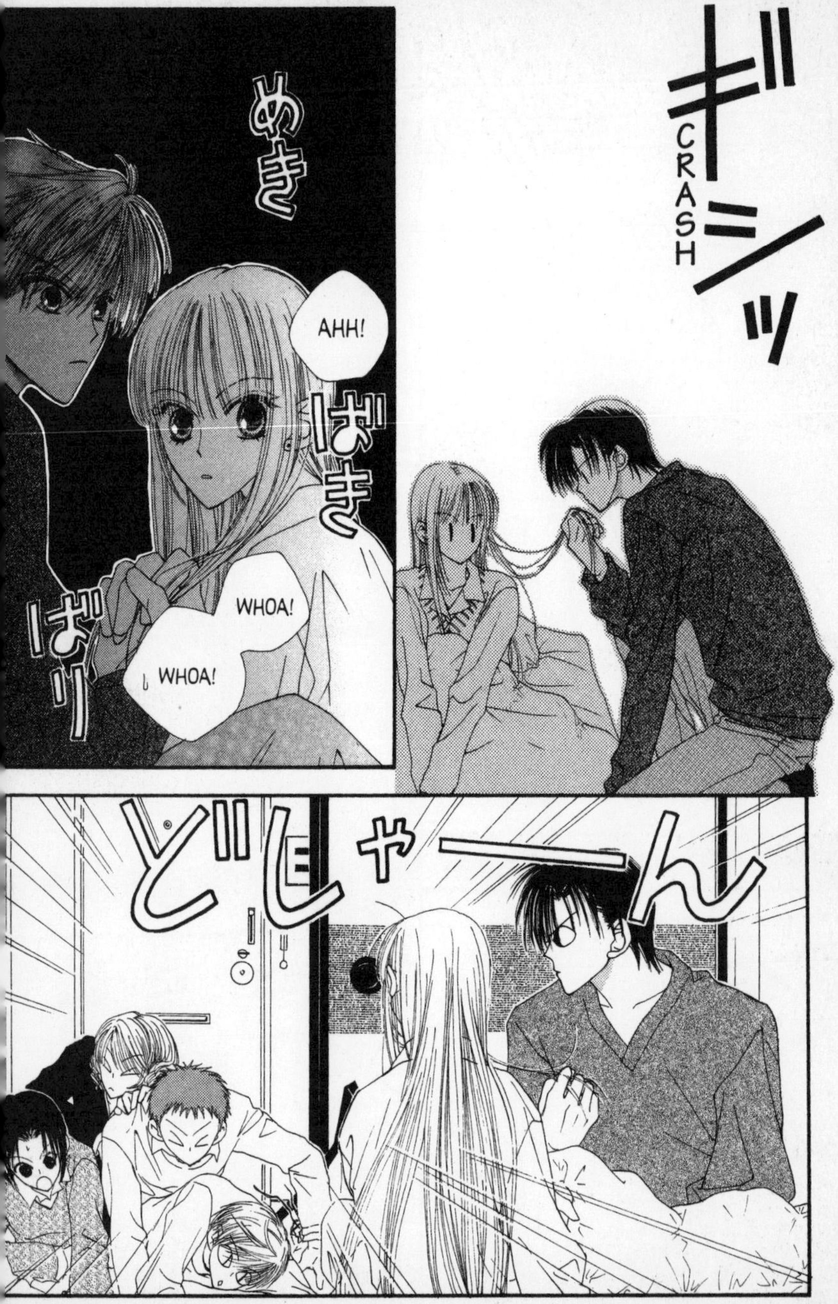
ギシッ
CRASH
AHH!
ぼき
めき
WHOA!
WHOA!
ぼり
どしゃーん

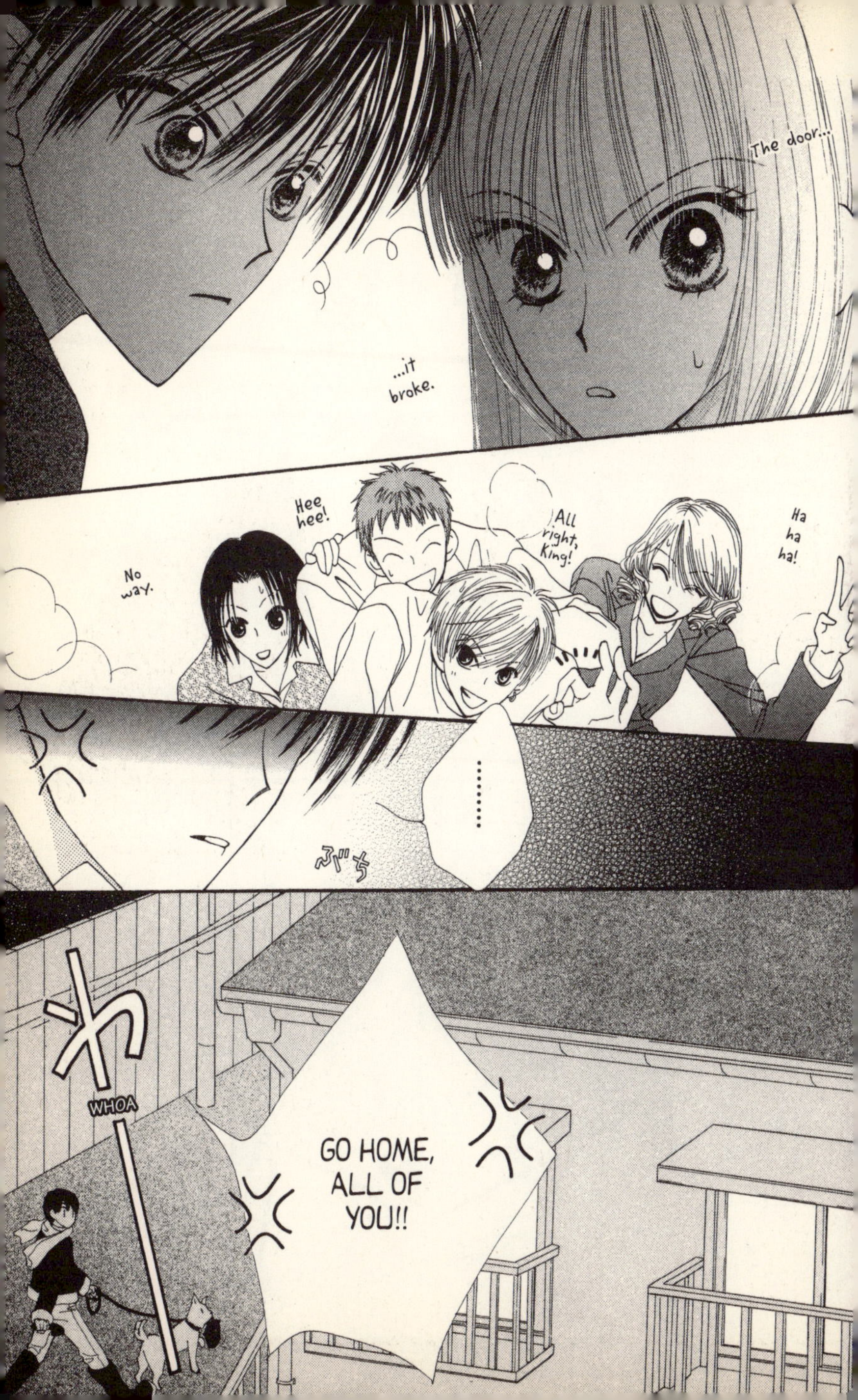

The door...
...it broke.
Ha ha ha!
All right, King!
Hee hee!
No way.
......
ぶち
GO HOME, ALL OF YOU!!
わ
WHOA

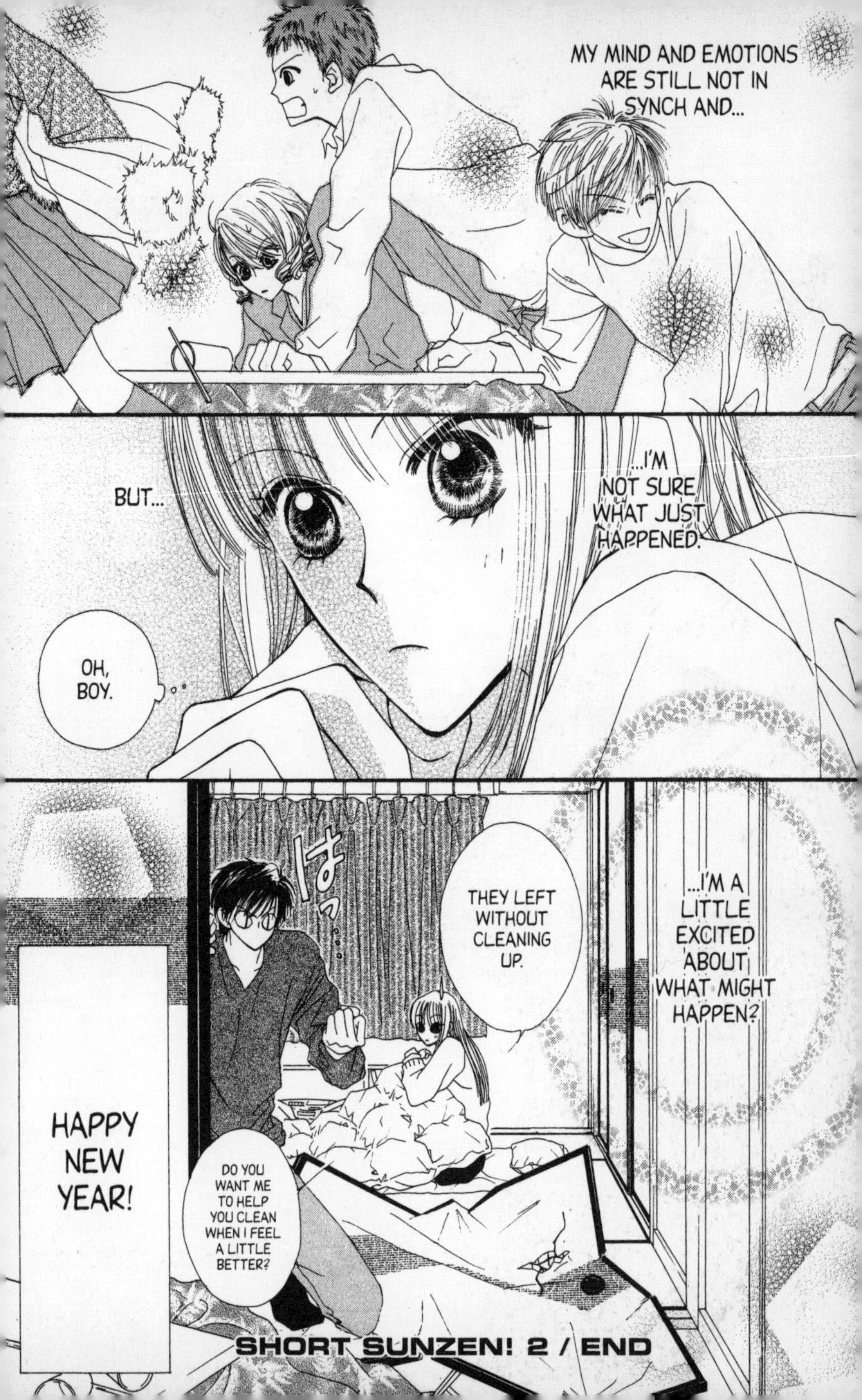

MY MIND AND EMOTIONS ARE STILL NOT IN SYNCH AND...
...I'M NOT SURE WHAT JUST HAPPENED.
BUT...
OH, BOY.
...I'M A LITTLE EXCITED ABOUT WHAT MIGHT HAPPEN?
THEY LEFT WITHOUT CLEANING UP.
はっ
DO YOU WANT ME TO HELP YOU CLEAN WHEN I FEEL A LITTLE BETTER?
HAPPY NEW YEAR!
SHORT SUNZEN! 2 / END

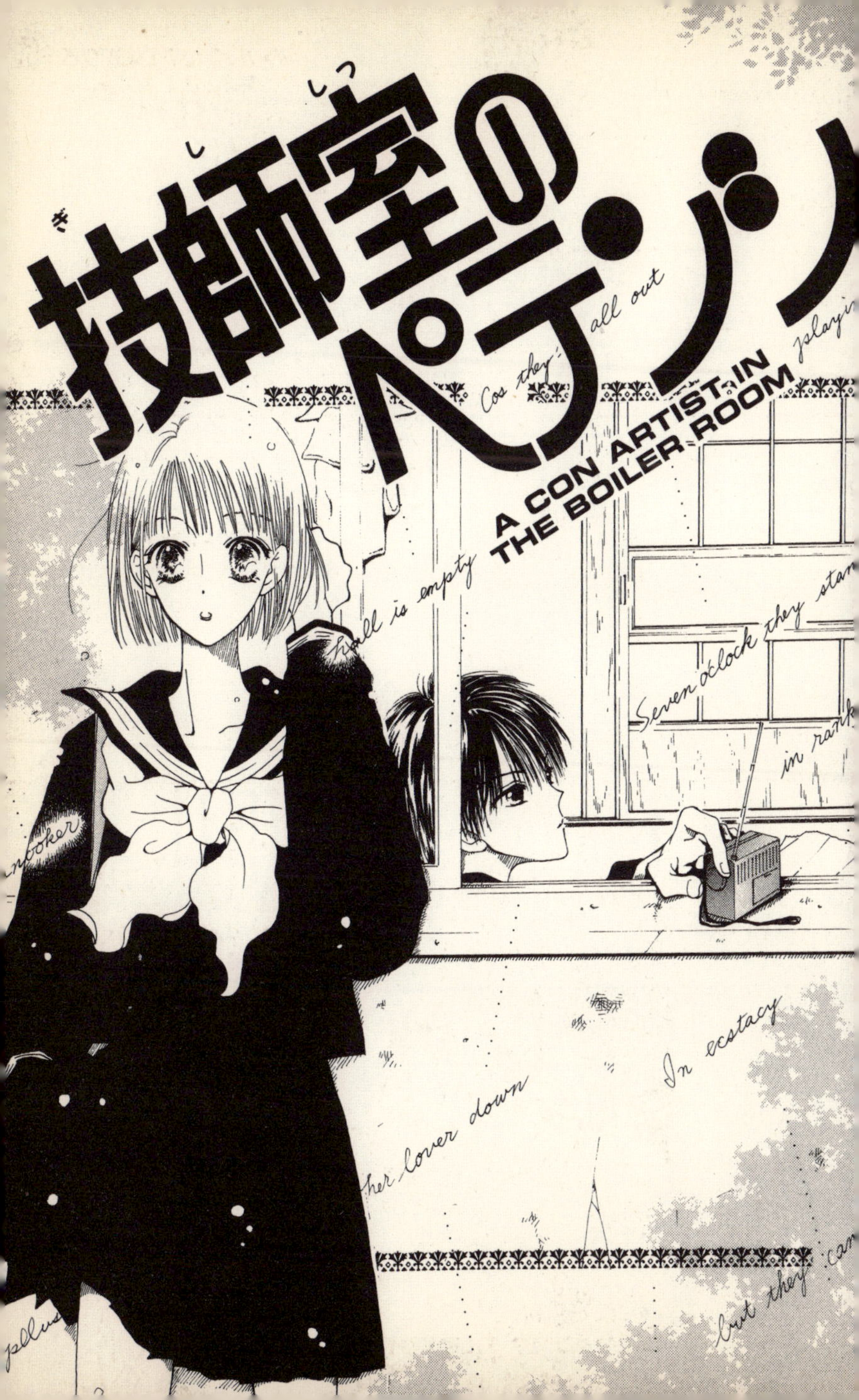

技師室のペテン
A CON ARTIST IN
THE BOILER ROOM

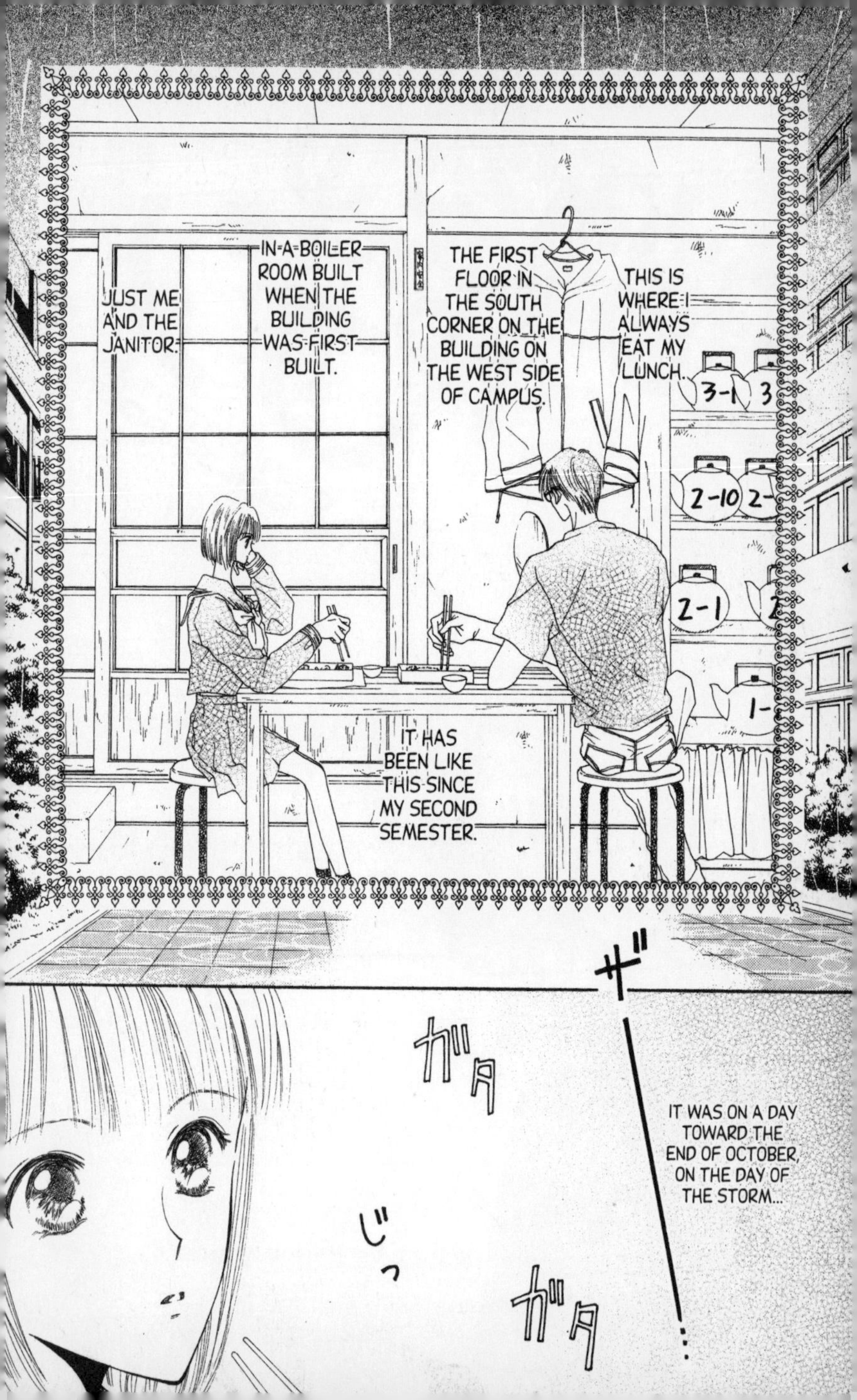
THIS IS WHERE I ALWAYS EAT MY LUNCH.
3-1
3
2-10
2-
2-1
2
1-
THE FIRST FLOOR IN THE SOUTH CORNER ON THE BUILDING ON THE WEST SIDE OF CAMPUS.
IN A BOILER ROOM BUILT WHEN THE BUILDING WAS FIRST BUILT.
JUST ME AND THE JANITOR.
IT HAS BEEN LIKE THIS SINCE MY SECOND SEMESTER.
ザ
IT WAS ON A DAY TOWARD THE END OF OCTOBER, ON THE DAY OF THE STORM...
ガタ
ガタ
じっ

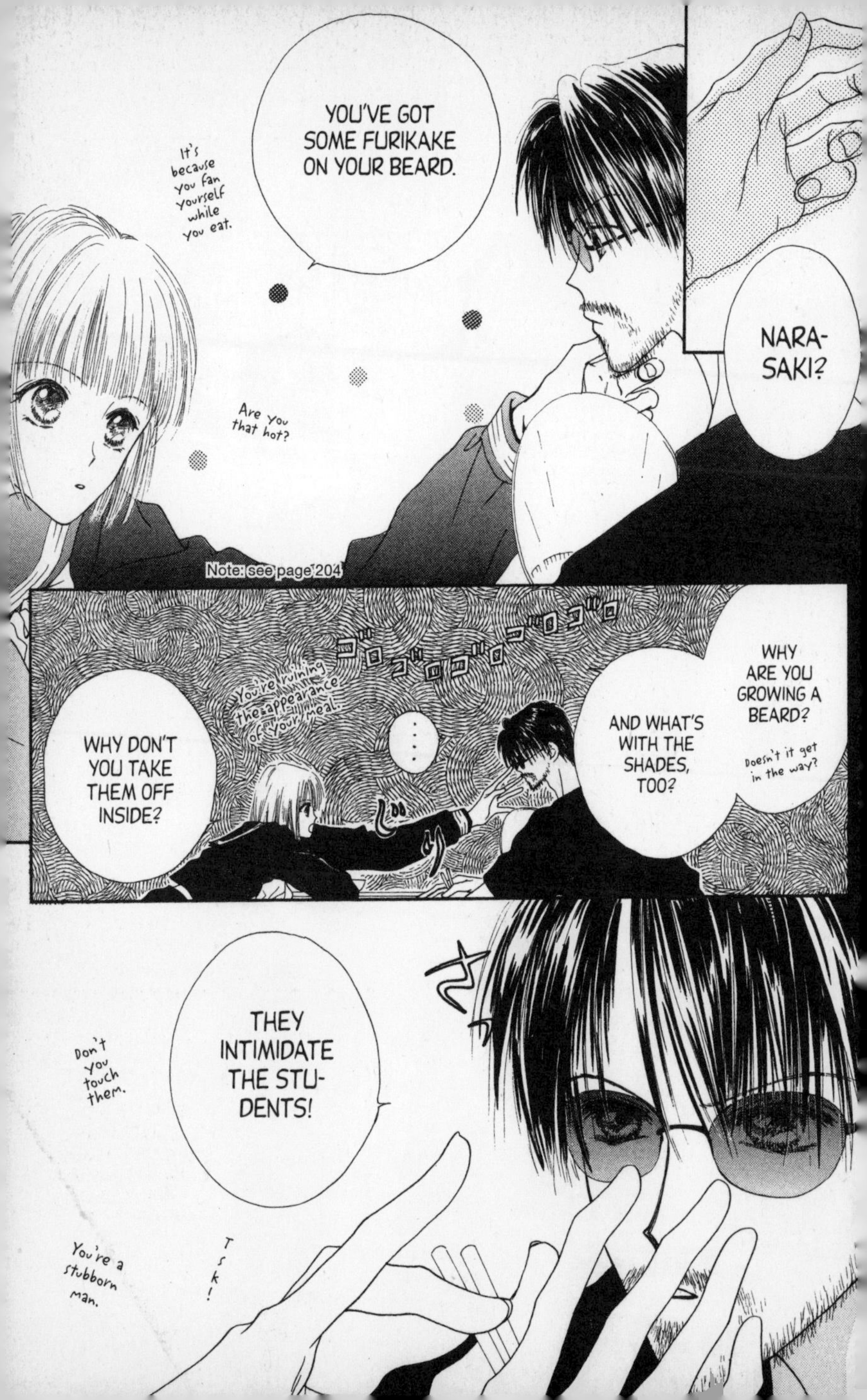
NARA-SAKI?
YOU'VE GOT SOME FURIKAKE ON YOUR BEARD.
It's because you fan yourself while you eat.
Are you that hot?
Note: see page 204
WHY ARE YOU GROWING A BEARD?
Doesn't it get in the way?
AND WHAT'S WITH THE SHADES, TOO?
You're ruining the appearance of your meal.
...
WHY DON'T YOU TAKE THEM OFF INSIDE?
THEY INTIMIDATE THE STU-DENTS!
Don't you touch them.
Tsk!
You're a stubborn man.

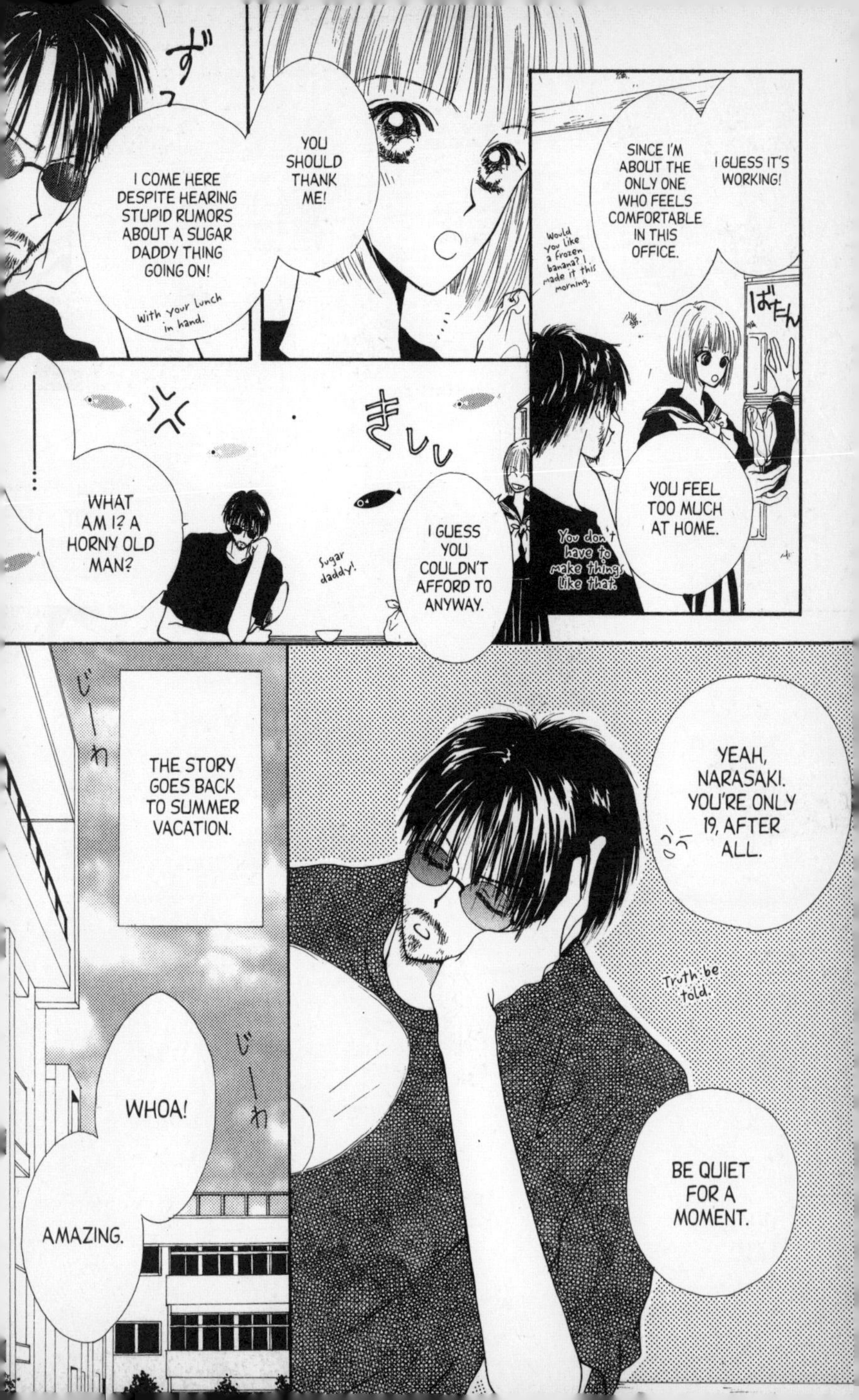
I GUESS IT'S WORKING!
SINCE I'M ABOUT THE ONLY ONE WHO FEELS COMFORTABLE IN THIS OFFICE.
Would you like a frozen banana? I made it this morning.
ばたん
YOU FEEL TOO MUCH AT HOME.
You don't have to make things like that.
YOU SHOULD THANK ME!
ずっ
I COME HERE DESPITE HEARING STUPID RUMORS ABOUT A SUGAR DADDY THING GOING ON!
With your lunch in hand.
きしい
I GUESS YOU COULDN'T AFFORD TO ANYWAY.
Sugar daddy!
WHAT AM I? A HORNY OLD MAN?
YEAH, NARASAKI. YOU'RE ONLY 19, AFTER ALL.
Truth be told.
BE QUIET FOR A MOMENT.
じーわ
THE STORY GOES BACK TO SUMMER VACATION.
じーわ
WHOA!
AMAZING.

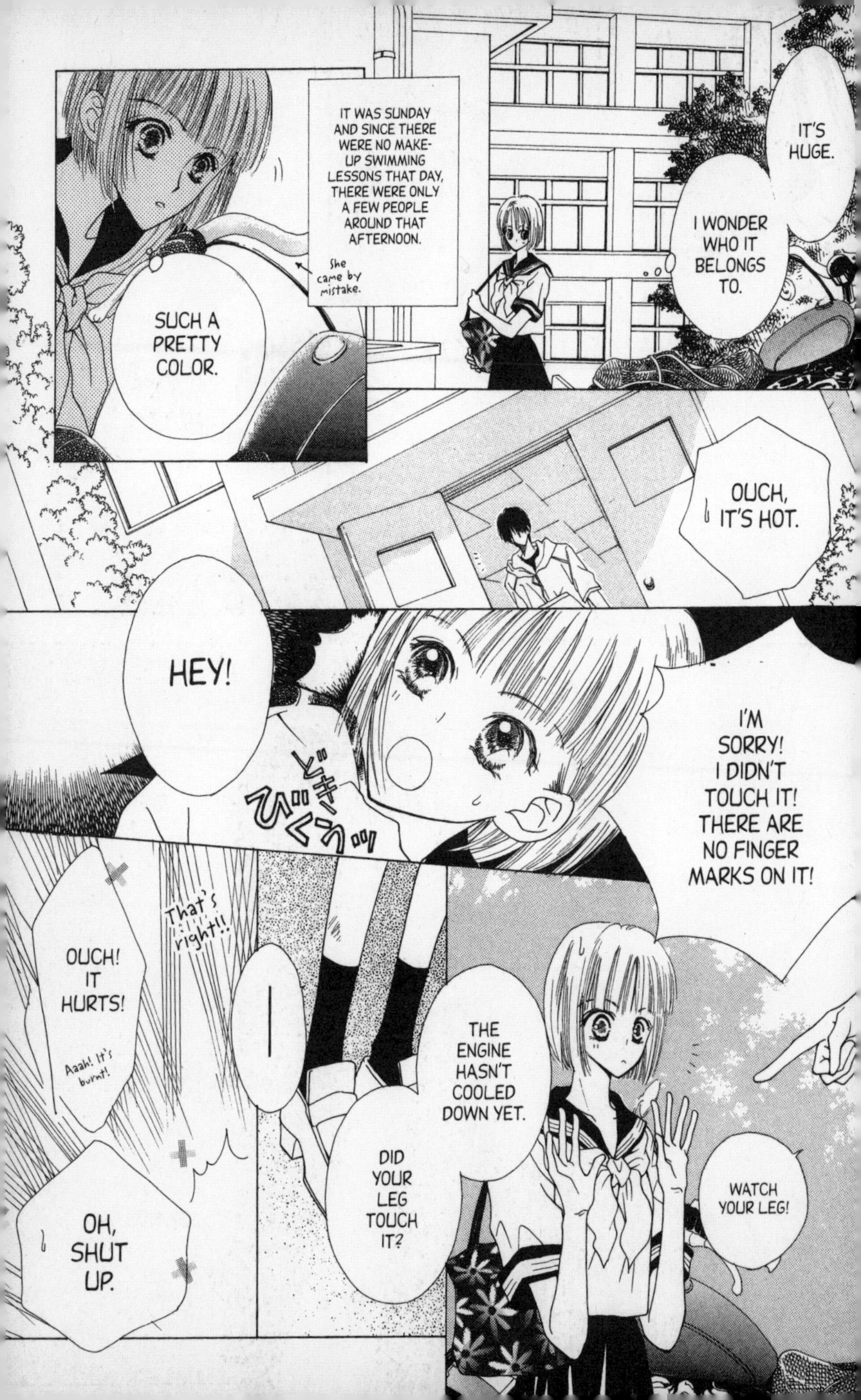
IT'S HUGE.
I WONDER WHO IT BELONGS TO.
IT WAS SUNDAY AND SINCE THERE WERE NO MAKE-UP SWIMMING LESSONS THAT DAY, THERE WERE ONLY A FEW PEOPLE AROUND THAT AFTERNOON.
She came by mistake.
SUCH A PRETTY COLOR.
OUCH, IT'S HOT.
HEY!
I'M SORRY! I DIDN'T TOUCH IT! THERE ARE NO FINGER MARKS ON IT!
THE ENGINE HASN'T COOLED DOWN YET.
DID YOUR LEG TOUCH IT?
WATCH YOUR LEG!
—
That's right!!
OUCH! IT HURTS!
Aaah! It's burnt!
OH, SHUT UP.

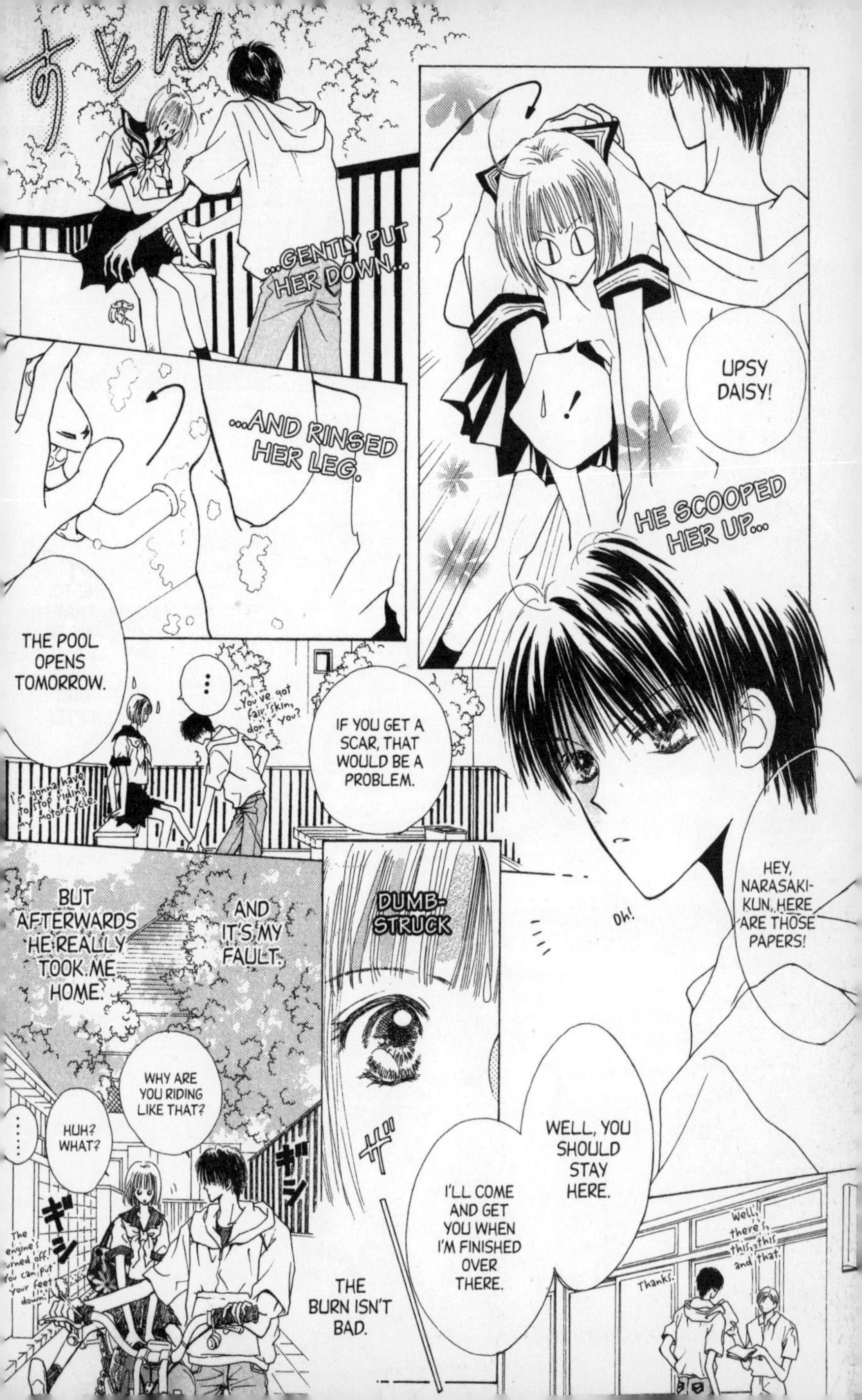
UPSY DAISY!
HE SCOOPED HER UP...
すとん
...GENTLY PUT HER DOWN...
...AND RINSED HER LEG.
THE POOL OPENS TOMORROW.
IF YOU GET A SCAR, THAT WOULD BE A PROBLEM.
...
You've got fair skin, don't you?
I'm gonna have to stop riding my motorcycle.
HEY, NARASAKI-KUN, HERE ARE THOSE PAPERS!
Oh!
WELL, YOU SHOULD STAY HERE.
I'LL COME AND GET YOU WHEN I'M FINISHED OVER THERE.
Well, there's this and that.
Thanks.
DUMB-STRUCK
ザッ
THE BURN ISN'T BAD.
BUT AFTERWARDS HE REALLY TOOK ME HOME.
AND IT'S MY FAULT.
WHY ARE YOU RIDING LIKE THAT?
HUH? WHAT?
......
ギシ
ギシ
The engine's turned off. You can put your feet down.

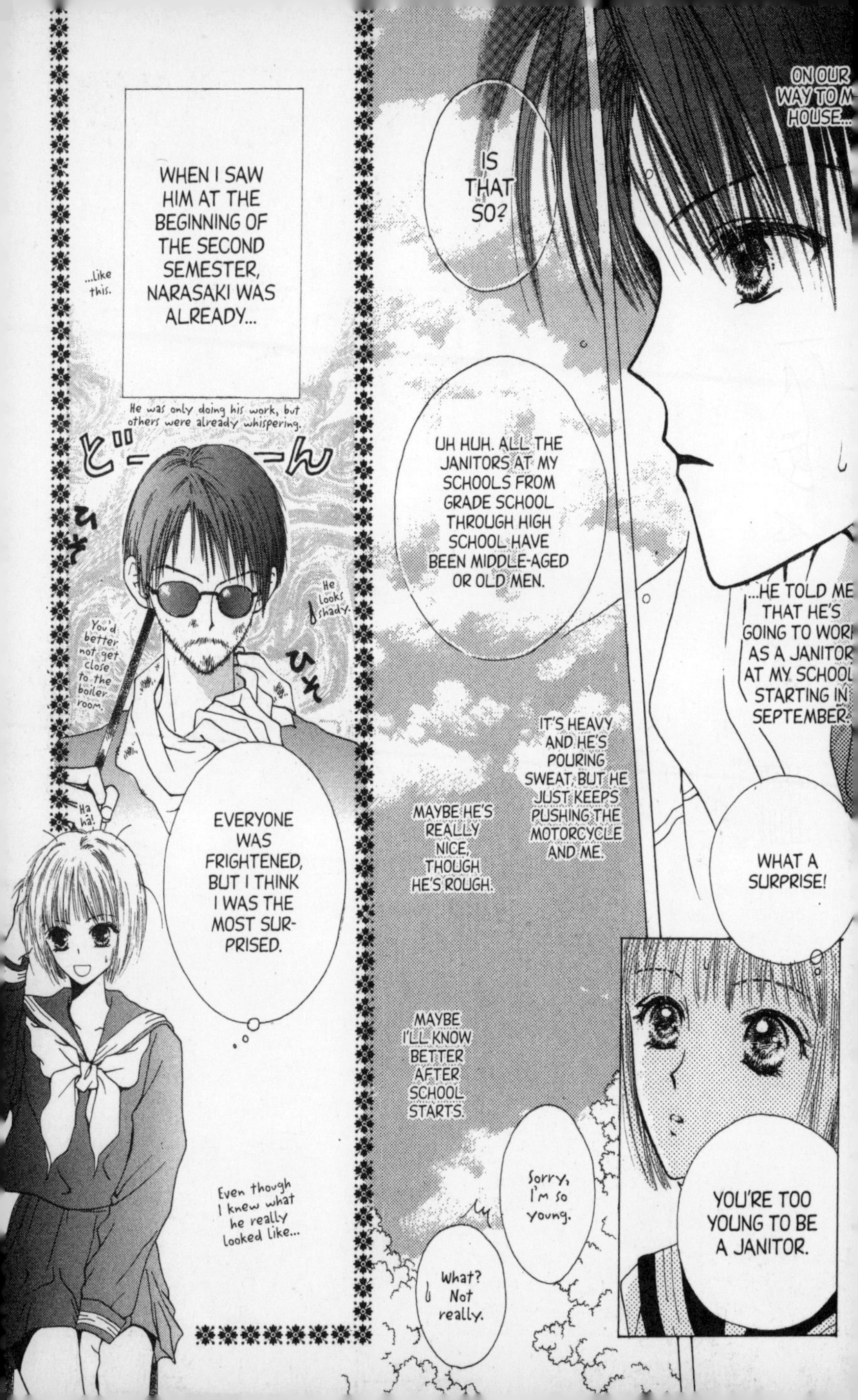

ON OUR WAY TO M HOUSE...
...HE TOLD ME THAT HE'S GOING TO WOR AS A JANITOR AT MY SCHOOL STARTING IN SEPTEMBER.
IS THAT SO?
WHAT A SURPRISE!
UH HUH. ALL THE JANITORS AT MY SCHOOLS FROM GRADE SCHOOL THROUGH HIGH SCHOOL HAVE BEEN MIDDLE-AGED OR OLD MEN.
IT'S HEAVY AND HE'S POURING SWEAT, BUT HE JUST KEEPS PUSHING THE MOTORCYCLE AND ME.
MAYBE HE'S REALLY NICE, THOUGH HE'S ROUGH.
YOU'RE TOO YOUNG TO BE A JANITOR.
Sorry, I'm so young.
What? Not really.
MAYBE I'LL KNOW BETTER AFTER SCHOOL STARTS.
WHEN I SAW HIM AT THE BEGINNING OF THE SECOND SEMESTER, NARASAKI WAS ALREADY...
...like this.
He was only doing his work, but others were already whispering.
どーーん
ひそ
He looks shady.
ひそ
You'd better not get close to the boiler room.
Ha ha!
EVERYONE WAS FRIGHTENED, BUT I THINK I WAS THE MOST SUR-PRISED.
Even though I knew what he really looked like...

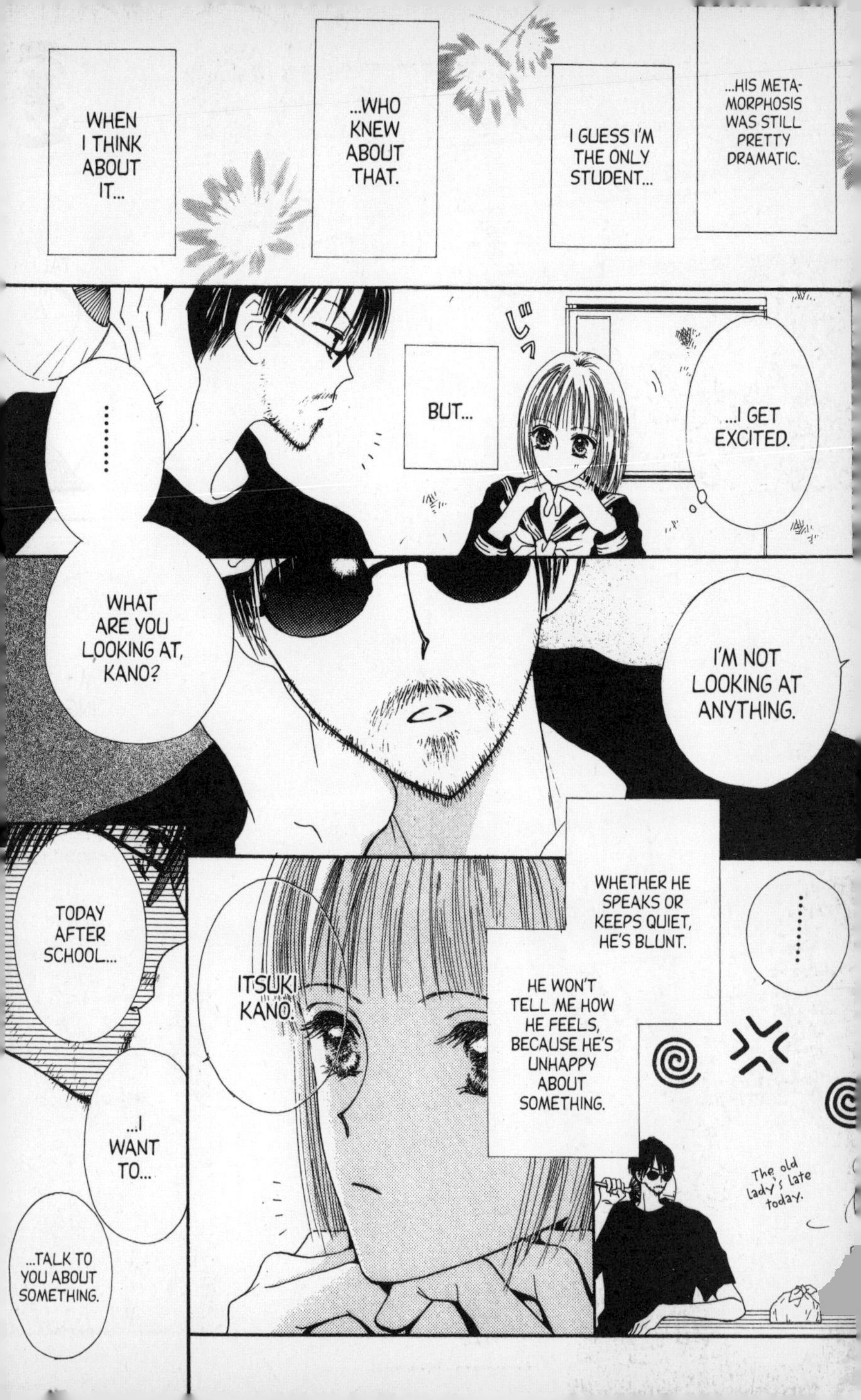
...HIS META-MORPHOSIS WAS STILL PRETTY DRAMATIC.
I GUESS I'M THE ONLY STUDENT...
...WHO KNEW ABOUT THAT.
WHEN I THINK ABOUT IT...
じっ
BUT...
...I GET EXCITED.
....
WHAT ARE YOU LOOKING AT, KANO?
I'M NOT LOOKING AT ANYTHING.
....
WHETHER HE SPEAKS OR KEEPS QUIET, HE'S BLUNT.
HE WON'T TELL ME HOW HE FEELS, BECAUSE HE'S UNHAPPY ABOUT SOMETHING.
The old lady's late today.
ITSUKI KANO.
TODAY AFTER SCHOOL...
...I WANT TO...
...TALK TO YOU ABOUT SOMETHING.

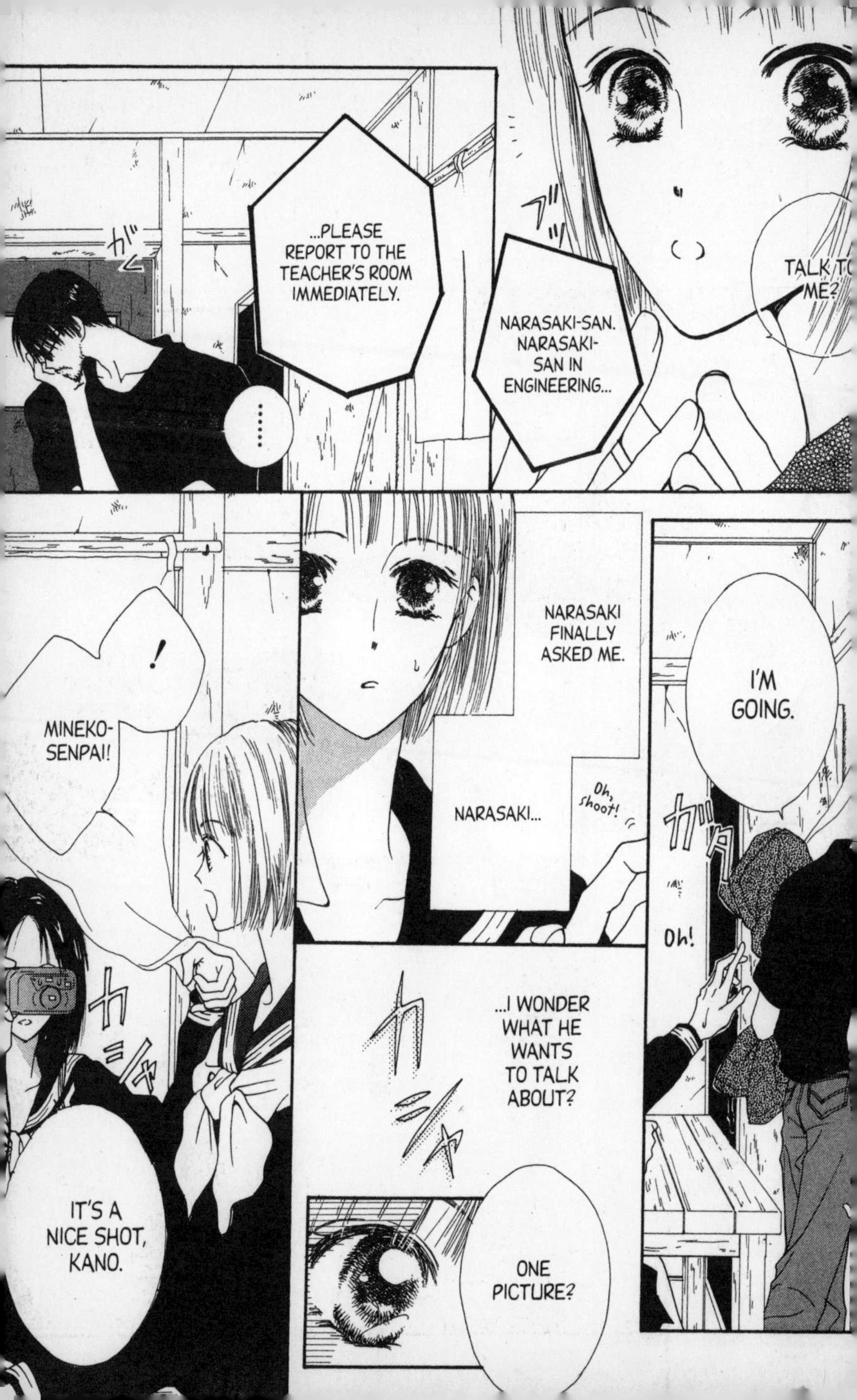
TALK TO ME?
NARASAKI-SAN. NARASAKI-SAN IN ENGINEERING...
...PLEASE REPORT TO THE TEACHER'S ROOM IMMEDIATELY.
......
I'M GOING.
Oh!
NARASAKI FINALLY ASKED ME.
NARASAKI...
Oh, shoot!
...I WONDER WHAT HE WANTS TO TALK ABOUT?
ONE PICTURE?
!
MINEKO-SENPAI!
IT'S A NICE SHOT, KANO.

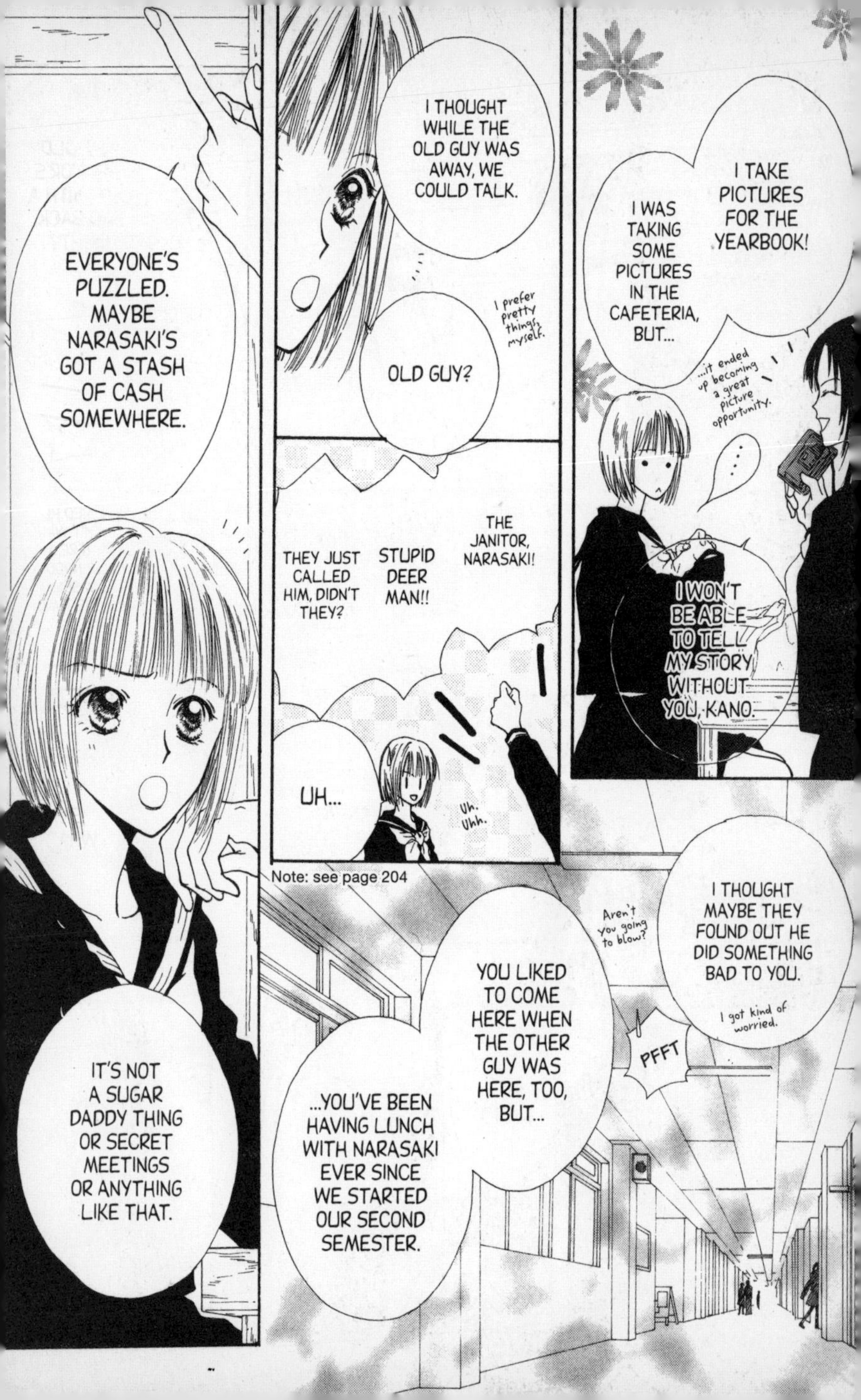
I TAKE PICTURES FOR THE YEARBOOK!
I WAS TAKING SOME PICTURES IN THE CAFETERIA, BUT...
...it ended up becoming a great picture opportunity.
...
I WON'T BE ABLE TO TELL MY STORY WITHOUT YOU, KANO.
I THOUGHT WHILE THE OLD GUY WAS AWAY, WE COULD TALK.
I prefer pretty things, myself.
...
OLD GUY?
THE JANITOR, NARASAKI!
STUPID DEER MAN!!
THEY JUST CALLED HIM, DIDN'T THEY?
Uh. Uhh.
UH...
I THOUGHT MAYBE THEY FOUND OUT HE DID SOMETHING BAD TO YOU.
I got kind of worried.
Aren't you going to blow?
PFFT
YOU LIKED TO COME HERE WHEN THE OTHER GUY WAS HERE, TOO, BUT...
...YOU'VE BEEN HAVING LUNCH WITH NARASAKI EVER SINCE WE STARTED OUR SECOND SEMESTER.
EVERYONE'S PUZZLED. MAYBE NARASAKI'S GOT A STASH OF CASH SOMEWHERE.
IT'S NOT A SUGAR DADDY THING OR SECRET MEETINGS OR ANYTHING LIKE THAT.

Note: see page 204

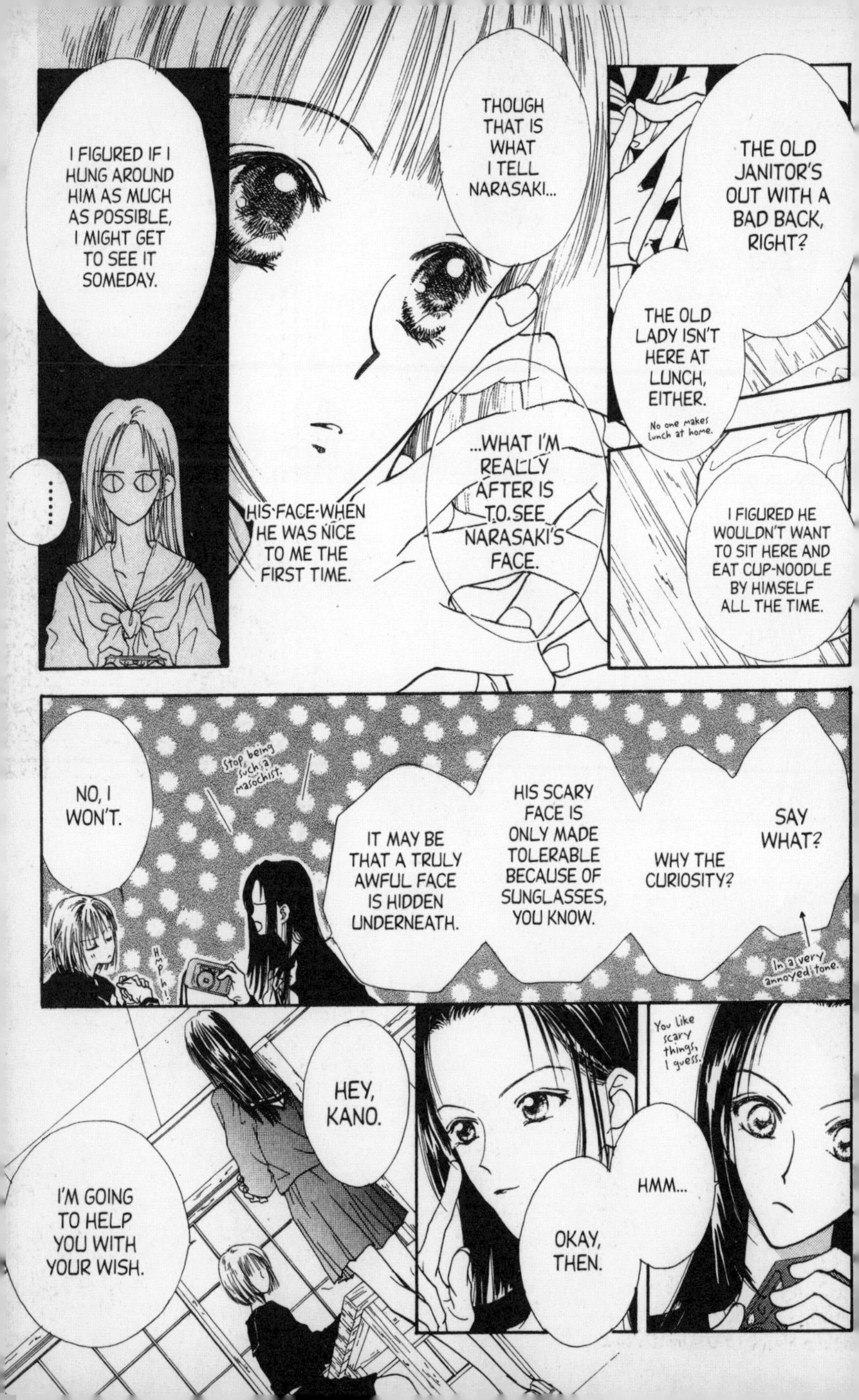
THE OLD JANITOR'S OUT WITH A BAD BACK, RIGHT?
THE OLD LADY ISN'T HERE AT LUNCH, EITHER.
No one makes lunch at home.
I FIGURED HE WOULDN'T WANT TO SIT HERE AND EAT CUP-NOODLE BY HIMSELF ALL THE TIME.
THOUGH THAT IS WHAT I TELL NARASAKI...
...WHAT I'M REALLY AFTER IS TO SEE NARASAKI'S FACE.
HIS FACE WHEN HE WAS NICE TO ME THE FIRST TIME.
I FIGURED IF I HUNG AROUND HIM AS MUCH AS POSSIBLE, I MIGHT GET TO SEE IT SOMEDAY.
......
SAY WHAT?
In a very annoyed tone.
WHY THE CURIOSITY?
HIS SCARY FACE IS ONLY MADE TOLERABLE BECAUSE OF SUNGLASSES, YOU KNOW.
IT MAY BE THAT A TRULY AWFUL FACE IS HIDDEN UNDERNEATH.
Stop being such a masochist.
NO, I WON'T.
Hmph!
You like scary things, I guess.
HMM...
OKAY, THEN.
HEY, KANO.
I'M GOING TO HELP YOU WITH YOUR WISH.

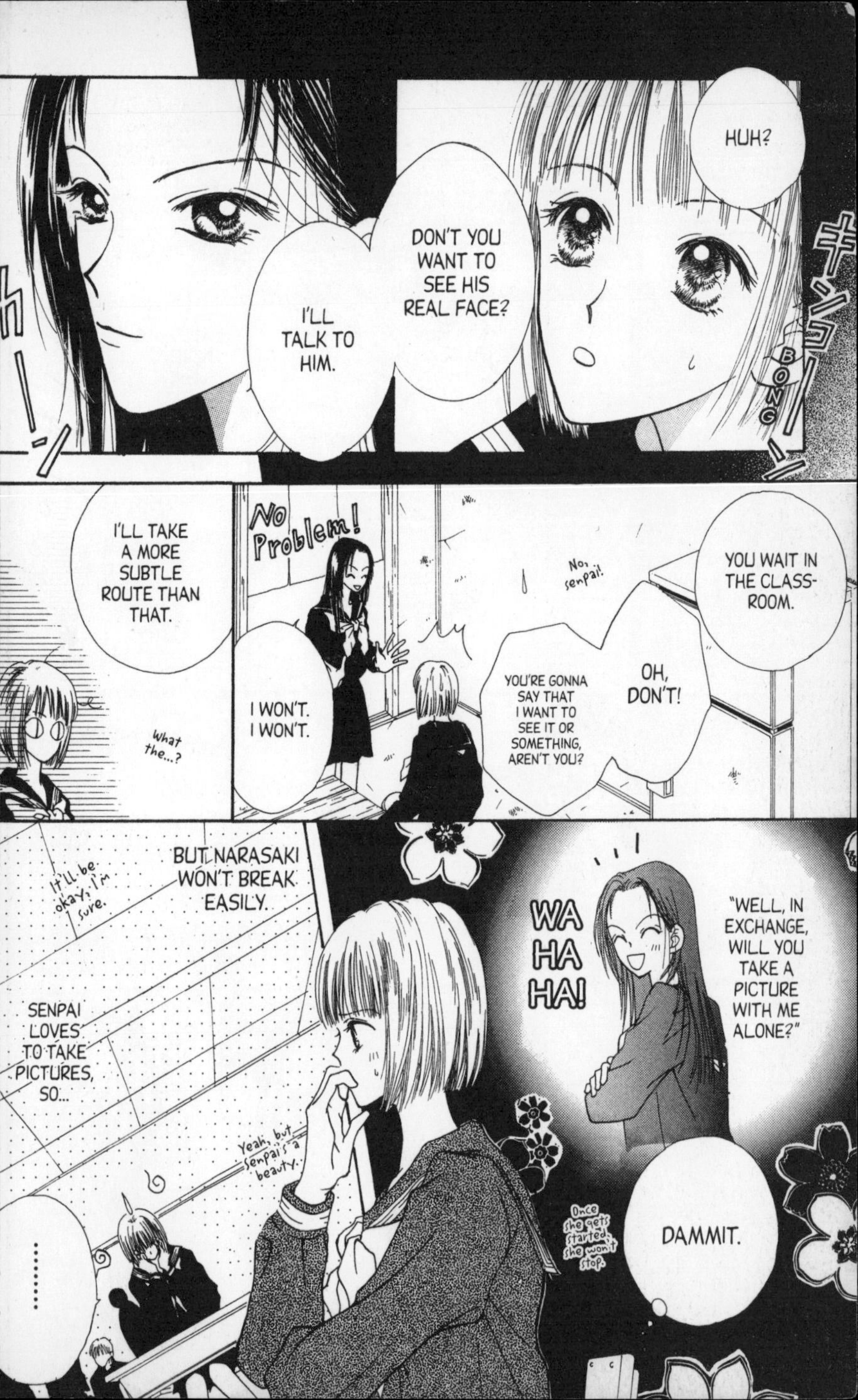
BONG
HUH?
DON'T YOU WANT TO SEE HIS REAL FACE?
I'LL TALK TO HIM.
YOU WAIT IN THE CLASS-ROOM.
OH, DON'T!
YOU'RE GONNA SAY THAT I WANT TO SEE IT OR SOMETHING, AREN'T YOU?
No, senpai!
I WON'T. I WON'T.
No Problem!
I'LL TAKE A MORE SUBTLE ROUTE THAN THAT.
What the...?
"WELL, IN EXCHANGE, WILL YOU TAKE A PICTURE WITH ME ALONE?"
WA HA HA!
DAMMIT.
Once she gets started, she won't stop.
BUT NARASAKI WON'T BREAK EASILY.
It'll be okay, I'm sure.
SENPAI LOVES TO TAKE PICTURES, SO...
Yeah, but senpai's a beauty.
....

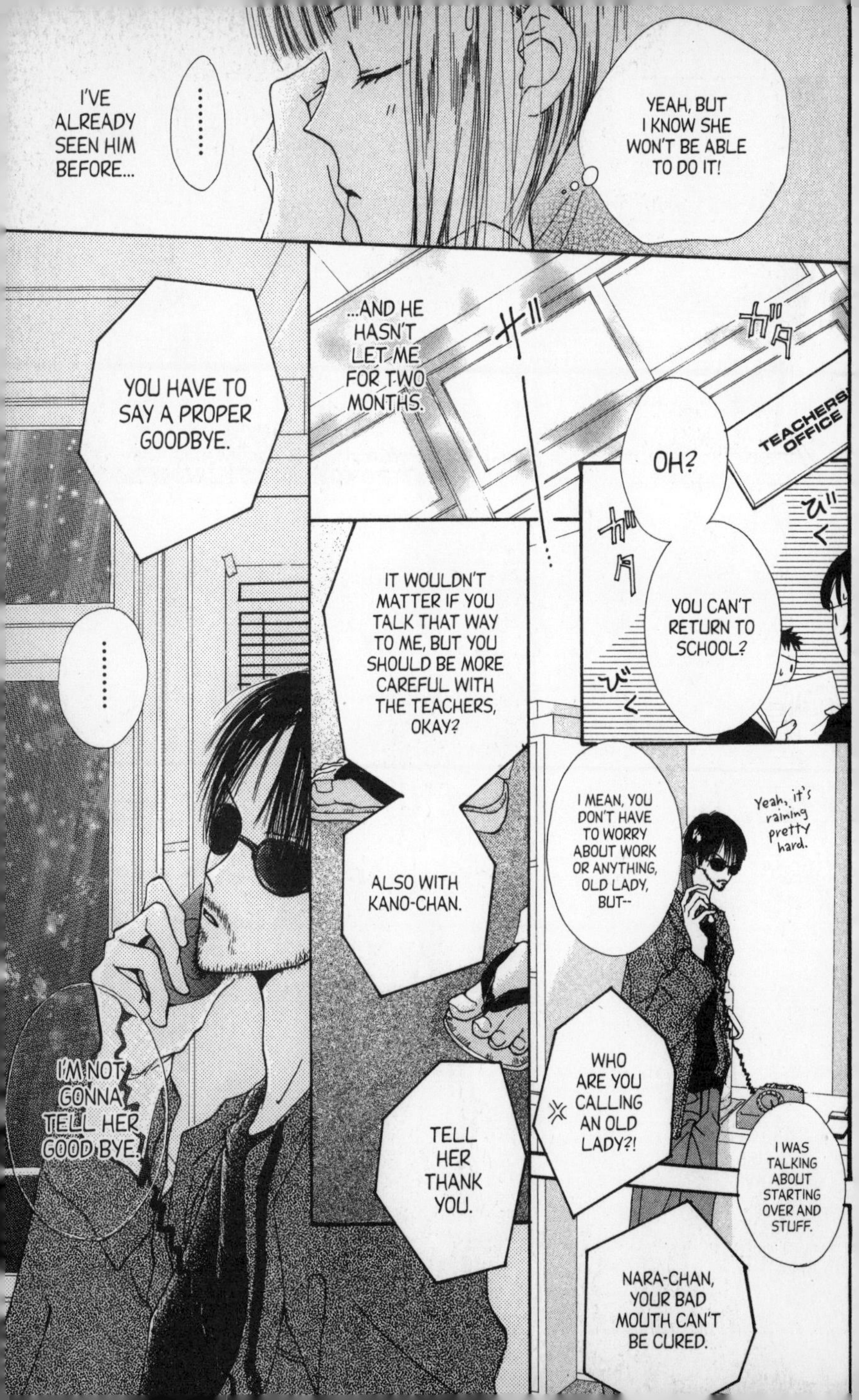
YEAH, BUT I KNOW SHE WON'T BE ABLE TO DO IT!
......
I'VE ALREADY SEEN HIM BEFORE...
ガタ
TEACHERS' OFFICE
OH?
YOU CAN'T RETURN TO SCHOOL?
びく
ガタ
びく
...AND HE HASN'T LET ME FOR TWO MONTHS.
Yeah, it's raining pretty hard.
I MEAN, YOU DON'T HAVE TO WORRY ABOUT WORK OR ANYTHING, OLD LADY, BUT--
WHO ARE YOU CALLING AN OLD LADY?!
I WAS TALKING ABOUT STARTING OVER AND STUFF.
NARA-CHAN, YOUR BAD MOUTH CAN'T BE CURED.
IT WOULDN'T MATTER IF YOU TALK THAT WAY TO ME, BUT YOU SHOULD BE MORE CAREFUL WITH THE TEACHERS, OKAY?
ALSO WITH KANO-CHAN.
TELL HER THANK YOU.
YOU HAVE TO SAY A PROPER GOODBYE.
......
I'M NOT GONNA TELL HER GOOD BYE.

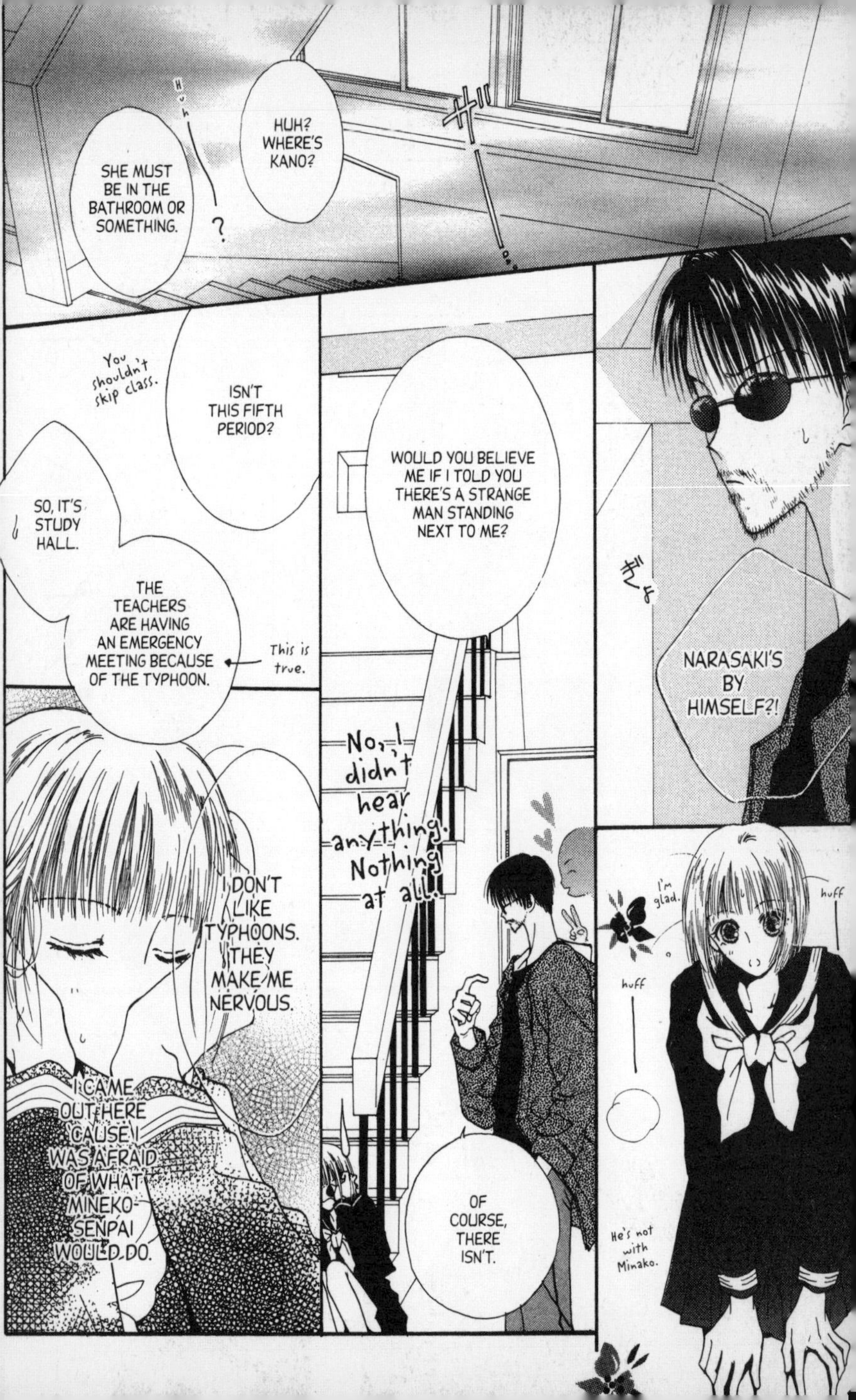
HUH? WHERE'S KANO?
Huh
SHE MUST BE IN THE BATHROOM OR SOMETHING.
?
NARASAKI'S BY HIMSELF?!
huff
I'm glad.
huff
He's not with Minako.
WOULD YOU BELIEVE ME IF I TOLD YOU THERE'S A STRANGE MAN STANDING NEXT TO ME?
No, I didn't hear anything. Nothing at all.
OF COURSE, THERE ISN'T.
ISN'T THIS FIFTH PERIOD?
You shouldn't skip class.
SO, IT'S STUDY HALL.
THE TEACHERS ARE HAVING AN EMERGENCY MEETING BECAUSE OF THE TYPHOON.
This is true.
I DON'T LIKE TYPHOONS. THEY MAKE ME NERVOUS.
I CAME OUT HERE CAUSE I WAS AFRAID OF WHAT MINEKO-SENPAI WOULD DO.

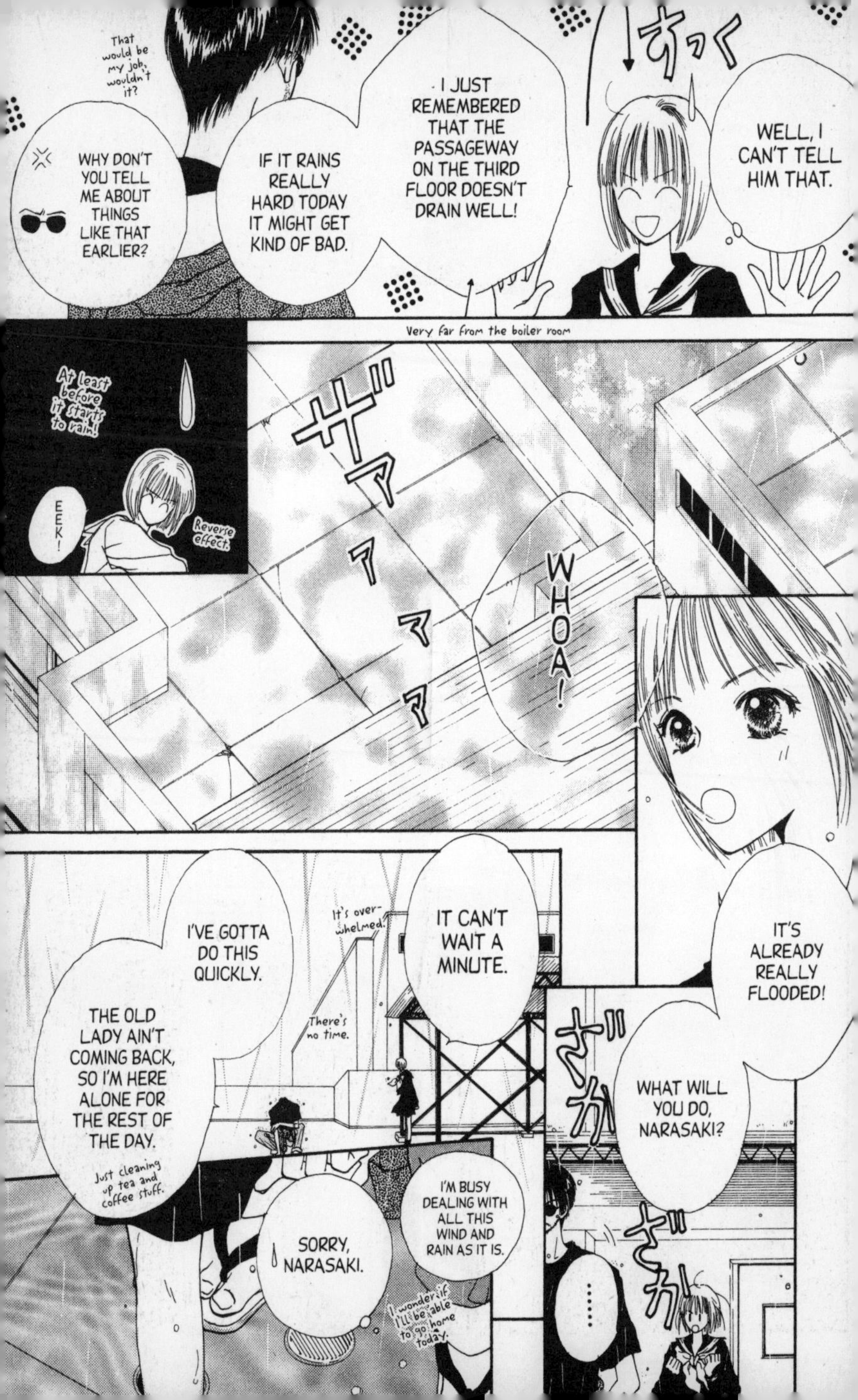
すっく
WELL, I CAN'T TELL HIM THAT.
I JUST REMEMBERED THAT THE PASSAGEWAY ON THE THIRD FLOOR DOESN'T DRAIN WELL!
IF IT RAINS REALLY HARD TODAY IT MIGHT GET KIND OF BAD.
That would be my job, wouldn't it?
WHY DON'T YOU TELL ME ABOUT THINGS LIKE THAT EARLIER?
Very far from the boiler room
ザァァァァ
WHOA!
At least before it starts to rain!
EEK!
Reverse effect.
IT'S ALREADY REALLY FLOODED!
WHAT WILL YOU DO, NARASAKI?
ざか
ざか!
......
IT CAN'T WAIT A MINUTE.
It's over-whelmed.
I'VE GOTTA DO THIS QUICKLY.
THE OLD LADY AIN'T COMING BACK, SO I'M HERE ALONE FOR THE REST OF THE DAY.
There's no time.
I'M BUSY DEALING WITH ALL THIS WIND AND RAIN AS IT IS.
SORRY, NARASAKI.
I wonder if I'll be able to go home today.
Just cleaning up tea and coffee stuff.

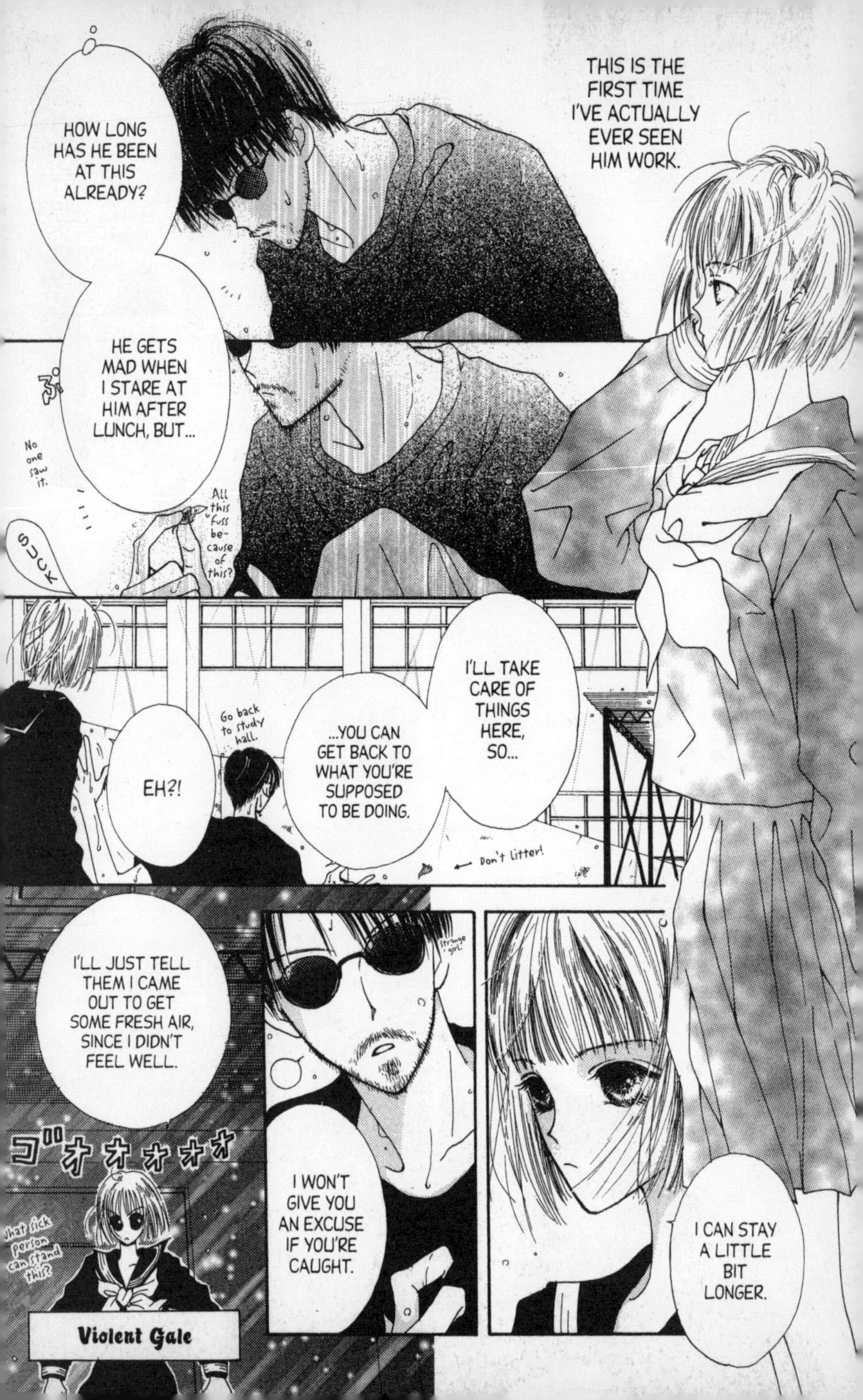
THIS IS THE FIRST TIME I'VE ACTUALLY EVER SEEN HIM WORK.
HOW LONG HAS HE BEEN AT THIS ALREADY?
HE GETS MAD WHEN I STARE AT HIM AFTER LUNCH, BUT...
ぶ
All this fuss be-cause of this?
No one saw it.
SUCK
I'LL TAKE CARE OF THINGS HERE, SO...
...YOU CAN GET BACK TO WHAT YOU'RE SUPPOSED TO BE DOING.
Go back to study hall.
EH?!
Don't litter!
Strange girl.
I WON'T GIVE YOU AN EXCUSE IF YOU'RE CAUGHT.
I'LL JUST TELL THEM I CAME OUT TO GET SOME FRESH AIR, SINCE I DIDN'T FEEL WELL.
ゴオオオオオ
What sick person can stand this?
Violent Gale
I CAN STAY A LITTLE BIT LONGER.

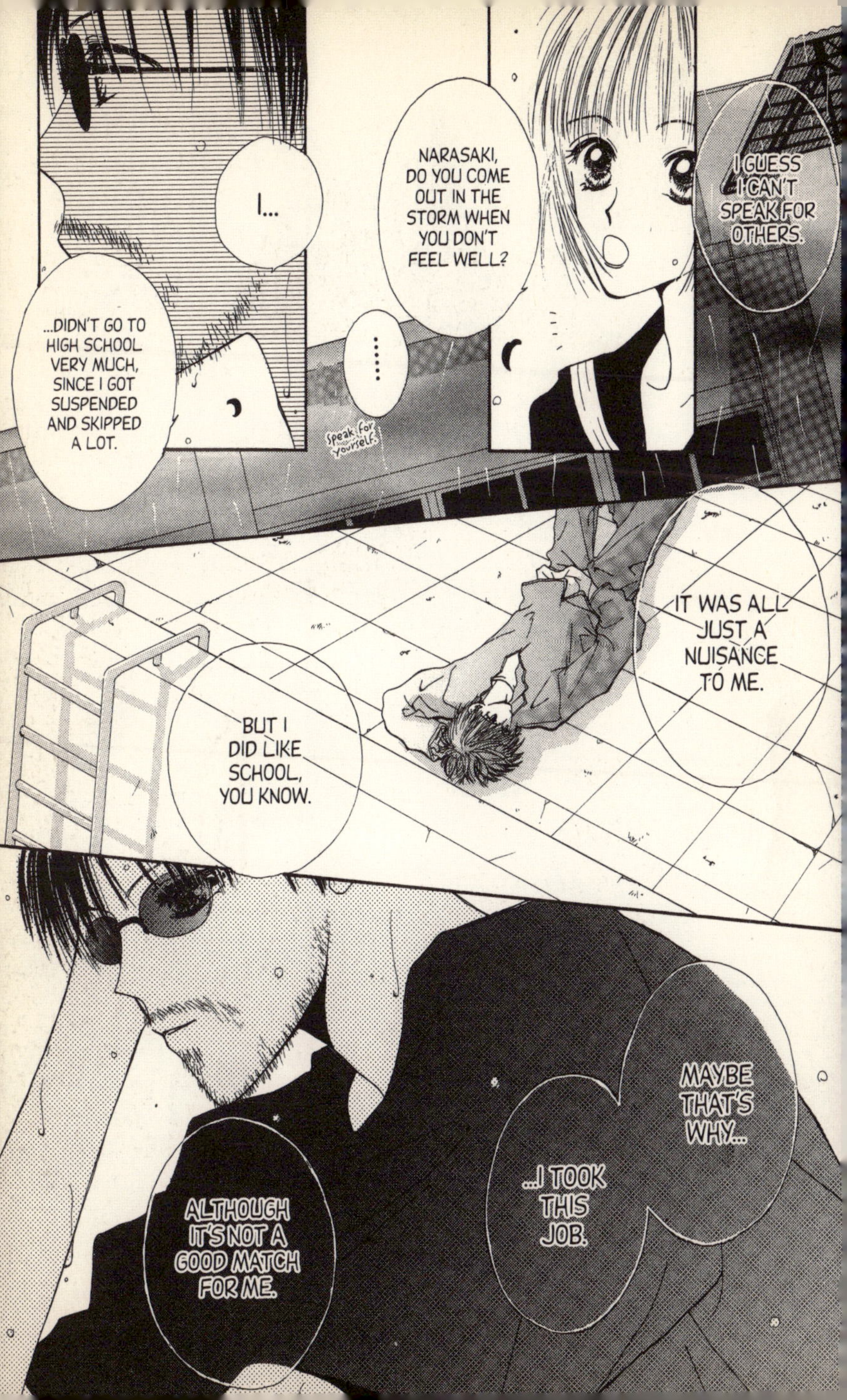
I GUESS I CAN'T SPEAK FOR OTHERS.
NARASAKI, DO YOU COME OUT IN THE STORM WHEN YOU DON'T FEEL WELL?
......
Speak for yourself.
I...
...DIDN'T GO TO HIGH SCHOOL VERY MUCH, SINCE I GOT SUSPENDED AND SKIPPED A LOT.
IT WAS ALL JUST A NUISANCE TO ME.
BUT I DID LIKE SCHOOL, YOU KNOW.
MAYBE THAT'S WHY...
...I TOOK THIS JOB.
ALTHOUGH IT'S NOT A GOOD MATCH FOR ME.

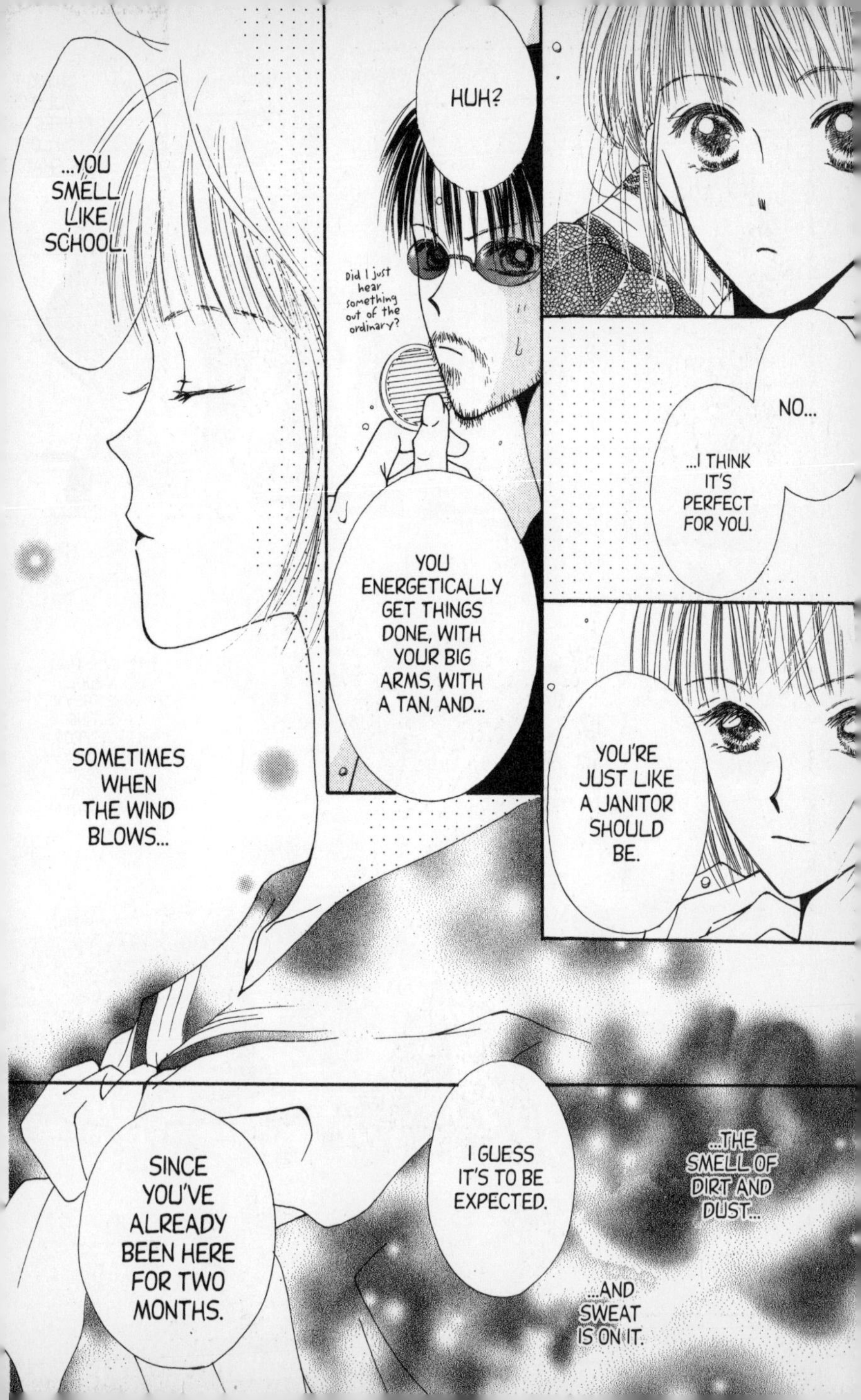
NO...
...I THINK IT'S PERFECT FOR YOU.
YOU'RE JUST LIKE A JANITOR SHOULD BE.
HUH?
Did I just hear something out of the ordinary?
YOU ENERGETICALLY GET THINGS DONE, WITH YOUR BIG ARMS, WITH A TAN, AND...
...YOU SMELL LIKE SCHOOL.
SOMETIMES WHEN THE WIND BLOWS...
...THE SMELL OF DIRT AND DUST...
...AND SWEAT IS ON IT.
I GUESS IT'S TO BE EXPECTED.
SINCE YOU'VE ALREADY BEEN HERE FOR TWO MONTHS.

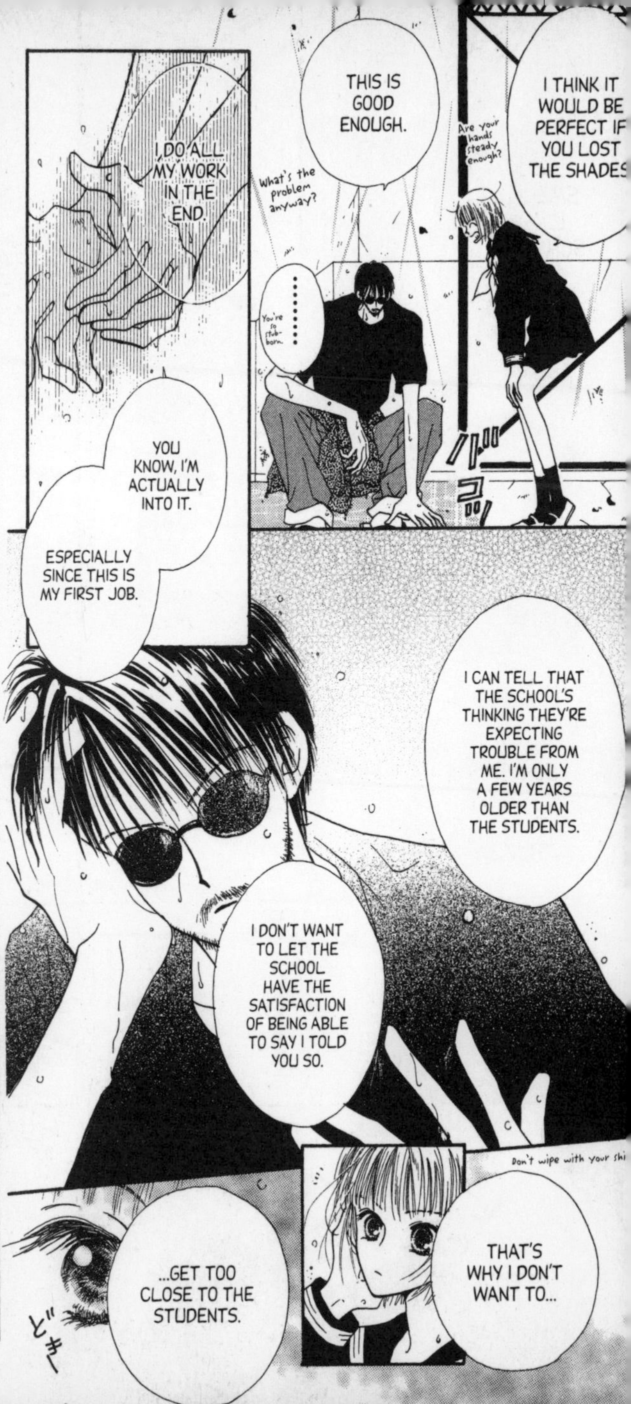
I THINK IT WOULD BE PERFECT IF YOU LOST THE SHADES
Are your hands steady enough?
THIS IS GOOD ENOUGH.
What's the problem anyway?
......
You're so stubborn.
I DO ALL MY WORK IN THE END.
YOU KNOW, I'M ACTUALLY INTO IT.
ESPECIALLY SINCE THIS IS MY FIRST JOB.
I CAN TELL THAT THE SCHOOL'S THINKING THEY'RE EXPECTING TROUBLE FROM ME. I'M ONLY A FEW YEARS OLDER THAN THE STUDENTS.
I DON'T WANT TO LET THE SCHOOL HAVE THE SATISFACTION OF BEING ABLE TO SAY I TOLD YOU SO.
Don't wipe with your shi
THAT'S WHY I DON'T WANT TO...
...GET TOO CLOSE TO THE STUDENTS.

WARDROBE

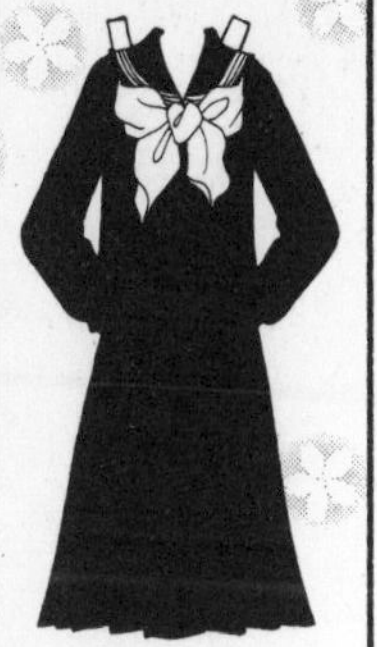

This is a bonus prize. (Ha ha!) The sailor suit uniform that Kano is wearing is a reflection of the reader's wish to have Satsuki wear a sailor suit-type uniform.

Also I get a lot of mail from my readers with drawings of their clothing designs. Thank you very much. Since there are no extra pages this time, I won't be able to introduce them to you, but I hope I will have a chance to in the future. I'm just hoping there will be more books published!

Satsuki is fun to draw, since I can put her in a lot of different type of clothing and arrange her hair in all different styles. Sometimes I think of stories so just to be able to draw a certain kind of clothes. On the other hand, there are times when I just don't have the time to think about clothes and the characters end up in half-baked clothes. I'm glad when my readers tell me they like certain clothes.

I'll do a Sendo doll when the mood strikes!

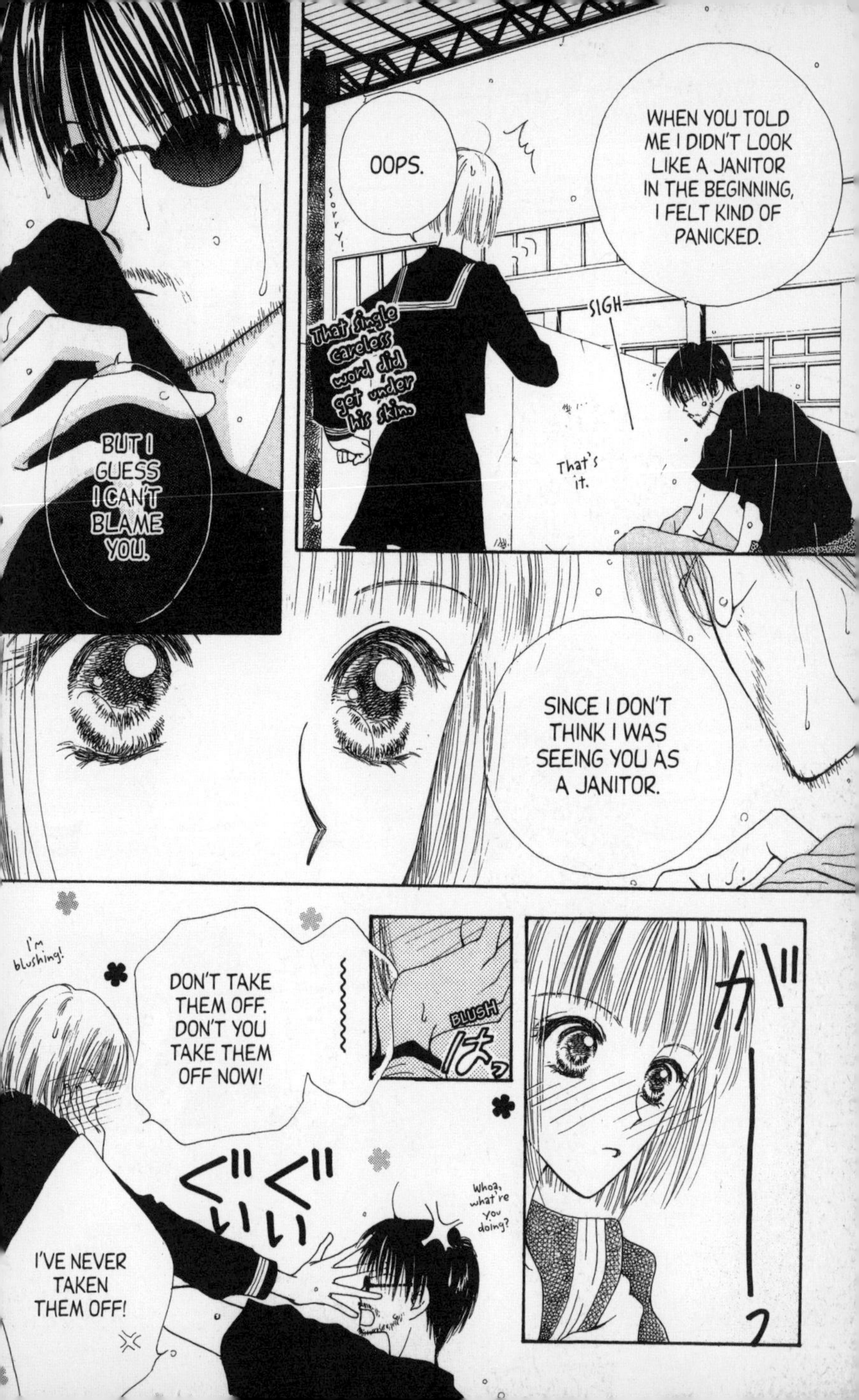
WHEN YOU TOLD ME I DIDN'T LOOK LIKE A JANITOR IN THE BEGINNING, I FELT KIND OF PANICKED.
SIGH
That's it.
OOPS.
sorry!
That single careless word did get under his skin.
BUT I GUESS I CAN'T BLAME YOU.
SINCE I DON'T THINK I WAS SEEING YOU AS A JANITOR.
ガーッ
BLUSH
はっ
DON'T TAKE THEM OFF. DON'T YOU TAKE THEM OFF NOW!
I'm blushing!
ぐいぐい
Whoa, what're you doing?
I'VE NEVER TAKEN THEM OFF!

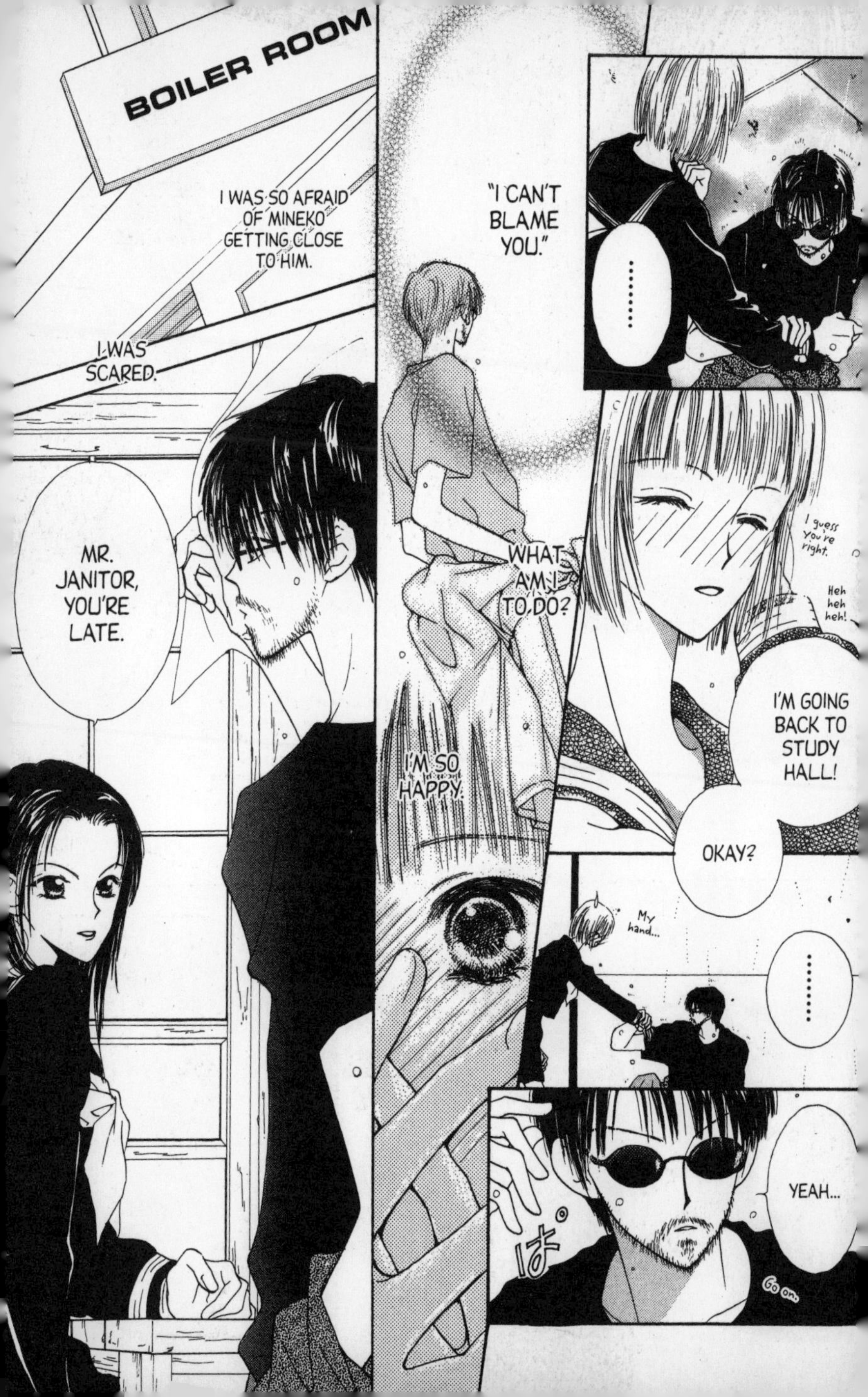

......
I guess you're right.
Heh heh heh!
I'M GOING BACK TO STUDY HALL!
OKAY?
My hand...
......
YEAH...
Go on.
は。
"I CAN'T BLAME YOU."
WHAT AM I TO DO?
I'M SO HAPPY.
BOILER ROOM
I WAS SO AFRAID OF MINEKO GETTING CLOSE TO HIM.
I WAS SCARED.
MR. JANITOR, YOU'RE LATE.

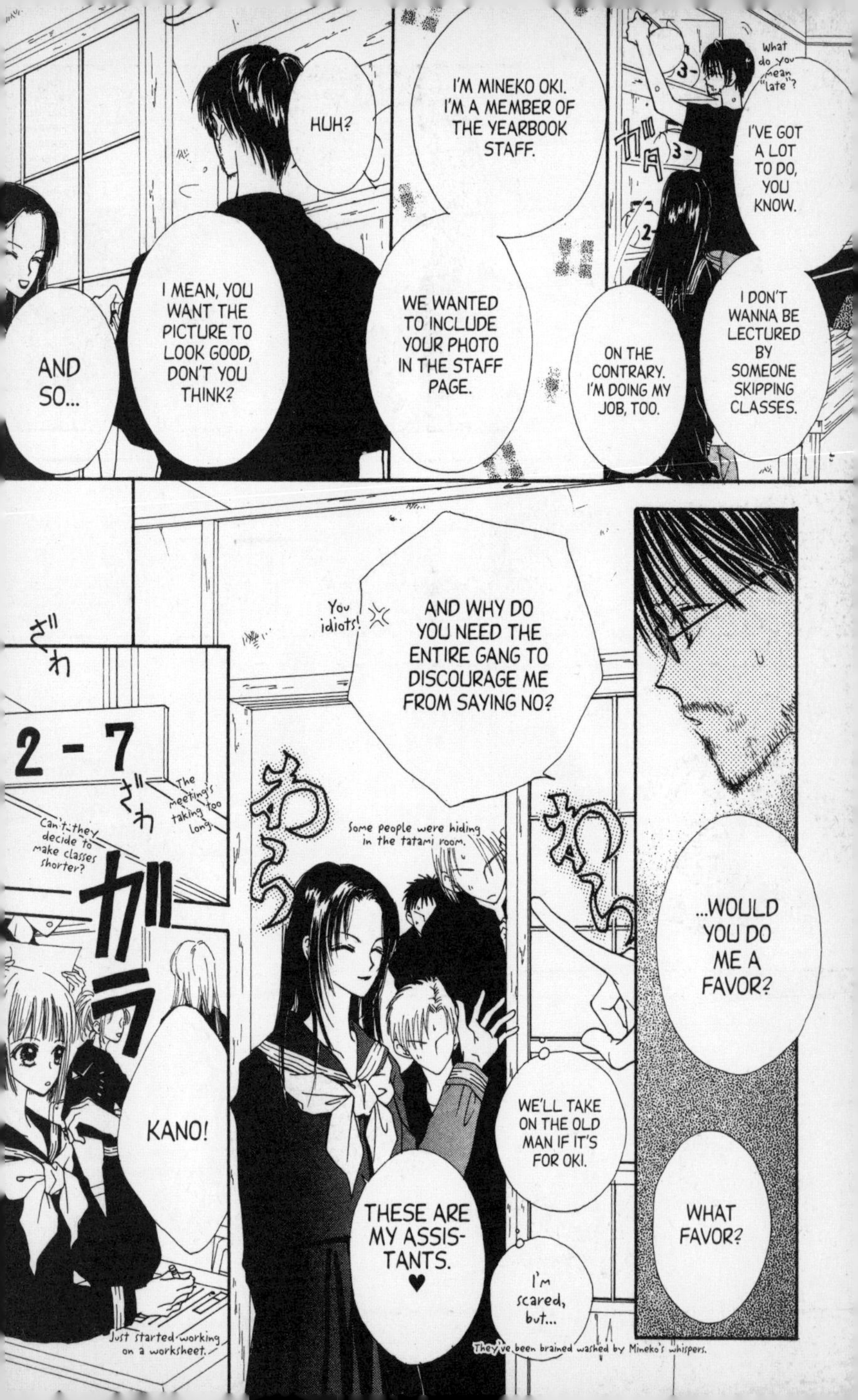
What do you mean "late"?
I'VE GOT A LOT TO DO, YOU KNOW.
I DON'T WANNA BE LECTURED BY SOMEONE SKIPPING CLASSES.
ON THE CONTRARY. I'M DOING MY JOB, TOO.
I'M MINEKO OKI. I'M A MEMBER OF THE YEARBOOK STAFF.
WE WANTED TO INCLUDE YOUR PHOTO IN THE STAFF PAGE.
HUH?
I MEAN, YOU WANT THE PICTURE TO LOOK GOOD, DON'T YOU THINK?
AND SO...
...WOULD YOU DO ME A FAVOR?
WHAT FAVOR?
You idiots!
AND WHY DO YOU NEED THE ENTIRE GANG TO DISCOURAGE ME FROM SAYING NO?
わら
わら
Some people were hiding in the tatami room.
WE'LL TAKE ON THE OLD MAN IF IT'S FOR OKI.
THESE ARE MY ASSIS-TANTS. ♥
I'm scared, but...
They've been brained washed by Mineko's whispers.
ざわ
ざわ
2 - 7
The meeting's taking too long.
Can't they decide to make classes shorter?
ガラ
KANO!
Just started working on a worksheet.

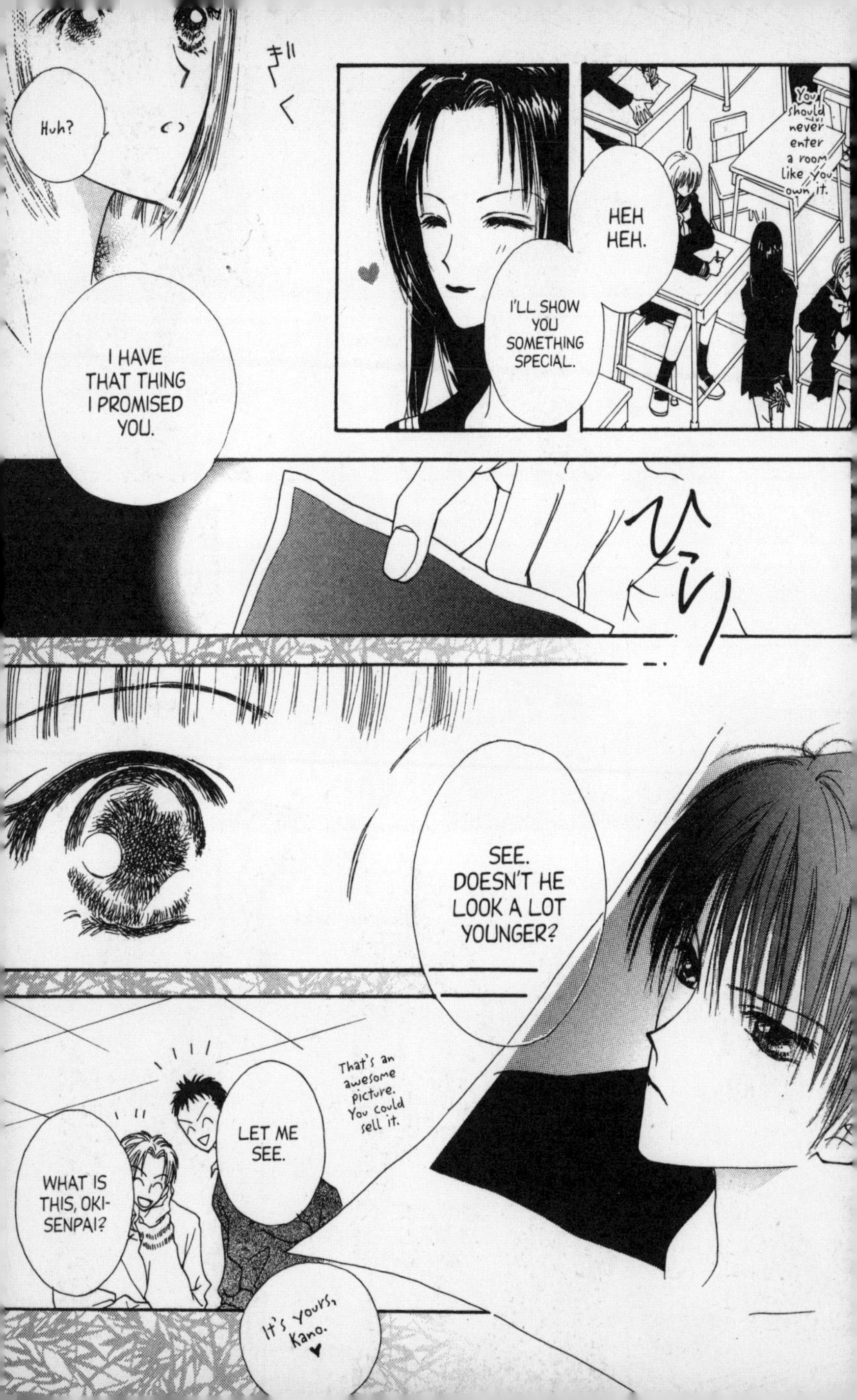
You should never enter a room like you own it.
HEH HEH.
I'LL SHOW YOU SOMETHING SPECIAL.
Huh?
I HAVE THAT THING I PROMISED YOU.
SEE. DOESN'T HE LOOK A LOT YOUNGER?
That's an awesome picture. You could sell it.
LET ME SEE.
WHAT IS THIS, OKI-SENPAI?
It's yours, Kano.

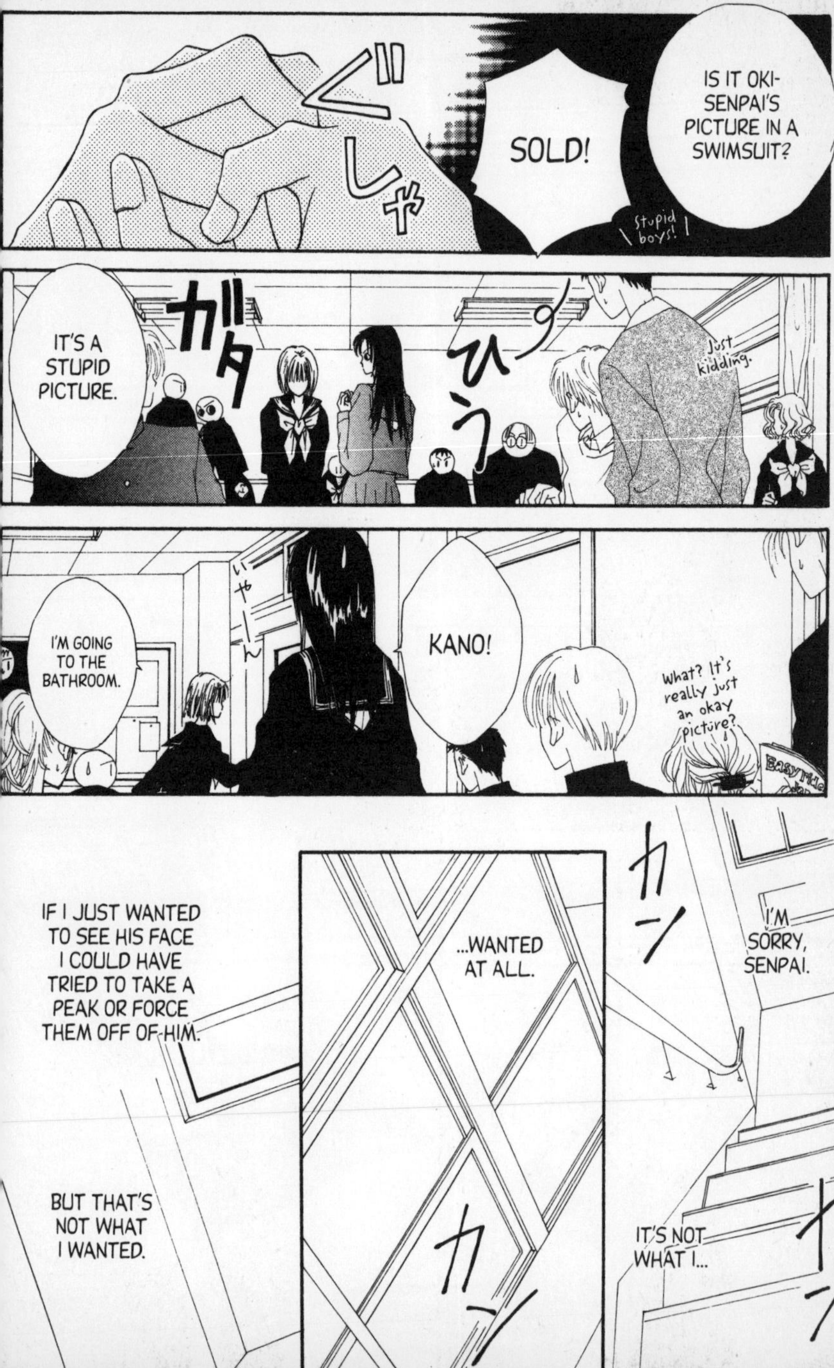
IS IT OKI-SENPAI'S PICTURE IN A SWIMSUIT?
stupid boys!
SOLD!
ぐしゃ
Just kidding.
ひう
ガタ
IT'S A STUPID PICTURE.
What? It's really just an okay picture?
KANO!
いやーん
I'M GOING TO THE BATHROOM.
カーン
I'M SORRY, SENPAI.
...WANTED AT ALL.
IF I JUST WANTED TO SEE HIS FACE I COULD HAVE TRIED TO TAKE A PEAK OR FORCE THEM OFF OF HIM.
カーン
IT'S NOT WHAT I...
カーン
BUT THAT'S NOT WHAT I WANTED.

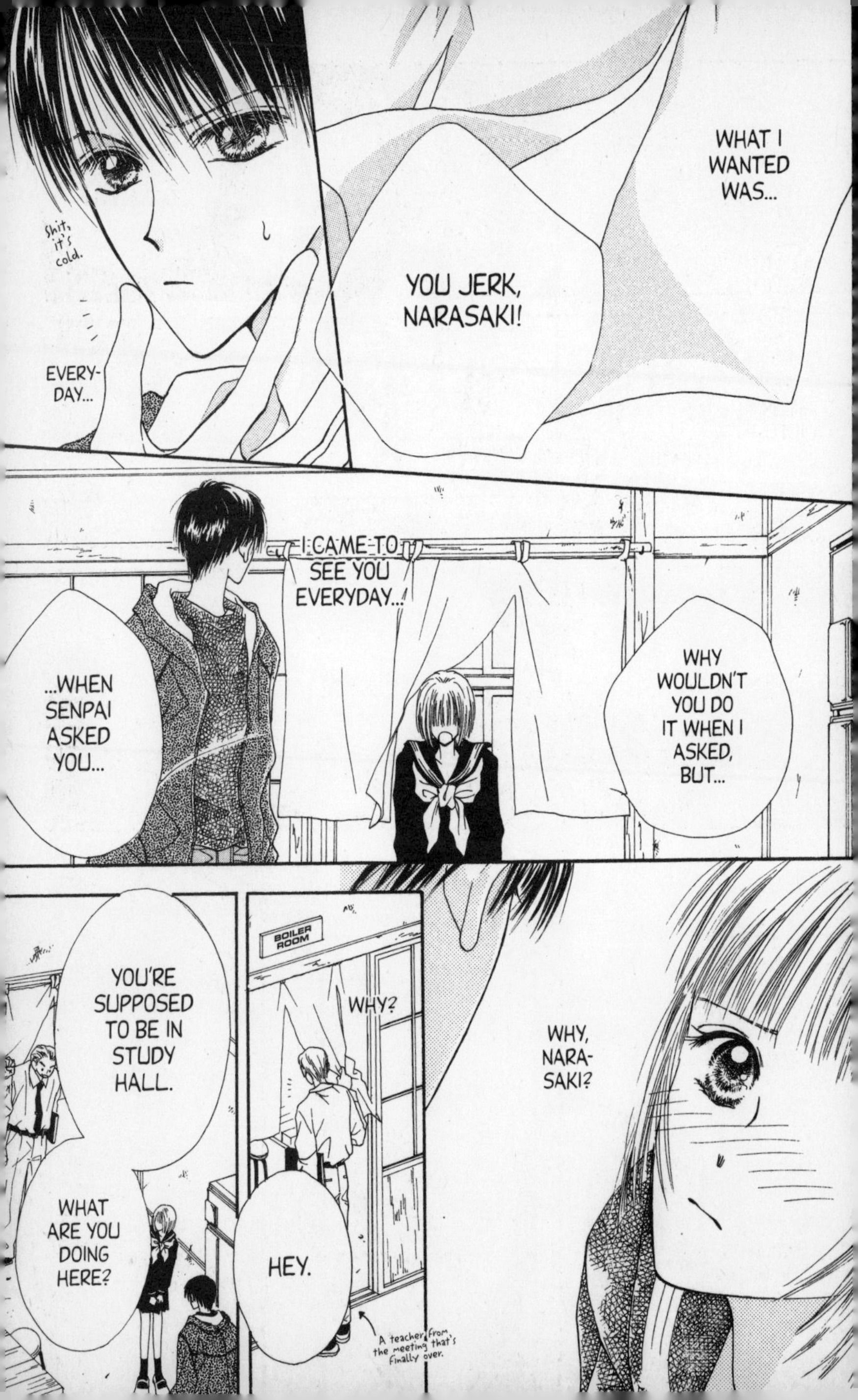
WHAT I WANTED WAS...
YOU JERK, NARASAKI!
Shit, it's cold.
EVERY-DAY...
WHY WOULDN'T YOU DO IT WHEN I ASKED, BUT...
I CAME TO SEE YOU EVERYDAY...
...WHEN SENPAI ASKED YOU...
WHY, NARA-SAKI?
BOILER ROOM
WHY?
HEY.
A teacher from the meeting that's finally over.
YOU'RE SUPPOSED TO BE IN STUDY HALL.
WHAT ARE YOU DOING HERE?

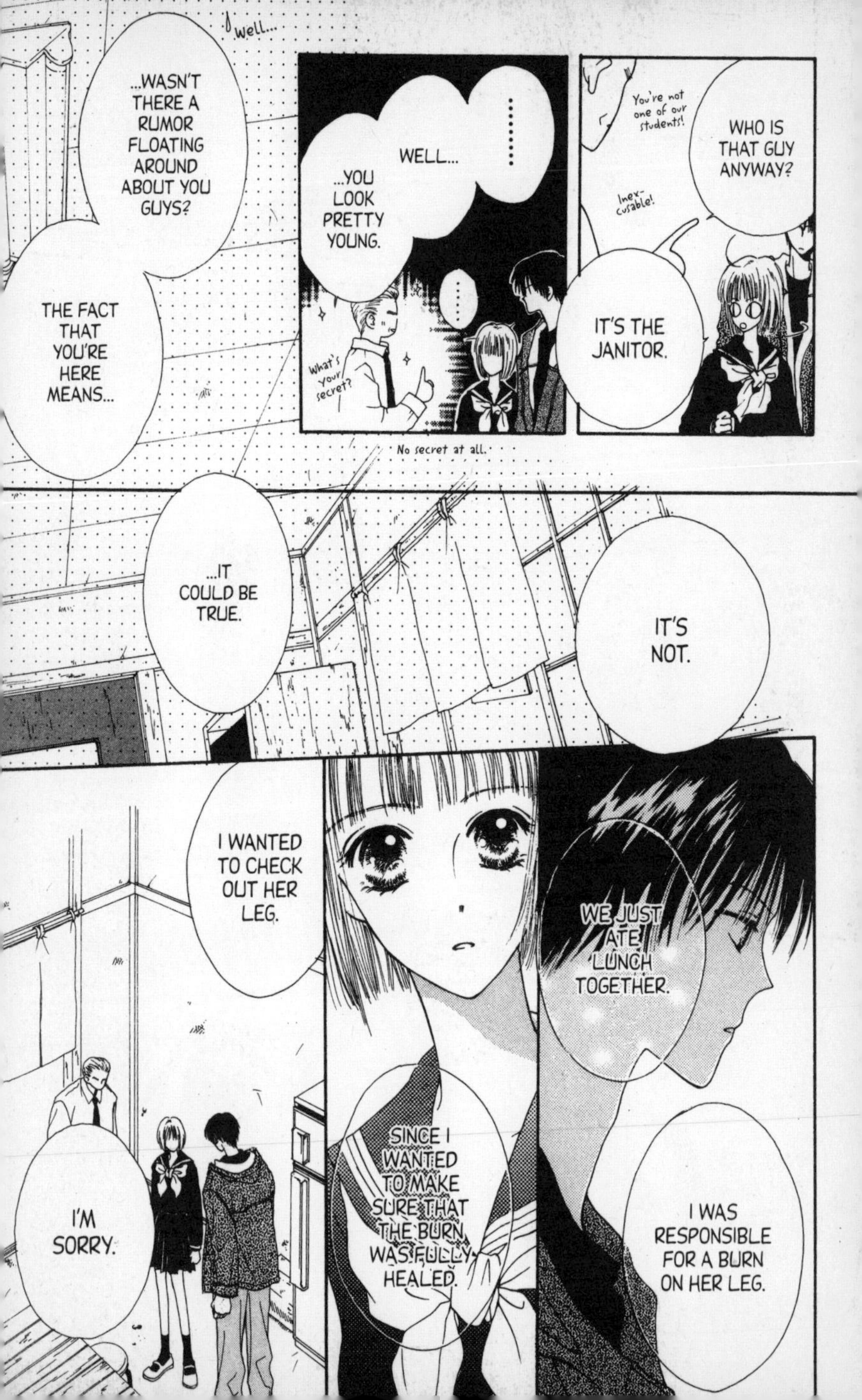
WHO IS THAT GUY ANYWAY?
You're not one of our students!
Inexcusable!
IT'S THE JANITOR.
WELL...
......
...YOU LOOK PRETTY YOUNG.
......
What's your secret?
No secret at all.
well...
...WASN'T THERE A RUMOR FLOATING AROUND ABOUT YOU GUYS?
THE FACT THAT YOU'RE HERE MEANS...
IT'S NOT.
...IT COULD BE TRUE.
WE JUST ATE LUNCH TOGETHER.
I WAS RESPONSIBLE FOR A BURN ON HER LEG.
SINCE I WANTED TO MAKE SURE THAT THE BURN WAS FULLY HEALED.
I WANTED TO CHECK OUT HER LEG.
I'M SORRY.

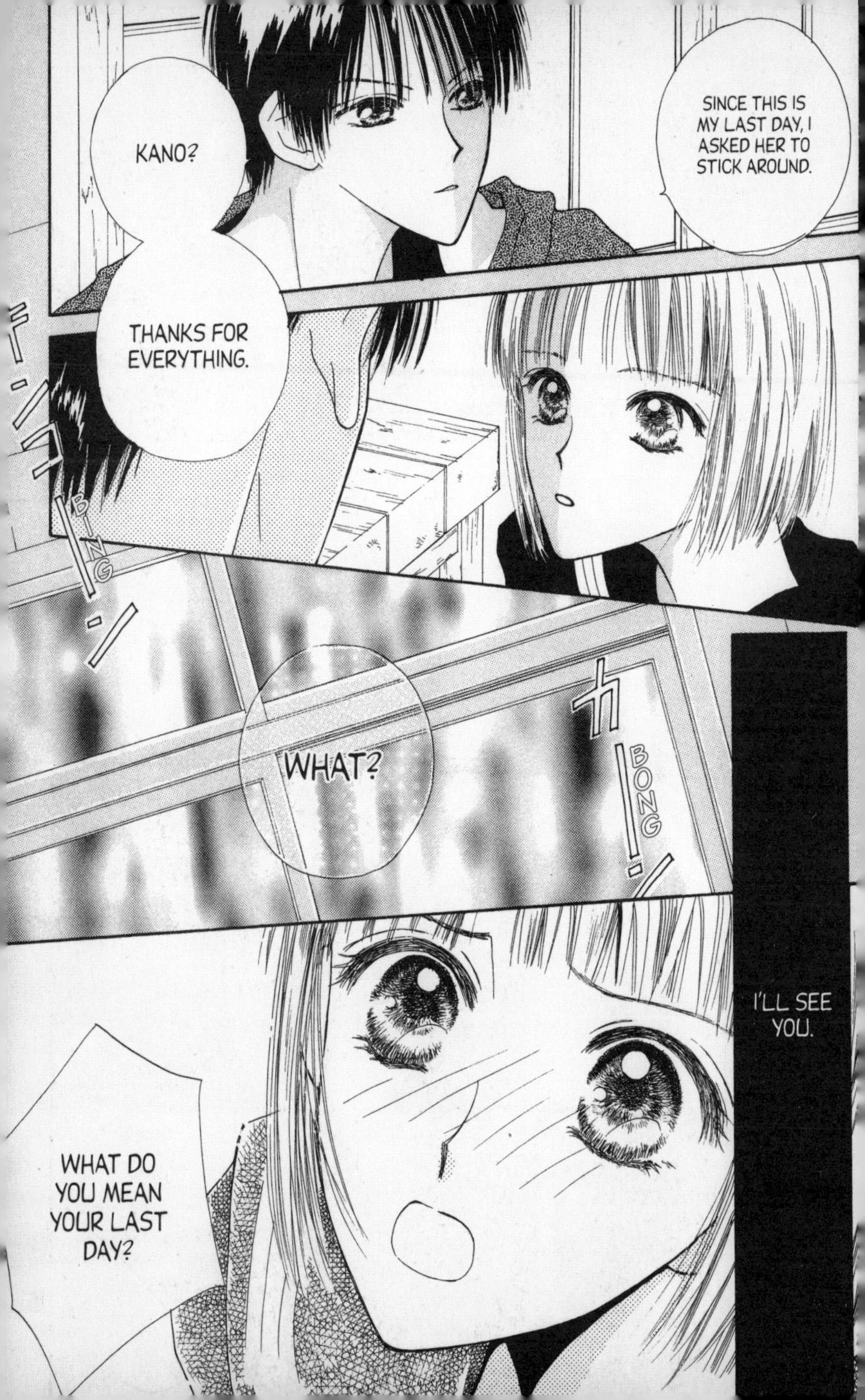
SINCE THIS IS MY LAST DAY, I ASKED HER TO STICK AROUND.
KANO?
THANKS FOR EVERYTHING.
BING
I'LL SEE YOU.
BONG
WHAT?
WHAT DO YOU MEAN YOUR LAST DAY?

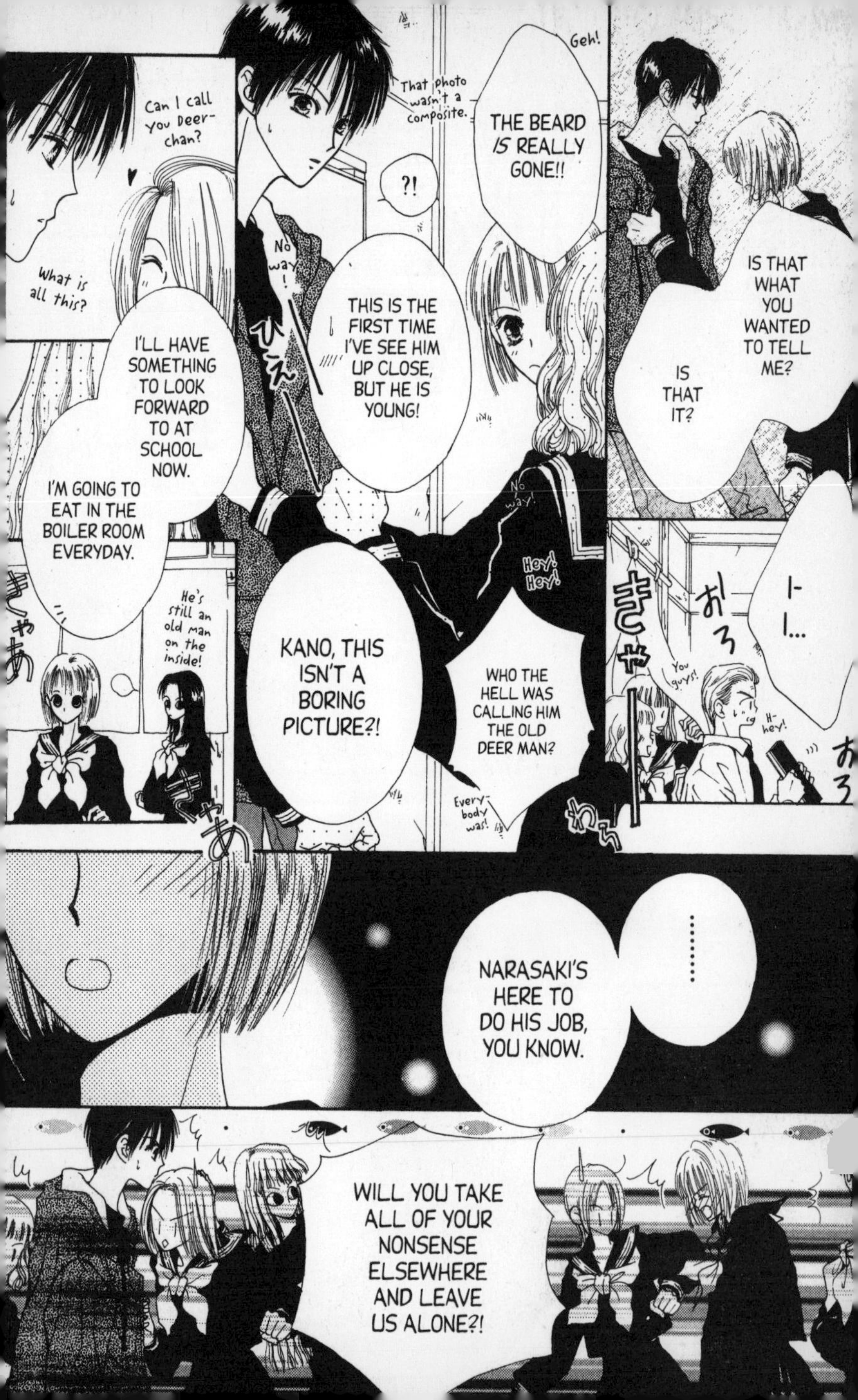
IS THAT WHAT YOU WANTED TO TELL ME?
IS THAT IT?
I-I...
You guys!
H-hey!
Geh!
THE BEARD IS REALLY GONE!!
That photo wasn't a composite.
?!
No way!
THIS IS THE FIRST TIME I'VE SEE HIM UP CLOSE, BUT HE IS YOUNG!
No way!
Hey! Hey!
KANO, THIS ISN'T A BORING PICTURE?!
WHO THE HELL WAS CALLING HIM THE OLD DEER MAN?
Every-body was!
Can I call you Deer-chan?
What is all this?
I'LL HAVE SOMETHING TO LOOK FORWARD TO AT SCHOOL NOW.
I'M GOING TO EAT IN THE BOILER ROOM EVERYDAY.
He's still an old man on the inside!
......
NARASAKI'S HERE TO DO HIS JOB, YOU KNOW.
WILL YOU TAKE ALL OF YOUR NONSENSE ELSEWHERE AND LEAVE US ALONE?!

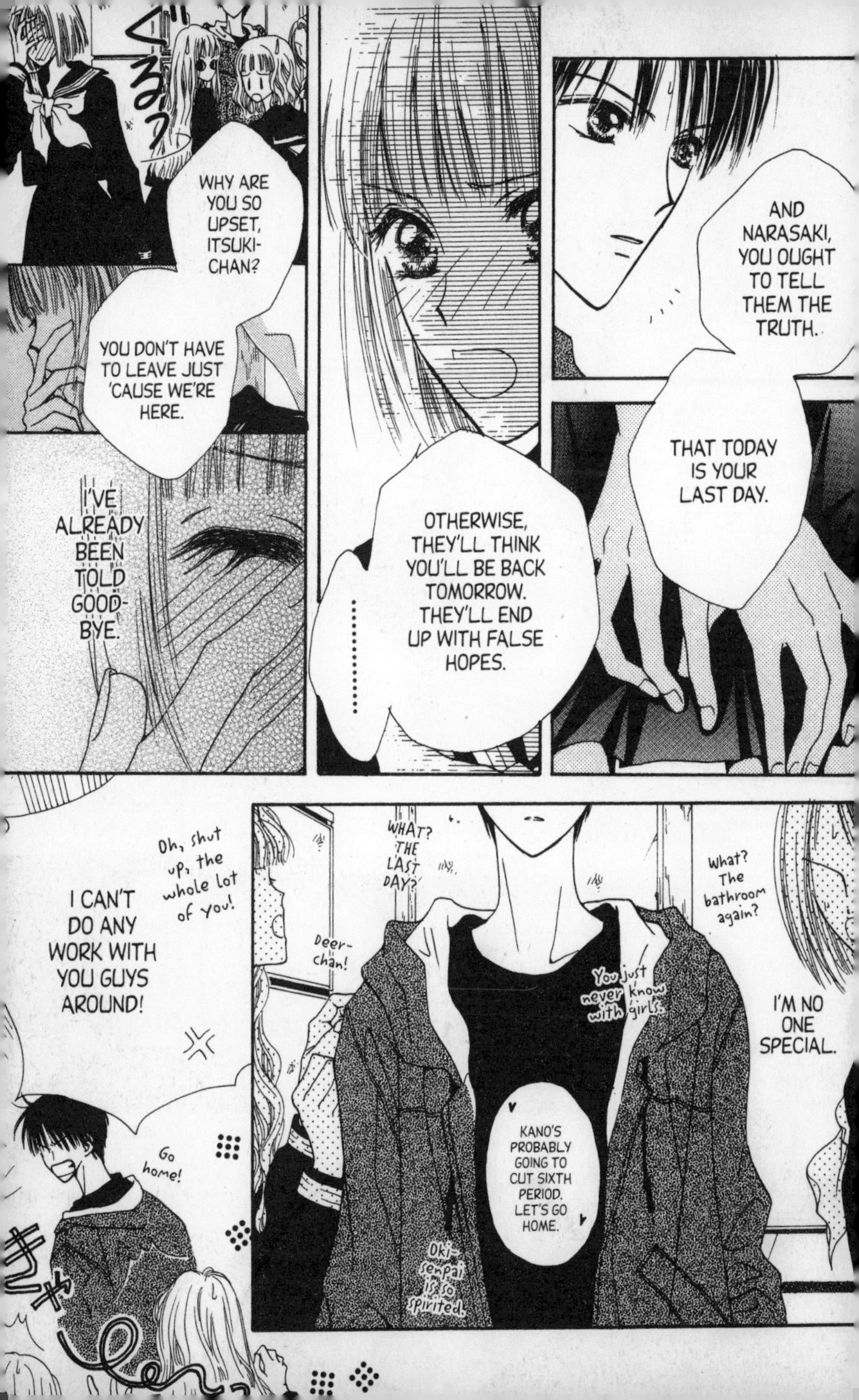

AND NARASAKI, YOU OUGHT TO TELL THEM THE TRUTH.
THAT TODAY IS YOUR LAST DAY.
OTHERWISE, THEY'LL THINK YOU'LL BE BACK TOMORROW. THEY'LL END UP WITH FALSE HOPES.
......
くるっ
WHY ARE YOU SO UPSET, ITSUKI-CHAN?
YOU DON'T HAVE TO LEAVE JUST 'CAUSE WE'RE HERE.
I'VE ALREADY BEEN TOLD GOOD-BYE.
I'M NO ONE SPECIAL.
What? The bathroom again?
WHAT? THE LAST DAY?
Deer-chan!
You just never know with girls.
KANO'S PROBABLY GOING TO CUT SIXTH PERIOD. LET'S GO HOME.
Oki-senpai is so spirited.
I CAN'T DO ANY WORK WITH YOU GUYS AROUND!
Oh, shut up, the whole lot of you!
Go home!

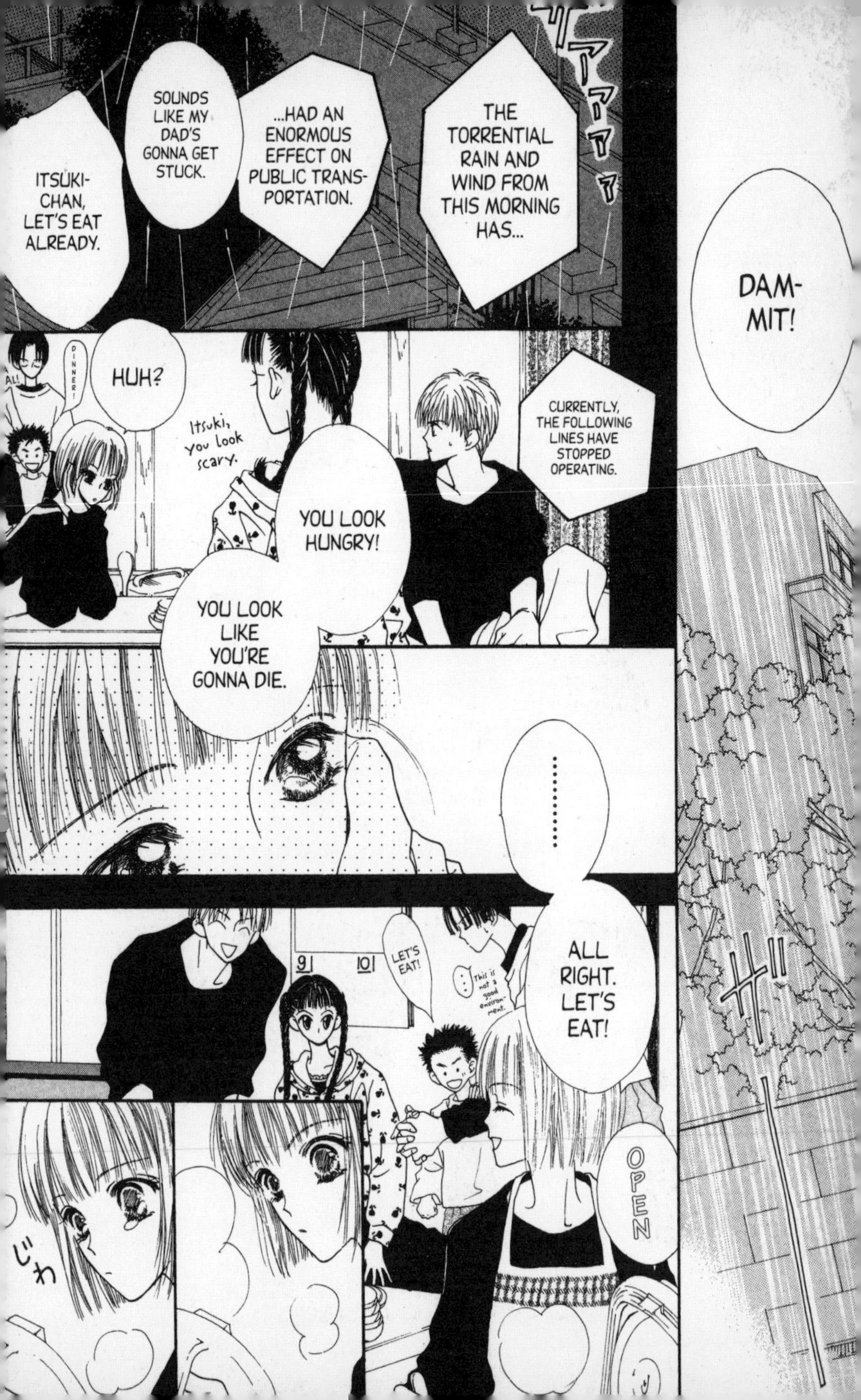
DAM-MIT!
THE TORRENTIAL RAIN AND WIND FROM THIS MORNING HAS...
...HAD AN ENORMOUS EFFECT ON PUBLIC TRANS-PORTATION.
SOUNDS LIKE MY DAD'S GONNA GET STUCK.
ITSUKI-CHAN, LET'S EAT ALREADY.
CURRENTLY, THE FOLLOWING LINES HAVE STOPPED OPERATING.
YOU LOOK HUNGRY!
YOU LOOK LIKE YOU'RE GONNA DIE.
Itsuki, you look scary.
HUH?
DINNER!
......
ALL RIGHT. LET'S EAT!
This is not a good environ-ment.
LET'S EAT!
OPEN
じわ

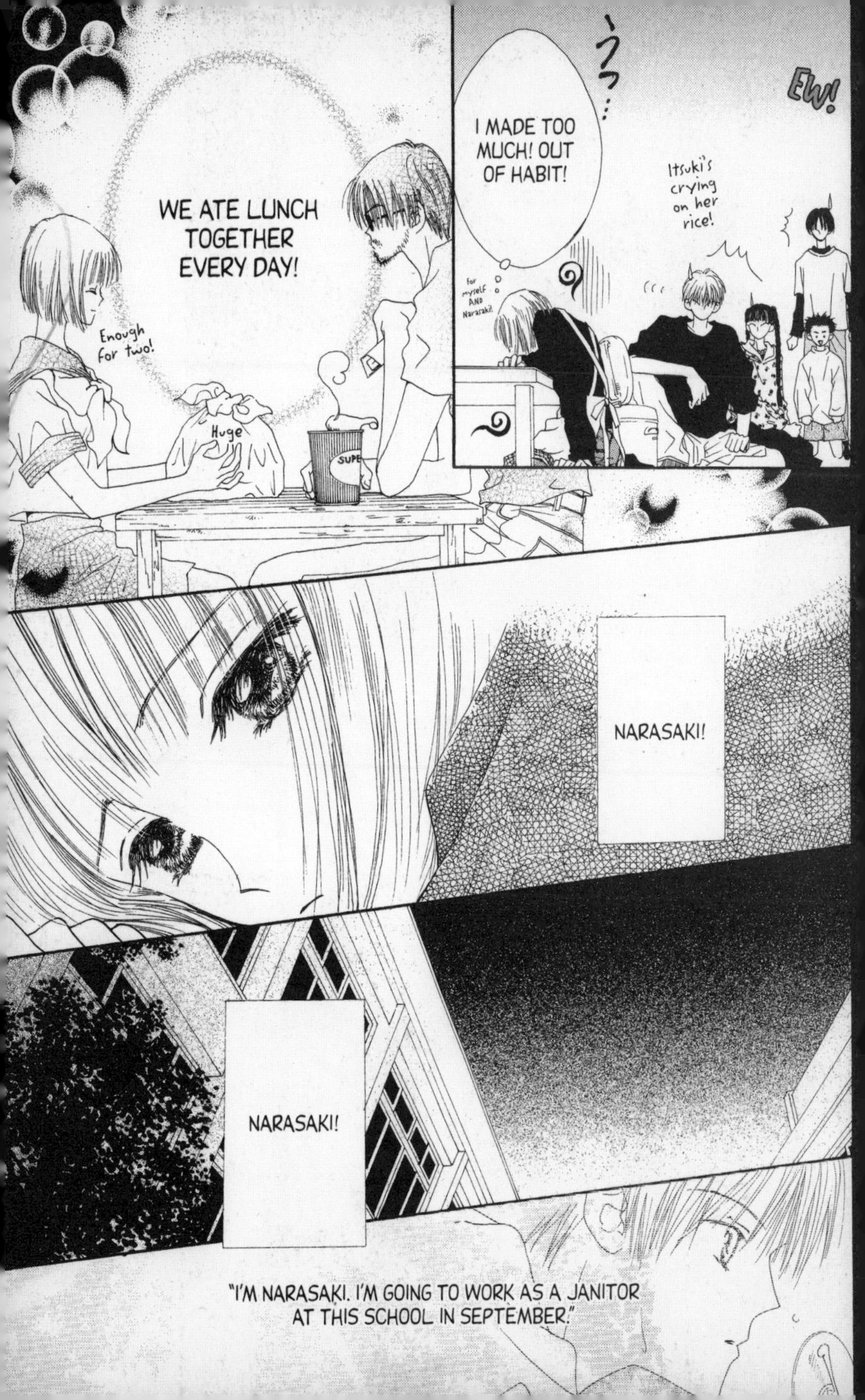
EW!
Itsuki's crying on her rice!
I MADE TOO MUCH! OUT OF HABIT!
for myself AND Narasaki!!
WE ATE LUNCH TOGETHER EVERY DAY!
Enough for two!
Huge
SUPE
NARASAKI!
NARASAKI!
"I'M NARASAKI. I'M GOING TO WORK AS A JANITOR AT THIS SCHOOL IN SEPTEMBER."

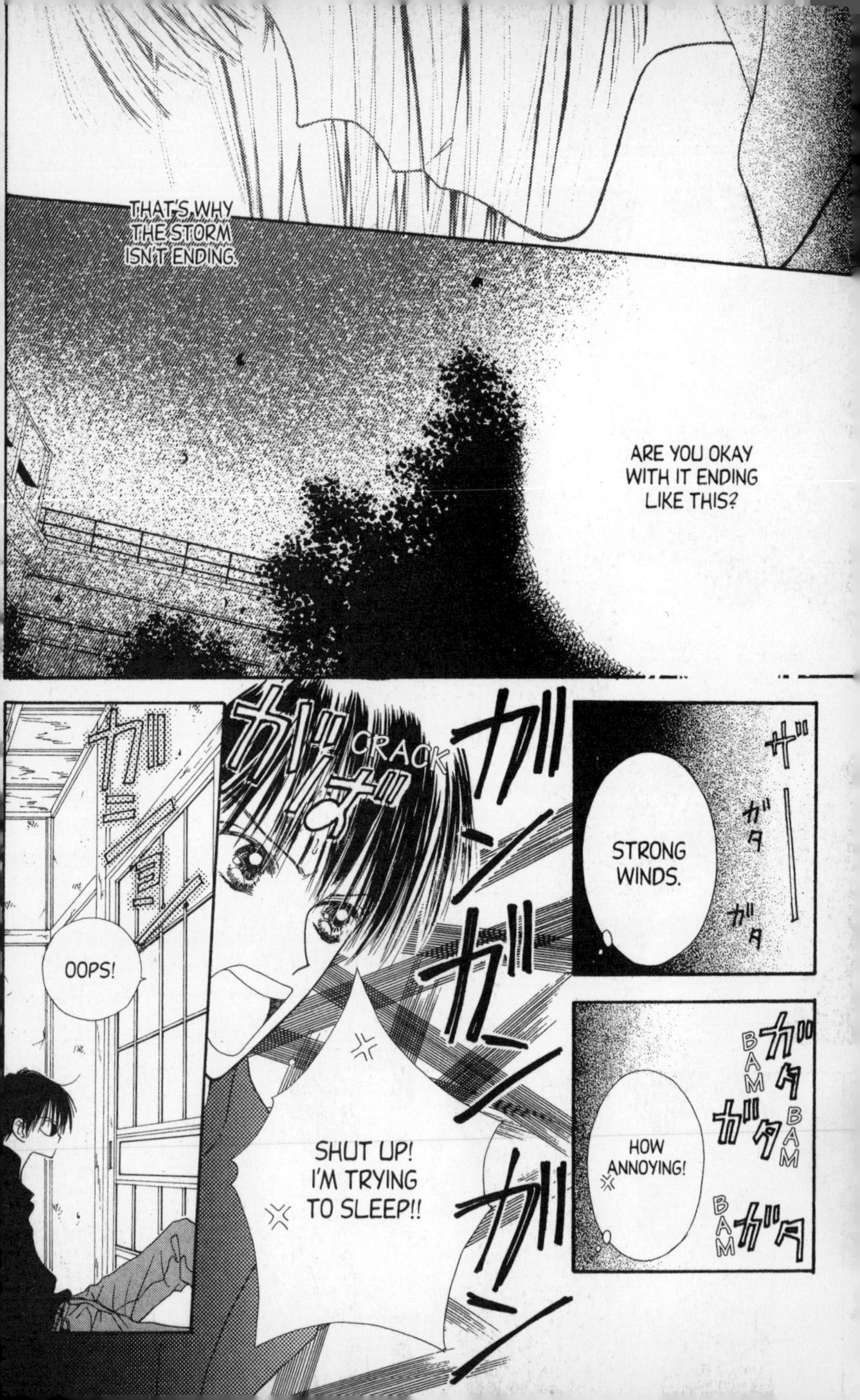

THAT'S WHY THE STORM ISN'T ENDING.
ARE YOU OKAY WITH IT ENDING LIKE THIS?
ザー
ガタ ガタ
STRONG WINDS.
BAM BAM BAM
HOW ANNOYING!
CRACK
SHUT UP! I'M TRYING TO SLEEP!!
OOPS!

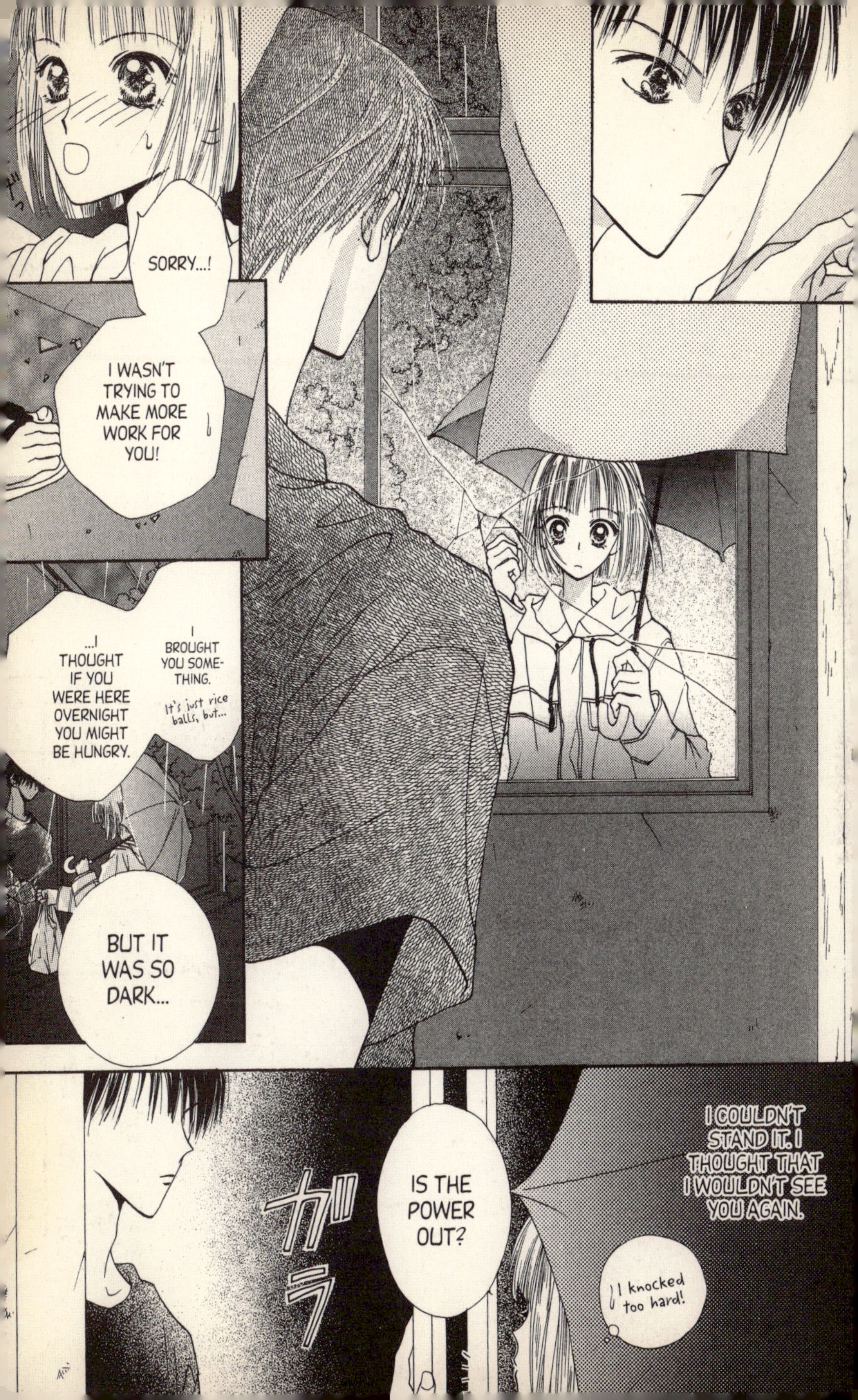

SORRY...!
I WASN'T TRYING TO MAKE MORE WORK FOR YOU!
I BROUGHT YOU SOME-THING.
It's just rice balls, but...
...I THOUGHT IF YOU WERE HERE OVERNIGHT YOU MIGHT BE HUNGRY.
BUT IT WAS SO DARK...
I COULDN'T STAND IT. I THOUGHT THAT I WOULDN'T SEE YOU AGAIN.
I knocked too hard!
IS THE POWER OUT?
ガラ

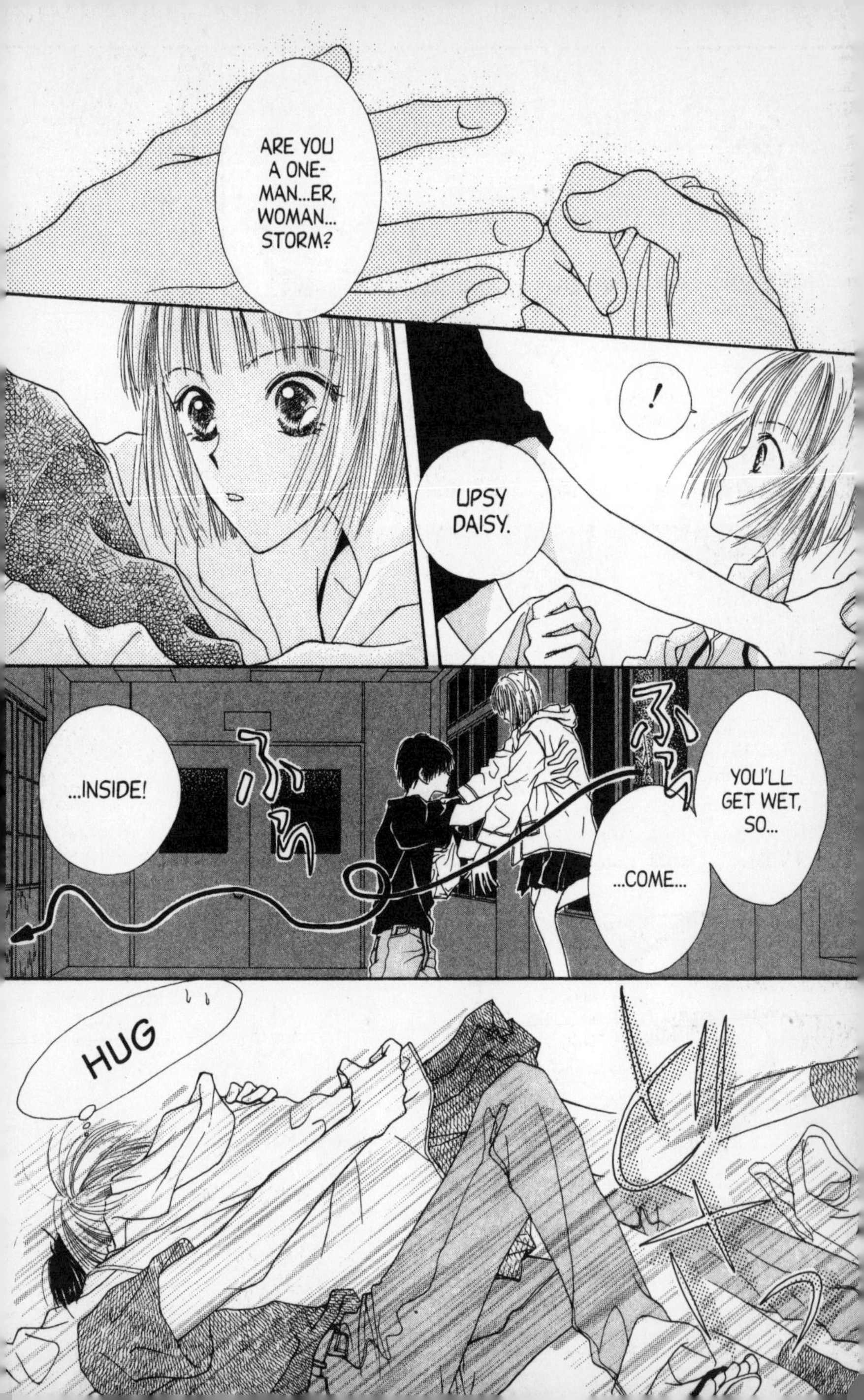
ARE YOU A ONE-MAN...ER, WOMAN... STORM?
!
UPSY DAISY.
YOU'LL GET WET, SO...
...COME...
...INSIDE!
HUG

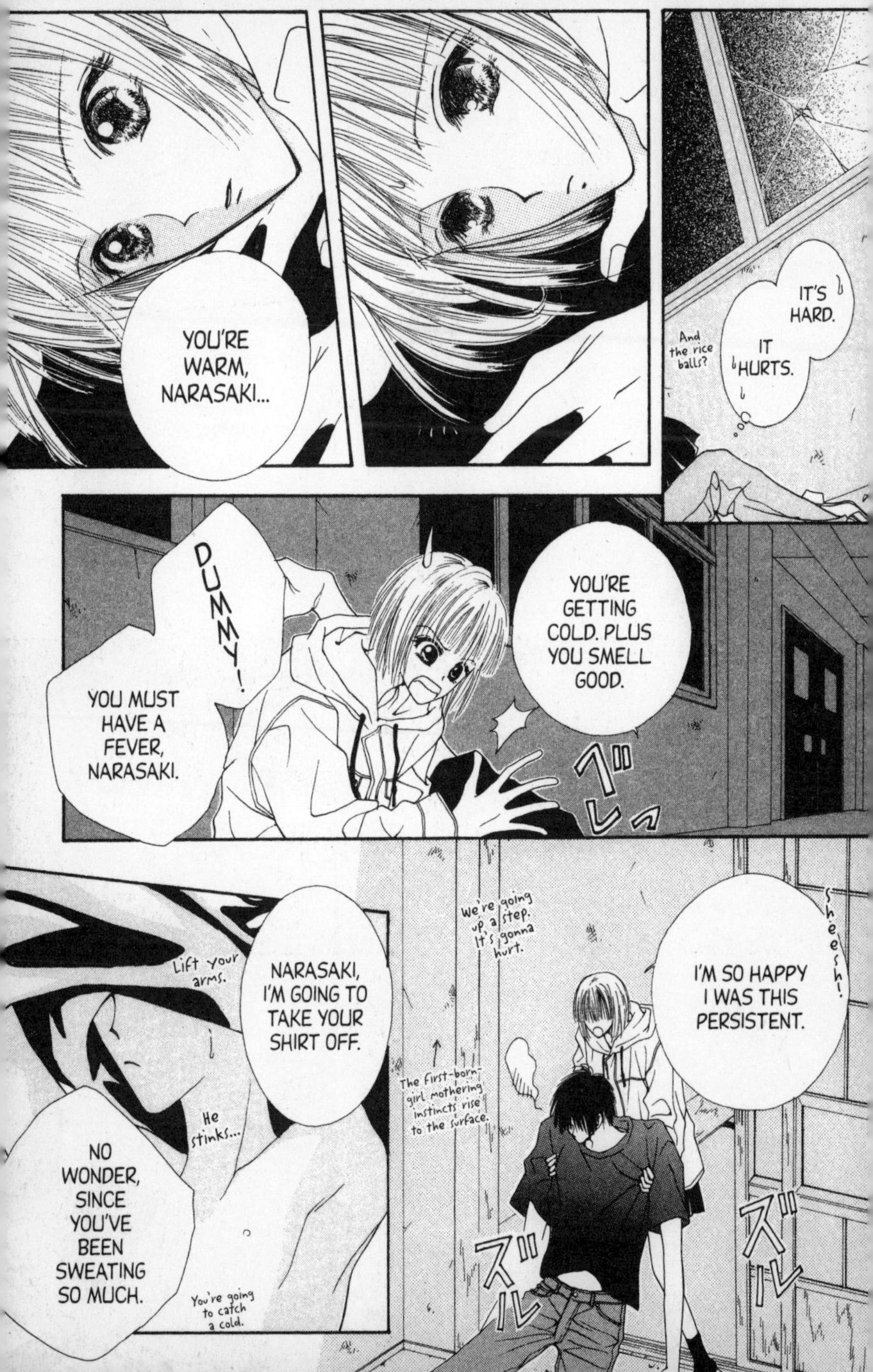

IT'S HARD.
IT HURTS.
And the rice balls?
YOU'RE WARM, NARASAKI...
YOU'RE GETTING COLD. PLUS YOU SMELL GOOD.
DUMMY!
YOU MUST HAVE A FEVER, NARASAKI.
sheesh!
I'M SO HAPPY I WAS THIS PERSISTENT.
We're going up a step. It's gonna hurt.
The first-born-girl mothering instincts rise to the surface.
ズル
ズル
NARASAKI, I'M GOING TO TAKE YOUR SHIRT OFF.
Lift your arms.
He stinks...
NO WONDER, SINCE YOU'VE BEEN SWEATING SO MUCH.
You're going to catch a cold.

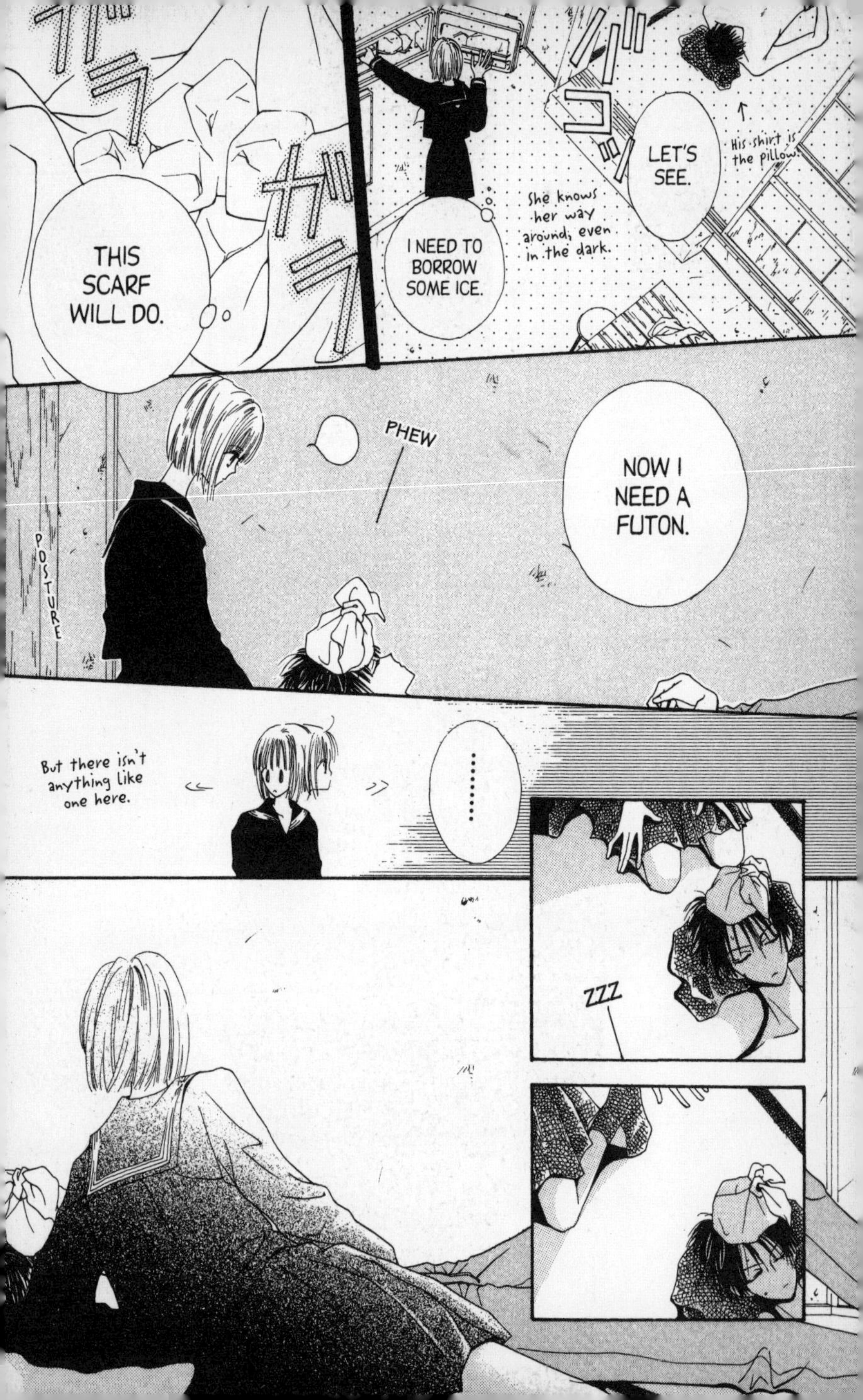
His shirt is the pillow.
LET'S SEE.
She knows her way around, even in the dark.
I NEED TO BORROW SOME ICE.
THIS SCARF WILL DO.
NOW I NEED A FUTON.
PHEW
POSTURE
......
But there isn't anything like one here.
ZZZ

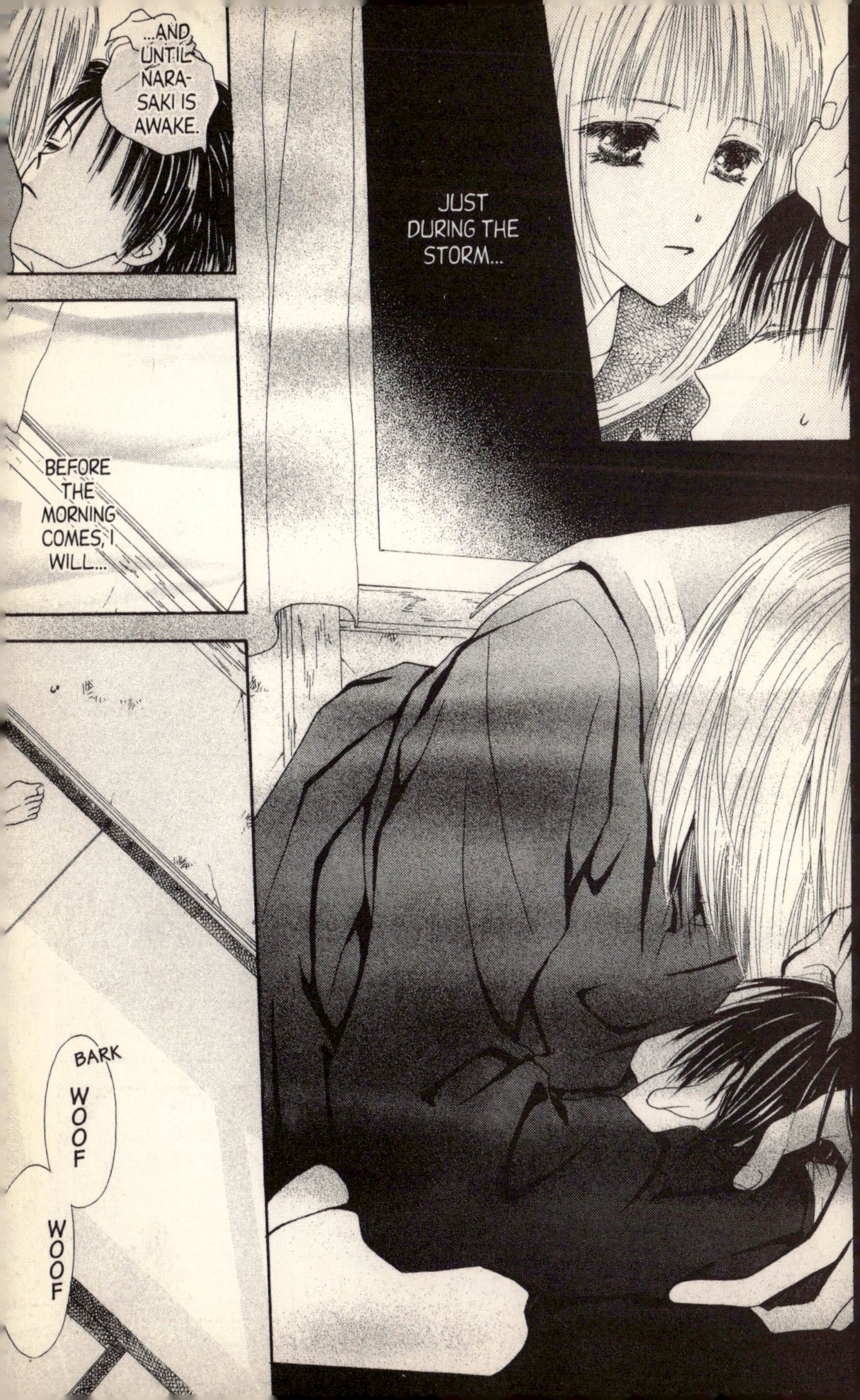
JUST DURING THE STORM...
...AND UNTIL NARA-SAKI IS AWAKE.
BEFORE THE MORNING COMES, I WILL...
BARK
WOOF
WOOF

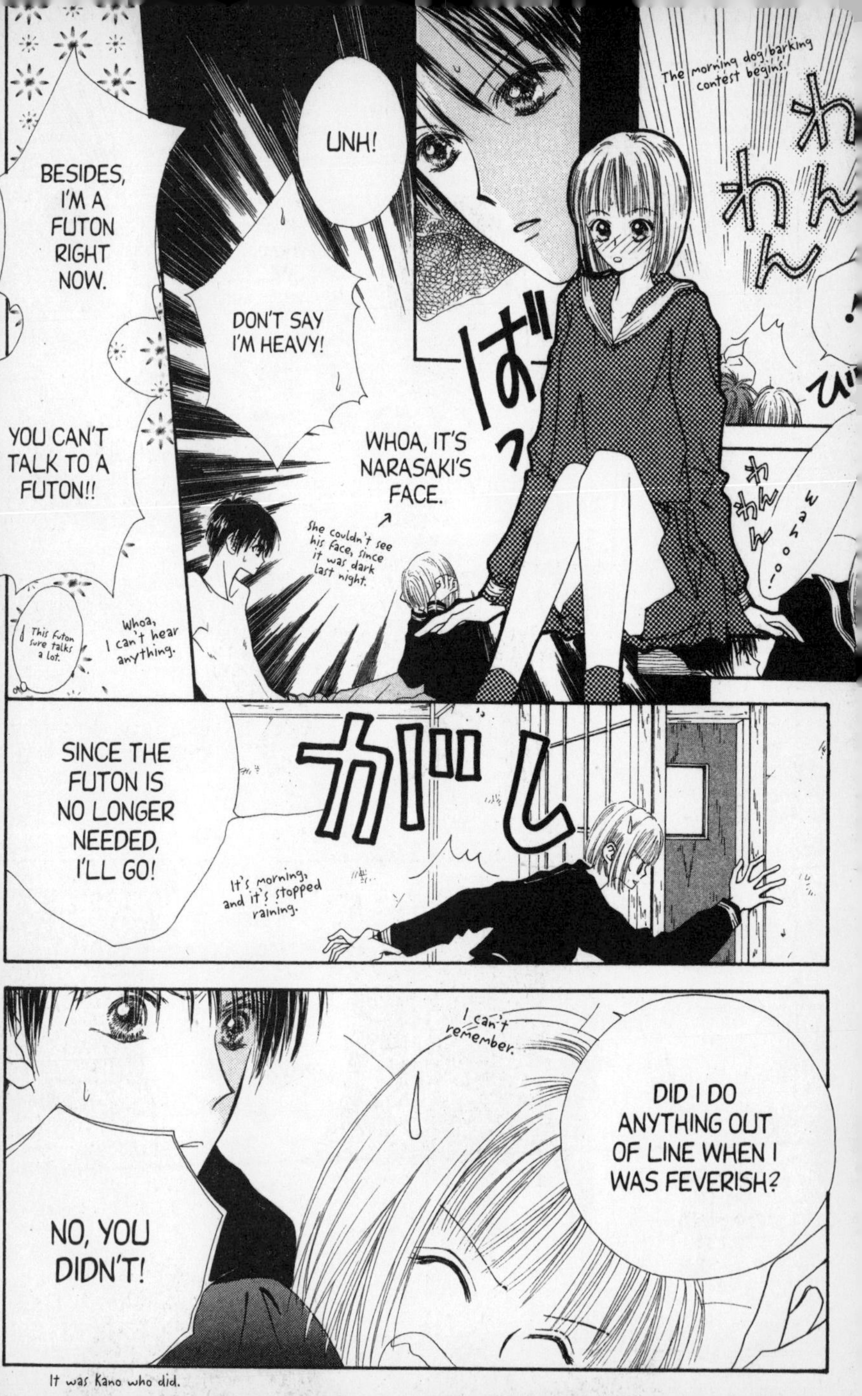
The morning dog-barking contest begins!
UNH!
DON'T SAY I'M HEAVY!
WHOA, IT'S NARASAKI'S FACE.
She couldn't see his face, since it was dark last night.
Whoa, I can't hear anything.
BESIDES, I'M A FUTON RIGHT NOW.
YOU CAN'T TALK TO A FUTON!!
This futon sure talks a lot.
SINCE THE FUTON IS NO LONGER NEEDED, I'LL GO!
It's morning, and it's stopped raining.
I can't remember.
DID I DO ANYTHING OUT OF LINE WHEN I WAS FEVERISH?
NO, YOU DIDN'T!

It was Kano who did.

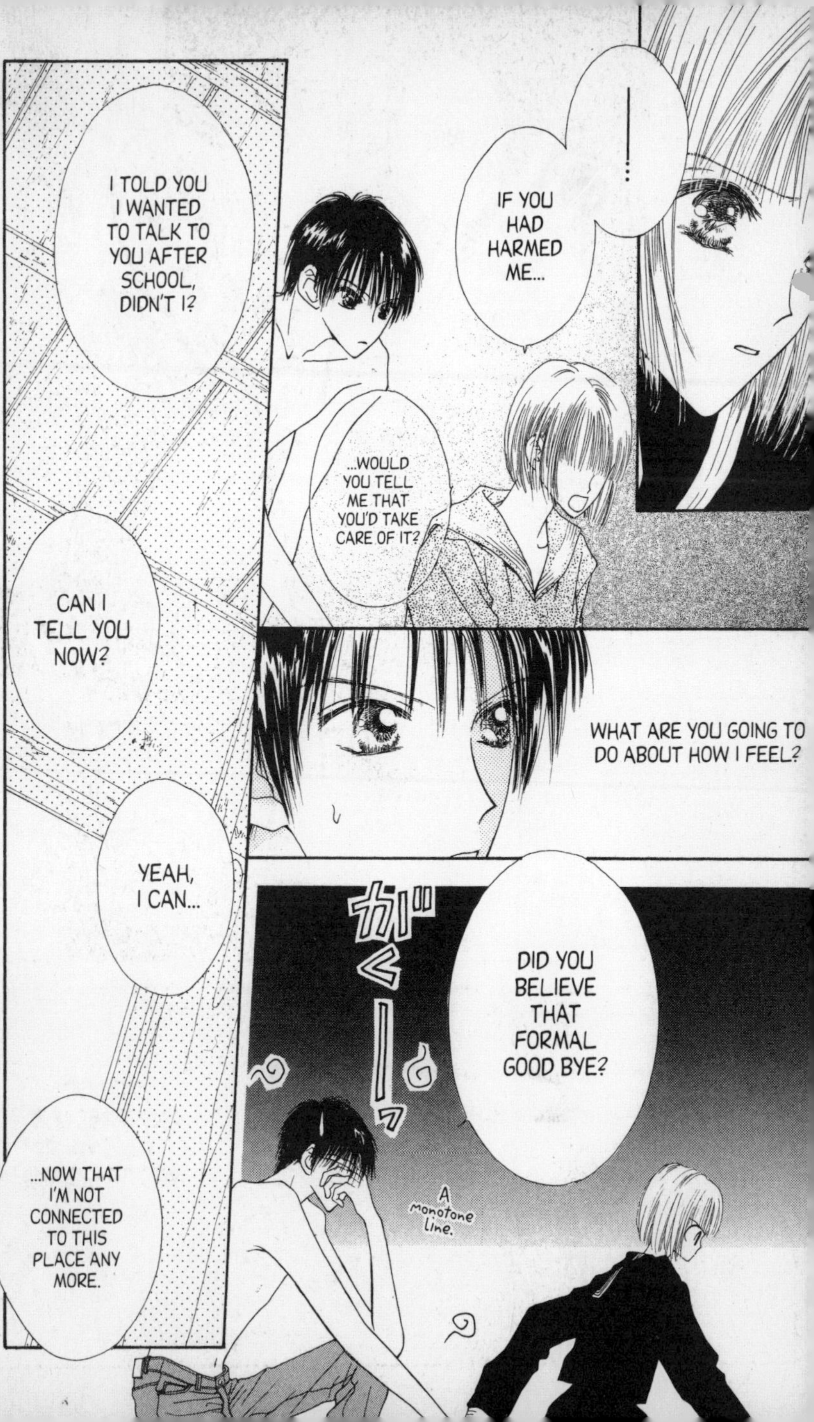

!...
IF YOU HAD HARMED ME...
...WOULD YOU TELL ME THAT YOU'D TAKE CARE OF IT?
WHAT ARE YOU GOING TO DO ABOUT HOW I FEEL?
DID YOU BELIEVE THAT FORMAL GOOD BYE?
がくーっ
A monotone line.
I TOLD YOU I WANTED TO TALK TO YOU AFTER SCHOOL, DIDN'T I?
CAN I TELL YOU NOW?
YEAH, I CAN...
...NOW THAT I'M NOT CONNECTED TO THIS PLACE ANY MORE.

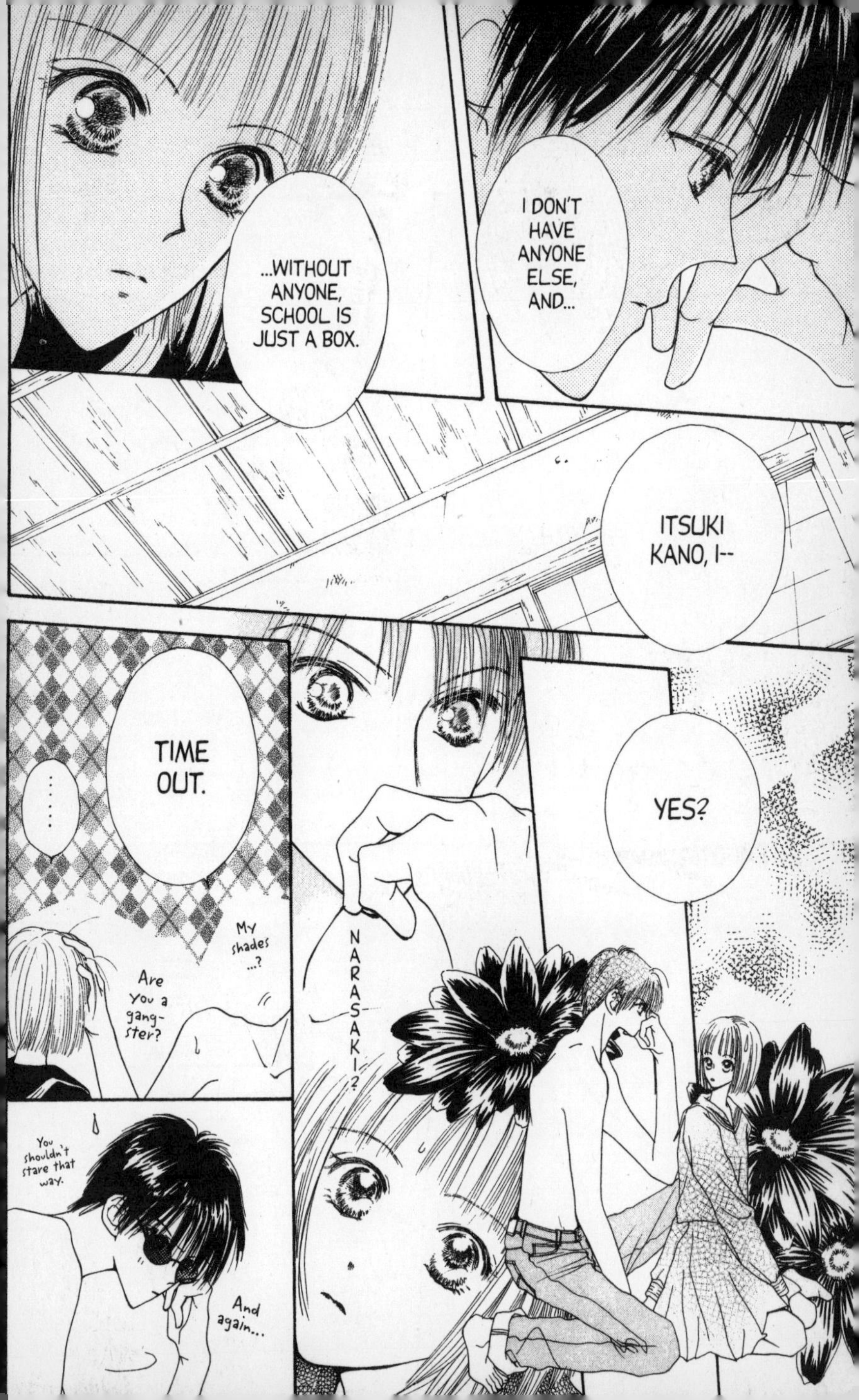
I DON'T HAVE ANYONE ELSE, AND...
...WITHOUT ANYONE, SCHOOL IS JUST A BOX.
ITSUKI KANO, I--
YES?
NARASAKI?
TIME OUT.
......
My shades ...?
Are you a gangster?
You shouldn't stare that way.
And again...

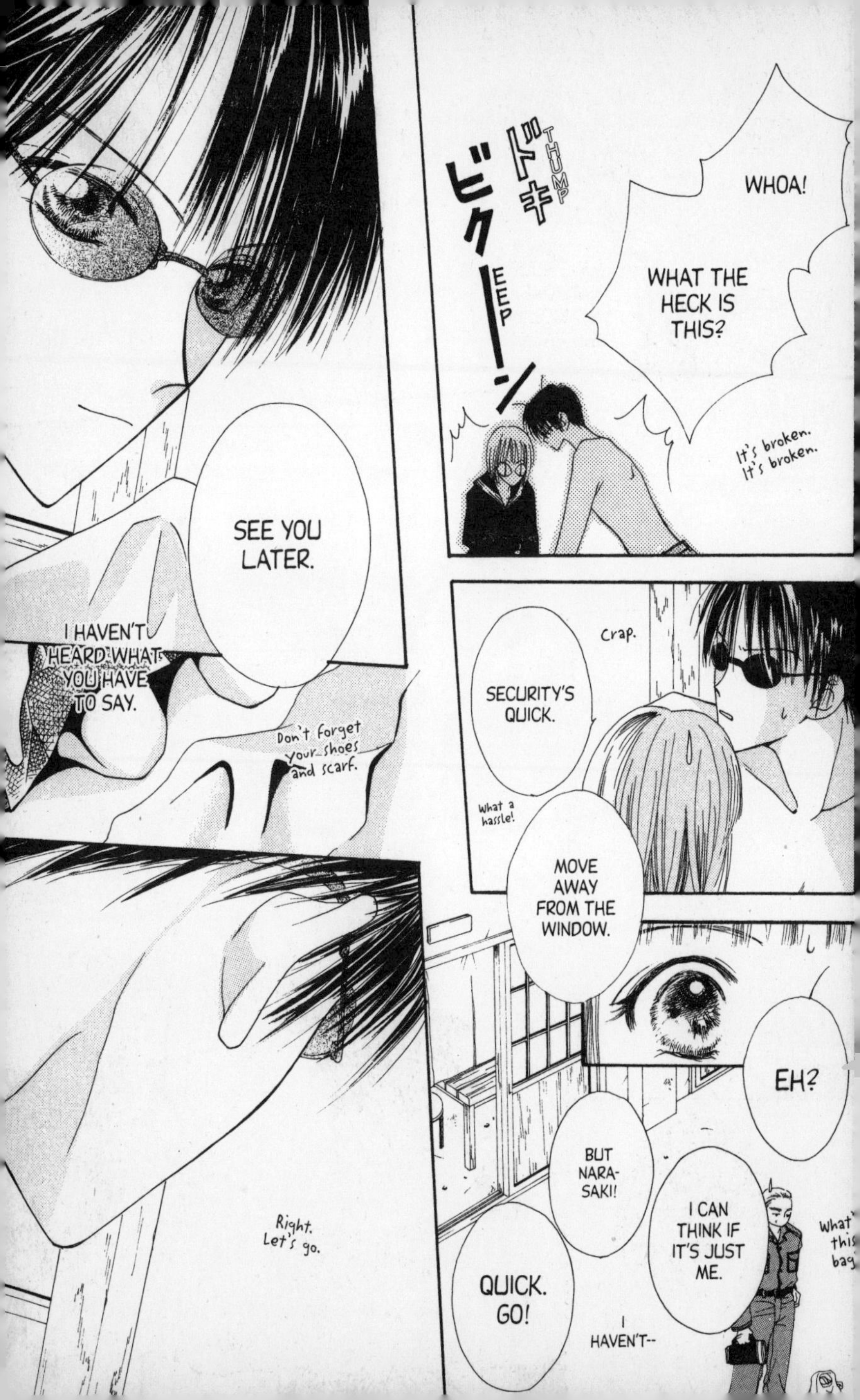
WHOA!
WHAT THE HECK IS THIS?
ドキ
THUMP
ビクーーン
EEP
It's broken. It's broken.
Crap.
SECURITY'S QUICK.
What a hassle!
MOVE AWAY FROM THE WINDOW.
EH?
BUT NARA-SAKI!
I CAN THINK IF IT'S JUST ME.
QUICK. GO!
I HAVEN'T--
SEE YOU LATER.
I HAVEN'T HEARD WHAT YOU HAVE TO SAY.
Don't forget your shoes and scarf.
Right. Let's go.

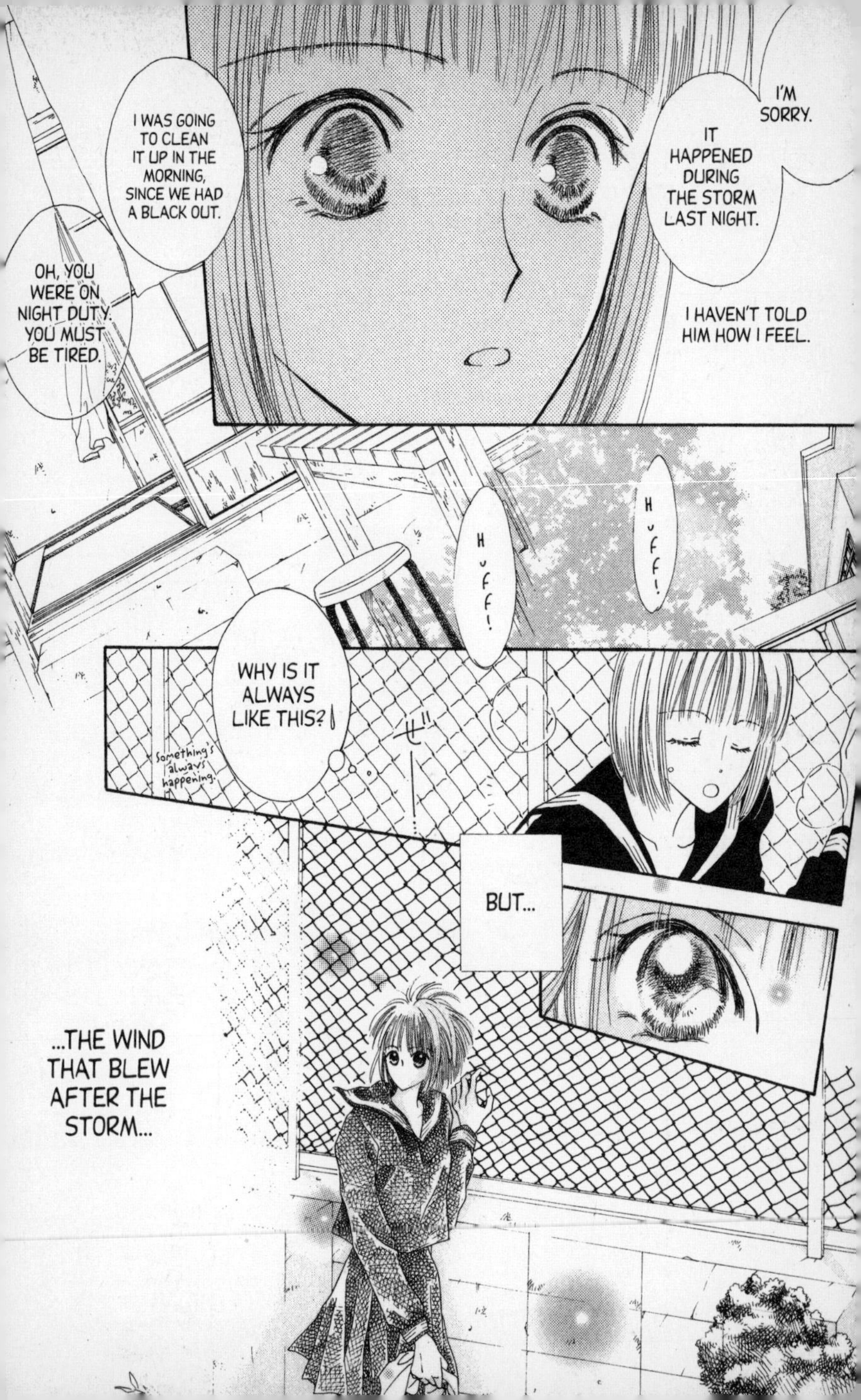
I'M SORRY.
IT HAPPENED DURING THE STORM LAST NIGHT.
I WAS GOING TO CLEAN IT UP IN THE MORNING, SINCE WE HAD A BLACK OUT.
OH, YOU WERE ON NIGHT DUTY. YOU MUST BE TIRED.
I HAVEN'T TOLD HIM HOW I FEEL.
Huff!
Huff!
WHY IS IT ALWAYS LIKE THIS?!
Something's always happening.
BUT...
...THE WIND THAT BLEW AFTER THE STORM...

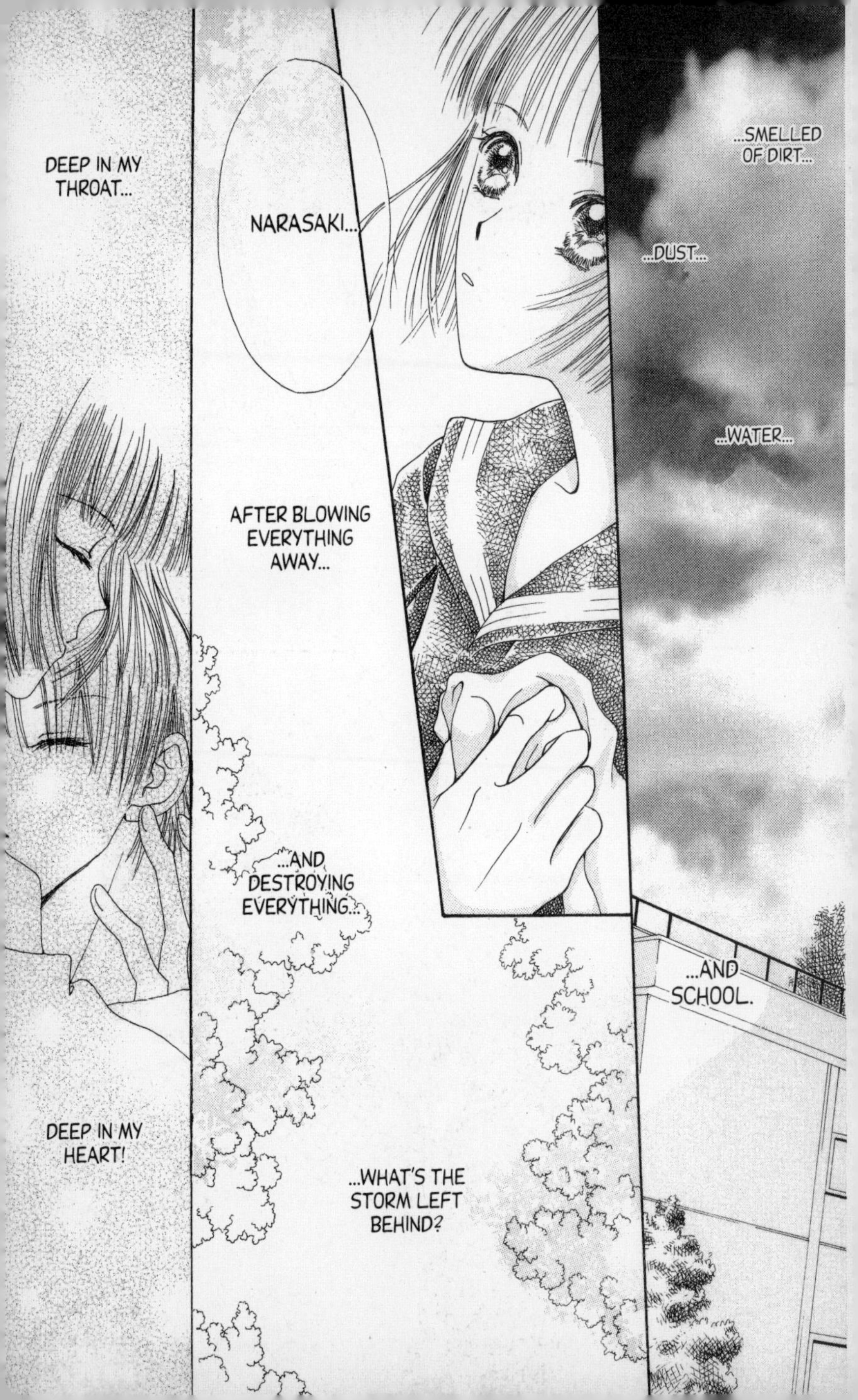
...SMELLED OF DIRT...
...DUST...
...WATER...
...AND SCHOOL.
NARASAKI...
AFTER BLOWING EVERYTHING AWAY...
...AND DESTROYING EVERYTHING...
...WHAT'S THE STORM LEFT BEHIND?
DEEP IN MY THROAT...
DEEP IN MY HEART!

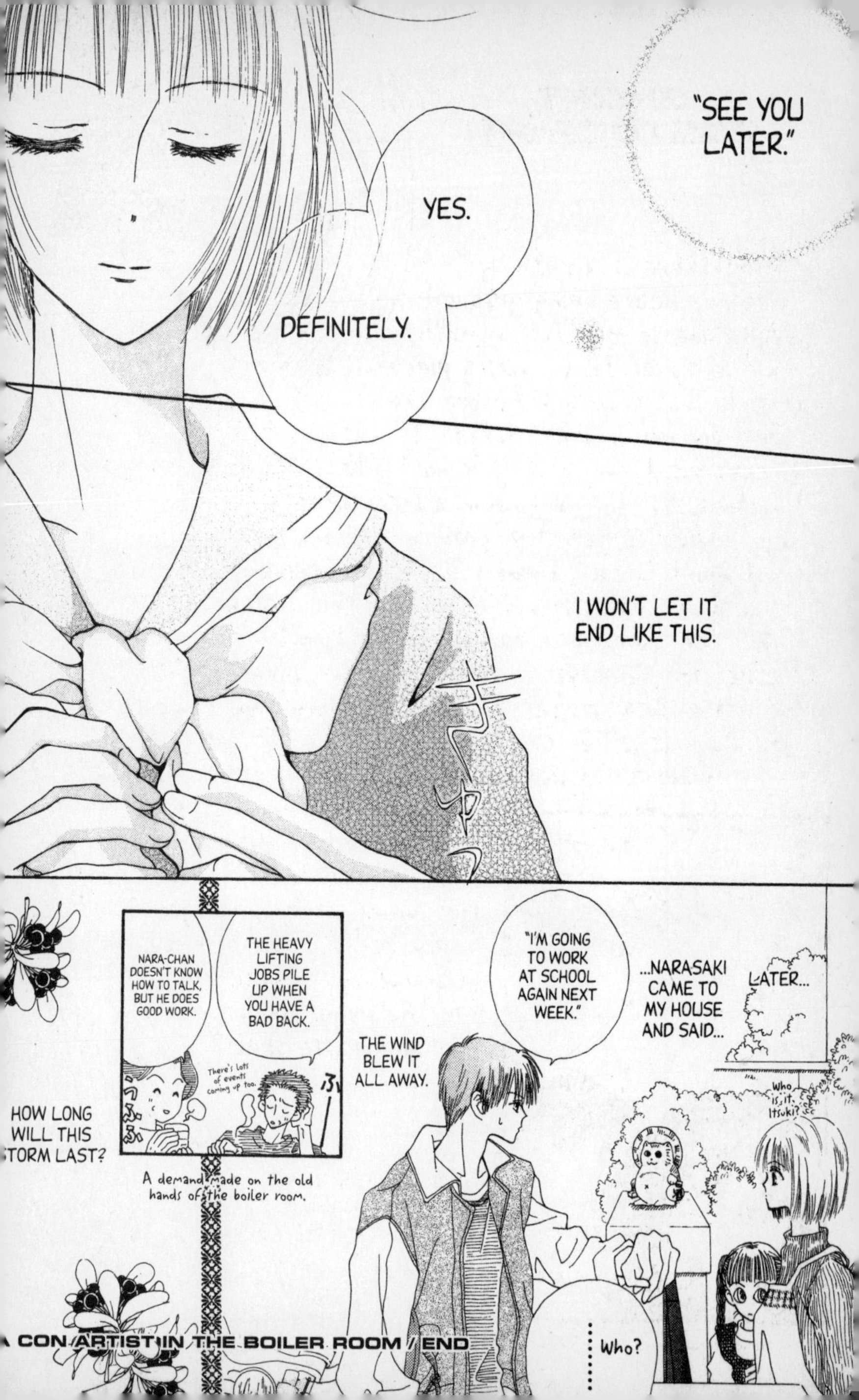
"SEE YOU LATER."
YES.
DEFINITELY.
I WON'T LET IT END LIKE THIS.
ギュッ
LATER...
...NARASAKI CAME TO MY HOUSE AND SAID...
"I'M GOING TO WORK AT SCHOOL AGAIN NEXT WEEK."
Who is it, Itsuki?
...Who?
THE WIND BLEW IT ALL AWAY.
THE HEAVY LIFTING JOBS PILE UP WHEN YOU HAVE A BAD BACK.
NARA-CHAN DOESN'T KNOW HOW TO TALK, BUT HE DOES GOOD WORK.
There's lots of events coming up too.
A demand made on the old hands of the boiler room.
HOW LONG WILL THIS TORM LAST?
A CON ARTIST IN THE BOILER ROOM / END

SHORT POSTSCRIPT!

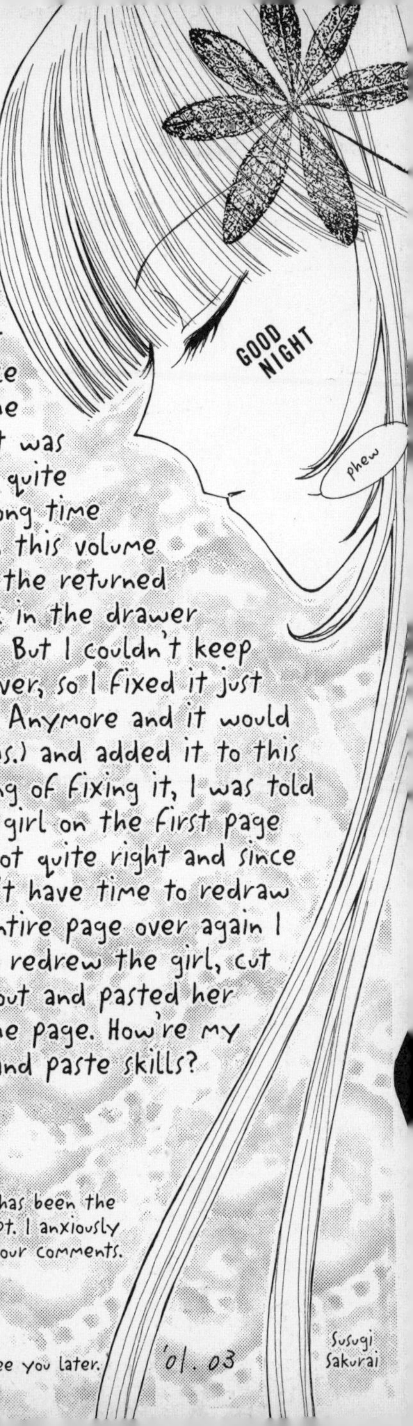
GOOD NIGHT
phew

Anh! There is something like my heart being grabbed happening to me. "A Con Artist in the Boiler Room" was a piece that was published before the first volume of Short Sunzen. It was created during a "this is not quite manga, but it was drawn a long time ago" phase. To get it printed in this volume of Short Sunzen, I had to use the returned artwork. I had to put it back in the drawer because I was so embarrassed. But I couldn't keep the story hidden away forever, so I fixed it just a little (Really...just a little. Anymore and it would be a whole other can of worms.) and added it to this volume. I'm sorry. Speaking of fixing it, I was told the girl on the first page was not quite right and since I didn't have time to redraw the entire page over again I simply redrew the girl, cut her out and pasted her onto the page. How're my cut and paste skills?

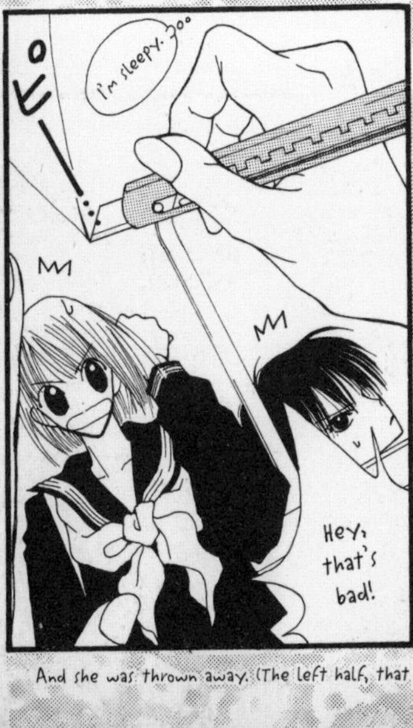
I'm sleepy.
Hey, that's bad!

And she was thrown away. (The left half, that is.)

So, this has been the postscript. I anxiously await your comments.

See you later. '01. 03

Susugi Sakurai

GLOSSARY

WELCOME TO OSAKA

Osaka, where Satsuki Kurokawa and Aya Sendo live, is a very special place in Japan, known for its unique food and customs. Here's a guide to make you feel more at home in the Kansai region of Japan, although lots of it applies to anywhere in Japan, and some is global.

HONORIFICS

In respect for the Japanese setting, the convention of name honorifics has been retained. In Japan, which suffix one uses when addressing another person, and whether or not one uses their first name indicates the level of respect between two people. When someone chooses not to use honorifics, that can be telling, too.

-san. Equivalent to Mr. or Mrs., but also used between coworkers, acquaintances and friends. This is the most common suffix and the default level of respect.

-kun. Indicates friendly familiarity. Also used by older students to address younger students.

-chan. Indicates friendly familiarity, and is often used for smaller, cuter things than oneself.

-senpai. Used by younger students when speaking to or about older students.

-sensei. Teacher.

-sama. Indicates a great level of respect and is used towards someone much older or of much higher standing.

No suffix: either said out of disrespect or because the speaker and subject are very close.

Page	
Page 1	Asobo: "Let's play!"
Page 5	3-12: Grade and classroom number are shown like this: Grade 3 of high school (hence 12th grade) classroom 12.
Page 8	Yoshinoya Gyudon: "Gyudon" is a beef bowl (rice with beef on top); Yoshinoya is a fast food restaraunt.
Page 9	Omake: Bonus content, a little something extra! In this case, a picture of Satsuki in a dress.
Page 11	Yen: 400 yen is about $4. That's about how much an average volume on manga costs in Japan.
Page 12	Hageshii Ame Agari: "End of the Pouring Rain," literally. We've replaced it with "I Can See Clearly Now (the rain is gone)."
Page 22	Bosozoku: Motorcycle gang.
Page 43	Kintaro: A hero of folktales. He is strong, fat, and likes sumo. Yukata: Summer cotton kimono. Dango: Japanese sweet made of rice flour that comes on a stick.
Page 61	Tamaya: In the old days, people used to yell out the maker of the fireworks as they went up. Tamaya was one of the major fireworks manufacturers. It may also be an intended pun with the name of Satsuki's high school, Tama High.
Page 62	Dora-pocket: Refers to the magic pocket of Doraemon from which he takes out all kinds of good
Page 66	Hanabi: A kind of firework that makes little noise.
Page 85	Satasuma, Kara Sawagi, Love and P-Night: All TV shows, obviously.
Page 96	Aka zubuton: Red cushion Aka-ten: Failing grade
Page 106	Yankee Santa: Yankee means juvenile delinquent-types; the word originated in the Osaka area where these kids ended their sentences and phrases with "yan-ke."
Page 109	Takoyaki: Also known as 'octopus balls,' these are made in a ball shape with a piece of octopus in each one of them. Usually eaten as a snack.
Page 123	Light House: This is a Japanese proverb meaning that you miss what is very close to you.
Page 129	Nabe: A dish made in a hot pot with vegetables, meats, seafood, etc. in a broth, eaten with a special sauce and noodles.
Page 131	Story of Hachiko: The story of a faithful dog named Hachiko. There's a statue of the dog in front of Shibuya Station is very famous and many people use it as a meeting place.
Page 134	Kotatsu: A table with a heating element on the bottom of the tabletop.
Page 136	Yakisoba: Fried noodles with a Japanese sauce.
Page 146	Tengu no mai: Tengu is a human-shaped monster with an elongated nose and red face. Literal tranlation: Dance of the Tengu.
Page 157	Furikake: Flavoring used on rice.
Page 164	Deer Man: Taking the "Nara" from "Narasaki" the girl is making a pun about Nara Park in historic Nara, Japan, home to a herd of sacred deer.

In the Next Volume of

SHORT SUNZEN!

FOR SATSUKI AND SENDO, SCHOOL IS GETTING A LITTLE OLD--AND THEY'RE GETTING A LITTLE OLD FOR SCHOOL. AS CLASSROOM 12 PREPARES TO TAKE THEIR HIGH SCHOOL EXIT EXAMS, ONE BIG QUESTION LOOMS: WILL ANYONE PASS? AND OF COURSE, WILL AYA BE ABLE TO CONFESS HIS FEELINGS TO SATSUKI BEFORE IT'S ALL CAPS AND GOWNS?

STOP!

This is the back of the book. You wouldn't want to spoil a great ending!

This book is printed "manga-style," in the authentic Japanese right-to-left format. Since none of the artwork has been flipped or altered, readers get to experience the story just as the creator intended. You've been asking for it, so TOKYOPOP® delivered: authentic, hot-off-the-press, and far more fun!

DIRECTIONS

If this is your first time reading manga-style, here's a quick guide to help you understand how it works.

It's easy... just start in the top right panel and follow the numbers. Have fun, and look for more 100% authentic manga from TOKYOPOP®!